THE
DIPLOMAT'S
WIFE

Also by Michael Ridpath

THE DIPLOMAT'S WIFE

Michael Ridpath

CORVUS

Published in trade paperback in Great Britain in 2021 by Corvus,
an imprint of Atlantic Books Ltd.

10 9 8 7 6 5 4 3 2 1

A CIP catalogue record for this book is available from the British Library.

Trade paperback ISBN: 978 1 78649 702 4
E-book ISBN: 978 1 78649 703 1

Printed in Great Britain by Bell and Bain Ltd, Glasgow

Corvus
An imprint of Atlantic Books Ltd
Ormond House
26–27 Boswell Street
London
WC1N 3JZ

www.corvus-books.co.uk

To the English country pub. May it open soon.

London, spring 2020

PART 1

ENGLAND

Chapter 1

'Mean bastard!' Phil muttered as he reread the first page of what had over the last six months become his favourite book:

> *The thing is that the road takes you. You can't dictate to the road. If you do you might as well be in a train. Hitch-hiking is the art of wondering what will happen to you between your starting point and your destination and taking from everything that does happen everything that you can.*

He pitched the already tatty paperback on to the floor next to his bed and stared down at the cover. The words *Hitch-Hiker's Guide to Europe* stood proud above an enticing red rucksack with bulges containing maps, a sleeping bag and clever survival tools, its fabric scattered with colourful stickers that were almost legible.

He glanced across the floor at his own brand-new rucksack, green, with a small Union Jack poorly sewn on to its centre.

This had been Phil's bedroom since the age of four. He was a bit of a hoarder, and a sucker for teenage nostalgia of lost childhood. He liked the random objects which traced his life dotted around the room: a Matchbox Ford Zephyr, a platoon of plastic Afrika Korps soldiers, an Airfix model of HMS *Victory*. Arsenal's Liam Brady crossed a football from one wall towards the stick figures of Lowry's satanic mills on the other. Phil's bookshelf traced a similar path, beginning with Enid Blyton,

3

Arthur Ransome and Biggles, moving through a row of war comics, on to Agatha Christie, Ian Fleming, John le Carré and Georges Simenon.

The bottom right-hand corner of the bookshelf was devoted to the eclectic gifts from his grandmother over the years: *Animal Farm*, *Homage to Catalonia*, *The Communist Manifesto*, *Atlas Shrugged*, *Njál's Saga* and *A Day in the Life of Ivan Denisovich*, as well as his eighteenth-birthday present, a copy in French of Zola's *Germinal*, a bleak story of coal miners in northern France. He had read them all. That shelf was where the *Hitch-Hiker's Guide* lived. Grams had given it to him for Christmas when he had told her of his plans to spend the summer holiday between school and university Interrailing around Europe with his friend Mike.

Phil loved the book. It was subtitled *How to See Europe by the Skin of Your Teeth* and it was full of tips for ways to travel around the Continent on as little money as possible. Everything about the book excited him. Phil was always hungry, and the *Guide* was like the menu of the biggest buffet Phil had ever seen. He could gorge himself on so many of the marvels of Europe in just a month: the impressionist paintings in Paris one week, the canals of Venice another, the sands of a Greek island the week after that.

But the *Hitch-Hiker's Guide* also told of freedom. The freedom of the open road. The freedom from a plan. The freedom to wake up in the morning and not know where he would spend that night. The freedom to sleep on a beach, under a tree or in a hostel. The freedom to talk to other travellers from other countries, and to the random generous strangers who would give him lifts. The freedom to eat a meal of bread, cheese and wine on the banks of the Seine, or on the stone bench of a Roman amphitheatre.

The freedom to escape Wittingcombe, the village wedged into a fold of the Chiltern Hills in which he had spent the whole of his life.

Mike had shared Phil's enthusiasm; they had decided to ditch the Interrail idea and hitch-hike instead.

They were leaving the following Saturday, taking the train to Sevenoaks in Kent and then hitching to the Channel from there. They had allowed themselves five weeks and three hundred pounds each, three hundred pounds that they had both saved toiling on a building site during the Christmas and Easter holidays.

Except now they weren't going. Or at least Phil wasn't going.

The mean bastard in question, Phil's dad, had seen to that.

'Phil! Grams is here!'

His mother's voice snaked up the stairs and through his closed bedroom door.

It was Sunday, and Phil's grandmother was dropping in for lunch before going on to London. She lived in Cornwall; Wittingcombe was on the way.

For a moment Phil considered staying in his room and sulking. But that wasn't his style. Plus he always wanted to see his grandmother.

Plus, he was hungry and the roast beef smelled really good.

'Coming!'

'So, when are you off on your adventure, Philip?'

'It looks like I'm not going,' said Phil as neutrally as possible. He was too proud to sound sulky or angry, even if that was exactly how he felt.

There were five of them around the gleaming dining table: Phil's parents, his grandmother and his sixteen-year-old sister, Mel.

'Oh. What have you done?'

Grams had realized immediately that Phil must have done something wrong. She was looking at him in that all-too-familiar way she had. Not exactly enquiring, more interrogating. She wanted to know the answer.

Grams always wanted to know the answer.

She was young for the grandmother of an eighteen-year-old – in her mid sixties, Phil believed. Nor did she really look like a granny: she was tall and long-limbed, and her thick short hair was still dark with only the odd strand of grey. Her voice was husky, clipped and old-fashioned, like something out of a black-and-white movie. She couldn't say her 'r's, a trait that had skipped a generation to her granddaughter, much to Mel's frustration. Grams's deep brown eyes, almost black, latched on to you over her large, imperious nose, and once they had fixed on you, they wouldn't let go until you had answered her question.

'I crashed Dad's car last week.'

'Oh dear. Was it your fault?'

'The insurance company thinks so,' said Phil's father.

'What do you think?' asked Grams.

Phil had borrowed his father's Rover to drive a couple of mates from school on a mini pub crawl around the best village pubs in the area. Phil had only drunk one pint at the first pub, the Three Castles in Wittingcombe, and that was going to be his lot for the evening. They were celebrating the end of A-levels and Elvis Costello was 'Watching the Detectives' as loud as the car's tape deck would allow. Phil was turning right off a main road into a narrow lane to the second pub. The driver of a Marina had slowed and signalled for him to go ahead, but as he turned, a Bedford van sped out of nowhere and caught the rear of the Rover, spinning it off the road and into a wall. No one was hurt, Phil passed the inevitable breathalyser test, the van was scarcely damaged, but the Rover was a write-off.

He recalled the woman in the Marina who had urged him on. He hadn't seen the van coming and perhaps he should have done. But wasn't it driving too fast?

'I don't know,' he said, honestly.

'Phil hasn't had much driving experience yet,' said his father. 'He only passed his test in February.'

'So it wasn't his fault?' Grams said.

'Oh, it was his fault all right.'

'And you won't let him go to Europe as a punishment, Caroline?' Grams directed the question at her daughter, Phil's mum.

'It's not that,' said Mum.

'We need him to pay for a new car,' said her husband.

'It's all my savings,' said Phil. 'I can't afford the trip now.'

'I see,' said Grams.

She popped a chunk of roast potato in her mouth and chewed it thoughtfully. Grams's inquisitions could be uncomfortable. Phil's mother, a small, slight figure a good five inches shorter than Grams, had learned in the course of her forty-two years how to defy her own mother. Phil's father, an affable man with a sweep of fair hair, a strong chin and a pliant character, had more difficulty. But Phil knew that this was an issue on which he was prepared to stand his ground.

Phil's father wasn't usually a mean bastard. David Dewar was a kind, eminently reasonable, reliable husband and father. But he didn't like risk; he was a little afraid of life. He had been unhappy when Phil had decided to hitch-hike rather than take the train. He had been disappointed when Phil had turned down the chance to work in an insurance company in London over the summer. Dad saw this as a great opportunity for Phil to see what the insurance business – his world – was like, and to secure the all-important bottom rung on a sturdy career ladder. Phil thought, feared even, that he would end up spending most of the rest of his life in an office and he didn't want to start now.

The replacement for the Rover was going to cost £550, in addition to the insurance money, and the previous evening Dad had informed Phil that Phil would have to pay. Three hundred now and the remaining £250 when he had earned it over the summer.

Phil had argued; he had pleaded. He had almost burst into tears.

But Dad had loved his brown Rover. He believed, deeply and passionately, in financial accountability. Phil would have to pay.

Now Phil wouldn't have the money to go to Europe. Not only that, he would have to go back to the building site to earn the £250 he was short – if there was still a job for him.

Grams fixed her son-in-law with those interrogating eyes. 'Didn't you insure the car, David?'

'Of course I did, Emma,' said Dad. 'You have to; it's the law. But with Phil on the policy, the premiums were high, so I took a five-hundred-and-fifty-pound excess. It always makes sense to do that if you can afford it, you know.'

'If *you* can afford it?' said Grams. 'Not if Phil can afford it?'

'I'm the one paying the premium.'

'Yes, I see that. But apparently Phil is the one paying the excess. And he demonstrably cannot afford it.'

7

One–nil to Grams! Phil did his best not to chuckle into his Yorkshire pudding. A quick glance at his father's reddening face told him two things. Dad immediately understood his mother-in-law's point. And he hadn't thought of it himself. Which, as the insurance executive, he should have done.

A glimmer of hope flared. Maybe Dad would admit defeat? Maybe he would pay the excess? Maybe Phil was still going to Europe?

Dad bit back whatever he was going to say and took a sip from his small wine glass.

'Phil has to learn financial responsibility at some point, and eighteen is the right age.' Dad's voice was uncharacteristically firm. Phil realized he had been backed into a corner; there was no way out to save face apart from sticking to his guns. He glanced at his son. 'I'm sorry, Phil, that's just the way it is.'

'Caroline? What do you think?'

'I think David's absolutely right, Mother.' Mum was sticking by Dad, as she always would in any argument with Grams. Reluctantly, Phil acknowledged the score was now two–one to his father.

Grams seemed about to argue, but then she threw in the towel. 'I do hope I can come and see you when you get to Edinburgh?' she said.

'If I get to Edinburgh,' said Phil. 'I've got to get my grades first. But, yes, I'd love to see you.'

'Anything for free food,' said Mum in an attempt to lighten the mood. Phil couldn't bring himself to smile. In fact, he almost didn't ask for seconds, to make the point that he was very unhappy. But the beef was very good. And so were the roast potatoes.

The conversation flowed as the three adults coped well with the grumpy teenager, however justified his grumps. Mel kept her head down until Emma questioned her on a new musical form she had read about in *The Times*, something called '2 Tone ska'. Phil had barely heard of it, but Mel was an avid reader of the *New Musical Express*, and was able to fill her grandmother in, while Grams told Mel all about Jamaican ska in the 1960s.

Not for the first time, Phil found himself wondering how the hell does she know that? He was sure his parents were asking themselves the same thing.

Phil was finishing his second helping of his mother's excellent Eve's pudding and custard when his grandmother took a sip of her wine.

'You know, David, I might have something for Philip.'

'Something?' said Dad.

'Yes. A job. A way for him to earn his two hundred and fifty pounds. Possibly a bit more.'

'Oh yes?' Dad was guarded. Phil was all ears.

'Of course, he might not want to do it.'

Dad looked pleased at this.

Grams glanced at Phil. 'For a while now, I have been thinking of driving around Europe myself. Visiting some of my old haunts from before the war. You know – Paris, Berlin, places Roland was posted.'

Roland was Phil's late grandfather, a former diplomat.

'I really thought this would be the summer to do it. In fact, I was intending to perhaps meet you and your friend and take you out to dinner in Paris or somewhere.'

Phil's father's brows knitted in a frown.

'I don't want to go by myself. And now it looks as if I will need a driver. So I wonder if you would oblige, Philip? I would pay for all your meals and accommodation, naturally. And perhaps three hundred pounds?'

'Why will you need a driver?' asked Mum.

'Philip isn't the only one in trouble, I'm afraid. I'm due for a visit to the magistrates' court on Tuesday. I was caught over the limit on the road to St Austell. Most embarrassing. We'll see, but I suspect I will lose my licence for a year. So I could do with a chauffeur. And the company.'

She smiled at Phil. It was an extraordinarily sweet, innocent smile, all the more affecting for its rarity.

'Mother!' Caroline looked shocked.

'I know. I won't do it again, I promise.'

'And you're planning to go in the Triumph?' Dad asked. 'Are you sure you are happy with Phil driving it?'

Grams's sleek green TR6 was visible through the dining-room window, a fine-looking two-seater convertible that Phil had long admired.

'That was my intention. Don't worry, David, I will make sure it's insured properly. But what do you think, Philip? I know it will be frightfully dull for you, carting an old woman around. Nothing like hitch-hiking with your friend.'

Phil grinned. 'I think that would be great, Grams. Thank you so much!'

Dad's frown deepened. 'I'm not sure that's such a good idea, Emma.'

'Oh come now, David. Philip's eighteen. He owes money. He needs a job. He's found a job. There's nothing more financially responsible than that.'

Dad glanced at Mum. The score was now three–two to Grams. Dad let the final whistle blow. 'Your grandmother is right, Phil. It's your choice.'

'When do we leave?' Phil asked.

'Next weekend all right for you?'

Chapter 2

Phil sauntered the couple of hundred yards through the village to the Three Castles. It was a lovely summer's evening. The rooks were settling themselves in the trees behind the vicarage; the narrow village street was quiet as the inhabitants watched *Coronation Street* or *Crossroads*, or, as in his parents' case, tucked into the first of the evening's gin and tonics.

Wittingcombe snoozed gently in its valley, bathed in soft evening sunlight. Ancient timbers supported the crooked bricks of the cottages that lined the road, as red, yellow and pink roses crept up the walls towards roofs that buckled and bowed. The Three Castles stood at the far end of the village, as it had done for centuries, at the point where the village high street became a country lane lined with high hedges and tangles of Queen Anne's lace.

Phil ordered himself a pint of Brakspear at the bar, and settled at his favourite table between the dartboard and the jukebox. Although school hadn't technically broken up yet, now exams were over the pupils didn't have to show up, so Phil had been surprised and a little flattered when his French teacher, Mr Parsons, had rung him to suggest they meet for a drink.

He had no idea why.

Phil sipped his pint. He was grateful for his grandmother's offer, but he was still angry with his dad that he had had to abandon his hitch-hiking plans. It wasn't as if travelling around Europe with Grams was going to be that great anyway. One of the things he had been looking forward to was chatting up girls with Mike around the bars of Europe. They probably wouldn't have had much success, but it would have been fun trying. Hard to do that with your grandmother.

Especially if your grandmother was a little weird. And it was hard to escape the fact that Phil's grandmother was more than a little weird.

He wished he had hesitated just for a moment at that turning to double-check the road when the woman had beckoned him to go forward. She looked like one of his friends' mums – he had just done what she had told him without questioning it. What an idiot!

'Hello, Phil.'

Phil recognized the voice of his French teacher and scrambled to his feet. Mr Parsons was a prematurely wizened sixty-year-old with a clipped, very English accent and a deep love of French literature, which over the previous two years he had managed to pass on to Phil and the rest of his A-level class. There was not much Phil wouldn't do for Mr Parsons.

Standing just behind him was a man a little older than the French master, bald with fluffs of grey hair sticking out above his large ears. Phil would have pegged him as another teacher, except he didn't recognize him, and he was wearing a suit. Apart from the headmaster, teachers at Phil's school stuck to old sports jackets and rumpled trousers. 'Hello, sir.'

'Sadly, Phil, I am no longer "sir" to you. And not even really "Mr Parsons". Call me Eustace.'

Naturally, Mr Parsons' pupils had gleefully been calling him 'Eustace' behind his back ever since they had discovered that was his first name, but Phil felt honoured to be permitted to call him that to his face.

'This is Charles Swann,' said Mr Parsons. 'Phil Dewar, one of my pupils. *Former* pupils. Going to Edinburgh in September.'

'Provided I get the grades.'

'As I said, going to Edinburgh in September.' Mr Parsons grinned with confidence. 'What will you have, Charles?'

'Oh, a pint of bitter, please.'

'Can I get you another, Phil?'

'Thank you, sir. I mean, Eustace. A pint of Brakspear's.'

The bald man sat down opposite Phil and pulled out a packet of cigarettes, offered Phil one, which he declined, and lit up. 'Nice pub,' he said, taking a puff. 'Your local?'

'My house is on the other side of the village. Do you live around here? I haven't seen you about.'

'Oh no. I live in Surrey. Woking.'

'Are you a teacher too?'

Swann grinned. 'Sometimes I wish I was. No, a civil servant.' He leaned back in his chair, examining Phil. 'Eustace tells me your exams are all finished now. Have you got any plans for the summer?'

'I was supposed to be spending a month hitch-hiking around Europe, but it looks like that's fallen through. I crashed my father's car last week, and now I can't afford to go.'

'My commiserations,' said Swann. 'I had a bad smash when I was your age. Lucky to get out alive. All my fault.'

'I suppose this one was mine,' said Phil.

Mr Parsons reappeared, clasping two pints. 'Here you are, Phil. I have to go, I'm afraid. I'll leave you here with Charles.'

Phil accepted the pint and put it down next to his existing glass. He looked at his teacher in confusion.

'Charles will explain. This is the first time I've met him. But he is a very good friend of a very good friend of mine. He is who he says he is.' Mr Parsons looked straight into Phil's eyes as he spoke.

'All right,' said Phil, confusion morphing into interest. 'Thanks for the pint.'

He turned to Swann, who was still watching him carefully as he smoked his cigarette. The man's gaze was shrewd, with a hint of steel. Definitely not a schoolteacher. 'What are you planning to do instead?' Swann asked. 'Now you can't go hitch-hiking.'

'My grandmother has offered to take me around Europe. I'm supposed to drive her. Technically it's a job, but actually she bailed me out.'

'That's decent of her,' said Swann.

'She's a decent woman,' said Phil. 'A little odd sometimes, but she has always been good to me.' He sipped the smaller of his two pints. 'What do you want? You said you worked for the civil service?'

'I do. I'm semi-retired now.'

'Which department?'

'I couldn't say.' Swann looked at Phil levelly.

Phil had read enough spy novels to know what Mr Swann *was* saying. A thought occurred to him. 'Is that Swann as in *À la recherche du temps perdu?*'

'It is, actually. Eustace thought you would appreciate it.'

Phil couldn't help grinning. Mr Parsons had overreached himself with inflicting Proust as an off-syllabus novel on his class the previous autumn term.

'So Swann is not your real name?'

'Obviously not,' said Swann. 'But it will do us for now.'

'OK.' Phil sipped his pint. His heart started beating faster. He was going to study languages at university and he had fantasized about how one day he would be approached by the secret service in exactly this way. Was it happening already? Phil knew that Mr Parsons liked him, respected him even. Would MI5 or MI6 or whomever Swann was with want him to learn Russian? Phil had always fancied the idea of learning Russian.

He decided to take the initiative. He had no idea whether he would agree to be a spy, but he knew he wanted to be asked. 'Are you recruiting me?'

'No,' Swann replied, with a smile revealing chaotic yellow teeth. 'Or not exactly. There is something that we would like you to do for your government. For your country. But before we talk about that, I want your word that you won't discuss what I am about to say with anyone. Not your family. Not your friends. Certainly not your grandmother.' The grin had gone.

Phil didn't want to keep this a secret. In particular, he wanted to tell his mates from school all about Mr Parsons' friend. But if he didn't promise he would never find out what 'this' was. Mr Parsons had trusted him.

'All right,' he said. 'I won't tell anyone.' And he meant it. He would keep his word and justify Mr Parsons' trust.

'Good man,' said Swann. 'This is what I would like you to do, if you are willing . . .'

Chapter 3

The train pulled into St Austell. Phil closed his hefty volume of *War and Peace*, which he had long planned to take with him on his European trip, since it was a book big enough to last him five weeks: 130 pages done, 1,270 to go. He grabbed his bulging green rucksack and dropped down on to the platform. He had one five-pound note in his pocket, borrowed from his mother, to pay for the taxi to Mevagissey, the fishing village near which Grams lived.

He emerged from the station entrance to find his grandmother, and her TR6, waiting for him.

'Stick your bag in the boot and hop in,' she said. She took the passenger seat, and Phil sat at the wheel. The boot was already two-thirds full of luggage.

'I thought I was supposed to go to your house. How did you get the car here?'

'I drove.'

'The magistrate let you off?'

Grams smiled. '*You* didn't really believe that? Your parents, maybe, but not you, surely?'

Phil grinned. 'So you weren't caught drinking and driving?'

'Of course not! I would never do such a thing. Now, let's get going.'

'All right. Where to? Dover?'

'Not quite yet. We're going to start in Devon. Chaddington Hall.'

Phil loved driving the TR6. They sped across Bodmin Moor with the roof down. It was a cool day for June with small white clouds chasing the car eastwards, scattering quick black shadows across the green moor. Phil usually drove his mother's dull, underpowered Renault 5 with the weird gearstick, and occasionally his father's big, heavy, slightly scary Rover. The TR6 beat both of them hands down, and along the straight bits of the A30 he was able to push above eighty without any complaint from his passenger.

Stupidly, Phil had forgotten to bring any of his tapes. Grams slotted in one of her own, some opera, and although Phil flinched at the first screech, he enjoyed the way the music swelled around them as they barrelled across the moor.

'Do you really need me to drive, or were you just being generous?' he asked.

'Oh, no. I'd much rather you drove. I've lost my confidence, recently. And I'm very glad you agreed to come.'

'Really?'

'Yes, really. I have a feeling I will need a fit young man with me.'

'To do what, exactly?'

'To deal with the unexpected.'

'Are we expecting the unexpected?' Phil asked with half a smile.

'Yes, I rather think we are.'

Phil slowed behind a line of cars following a caravan. 'Where are we going? You said you were posted to Paris and Berlin?'

'That's right. Or rather Roland was.'

Phil remembered his grandfather well: he had died five years before, when Phil was thirteen. Phil had liked the old man. The family had visited his grandparents a few times in Mevagissey, and Grandpa usually took Phil out fishing around the local coves in a little motor-boat. They never caught much, but it had been fun.

'Will we be going anywhere else?'

'Possibly. Probably. I don't know yet.'

'This all sounds very mysterious.'

'Oh, it is,' said Grams. She was silent for a moment. 'One of the reasons I asked you to accompany me is that I want to tell you a story. My story. The story of what I did before the war. I mentioned I've

16

been thinking of revisiting my life then. But I also want to share it, so someone knows about it when I'm gone.'

'But you're not going anywhere, Grams,' said Phil. 'I don't know how old you are, but you can't be much more than sixty.' Phil tactfully lopped a couple of years off his best guess.

'Sixty-four,' said Grams. 'And you never know. Roland was only seventy-two when he died.'

That still seemed to give Grams another eight years at least. She looked pretty healthy to Phil. Not even really an old lady.

'Why me?' said Phil. 'Why not Mum?'

Grams smiled. 'My story would be difficult for your mother. It might be difficult for you. But I think you are the right person to hear it. I'm sure you are.'

Phil wasn't completely convinced by that explanation, but his curiosity was aroused, as his grandmother had no doubt intended.

'All right. We start at Chaddington Hall? That's where you grew up, right?'

'That's right.'

'And your father was a lord?'

Phil's parents had discussed Chaddington Hall once or twice, but when he had pressed his mother for details of her grandparents, she had been evasive, to the point that Phil had almost doubted their existence. The idea that his family could have had any lordly ancestors seemed faintly ridiculous to him; his mother behaved in a resolutely middle-class fashion. But Grams? There was a touch of the aristocrat to her. And she had become a 'lady' herself when Grandpa had been knighted for his services to diplomatic cocktail parties or whatever. Dad's father, who still lived with his wife in a nice village outside Glasgow, had been in insurance.

'He was Lord Chaddington,' Grams said.

'Is there a Lord Chaddington now?'

'No. I did have a brother. Hugh. But he died, so there was no heir to the title.'

Phil hadn't heard anything about a Hugh. He would have been Phil's great-uncle. Why had his mother never mentioned an uncle? There was a Great Aunt Sarah in Australia, presumably Grams's sister, but Phil had only met her once, and couldn't remember that very clearly.

'So who owns Chaddington Hall now?'

'It's a prep school. My sister and I sold it in 1967. Most of the proceeds went in death duties. I telephoned and they are expecting us. It will be the first time I have been back since my father died. And it's the place where my story starts.'

Soon after they crossed the River Tamar from Cornwall into Devon, they turned off the A30, and followed a number of ever-smaller roads that twisted and turned through little valleys and wooded lanes where the trees met overhead. Grams did the navigating without the aid of a map, which was fortunate, because Phil had completely lost his sense of direction. They emerged from a wood and over an uncharacteristically low hedge he caught sight of a broad bare hillside about five miles away.

'Dartmoor,' said Grams.

'Are we going up there?'

'Not quite.'

They meandered closer to the hills, until they passed a small sign announcing Chaddington. The village was tiny, just a few cottages, a couple of farms and a squat stone church with a squat stone tower. Trees encroached from all sides.

'Let's go the back way,' Grams said. 'Turn left here.'

She indicated a tiny lane opposite the church.

'There's more of a back way than this?' said Phil, but he did as she suggested. He wasn't sure why: even though they were heading towards the moor, it was impossible to see much above the high banks and hedges. The lane twisted and turned, passed a farm, and then straightened up for a hundred yards or so. Phil braked as the lane lurched over a small rise, and plunged into a hollow surrounded by trees, where it turned sharply to the right. Grams seemed to shiver and looked over her shoulder at the curve. Phil felt a flash of irritation: he had braked in plenty of time.

They emerged from the trees and soon came upon a slightly bigger road and a pair of grey gateposts, guarded by a tiny lodge. A large blue painted sign proclaimed: 'Chaddington Hall School' and underneath it: 'Preparatory School for Boys 7–13 Years'.

Phil turned in, and guided the TR6 along a driveway running through a sports field split up into a number of cricket pitches. Boys of different sizes were playing – it was a Saturday afternoon in summer, after all.

'This used to be the park,' said Grams. 'It makes sense they would turn it into playing fields.'

Chaddington Hall appeared ahead of them at the end of the long drive: a rambling house surrounded by lush vegetation. Plants climbed to left and right of the front door up towards the roof, and a thick, ancient tree stood on a circle of lawn to one side, its long branches stretching out towards them. The house appeared kindly rather than imposing, ancient grey brickwork wrinkling the façade.

'That's a chestnut,' Grams said. 'We used to love climbing it. I bet the schoolboys still do.'

'I bet it's out of bounds,' said Phil. 'That's what schools do: ban the stuff that's fun.'

He drew up next to a line of cars and a couple of minibuses parked on a tarmac apron to one side of the drive.

'I'm pleased to see they haven't messed the house up,' Grams said. 'At least on the outside.'

'If they've turned it into a school, it's bound to look different on the inside,' Phil warned.

'I know.'

As they walked up to the entrance, a small boy in grey shirt and shorts charged past, then stopped and pushed open the heavy door for them. They entered a square black-and-white-tiled hall, an imposing wooden staircase rising opposite. To their left, an open door marked 'School Office' revealed a large desk, behind which sat a middle-aged woman in a tweed skirt. She rose and approached them.

'Lady Meeke? I'm Mrs Woodfield, the school secretary. We spoke on the telephone.'

Grams shook her hand and introduced Phil.

'Would you like a tour? I'm sure the place has changed a lot since you lived here, but I hope some of it will bring back memories.'

'Thank you, I'd love one.'

And so Mrs Woodfield showed them around the house, or rather the school. Phil had never been in a boarding school before, and he felt sorry for the kids who were shut away there for weeks on end, especially the smaller ones. But he had to admit the place had a friendly feel to it – this was no Dotheboys Hall. It did smell of small boys: strains of socks, body odour, school food, old books, ink and carbolic twisted through the corridors, dormitories and classrooms.

It wasn't a large school, but Phil was amazed at how dozens of children could eat, sleep and work in a home that had been built for just one family. His grandmother's family. They passed through the dormitories upstairs.

'This was my room,' said Grams. Phil could see how it might once have been a delightful bedroom, looking out over a lawn sloping gently down to a stream, with Dartmoor rising behind it. Now four small single beds and two bunk beds took up almost the entire floor space.

They passed through other dormitories that had belonged to Hugh and Sarah, although they weren't permitted to see Lord and Lady Chaddington's bedroom, which was now part of the headmaster's quarters.

Downstairs, the dining room was still a dining room, but narrow tables and benches had replaced the Chippendale table and chairs, and most of the other rooms had been turned into classrooms, as had the stables outside. Scrappy notices and solemn wood-and-gold honours boards proclaiming scholarships to minor public schools adorned the corridor walls, along with a random selection of prints: county maps, local churches, Indian hunting scenes. The classroom art was more educational: posters of an internal combustion engine and Roman legionaries marching along a straight road.

Finally they came to the school library.

This was a magnificent hexagonal room of bookshelves reaching two storeys high, a wrought-iron gallery giving access the higher shelves. A hexagonal skylight let in the June sunshine.

'I'm so pleased you kept this!' said Grams, her eyes shining. 'Oh, this was my favourite room in the house, Philip! My grandfather built it in the last century. And stocked it. There were wonderful books here.' She cast her eyes along the shelves. 'They've all gone, now.'

Mrs Woodfield sniffed. 'We're very proud of our library.'

'Oh, of course!' said Grams. 'Every school should have a library.' She glanced along a row of history textbooks. 'It's wonderful that children learn to love books here. It's just . . . it's different.'

'The grounds will have changed too,' said Mrs Woodfield. 'Although I suspect what we now call the headmaster's garden will be pretty much the same as it was. You are welcome to wander around outside, if you wish.'

And so they did. The stable yard had been turned into a playground, a pair of wonky football posts defied the summer term on the lawn, class-rooms had been built in the walled garden, but a square of grass survived, lined on one side with a border of flowers of different shapes and sizes and on the other with an arbour bearing a massive green plant.

'Ah, they've kept the wisteria!' said Grams. 'A couple of weeks ago this whole thing would have been purple.'

'It's very pretty,' said Phil. His enthusiasm for gardens lagged way behind his grandmother's, but even he could appreciate the beauty of the setting.

They walked over to the arbour. 'Let's sit here for a bit,' she said as they approached one of those benches engraved with the name of a past pupil which adorn all schools. They looked out over to the moor rising not more than a couple of miles away. They could hear the rustle of a brook at the bottom of the garden, and in the distance the squeals and cheers of small boys playing cricket.

'Are you sorry you came?' Phil asked.

'No,' said Grams. 'Well, partly. But I wanted to see it. I *needed* to see it.' She sighed. 'I loved it here. At least when I was a child. I'm not sure I came back here at all after about 1939. Until Sarah and I had to sell it.'

'Why was that?'

'You'll find out,' Grams said. She turned to her grandson. 'I think I need to begin my story, don't you?'

'Yes, I do.'

'We'll begin here, the weekend Hugh died.'

Chapter 4

February 1934, Chaddington Hall, Devon

I WAS NINETEEN, and I was waiting to get married. To whom, I had no idea.

The project had started the year before, my first season. My mother and I had decamped to our London house in Hill Street in Mayfair. Several weeks were given over to Mama visiting the mothers of other debutantes and both of us trying on a series of dresses, before the gruelling schedule of ball after ball began. Although I was her raw material, my mother was strangely confident. My elder sister Sarah's season had been a triumph; she had nabbed Tubby Partington-Smythe, a skinny cavalry officer who was the son of a marquess and a genial, considerate young man who had fallen instantly and heavily in love with her. They were now married – happily married. Although my mother considered me not nearly as good a catch as Sarah, she felt I had nice eyes, and her dressmaker could make something of my full figure. Although unfashionable, quite a few men liked a full figure, apparently.

And I was clever, she said. A much smaller number of men would like that.

The whole thing was the disaster I had expected it to be. The balls involved dance cards, which were carried around by the debs. The dance cards were filled in with the names of young men. Or not.

In my case not.

My mother soon got fed up with sitting out dances with me, and I ended up with a girl called Edwina, the daughter of an ambassador to a Balkan country who had seen the world and was interested in it. Her figure was 'full' top to toe, and she had unfortunate buck teeth, so she and I spent a lot of time together on the edges of the balls, much to Mama's annoyance. The one good thing was that eventually I got to go to Buckingham Palace to see the king. That was fun.

But now I was stuck in Chaddington Hall, with nothing but the library and Tallow, my beautiful grey mare, to amuse me.

And my brother Hugh, whenever he put in an appearance.

Luncheon was over and I was sitting in the small drawing room, reading my book, waiting for him to arrive from London. The small drawing room had a good view of the drive. Hugh was arriving 'some time after luncheon', and I was excited.

Sure enough, his dark blue Riley sped up the drive. I rushed out to meet him, overtaking Jecks, the butler, on the way.

Hugh waved and hopped out of the car, before giving me a hug. He was short for a man, about my height, with thick dark hair, blue eyes and a wide, wide smile that he now bestowed on me. He was desperately good-looking, according to the debs and their mothers, so Mama had come under pressure to procure him for a number of the balls last summer. He had liked Edwina too.

'*Ciamar a bha an turas agad?*' I said.

'What?'

'*Ciamar a bha an turas agad?*' I repeated.

'Ah!' Hugh gave me a wide grin. '*Bha turas math agam,*' he replied. 'I'm sorry, I didn't recognize your Gaelic pronunciation.'

'I was just guessing,' I said. 'It's difficult when you only have a textbook to go from.'

'Not bad, then,' said Hugh. 'I'm impressed.'

I grinned. Hugh had written to me that he had started learning Scots Gaelic for the fun of it, and I had wanted to surprise him. 'I

24

got Hatchards to send me MacLaren's *Gaelic Self-Taught*. It's fiend-ishly difficult, isn't it?'

'It is,' said Hugh. 'Which makes it more fun, don't you think?'

Unlike Hugh, I had never been to school. My parents had employed a succession of tutors and governesses. I had learned French and German from them. Hugh had taught me Latin and Greek, or at least got me started, and with Hugh's help I had had a bash at Italian. We both loved languages and were good at them, but Gaelic was a cut above the rest, even Greek.

Mama came down to greet her son, but Papa remained snoozing in his business room. Jecks took Hugh's suitcase up to his bedroom, and Hugh glanced at the sky.

'After that drive, I'd love to get some fresh air before it gets dark. Do you want to come with me, Ems?'

'Rather!' I said. Twenty minutes later we were crossing the brook at the bottom of the garden and heading across the fields towards the moor. It was a cloudy damp February day, and the top half of Dartmoor merged into the grey. The going was muddy, especially by the gates where the red South Devon cows had churned up the red south Devon soil. Hugh headed for a gully scored into the flank of the moor, from which a stream tumbled down to join the brook that ran by the Hall. It was a walk we had both done many times.

'Have you read *Down and Out in Paris and London*?' I asked. 'George Orwell. I've almost finished it. It's really very good.'

'I've heard good things about it.'

'Did you know that tramps are called tramps because they have to spend all day tramping from one parish to another? They are not allowed to spend more than one night in a parish. It's beastly!'

'I think I did know that,' said Hugh. 'And it does sound beastly.'

'Mind you, Paris is just as bad. The restaurants there are like the Black Hole of Calcutta, at least for the kitchen staff. I'm not sure I could bear to eat a meal there. Do you know this man Orwell?'

'I haven't met him,' Hugh said. 'I think Orwell isn't his real name. It's Blythe or Blair or something. And I believe he went to Eton.'

'Really? I find that disappointing.'

Our father had attended Eton and loathed it. Which is why he had sent Hugh to a public school in Wiltshire instead. I had imagined George Orwell as a crusading man of the people – certainly not someone who could have touched his relatives for the odd fiver if he was in real trouble.

'How is the cramming going?'

'All right, I think.' Hugh was cramming for the Foreign Office exam, which involved spending most of his days at an establishment near the British Museum, brushing up on his languages and learning economics and history.

'Are you confident? For the exam?'

'As confident as I can be,' said Hugh. 'But it's frightfully competitive. Last year they only took the top seven out of eighty-two applicants.'

'Well, I'm sure you'll pass,' I said. And I was. Top seven was easy for Hugh.

'What are your plans?' Hugh asked.

'I have no plans. I'm waiting for a big fat husband to come down the chimney.'

'Is Mama making you do the season again this summer?'

If a deb failed to snare a husband in her first season, the rule was she could have another go the following year. 'She's trying. But not as hard as I would have expected. I think she may have given up.'

'Good. It really isn't your thing, is it?'

'They're all chumps, Hugh. Every single one of them.'

Hugh laughed.

We crossed a stile into open moorland, and the path pointed steeply uphill, along the edge of the brook. We were both panting. The gully stretched up into the mist.

I felt outrageously happy, being with my brother, alone, up on the moor we both knew so well. I started to sing: '*Oh, 'tis my delight on a dirty night, to bomb the bourgeoisie!*'

It was a song Hugh had taught me when I was fifteen. He laughed and joined in as we climbed.

'I think we should stop here,' he said at last, panting.

So we paused and turned to look back at Chaddington Hall in its wooded valley, two plumes of smoke twisting up in the still, damp air, the parish church squatting a short distance from it.

Hugh took a deep breath. 'I do miss this. Especially after London.'

I glanced at my brother. 'I do have a plan. But I'll need your help.'

'Oh yes?' Hugh grinned at me, as if expecting an idea that was a little odd.

He got one.

'I'd like to visit the Soviet Union.'

'What! Mama and Papa would never let you.'

'But you went last year.' Hugh had gone for three weeks with two old friends from school and Cambridge.

'Yes. And they didn't like that much either.'

'Well, if they let you, why shouldn't they let me? And don't say it's because I am a girl.'

'Because you are a girl.'

'I told you not to say that!'

'I know you did, but it's true.'

'It may be true, but it's wrong.'

'It may be wrong – it *is* wrong – but where are you going to get the money from if they don't give it to you?'

'I've been saving up. And . . .'

'Yes?' Hugh looked at me suspiciously.

'And maybe you could lend me some? When my fat husband comes down the chimney I can pay you back.'

Hugh didn't say yes. But then he didn't say no either. 'You can't go by yourself.'

'Well, that's the other thing you can help me with. Could you put me in touch with people? Women, preferably. You must know heaps of people who'd like to go.'

Hugh set off down the hillside. 'I'll lend you the money – no, I'll *give* you the money, as long as you promise not to tell Papa where it came from. Or anyone else for that matter.'

'Oh, you are a darling!'

'And I can give you the names of a couple of people to write to. But you must keep my name out of it. You see . . .'

'What?' I asked. I didn't like the sound of Hugh's voice. 'What is it, Hugh?'

'I know you are not going to like this, Ems, but I've changed my mind about a few things. Political things.'

'Yes?'

'You see, as I've got a bit older, I've come to realize that some of my thoughts on politics were a little naive. Fine in theory – admirable in theory – but not practical in the real world.'

'I don't understand.'

'I'm still a socialist. I believe in helping the poor. It's just I'm no longer sure that communism is the right way to do it.'

'But . . . Hugh! What about all the stuff we've talked about for the last couple of years? The books you've made me read! I read the whole of *Capital*, for heaven's sake! You're not saying that's naive?'

'I suppose I am a bit.'

'Well, what about Russia? You came back saying the Soviets have really got the answer. Everyone is equal. The farms are modernizing. The Five Year Plan is bringing prosperity. You saw it with your own eyes!'

'We saw a lot of starving people in Russia. And they lock a lot of people up. Dick came away with a different opinion; I think he may be right.' Dick was one of the two old school friends who had travelled with Hugh.

'Those were all kulaks, you said!'

'Maybe. But, as Dick says, kulaks are people too.' Kulaks were rich Russian peasants whom Stalin had accused of profiteering off poor Russian peasants. 'Warnes of Tumphill Farm is a kulak. Why should he starve?'

We trudged down the hill in silence, as I tried to make sense of it. Tumphill Farm was one of the most successful farms on the estate, and Mr Warnes was generally admired for his expertise. I liked Mr Warnes; everyone did.

And if that's what the Soviets did to the kulaks, think what they had done to the landowners. Like us.

But that wasn't the point! I had to recognize I was being brainwashed by my class when I should be worrying about the people, the masses.

'Is it because you are applying for the Foreign Office?' I asked. 'You don't want them to think you are a communist?'

'That may be part of it,' Hugh said. 'I knew you would be upset. You don't have to change *your* mind.'

'Why? Because it's all right if *I* am naive?'

'No. Because it's all right if you make up your own mind. It might even be a good thing.'

That last comment stung me, and I spent the whole time until dinner stewing. It stung because it was true. I was and always had been totally dependent on Hugh for my education, and hence for my opinions. So I agreed with him. Probably always. Which, as he said, was probably not a good thing.

But what choice did I have? My parents had refused to allow me to go to school. Although he never came right out and said it, my father seemed to think that money spent on educating girls was money wasted. My mother seemed to think it was positively harmful, especially for me. She was suspicious of my reading, of my love of learning new languages, of the awkward questions I had been asking people since the age of five. She lived in fear of me becoming a 'bluestocking', one of those females to be pitied who went to university, scared off eligible men and reached premature old maidenhood at thirty. Sarah was my mother's model of what a young woman should be: witty, charming, well dressed, an excellent horsewoman, capable of conversing with anyone, but unburdened with too much education. Sarah had made a fine marriage.

Why couldn't I be more like Sarah?

I often wondered that myself. I loved my sister, and I agreed with my mother that she was a great catch for the lucky Lord Tubby. But I was different. Hugh understood that.

Hugh was my window on the world of ideas. He brought them back with him from school or university, smuggled them into the house and unpacked them to show to me. Poetry – Kipling at first, then Hardy and Swinburne, and now Brooke, Eliot, Yeats and Pound. Literature – Dickens, Tolstoy, Dostoevsky, Hugo, Zola; and then Bloomsbury: Woolf, Forster, Strachey – some of whom Hugh had actually met. He brought me languages, economics, history, even physics.

It wasn't just Hugh, it was also my grandfather, whom I barely remembered, but who had stocked our wonderful library with many of the tools I needed to follow where Hugh led.

In Hugh's second year at Cambridge, he had become interested in socialism and then communism. So I had read Marx and Engels, articles by Lenin, and *The Intelligent Woman's Guide to Socialism and Capitalism* by George Bernard Shaw. I read about the General Strike, the breakdown of capitalism in 1929, the Hunger Marchers from Jarrow, the rise of Mussolini in Italy and Hitler in Germany. I shared my brother's anger at all this. I wanted to do something about it – but stuck in Devon I didn't know what I could do, apart from read and learn.

And now he tried to tell me it was all naivety.

I felt betrayed. I felt angry. I felt used.

It wasn't just that. I felt that a bond between me and my brother had snapped. Until that moment, he and I were two young twentieth-century right-thinking rebels together in a nineteenth-century household of obsolete aristocrats. Now there was just me.

I felt abandoned.

I slunk off to the library until it was time to change for dinner. I was late to the drawing room to welcome our guests, Sir Ivor and Lady Growcott, who lived about ten miles away, and Roland Meeke, a diplomat who had taken a cottage on the estate for a couple of weeks to go hunting. The purpose of the dinner was ostensibly to introduce Mr Meeke to the Growcotts, but was of course really to introduce him to Hugh. The scheme had been cooked up by Mama, who had urged Mr Meeke to come down to Devon, tempting him with the use of one of our hunters, in the hope of helping her son become a diplomat.

The Growcotts, affable gentry pushing sixty, I had known since childhood, but I had never met Mr Meeke before. The first thing I noticed was how dark he was: black hair, black eyebrows, deep brown eyes, even his skin was an unseasonable shade of brown. He was about the same height as Hugh, but whereas my brother was broad of shoulder and face, Mr Meeke was slim: narrow face, thin fingers, delicate gestures.

And charm. Oodles of effortless charm.

It was quite difficult to charm me in those days, and Mr Meeke didn't seem to try. We were seated next to each other at dinner. I was curious about a diplomat's life, a curiosity springing from those hours of conversation with my friend Edwina, and Mr Meeke did not disappoint. He came from a diplomatic family; like Edwina his father had been an ambassador – he'd served in Vienna and Brazil. Mr Meeke's first posting had been to Prague and, after a couple of years in Whitehall, he was about to head off to the embassy in Paris. He had a couple of weeks' leave before he went, and he wanted to get in some foxhunting.

Before I knew it, I had agreed to ride around the estate with him the next morning.

'Do you think the Schutzbund will succeed against Dollfuss?' I asked him.

Mr Meeke blinked at the sudden change of subject, a small smile flickering beneath his narrow moustache.

'I think the socialists are falling into a trap,' he replied. 'Dollfuss is provoking them so that he can come down hard on them. It will give him an excuse to lock up their leaders and ban the socialist parties.'

'Do you approve of Dollfuss?'

'No. But I don't approve of the Schutzbund either.' We spent several minutes discussing the details of Austrian politics, before Lady Growcott 'rescued' him. I am sure that's what she thought she was doing, although it seemed to me that Mr Meeke was interested in my opinions, even if they were gleaned from no more than a careful daily reading of *The Times*. But perhaps he was just being charming.

'Did you see Bettinson, Hugh?' Papa asked his son.

'Yes, I did, as a matter of fact,' Hugh replied. 'He gave me luncheon at the Carlton last week.'

Sir Patrick Bettinson was an MP for a constituency in the north of the county.

'And?'

'He's offered me a post as his secretary until the FO exam results. And I think he'll keep me on if I need to retake.'

'Good man, Bettinson,' said Sir Ivor. 'You can learn a lot from a fellow like that, Hugh.'

'That's what I thought,' said Hugh.

'You didn't take the job?' I asked. I sounded more horrified than I meant to, but less horrified than I felt.

Hugh looked at me uncomfortably. 'Yes. I did.'

'Excellent!' said Papa. 'Ivor's right. You can learn a lot from Bettinson. Do you know Sir Patrick, Mr Meeke?'

'But Sir Patrick is a Conservative!' I interrupted, before Mr Meeke had a chance to answer.

'And the Conservatives are in power,' said Mama, glaring at me. 'Or the National Government is, which is pretty much the same thing.'

'Hugh!' I beseeched my brother. 'I know you told me you had changed your mind about politics, but you said you were still a socialist. Bettinson's a dinosaur. He should be extinct! You can't possibly work for him.'

Hugh's expression of discomfort turned to pain. 'If I am going to represent my country abroad, I am going to have to represent the government, whatever their political persuasion. Working for Sir Patrick will help that.'

Something inside me snapped. I profoundly disagreed with Hugh, but it wasn't that which ignited my anger, or not just that. It wasn't even that Hugh had betrayed me, although by now I believed he had. It was that my brother had shown himself to be a weaker man than I had always believed him to be. He was a hypocrite, a moral coward. The most important person to me in the world had let me down, and I didn't like it one bit.

He was leaving me all alone.

'You are going to throw over all your beliefs, Hugh, just like that?' I was shouting now. 'What about me, Hugh? What about me?'

'What *about* you?' said Mama sharply. 'This has nothing to do with you. Behave yourself!'

'All right then, Hugh. What about you?'

Everyone stared at me. Including Hugh. The others were staring in incredulity, but Hugh understood, and I could see he was ashamed.

I wanted to scream at him. A voice at the back of my head started to yell, and I wanted to open my mouth to let the sound out. My eyes stung; I could feel the tears coming.

I couldn't bear the humiliation of crying at my brother's betrayal of me.

'I'm sorry, please excuse me,' I said, pushing my chair back and rushing from the room.

Chapter 5

I DIDN'T SLEEP well, and I was awake when the world outside my bedroom curtains turned from black to grey, although when I drew them, the clouds had all gone and the sun was peeking over the moor.

I expected I would be the first down to breakfast, but I passed Hugh on his way out, clutching the flat cap he wore when driving.

'Morning, Emma,' he said with a tentative grin.

'Morning.' I tried to sound non-committal, but it probably came out sullen.

'I'm off to Okehampton. I'm convinced there's a problem with the carburettor, but they can't spot it in London, so I'm going to try Wilkins. If anyone can find it, he can.'

'Right you are,' I said unenthusiastically. I am interested in a lot of things, but I have never been interested in car engines.

I kept moving towards the breakfast room, but Hugh stopped me. 'Ems?' He grabbed my sleeve. 'Ems!'

I turned to him.

'Look. I'm sorry. I really am.'

I met his eyes. I could tell he was indeed sorry.

And so he should be.

I brushed his hand away, and went in to breakfast.

I was concerned that Mr Meeke wouldn't appear at the stables, given my behaviour the night before, but he arrived fifteen minutes after me. Jonny the groom got Tallow ready for me, and Merlin for Mr Meeke, and we set off through the woods behind the Hall. It was a glorious morning. No sign of the clouds of the day before, and the clearing skies had brought a light brush of frost. The birds seemed happy: blackbirds, thrushes and robins were yelling their heads off, with a woodpecker somewhere deep in the wood providing a percussion accompaniment.

'Can we go up on the moor, do you think?' Mr Meeke asked.

'If you like,' I said. 'It will be lovely up there this morning.'

We left the wood and cantered across an open field to a bridle path that would lead us up and on to the open moor. Mr Meeke was graceful on a horse, and Merlin took to him.

'Do you get the chance to hunt much?' I asked him.

'No. That's the problem with being a diplomat, and the child of a diplomat. I have spent my entire life in capital cities. It's why I like to get out when I can, and hunting blows away the cobwebs.'

'You ride well.'

'Thank you. I learned in Vienna when I was a small boy. They know how to ride there.'

'Did you see the Lipizzaners?'

'Many times. And they are more beautiful in the flesh than they look in photographs.'

'Have you ever ridden one?'

'Sadly, no.'

'I'd love to go to Vienna,' I said.

'You should. Can't you get your parents to send you? I'm sure I could arrange someone for you to stay with. But then I'm even more sure your mother could.'

'She could if she wanted to,' I said. Mother knew everyone. She spent at least half her time up in London, often leaving Papa behind at Chaddington.

'I assume it was she who invited you down here?' I asked.

'Oh, yes. Jolly kind of her, really.'

I glanced at him. Did he realize *why* she had invited him?

He smiled at me. 'I enjoyed meeting your brother last night. Nice chap. I'm sure he will do very well in the FO.'

I returned his smile. Of course he realized; Mr Meeke was no fool.

'I'm so sorry I made such a frightful idiot of myself last night,' I said. 'I hadn't thought about it until just now, but Mama will be furious with me for telling you Hugh is a communist. Or *was* a communist.'

'I doubt your brother will need my help. He seems very capable.'

'Yes, but you should know that when he says he has given up on communism, he really means it. That's what has got me so upset.'

'But you are still a believer, I take it?'

I glanced at Mr Meeke to see whether he was teasing me, but he seemed to want to know the answer. So I told him. I told him what I thought about Marx. What I thought about Lenin. How I longed to visit the Soviet Union. How I admired Beatrice Webb and Rosa Luxemburg. How I admired the Austrian Schutzbund. And how I *hated* our own National Government.

He listened. He asked me questions. He knew a lot.

'But does it matter to you if Hugh has changed his mind?' he said. 'You don't have to change yours.'

'I know. I know I rely too much on my brother. In fact, he said just the same as you. Hugh has taught me virtually all I know. He has made me who I am, and I'm grateful for it. But now I feel as if he has abandoned me. I know it shouldn't, but it just makes me angry. So very angry.'

'I see,' said Mr Meeke. 'But he's still your brother. He'll always be your brother.'

'Yes,' I said. 'Yes, he will. I'm just being silly.'

'No. I can see how important he is to you. You're not being silly.'

We climbed the flank of Dartmoor, rising high above where Hugh and I had walked the day before. Eventually, we reached the top. On one side, Dartmoor stretched out bleak and desolate, folds of grass and bog scattered with its famous tors, stacks of stone that had been dumped on the moor by a long-forgotten giant. On the other, we looked out over the hedgerows and wooded valleys of

Devon towards Cornwall and Bodmin Moor in the distance. Thin February sunshine brought golden life to the leafless trees and bracken below us.

'See that tor over there?' I said, pointing to a cluster of rocks about three-quarters of a mile away. 'I'll race you.'

Tallow and Merlin were usually evenly matched, but Mr Meeke urged Merlin ahead of my mare, without using his crop, I was pleased to see. The speed, the countryside beneath me, Tallow's muscles at full stretch invigorated me as they always did. We zipped past the tor, and I pulled up next to Mr Meeke, whose clever smile had turned into a broad grin.

'God, I love this!' he said.

'So do I.'

'Are you hunting on Thursday?'

'I don't hunt any more,' I said. 'I used to really enjoy it, but I stopped last year.'

'That's a shame. It would have been fun to ride out together.'

'We can do that anyway,' I said. 'Papa would never believe this, but I've discovered it's perfectly possible to enjoy riding a horse without killing a fox at the end of it.'

'But what about the thrill of the chase? You can't deny that's real.'

I did know it was real. 'It's true: I do miss the thrill. But I never enjoyed seeing the hounds tearing foxes apart. And one day I realized I couldn't pretend all that needless bloodshed wasn't happening.'

'But don't you think it's natural? For man to hunt an animal? That's why it is so exciting; we've been doing it for millennia.'

'I think it's natural to hunt an animal for food. But not for sport. Or it's natural in the same way it's natural for men to be cruel, that it's natural for men to demand the death of a gladiator in the ring. Natural isn't necessarily right. Is it?'

I had tried this argument out on a number of people over the previous year. Mostly it only served to irritate them, so I had given up. But I didn't want to hide my opinion from Mr Meeke, and I was curious how he would react.

He looked thoughtful for a moment. 'No. It isn't.'

We rode on in silence. I was not sure whether I had won my argument, or whether he was just being diplomatic, but he had listened to me.

It was a long time since I had spoken to a man apart from Hugh who had really listened to me. In fact, Hugh was the only one.

We left the moor, dropping down towards the Hall, passing Dockenbush Farm and trotting along Dockenbush Lane, a tiny road bordered by high banks and hedges.

We crested a small hump, two abreast.

'Hello. What's that?' said Mr Meeke.

The lane ducked down and then turned sharp right. A knot of four or five people, one of whom wore a policeman's uniform, was gathered around a car, the bonnet of which was crumpled into the trunk of a large oak tree right on the bend.

The car was blue. I recognized the make. A Riley.

Something was stretched out on the road, something covered by a travel blanket. The travel blanket I had given Hugh for Christmas two months before.

'Oh no. No!' I cried.

I jumped off Tallow and ran to the car.

The policeman, PC Melluish, stood in my way as I rushed towards the body. 'Now, miss, best not to look.'

'I must see him!' I shouted.

'No, miss.'

I kicked PC Melluish hard in the shin and pushed past him.

I pulled back the rug from Hugh's face. I will never forget what I saw – it was a mess. His forehead and cheek had been smashed. There was blood, but there was also bone and pinkish stuff, which I realized later was brain matter.

It was truly horrible. But I'm glad I saw him that last time, in Dockenbush Lane.

Chapter 6

June 1979, Chaddington Hall

'Dockenbush Lane was the back way you made me take coming here?' Phil asked.

'That's right. That's where Hugh died.'

'It's a shame I never got to meet him.'

'A great shame.'

'I'm sorry, Grams,' said Phil, reaching over to touch his grandmother's hand.

Emma seemed surprised by the gesture, but squeezed Phil's hand gratefully.

'How did it happen?'

'They said it was ice on the road. That he skidded.'

'You sound doubtful?'

'There had been a tiny bit of frost on the ground early that morning, but there was none on the road by then. And I couldn't understand at that point why Hugh had taken Dockenbush Lane. You've seen it. It's not exactly more scenic, it just takes longer than the Tavistock Road.'

Phil frowned. '"Understand at that point"? You mean you understand now?'

'I think so. Come on. Let's go and see his grave. It's in the churchyard.'

They left the bench under the wisteria, and Emma led Phil to a small path at the side of the house that passed some sheds on the way to the church. Emma stumbled and grabbed at Phil's arm for support.

'Sorry,' she said. 'I seem to be unsteady on my feet these days.' She clung on to his arm.

'I didn't realize you were a real communist,' said Phil. 'Mum never told me. Does she know?'

'Of course she knows. I think she's ashamed of me. A loyal Conservative, your mother, always has been. It's her form of rebellion. Against me.'

'Are you still a communist?'

'No. What with one thing and another, it lost its allure. But I still vote Labour. What about you? Presumably last month was your first election. What did you vote?'

'Conservative,' Phil said.

'Just like your parents.' Emma made no attempt to keep the disappointment out of her voice.

Sod you, Phil thought with a flash of irritation. I'll vote the way I want.

They passed through a gate in a low wall into a churchyard. Tall oaks guarded the perimeter, throwing most of the yard into shadow, and three or four smaller, twisted dark green yews dotted the uneven ground. The church lurked a few feet away, and another gate at the far side of the yard led out towards the village. One large corner was given over to memorials of varying degrees of ornamentation to Chaddingtons and Breartons.

'Here it is.' Emma stopped in front of a relatively simple stone.

Hugh Brearton 1911–1934

'I have spread my dreams under your feet'

'It's Yeats,' Emma said. 'I chose it.'

'Why was he called Brearton, not Chaddington?'

'We all started off as Brearton – it was my maiden name. Hugh should have become Lord Chaddington eventually.'

Emma stood staring at the stone.

Phil noticed a wooden seat a few yards back against the wall of the churchyard and withdrew. Next to Hugh's grave he saw another for

Lord Chaddington, but there seemed to be none for Lady Chaddington. Phil wondered where she was. Was it possible she was still alive? Surely someone would have told him if she was.

Given what he was coming to know about his family, probably not.

He watched his grandmother stand straight but perfectly still at the grave of her brother.

He didn't yet understand what she was doing. He knew whatever it was was really important for her, and he was pleased that she had decided to share it with him. He was becoming increasingly curious where all this was leading, and happy to go along for the ride.

The churchyard was peaceful, and Phil was content to wait in the late-afternoon sun peeking beneath the leaves of the oaks. After ten minutes or so, Emma turned and joined him on the bench. Her eyes were dry and her expression thoughtful, rather than miserable.

'Let me tell you about Hugh's funeral.'

Chapter 7

February 1934, Chaddington

WE WERE ALL devastated, Mama, Papa and me, but we were all devastated alone.

I felt numb. I felt as though I was floating six feet above everything in a daze. I didn't cry for twenty-four hours. I was lost.

I didn't hug my parents, and they didn't hug me, or each other, from what I could tell. I'm ashamed to say I was polite to them. Polite! What was I thinking? What were we doing?

Papa crumpled. Everything about him sagged: his face, his shoulders, his spirit.

My mother was immediately angry. Her eyes were aflame. Every interaction with my father or me seemed to consume her with irritation, irritation which she could barely restrain with politeness. Whereas my politeness was a hazy indifference, hers was a fiery cold.

We needed Sarah to unlock our grief. We took too long to track her down and tell her, but when we eventually found her, at a friend's house in Northamptonshire, she came at once. She hugged us all. She made us all cry. She made us talk about Hugh. I was so relieved to see her; we all were.

The other person who was a help was Roland Meeke. He helped my father with the practicalities. He helped my mother with her frustration. He helped me talk about my brother, explain him, remember him. There was no foxhunting for Roland, but he and I did go for a couple of long rides together.

Sarah and he organized the funeral, which was a major event. Hugh had had lots of friends, from school, from Cambridge, from all sorts of unlikely places. As did my parents from London, and then there were all the county people, and relatives young and old, some of whom I couldn't remember ever meeting. Hugh's death touched a multitude.

St Mary's Chaddington was overflowing – barely a third of those present could fit in the church. The churchyard was heaving; I was glad that I had a place in the procession directly behind the coffin.

My family stood together, together really for the first time since his death, as we watched him go into the ground, dust to dust.

I was standing in the crowd in a daze, waiting for my parents to lead everyone back to the Hall, when I heard my name.

'Emma?'

I turned to see a tall man with a slight stoop and fair hair brushed back from a high forehead.

'Dick?'

'That's right. I had no trouble recognizing you. Though you must have been eleven when I last saw you.' Dick Loxton had come to stay with us a couple of times during school half-terms.

'Oh, I remember. You put up with me manfully.' I recalled I had interrogated him about the hypocrisy of the Church of England. Dick's father was a vicar.

He grinned. 'You took me aback a bit.'

'I warn you, I haven't changed much.'

'I know. Hugh talked about you a lot.'

'Did he?' For the first time in over a week, I could feel myself smiling. 'Thank you for telling me that,' I said.

Dick's blue eyes looked on me kindly. 'I'm sorry.'

'And I'm sorry for you. You were friends for a long time.'

'Yes.' Dick took a deep breath. 'He was my best friend. He made me see the world differently. Understand the world differently.'

'I know what you mean.'

The crowd began to shift as Mama and Papa made their way stiffly along the path back to the Hall, Papa's shoulders drooping, Mama standing erect, a good two feet distance between them.

Dick gave me his arm and we followed.

'I must ask you something, Dick,' I said. 'Did Hugh say anything to you about renouncing communism?'

'No,' said Dick. 'Mind you, I haven't seen him for ages. Not since last summer. I've been stuck teaching history and scripture in a school in Leeds. But we have corresponded.'

'Did he write to you about politics? The thing is, he was always so enthusiastic about Marxism. And after he came back from the Soviet Union, he seemed all the more excited about it. But then he said that you had persuaded him he was wrong. That the kulaks deserved to be let off.'

'It wasn't that, exactly. It was odd. Hugh, Freddie Pelham-Walsh and I all went on the same trip. We all saw the same things. But they thought they were experiencing a socialist paradise where everyone was equal and the government had worked out how to provide good jobs for all the workers.'

'And you didn't see that?'

'I saw a massive prison, where everyone was being spied upon, everyone had to do what they were told, and people were starving in the streets.'

'It sounds like you won him round. The other day he told me he had given up on communism completely. I thought it might have something to do with trying to get into the Foreign Office. I must admit, it upset me.'

'Why?' said Dick.

'Because I am just as much a communist as Hugh is. Was. And because I was afraid he was giving up on his principles because they were inconvenient to his new career.'

'That sounds very unlike Hugh.'

'That's what I thought.' I sighed. 'I wish I could talk to him about it now.' I swallowed. 'The last time we spoke I shouted at him. And then I ignored him the next morning. The morning he died.'

Dick touched my arm. His kind blue eyes studied me. 'Hugh was always so fond of you. Incredibly proud of you, actually. He was always a man of principle and he loved you. That's all you need to remember.'

His words were immensely comforting. The tears I could feel coming receded.

Drinks were being served in the Hall: cups of tea, sherry or something stronger for those who needed it.

A very tall woman and a slightly shorter man made their way towards Dick and me, clutching glasses of what looked like brandy and soda.

'Freddie!' Dick pumped the hand of his old school friend, whom I had met briefly once or twice before. Freddie's suit was much better cut than Dick's, and a gold watch chain sneaked across the beginnings of a tiny bulge in his tummy. I noticed he was wearing pink socks. He shook Dick's hand with a sad smile, the two red spots on his round cheeks glowing dully.

'Hello, Kay,' said Dick. 'I am so sorry.'

Kay was the tall woman, slim, dark, aloof, a few years older than Freddie and Dick. 'Thank you, Dick,' she said.

I was puzzled. Why was Dick, Hugh's oldest friend, proffering condolences to this strange woman and not the other way around?

'Have you met Kay, Emma?' Dick said.

Emma shook her head.

'This is Kay Lesser. Kay, this is Emma, Hugh's sister.' Dick looked at me, seeming to understand something. 'Kay was a . . . good friend of Hugh's. We met her in Russia, but she is living in London now.'

What!

'Hugh told me a lot about you,' said Kay. Her accent was American. Rough American. There was a touch of haughtiness in

45

the way she drew from her cigarette, looking down on me as she did so. I was taller than average myself; not many women looked down on me.

'Well, he hasn't told me anything about you,' I said coldly. Who on earth was this woman, and what had she been doing with my brother?

Kay assessed me under thick eyebrows, taking in the hostility which I was making no attempt to hide. There was something odd about her, a dark unconventional beauty based upon intriguing imperfections of her features, imperfections that would have rendered her ugly if she had carried herself differently. I could see what Hugh might have seen in her – if indeed he *had* seen anything in her.

'I'm not surprised. He told me his family wouldn't like me.'

'Why ever not? We are perfectly hospitable.'

'I'm sure you are,' said Kay. 'Because I am a communist. And because of my race.'

'Your race?'

'I'm Jewish. And I'm American.'

'So what?' I said.

'So Hugh thought your family would have difficulty with that.'

'Why should I have difficulty with that?' I said.

'I don't think he meant you. I think he meant your parents.'

The frustrating thing was that she might well have been right.

'Did you know Hugh well?' I asked her. I both dreaded the answer and needed to know it.

Kay Lesser looked at me. I realised she was, in some ways, a kindred spirit. We both loved Hugh and we were both angry at his death. But, at that moment, I hated her, and I don't think she liked me much either.

'He asked me to marry him a couple of weeks ago,' Kay said, quietly.

That, I wasn't expecting. My mouth fell open in shock. Kay seemed to enjoy my confusion.

At last I managed to spit out the obvious question. 'And what did you say?'

Before Kay could answer, Freddie Pelham-Walsh, who had been talking to Dick, interrupted. 'Poor Emma,' he said. 'I know how close you and Hugh were. He was a good man. A bloody good man.'

Freddie was Irish, or Anglo-Irish, which was why he had been sent to an Anglican boarding school in Britain. His voice was a unique creation, deep, rich and plummy, with a touch of Irish in his 'r's and his 'a's. I thought I detected a slight slur and I suspected that he had drunk more than the half-glass of brandy and soda he was holding.

'He was,' I said. Although I knew Freddie genuinely meant what he said, I was irritated that he had shown up to my brother's funeral tight.

'Have you noticed the socks?' Freddie said, raising his ankle. 'Hugh and I used to wear pink silk socks at school. Our little bit of rebellion.'

'I remember those socks!' I said, smiling now. 'Papa hated them.'

'So did our housemaster. But I always thought they were rather fine. I gave Hugh his for his sixteenth birthday.'

One of those uncomfortable funeral-conversation silences descended on us. Freddie crashed into it. He leaned in towards me, and spoke in a loud stage whisper. 'Look here,' he said. 'Are they sure it was an accident?'

'Of course they are sure,' I said. But I was thinking of the lack of ice on the road and Hugh's strange decision to take the back lane instead of the simpler, straighter and much quicker Tavistock Road to come home from Okehampton.

'Maybe he was killed. Have they thought of that?'

'Killed?' I said. 'Who would kill him? And why?'

'That's easy,' Freddie said. 'The secret service. Because he was a Russian spy.'

'Don't be an ass, Freddie,' said Dick. 'Hugh wasn't a spy. He wasn't even a real communist. Emma says he had given it up.'

'What do you think, Kay?' Freddie said. 'Am I right? Some spook killed poor Hugh and made it look like a car smash?'

Kay sighed. 'You're just making that up.' She glanced at me with the first glimmer of sympathy. 'You are a dumb son of a bitch, Freddie.'

But . . . I wondered.

Chapter 8

June 1979, Chaddington

'Have you got a photo of Hugh?' Phil asked.

'I have, as a matter of fact,' Emma said. Phil had known she would. She reached into her handbag and pulled out a dog-eared black-and-white photograph of a man of about twenty wearing a cricket sweater and a blazer, staring at the camera with a broad friendly grin.

He reminded Phil of someone. With a start he realized who it was.

'Looks a bit like me, doesn't he?'

Emma smiled and took the photo back. 'Yes,' she said. 'He does. I noticed that about you from when you were five.'

'*Was* Hugh a spy?'

Emma stood up and smoothed her dress. 'Shall we go?'

Phil shouldn't have expected his grandmother to answer such a straightforward question. But he was confident she would tell him. In time.

'Where to next?' he asked.

'The ferry.'

'We're going all the way to Dover tonight?'

'Not Dover. Plymouth. I've booked a night crossing to Brittany.'

So they left Chaddington and drove the twenty-five miles to Plymouth, in plenty of time for the ferry. As the boat pulled away from the ferry terminal and steamed through the Sound and past Plymouth Hoe out into the English Channel, Phil thought of how he had been looking forward to this moment for nine months, since he and Mike had cooked up their European trip one break time after German. It was supposed to have been an adventure, marking the transition from childhood to adulthood, or at least to studenthood. Instead of which, he was babysitting his old gran around the more staid parts of two European capitals.

And yet. Phil liked his old gran, who wasn't even really that old. And he had a feeling that this might turn into an adventure after all.

They were sitting on deck, watching the land recede. He heard a thump and a yell behind him, and he turned to see a man who looked rather like Frank Stapleton, the Arsenal striker, tripping into an English family eating sandwiches. It was the ten-year-old daughter who had yelped and she looked cross. The man apologized, and the mum smoothed things over. On closer inspection, Phil could see that the guy was not really that much like Frank Stapleton after all – he was shorter and his hair was a bit longer. But he was no doubt doing the same thing Phil was doing, but in reverse. He didn't look English – probably German or Dutch. A student going around Europe on his own. Maybe he had been hitch-hiking in England? Phil wondered how England would seem to a foreign student. Could the oh-so-familiar Chiltern Hills seem exotic?

Perhaps.

'Did you know you used to be able fly a car to France?' Emma said. 'In the fifties. Roland and I did it a couple of times. From Lydd Aerodrome to Le Touquet. Very luxurious.'

'I can't imagine that,' Phil said.

'Yes. They just opened up the front of the aeroplane, and drove your car up a ramp. Much quicker than a crane winching it on to a boat.'

'You married Mr Meeke, then,' Phil said. 'Grandpa.'

'I did. It was not at all surprising I fell in love with him. He was intelligent, good-looking, charming. He treated me seriously. I was bereft with the loss of Hugh. There was an enormous gap in my life, and Roland was there to fill it. He knew about life. He knew about many of the things I was interested in. He listened to me.

'What was less clear to everyone – except me – was why he liked me. He was as eligible as they come. A successful diplomat with a promising career, he was thirty-two, thirteen years older than me, but of eminently marriageable age. He could have had his pick, and he chose the strange Brearton girl – me.

'I thought I understood it. I had my own vanity: I thought I was intelligent and fascinating. I believed that the reason none of the young men had shown any interest in me so far was that they were too stupid to realize it. Chumps. All it took was for a man of the intelligence of Hugh to meet me, and he would be smitten. Roland was that man.' Emma smiled ruefully at Phil. 'My brother was right – I *was* naive.'

'Sounds to me you got it about right,' Phil said.

'We saw a lot of each other in the couple of weeks after Hugh's death. Then Roland headed off for Paris, but he came back to Devon as soon as he could get some leave. The next time I saw him was in London. He had invited me to dinner at Boulestin, and I had gone up to town with Mama. He proposed! I accepted. Mama was thrilled.

'Roland's father had died, but I met his mother, who was almost as dark-skinned as he was. It turned out that she was Anglo-Indian, her mother had been the daughter of a Rajput maharajah. Papa was a little taken aback by this, but Mama persuaded him that royal blood, however minor, was on the whole a good thing, even if it was Indian. We were married five months later in the village church, and I was off the books.'

'And you went to Paris?'

'And I went to Paris. Where we are going tomorrow.'

Hold on a moment, Phil thought. 'So that means my, er, great-grandmother was an Indian princess?'

'Great-great-grandmother, I think,' said Emma.

'Oh yes,' Phil said, doing the calculation. 'That's quite a long way back, isn't it? It doesn't exactly make me a prince. But I like the idea.'

Another thing his mother had omitted to tell him.

Emma winced. For a moment, Phil thought he had said something wrong, but then she touched her forehead.

'You OK, Grams?'

'I don't know. Wait a moment.'

Phil waited. Emma winced again. 'I think I'm getting a headache. Do you mind if we go in?'

They left the deck and entered one of the lounges, sitting on a plastic seat looking out at the grey Channel.

The headache got worse. 'I think I'm going to have to turn in,' Emma said.

'Here, I'll come with you.' Phil led her to the cabin Emma had booked. She had reserved one for each of them; Phil was quite sure that he and Mike would have just kipped on the seats in the lounge.

Emma emitted a groan as she flopped on her bunk.

'Is it a migraine?' Phil asked.

'No.'

'Shall I see if there is a ship's doctor?'

'No.'

'Are you sure?'

'Yes. I know what it is, and there is nothing anyone can do about it.' She closed her eyes. 'Apart from take a pill. Can you look in my bag? There's a box of pills.'

Phil opened Emma's suitcase and began rummaging.

'Not my suitcase, you idiot, I said my bag. My handbag!'

He turned to see his grandmother glaring at him. He snapped the suitcase shut.

'Did you see anything?' Emma demanded.

Phil blushed. 'I saw your underwear. I'm sorry, Grams. I just got a bit flustered.'

'You cannot afford to get flustered on this trip, Philip!' said Emma. 'Now look in my handbag.'

Phil swiftly found the pills, and gave her two with a glass of water. He offered to stay with her while she slept – there was an empty bunk – but she told him to go and get himself some supper. He did so, promising to return to check on her.

Her headache worried him.

So, too, did what he had seen in her suitcase.

It wasn't his grandmother's underwear, which wasn't particularly remarkable. It was something else that definitely was remarkable.

At the bottom of the suitcase, underneath the underwear and wrapped in a green dressing gown, had nestled a long, grey revolver and a box of ammunition.

PART 2

PARIS

Chapter 9

June 1979, Roscoff, Brittany

Phil knocked on Emma's cabin door as the ferry approached the rocky Brittany coast. He found his grandmother smartly dressed in a light blue jacket and skirt, but looking pale.

'How's your head?'

'Better,' said Emma. 'Much better.' She forced a smile. 'But would you mind carrying my suitcase?'

They both perked up as Phil drove the TR6 off the ferry and into the pretty little Breton town of Roscoff. Emma was doing the navigating, and she had chosen the scenic route to Paris, avoiding the autoroute, and stopping for breakfast in Saint-Malo and lunch in Pont-l'Évêque in Normandy.

The sun was shining, the top was down, and Phil was enjoying himself. Emma had brought a couple of Édith Piaf tapes, who he had never heard before, but who was undeniably and intoxicatingly French. After ten minutes, he got used to driving on the wrong side of the road, but overtaking was a bit tricky. He didn't push it, waiting until there was a long straight stretch and confirming with his navigator before passing other cars.

They found a restaurant near the *pont* of Pont l'Évêque, where they sat on a terrace overlooking the River Touques. Phil ordered pâté to start followed by coquilles Saint-Jacques. Emma ordered a cold bottle of the most delicious white wine Phil had ever tasted. He remarked on it, but Emma explained its deliciousness wasn't because the bottle was expensive, it was merely that wine tasted better in France, especially when drunk outside a restaurant in summer.

'Here, I've got you something,' Emma said. She reached down to a plastic WHSmith bag Phil had noticed she had brought with her from the car, extracted a yellow book and handed it to Phil.

Phil picked it up and examined the cover. *'Teach Yourself Gaelic,'* he said. He opened up the book at chapter one. 'This is ridiculous! What are all these 'bh's and 'dh's?'

'It's quite fun,' Emma said. 'But very difficult. You don't have to learn it if you don't want to. It's just I know you like languages.'

'And Hugh and you learned it forty years ago?'

Emma smiled. 'Yes.'

'Can you still speak it?' Phil asked.

'Chan eil fios agam. Faodaidh mi feuchainn.'

'All right. I have no idea what that means. But I'll give it a go.'

'Good.' Emma smiled. 'I wasn't sure . . .' She seemed uncharacteristically uncertain.

'No, it'll be fun,' Phil said. 'I'll take a look at it tonight.' So he would be alternating *War and Peace* with Gaelic grammar over the next few weeks. That sounded a bit heavy. But he didn't want to disappoint his grandmother.

'No sign of your headache?' he asked.

'No,' Emma replied, frowning.

'You've seen a doctor about it in England?'

'Yes.'

Phil wanted to find out more. He had been worried, and Emma had clearly been shaken.

'Philip. I need to tell you something, something I haven't told anyone else. But when I do, I will want you to do exactly as I ask, even though that may be difficult for you. Do you understand?'

'Yes,' said Phil. Part of him was excited that he was being cut into a big secret. But actually, more of him was scared it was a big bad secret.

It was.

'I have a brain tumour. That's what gave me the headache last night. That's what may give me a headache tomorrow night. Or it may not.'

'Oh no! Grams! How long have you had it?'

'Who knows how long it's been sitting there, biding its time? I started getting headaches about three months ago, and I noticed I was having difficulty with my balance. Eventually my GP sent me to Plymouth for a brain scan, and they found a big fat tumour sitting there, in my cerebellum, which is the bit of the brain that controls co-ordination, motor control and balance. It's growing: I'll need regular scans to monitor it.'

'Is there anything they can do? Can they chop it out?'

'No. Nothing. They can't chop it out because of where it is – they would do too much damage getting to it. They want to give me radio-therapy when I get back, but they don't think it will help much. It's going to kill me.'

'Christ! When?'

'I wish I knew. Tonight? Next month? Next year? Maybe two years. If it stops growing, I might be OK, but that's unlikely.'

The news hit Phil hard. He bit his lip. Suddenly the wine and the scallops didn't taste so good.

Emma reached across the table and grasped his hand. 'I'm sorry to give you this news, Philip. I know it can't be easy for you. I intended not to tell you. But that's not fair, especially if I start getting more headaches. And especially if something sudden happens. My balance might get worse, or my ability to move properly. Tumours can affect judgement and mood. I might become erratic, so my doctor says, or bad-tempered, or socially inappropriate, whatever that means.'

'I see,' said Phil, dully.

'That's why I wanted to go on this trip now. It might be the last chance I'll have, and I want to do it before I die. It's also why I asked you to come and drive me. I need a companion, and someone with me if something goes wrong.'

'But I'm only eighteen,' Phil said. 'Surely Mum would have been better? Or one of your friends?'

59

'You underestimate yourself,' said Emma with a grin. 'And remember I asked you to do exactly as I asked?'

'Yes.'

'OK. I understand you are upset now. But I want you to put that out of your mind. I don't want sympathy, I don't want pity, and above all I don't want us both to be miserable for the next couple of weeks. This will be my last holiday and I want to enjoy it. Your job is to help me enjoy it. I'm not sure your mother would be able to do that, but I think you can. Do you understand?'

Phil took a deep breath. 'Yes. I understand.' He closed his eyes. He didn't want to think about his grandmother dying. So he wouldn't.

He would do what she asked.

He opened his eyes, forced a smile and picked up his glass of wine. 'To a wonderful holiday, Grams!'

His grandmother smiled back, a genuine smile of pleasure and gratitude. 'Cheers, Philip.'

The journey to Paris from Pont l'Évêque was less cheery than the morning drive. Emma's news had shaken Phil. He thought about the gun he had seen in Emma's suitcase. Was she planning to use it on herself?

No. Phil was being paranoid.

But if not herself, whom was she planning to use the gun on? Old English ladies didn't usually pack heat to protect themselves.

Was she planning to shoot him? No, that really was ridiculous.

Could it have something to do with that little chat with his French teacher's friend Mr Swann in the Three Castles earlier that week?

Possibly.

He recalled the conversation. Swann leaning forward to sip his pint as he fixed Phil with his calm brown eyes, the soft yellow pub lighting reflecting off his smooth forehead.

'This is what I want you to do, if you are willing,' the mysterious civil servant had said.

Phil nodded.

'I know about your grandmother's trip. I believe she plans to revisit old haunts. Places she lived before the war. And she intends to see people she knew then.'

'That's the impression I got.'

'One of them may be a man called Lothar. Lothar isn't his real name; it's a code name. He used other aliases. Bruno Fleischmann. Anton Bartkowicz.'

'Is he some kind of spy?'

Swann nodded. 'Or at least he was. A long time ago. We don't know very much about him, or where he lives now. If your grandmother finds him, we would like to know about it. We would like to know where he is.'

'If you can't find him, how do you think my grandmother will?'

Swann grinned. 'I'm sure it hasn't escaped your notice, Phil, but your grandmother is a very intelligent lady.'

'Why don't you ask her directly?'

'We have.'

'And she said no?'

Swann nodded.

'Yet you want me to tell you where this Lothar is behind her back?'

'Yes. It's very important to us. To our country.' Swann hesitated. 'To *your* country.'

'Can you tell me why?'

'I can. But when I do, you will realize why I insist that you keep quiet about this conversation to everyone, especially to your grandmother.'

Phil swallowed. He felt a little as if he was betraying Grams by just listening to this. On the other hand, it intrigued him. How could he not listen to it? There were few people he trusted more than Mr Parsons, and Eustace had vouched for this man.

'OK.'

'We believe that Lothar knows of the identity of a spy. Someone who has been working for the Russians since before the war. Someone who is now high up in our government or the intelligence services.'

'You mean like Philby?'

'Yes. Like Philby. Or Maclean or Burgess. And a number of others whom the public doesn't know about.'

'A mole?'

Swann grinned. 'I see you have read your le Carré. We don't call them moles, but yes, that's exactly the kind of person we are looking for.'

'And this Lothar can tell you the identity of your mole?'

'We believe so. It's even possible that you might come across some clues as to who this man might be. Keep your eyes and ears open and your wits about you. And Phil?'

'Yes?'

'I meant what I said about not telling your grandmother. It's for her own safety – and yours. I'm sure you know how wilful she is. If she thinks that we are looking for Lothar, she might do something she will later regret. Something that puts her in danger.'

'Like what?'

'I can't be specific. Just trust me.'

'What do I do if we find Lothar? Or I discover who your mole is?'

'How good is your memory?'

'Pretty good.'

'All right. Here is a telephone number.' He reached into his breast pocket and extracted a simple file record card, on which a number was written in clear pencil. 'Memorize it and then rip up this card. If you come across any information that might be useful, ring this number, reversing the charges if necessary, and ask for me by name.'

'Mr Swann?'

'That's correct. Whoever answers the phone will know who you are, and put you through to me if they can. Otherwise, leave a message.'

Phil took the card.

'Will you do that?'

Phil was eighteen. This was exciting. There was some risk – that was exciting too. He would be working behind his grandmother's back, but he would also be doing something for his country. Phil was well aware that young men his age had done a lot more for their country in the past than travel around Europe with their grandmothers and make phone calls, even ones where you had to reverse the charges in a foreign language.

'Yes,' he said. 'Yes, Mr Swann. I'll do it.'

Chapter 10

Emma was watching him. She didn't know what he was thinking, but she knew he was thinking something.

Phil remembered he was supposed to be cheering her up. He forced a small smile. Then with a supreme effort of will, he transformed it into a big grin.

'Come on, Grams, let's have some French pop.'

'French pop? And where would I find that?'

'On the radio.'

Emma twiddled the knobs and soon loud French punk music filled the car.

Or not exactly French. Phil recognized the song. 'This is Plastic Bertrand, you know, Grams,' he said.

'Oh really?'

'Yeah. But he's not French, he's Belgian. Not many people realize that. Or not English people anyway. I just wanted to impress you with my musical knowledge.'

'I am impressed,' said Emma. 'Do you like it?'

'I do,' Phil admitted. 'But for God's sake don't tell Mel. It will ruin my street cred.'

'And what's your street cred?'

'That is a very good question.'

They drove along listening to 'Ça plane pour moi' belting out across the Norman countryside.

When the song had finished, Emma spoke. 'Not really my cup of tea, Philip. I think I agree with your sister.'

'That is your right.'

'Also – I think you'll find that although Monsieur Bertrand was born in Belgium, his father was in fact French. Am I correct? I read an interview with him in *The Times* a couple of years ago.'

Phil shot his grandmother a quick glance. Her eyebrows were raised in serious curiosity.

Phil shook his head. 'I don't know, Grams. Somehow I suspect you are correct.'

She reached into her handbag and pulled out a packet of cigarettes. Embassy. She lit one.

'I didn't know you smoked?' said Phil.

'I gave up nearly ten years ago. But now . . . what the hell? Want one?'

'No thanks,' said Phil.

'Very wise.'

The driving became much trickier as they entered Paris. The traffic was heavy, which was probably a good thing because it slowed everyone down. Nevertheless, Phil seemed to attract more than his fair share of blasts from other drivers' horns.

Emma navigated flawlessly from some map in her head. She said she knew exactly where their hotel was. Soon they were driving along the Seine, on the north bank as far as Phil could tell, although he couldn't remember whether north was 'left' or 'right'.

The traffic moved in fits and starts involving rapid gear changes, hooting and acceleration and then braking and more hooting. Phil had never been to Paris before, but he recognized the Arc de Triomphe and the Eiffel Tower. They crawled down the Champs Élysées with its glitzy cafés and cinemas and approached a maelstrom of metal with a big stone needle in the middle of it.

'This is the Place de la Concorde,' said Emma. 'Keep up your speed, don't look in the mirror and go for it.'

Phil did his best. Swarms of Deux Chevaux and tiny Renaults driven by lunatics buzzed around the poor TR6, horns blaring, but somehow they all missed him.

Phil was spat out on to a smaller street. 'Jesus! We won't have to do that again, will we?'

'Don't worry,' said Emma. 'Once we get to the hotel, they will take care of our car for us. We'll take taxis around the city – or the Métro.'

'Thank God for that.'

They plunged deeper into the heart of Paris, turning into a cobbled square with some kind of obelisk in the middle.

'Just here, Philip.'

'Are you sure?' Phil drew up beside a pair of grand doormen guarding an elegant facade from which white awnings proclaimed one word: *Ritz*.

Phil was wearing jeans and his David Bowie T-shirt. Lady Meeke looked appropriately elegant in her light blue suit. The scary doormen were clearly entirely used to elegant English ladies arriving with scruffy grandsons. As Emma had promised, a lesser, smaller flunkey whisked the car away somewhere and they entered the grandest hotel lobby Phil had ever seen.

Emma glanced at her grandson.

'I think you and I might be going shopping tomorrow, Philip.'

Clothes shopping with your grandmother is always going to be excruciating, but Emma approached the problem sensibly, and Phil ended up with two jackets, a couple of shirts and a pair of nice trousers, to go with the black cords and beige V-necked sweater he had stuffed into his rucksack for smart occasions. All paid for by her. He also got his hair cut.

All in all, he didn't look too bad, he was surprised to acknowledge.

After lunch in a small bistro, they walked along the smart Rue du Faubourg Saint-Honoré until they came to a high stone archway from which a Union Jack fluttered proudly. Emma had a word with the porter at the lodge by the gate, and they strolled through a courtyard into the impressive building itself. A secretary with a pleasant Yorkshire accent, which seemed oh-so-English in the Parisian surroundings, led them to a small room dotted with ornate green and gold furniture. Impressively bewhiskered and besashed Englishmen looked down on them from large oil portraits in heavy frames.

'That one was the ambassador when I was here,' said Emma, pointing to a distinguished if slightly raffish-looking grey-haired gentleman with a trim moustache and a monocle. 'Sir George Clerk. Very charming, but a bit of a plonker, as you might say.'

'Might I?'

'Emma!' They turned as a sleek man with a dark grey suit and thick, light grey hair swept into the room.

Emma rose to her feet and accepted his kiss on the cheek.

'How lovely to see you!' the man gushed. 'I'm sorry I couldn't give you lunch – my lunches are spoken for weeks in advance these days. But you will have a cup of coffee with me?'

'This is my grandson, Philip. Philip, this is Sir Cyril Ashcott, the ambassador.'

'And former third secretary, a long time ago,' said the ambassador with a grin.

'You have done very well for yourself,' Emma said. 'The Paris ambassadorship is *the* plum posting, you know,' she said to Phil.

'I had a slight hiccup in my career here before the war,' Sir Cyril explained to Phil. 'But thanks to your grandfather, and your grandmother here, I survived. And prospered.'

'I understand there is a Lady Ashcott?' said Emma.

'Yes, there is,' said Sir Cyril with a grin. 'And very happy she is too.'

'Really? I am surprised.'

His grandmother's rudeness shocked Phil, but Sir Cyril took it in his stride.

'As blunt as always, I see, Emma. Have you never met Penelope? We've been married ten years now.'

'No, I haven't. I think Roland did.'

'Sure to have. Perhaps we can rectify that while you are here. Where are you staying?'

'The Ritz.'

'Jolly good. I'll be in touch. I am sorry about Roland. And that I wasn't able to attend the funeral. I think I was in BA at the time.'

Emma smiled.

'Your grandfather was a fine man,' said Sir Cyril to Phil. 'Are you thinking of joining the diplomatic service?'

Phil looked confused. He had no clue what he wanted to do after university, beyond ensuring it wasn't insurance. He suddenly realized this was 'the old boy network' in action, and was a bit surprised to see it involved him.

'Oh, don't worry about Philip,' said Emma. 'He can find his own job when the time comes. That's not why we're here. I just wanted to look around the place again. It was an interesting time.'

The ambassador examined Emma carefully. Then he smiled. 'It was certainly that.'

They spent half an hour chatting about people in Paris in the 1930s, before the ambassador took his leave. But he suggested that they wander around the embassy, accompanied by Miss Stott, who, it turned out, was not just a secretary, but a modern-day third secretary. She was blonde and long-legged, and really quite attractive, Phil couldn't help noticing. Twenty-five, at least. Way out of his league, obviously.

Miss Stott immediately realized, diplomatically, that Emma wanted to do the explaining, and kept quiet and listened as they walked around the embassy.

It was extraordinarily elegant, if not opulent. Known as the Hôtel de Charost, it had been purchased in the early nineteenth century by the British government from Napoleon's sister, Pauline Borghese, and still retained the ambience of a city palace, imperial rather than royal. The overall effect was a mixture of French grandiosity and British pomposity, which Phil found overwhelming. Everywhere you looked there were delicate chairs, ornate lamps, brilliantly polished tables, extravagant flower arrangements, grand portraits of grand diplomats and melodramatic classical landscapes. The prevailing colours were gilded yellow, polished brown, and green and crimson fabric. The Hôtel de Charost had been home to a succession of peers and knights of the realm, in a line from the Duke of Wellington to Sir Cyril, all of whom had dined for England.

Emma led the way outside to a semi-circular courtyard. 'This used to be the stable block,' she said, pointing to a block emblazoned with two fine stone horses above its entrance. 'Before they turned it into the Chancery. Has that changed?' she asked the third secretary.

'Oh no,' she said with a smile. 'The funny thing is, I always wanted to work in a stables when I was a girl.'

'This is where all the work gets done,' Emma said. 'Roland had his office here on the top floor.'

They went around the side of the house to the garden. This was a little patch of England in the middle of Paris. Lawns, ancient spreading trees, beds of roses and exuberant borders of other flowers that Phil couldn't name. All was quiet behind the garden's high walls. The only signs of the city outside were the top of a gilded dome and the tip of the Eiffel Tower in the distance. The Faubourg Saint-Honoré itself was a relatively narrow road for Paris, certainly not one of Haussmann's grand boulevards, and it was extraordinary how this oasis of calm and beauty could exist right next to it, in the midst of the Parisian bustle.

Emma could see what Phil was thinking. 'I know. Amazing, isn't it? Do you mind if we sit here for a while?' she asked Miss Stott.

'Of course. I'll leave you to it. I've got one or two things to catch up with back in the Chancery.'

'Nice girl, don't you think, Philip?' said Emma with a grin.

'Yes, Grandmother, I thought she was very nice,' he replied with fake primness.

'Glad to see you have good taste. When Roland and I were here, they would never have allowed a woman to be third secretary. I hope she goes far. Maybe one day in thirty years' time you'll come back to Paris and she'll be ambassador. I like the northern accent too.'

The shade of a large chestnut protected them from the afternoon sun, birds mumbled lazily from the bushes, and the leaves around them rustled in a gentle breeze. Emma lit a cigarette.

'Now, Philip. I need to tell you about Paris.'

Chapter 11

May 1936, Paris

I WAS REMARKABLY undiplomatic for a diplomat's wife. I tended to say what I thought. If a question came into my head, I would ask it. If someone was evasive, or claimed to know something when they clearly didn't, I would point that out. Poor Roland hadn't anticipated that. I think he thought with my languages and my inquisitiveness I would be able to hold my own in conversation, and indeed I could. I know some diplomats actually liked me. But then again, some didn't.

One of those that didn't was the ambassador, Sir George Clerk. He was known for his charm and his urbanity. He seemed to me to be lazy and a little bit stupid. I think he realized I thought this, and unsurprisingly he didn't appreciate such lack of respect from a twenty-one-year-old.

Poor Roland.

What was worse, his wife liked me. Lady Clerk was a nutcase. The previous ambassadress, Lady Tyrell, had also been a nutcase, but Lord Tyrell had been able to keep her away from Paris. This had raised eyebrows locally, so the Foreign Office had insisted that Lady Clerk be present in the embassy with her husband. They detested each other.

She was crazy, but I liked her. She was a painter and a sculptor. She set up shop in a room at the top of the building that had previously been occupied by a third secretary. She was also a faith healer. To the annoyance of the ambassador, all kinds of odd people would tramp through the embassy to see her: models, patients, fellow artists. I once bumped into Marc Chagall on the stairs on his way down. She offered to heal my twisted ankle for me, but I refused. I modelled for her once, naked, which was probably a little bit stupid on both our parts, but fortunately I couldn't recognize myself in the resulting picture, and I assume no one else could either. Roland never knew.

Poor Roland's job was to keep tabs on her at all times, so that the ambassador could make sure he never bumped into her. Roland frequently acted as an intermediary, passing messages about domestic arrangements between husband and wife. It was absurd.

Most of the other embassy staff were polite to me, as were their wives, who I suspected thought me a queer fish. Only Cyril Ashcott was friendly. I think he found my faux pas amusing, which was perfectly all right with me. He was a third secretary, and at twenty-six he was the nearest in age to me. He followed the ambassador's lead in enjoying the good life that Paris had to offer, but perhaps not in exactly the same way.

Roland worked hard. He was first secretary, which meant he organized everything. He was clearly very good at his job, and well respected by the embassy staff and the wider diplomatic corps in Paris. We were invited to countless functions, where he gently prodded me into behaving a little more diplomatically. He was popular; I was tolerated, mostly, although I must have said something particularly nasty once to a Japanese diplomat without realizing it, for all the Japanese seemed to loathe me. I didn't like them much either, or what they were doing in China.

Roland explained that while my assessment of the Chinese situation might make sense, it was exactly the kind of opinion I should keep to myself.

Despite all the parties and all the diplomatic chatter, I was lonely. Can you be lonely if you don't really mind it? Perhaps I mean I was alone. Roland worked, and naturally I couldn't possibly be allowed to get a job – that was frowned upon for a diplomat's wife – so I had the days and most of the evenings to myself. Of course, I read. I obtained a reader's ticket to the Bibliothèque nationale, I discovered the American Library on the Rue de Téhéran and I spent a lot of time and quite a bit of money at an English-language bookshop on the Rue de l'Odéon on the Left Bank. I found plenty of good books to read, and so I was content.

But I missed Hugh so much. I missed him because he was my brother and I loved him and he was dead. I missed him because I had no one to discuss my reading with: without him it had all become strangely purposeless. I missed him because I wanted someone to tell about all that I saw and heard at the embassy.

I did talk to Roland about my reading, and we certainly gossiped about the embassy, but it wasn't quite the same.

I saw my mother frequently. She had taken to getting her dresses made at great expense in Paris, at Schiaparelli's, and she was constantly coming for fittings. She had a number of friends in Paris, and she sometimes stayed with them, or at the Crillon, but never with me. She usually took me out to dinner, with Roland if he was available. I tried once to speak to her about Hugh, to remember him with her, but she was having none of it.

I had questions about Hugh. About his renunciation of communism. About the car accident. About the mysterious American woman. Why had he been on Dockenbush Lane? Was he really a spy? Had he really been murdered by the secret service?

I had thought Hugh was the person I knew best in the world, and then suddenly, right after his death, all that had been thrown into doubt. If I couldn't answer those questions, did I know who he truly was? What kind of sister was I?

It unsettled me. It gnawed at me.

I told myself such speculation was preposterous, and tried to force it out of my head, but my questions needed answers more sensible than Freddie's drunken ravings.

So I was pleased when I received a telephone call from Dick. He was in Paris and he wondered if he could drop by and see me.

He came for tea at our flat, a first-floor apartment with big shuttered windows that let in masses of sunlight. We lived in the Rue de Bourgogne, a quiet street near Les Invalides on the Left Bank. Dick wore grey flannel trousers, an open-necked shirt and a jacket with elbow patches. He looked so badly dressed and *so* English. I rather liked that. The embassy staff were all beautifully turned out at all times, the men in black coats and striped trousers from Savile Row, the women outfitted by local Parisian dressmakers.

Dick seemed pleased to see me too. He was writing a novel about the downfall of capitalism and had decided that Paris was the place to do it. He was planning to stay for three months.

We talked about Orwell's *Down and Out,* which he too had read and claimed as the inspiration for his own novel, and then I asked him what was uppermost on my mind. I did that in those days. I still do that now.

'You remember what Freddie said at Hugh's funeral? That Hugh was a spy for Russia and that the secret service killed him? Was there any truth to that?'

Dick snorted into his cup of tea, a good English bone-china cup received as a wedding present from Roland's aunt. 'Absolutely not! Total tosh. Freddie talks absolute rot, especially when he's tight. He was tight, you know?'

'I thought perhaps he was.'

'Appalling behaviour, I'm afraid. I say, you haven't been worrying about that, have you?'

'I'm afraid I have, rather. You see, Hugh and I had had a dreadful row the evening before he died. I told you about that – he claimed to have given up on communism – but it didn't make sense to me. And I don't know what he was doing on that back lane.'

'Did the police have any suspicions?'

'No, but they wouldn't if the secret service had killed him, would they?'

Dick put down his cup. 'I don't know much about the secret service, but I don't think they murder people whom they suspect of being spies. They try them and hang them. That's different.'

He looked right at me. 'And I really don't think Hugh was a spy. I wouldn't necessarily know for sure if he was, but I suspect I would have an inkling. I had none.'

I listened and sipped my tea. 'Tell me about him,' I said. 'What was he like at school?'

Dick took out a pipe. 'Do you mind?'

I shook my head and lit up a cigarette.

'Everybody liked him,' Dick replied as he filled the bowl with tobacco. 'As at most schools, there was a split between the arty types, the "aesthetes", and the hearties who played rugger, but Hugh seemed to span that. He played cricket and he wrote poetry and rebellious essays. The beaks liked him too.'

'And which were you?'

'I suppose I was an aesthete. I shared a study with Hugh in the Upper School. But Freddie was the one the hearties really loved to hate. He would wear silk scarves around his wrist and quote obscure Latin poetry at them. They loathed it.'

'But Hugh and Freddie were good friends?'

'Very good friends. I think Hugh admired Freddie's rebellious streak. The way he didn't care about authority. They started a magazine together, *The Light of Youth*. I contributed. Bad poetry, earnest essays, satire that we thought frightfully clever. It was banned in the end, but they gave it a good run.'

'Is Freddie a homosexual?' I asked.

Dick looked shifty. 'Yes.'

'Was my brother a homosexual?'

Dick blushed. I wasn't sure if that was because he was embarrassed discussing the subject with a young lady, or if he was hiding something.

'No,' he said. 'At least I don't think so.' He paused, puffing on his pipe. 'No, I'm sure not.'

'Sorry, I'm embarrassing you,' I said. 'Given all the books I read, I couldn't help coming across homosexuality. I couldn't possibly ask my parents about it, but I could ask Hugh, and he explained all. But there's one thing I never understood. If you are a homosexual, does that mean you will always like just men, or can you change?'

Dick smiled nervously. 'I'm not sure I completely understand that either. Many of the boys who experimented with it at school are now frightfully keen on girls. Others, like Freddie, have no interest in women at all.'

'And my brother?'

'He liked women. I think he always did. I really don't think there was anything physical between him and Freddie, if that's what you are asking.'

'I was thinking more about Kay.'

'He was desperately keen on her. He never mentioned her to you?'

'No, I wish he had. I find it hard to forgive him for keeping her a secret from me. Who is she?'

'She's an American, from Chicago originally, I think, but then she moved to Vienna where she studied German. She went from there on the same Intourist trip as Freddie, Hugh and me. Hugh and she hit it off right away. After the trip, Hugh returned to London and they wrote to each other. Then she got herself a position as an assistant to an Austrian photographer in London, and moved there to be with Hugh. Hugh and she saw a lot of each other.'

'Did you know he had asked her to marry him?'

'No. I'm a bit surprised. But I can't imagine she would lie about something like that.'

'What did *you* think of her?'

'She's very attractive in an odd way. She's earnest and sincere. Self-taught. A little like you. Perhaps that's why Hugh liked her.'

Dick reddened again. 'Sorry. That came out wrong. But I told you before how frightfully proud of you Hugh was.'

I smiled reassuringly. 'That's all right. What about Hugh's communism? Had he really given it up? Did he ever actually join the party?'

'When we went up to Cambridge in 1929, everyone was talking about poetry. By the time we did our finals, everyone was talking about Marx. It all changed. And it was the crash that did it, first on Wall Street in 1929 and then the banks in 1931. Capitalism is broken, that's clear now. Suddenly socialism seemed the answer, or even communism.

'Freddie was at Trinity reading History, but he switched to Economics so that he could be taught by a don named Maurice Dobb.'

'I remember that name. Hugh mentioned him in his letters.'

'He's a Marxist, and he taught Freddie all about dialectic materialism and the dictatorship of the proletariat. Then Freddie joined a dining club called the Apostles – it's supposed to be secret, but everyone knows about it. Keynes is the president, you know, the economist?'

I nodded.

'Hugh was at King's, Keynes's college, and Freddie soon got him in. I was never a member, but I believe the idea was that someone gave a paper at each dinner and it was discussed. A lot of the undergraduate members were taken with Marxism, and they began to spread it around the university. Very effectively: we were all receptive. A former coal miner started the Cambridge University Socialist Society, and we all joined – I think they have a thousand members now. Freddie joined the Communist Party and got his little green party card, but I don't think Hugh ever got around to it.'

'Did you sign up?'

'No. Almost. My father is a vicar, you may remember. He had a parish in rural Hampshire, but the General Strike made him think, and he asked to be transferred to a mining village in Durham. Which he was. It was quite a shock to the rest of the family. It wasn't just that we were middle-class southerners; those villages are very Methodist – the Church of England is the enemy. But my father did a good job. I learned to play the trombone and the miners let me play in one of their bands. The poverty shocked me, the houses, the children going down the mines at fourteen, the coal dust everywhere.

'So I listened to the likes of Maurice Dobb, and I read the essays and the books, and I stayed up till two in the morning drinking college port and discussing Lenin. But I found the atheism of Marxism a problem. I still think "love thy neighbour" is the commandment to live by. Atheism appealed to most of the communist undergraduates; they believed the Church of England was hypocritical. That's certainly what Hugh thought.'

'All right, I understand,' I said. 'That's how Hugh became a communist, but why did he give it up? He suggested to me that it was after your trip to Russia, but I remember him coming back from that more fired up than ever.'

'He and Freddie seemed very taken with the Soviet system, as I told you, and Kay certainly was. We went to Leningrad and Moscow and then Kiev and Kazan. We saw the Hermitage and the Kremlin and we visited tractor factories and collective farms. It's true that there isn't a class system as far as we could tell, and the workers run things not the capitalists, and they are building all kinds of wonderful projects, and the people seem dedicated to making their country work. But we weren't allowed to talk to anyone, or rather they were too scared to talk to us. The trains were terrible – I remember a nightmare journey to Kiev that took forever with no food or water. Life is tough and people are seriously poor, poorer even than the mining village at home, and that's saying something. In Kiev they were literally starving, dying in the street.

'Of course, Freddie and Hugh said it was because the economy had been broken under Tsarism, and it would inevitably take a while to sort it out. That may be true. But essentially they claimed that everything they didn't like was a result of the Tsars, and everything they did like was a result of the new communist world order.

'The thing is, it isn't a free country.' Dick grinned. 'I remember Freddie leaping off the boat in Leningrad shouting "Free at last!" and tripping over a notice in Russian saying "Keep off the grass". He was probably drunk.'

I laughed. 'But you changed Hugh's mind?'

'My history tutor at Cambridge was originally from the Ukraine. He told me that there was a famine in the Ukraine that the government wasn't admitting to. He said the secret police was at least as bad as under the Tsars, and that the country was just a giant prison.'

'He must be a counter-revolutionary, then,' I said.

'That's what Hugh said. At first. But I introduced them and I think he may have convinced Hugh.'

I frowned. 'This history don sounds to me like a Russian bourgeois who can't bear the people taking his property and giving it to the workers.'

Dick was taken aback. I don't think he quite realized how closely I followed Hugh's beliefs.

'Emma. Don't be hard on Hugh for changing his mind. He was a good man, probably the best man I know. Or knew. He was always concerned about the poor in our society, the people who have nothing.'

'Then why did he want to become a diplomat?' I protested.

'What's wrong with that?'

'It's about as bourgeois as they come. Eating and drinking in the pursuit of monopoly profits for an imperialist country.'

Dick raised his eyebrows. 'Isn't that what your husband does?'

'I know,' I said. 'And it makes me sick sometimes.'

'Oh.'

'Look, I'm sorry, Dick,' I said, afraid I had gone too far. 'I am a hypocrite, I know it. At least you have lived in a mining town and tried to help the people there. I just read books and have servants wait on me. I hate myself for it. And sometimes I hate Hugh for it.'

I felt my eyes sting with tears. I didn't cry often. When I did, it usually had something to do with Hugh or his memory.

Dick put down his cup. 'I must be going. It was lovely to see you again, Emma.'

'Oh, Dick. I am sorry. I've scared you off! As you can see, I am still upset about Hugh and it affects me in silly ways. But I did enjoy talking to you. Can I see you again?'

Dick smiled, what seemed to me a genuine smile, although I'm not always very good at telling. 'Yes, I'd like that.'

'Tell you what. There is a gruesome cocktail party at the embassy tomorrow night in honour of a whisky distillers' delegation from Scotland or something. We're trying to get the French to drink more whisky. Can you come? They always want people to make up the numbers.'

'When you put it like that, how can I refuse?'

Chapter 12

THE ROOM WAS heaving. I should have anticipated that a delegation of whisky distillers would be more popular than the screw manufacturers from Birmingham who had visited the embassy the week before.

Roland was working hard introducing Scotsmen to French politicians and wine merchants. I was sipping malt whisky with Dick and Cyril. And coughing.

'You must remember never to put ice in a good malt,' Dick said. 'And no soda either. Just a drop of water.'

'This is good stuff,' said Cyril, who seemed to have taken to Dick. Cyril was so slim he was almost emaciated, his body long and concave, but in a room full of elegant men, Cyril was one of the most elegant.

'Ah, there is the Vicomte de Montfaucon. I must introduce him to Mackenzie. I know the vicomte likes his Scotch.'

Cyril left us to attend to his duties.

'You know what we were saying about Freddie,' said Dick, nodding after Cyril's retreating figure.

'No,' I said. 'Really! How can you tell?'

'It's just a feeling. I may be wrong, of course.'

'I never would have guessed. I have always thought Cyril was quite good-looking.'

'So does the vicomte,' said Dick. It was true: the middle-aged elegant Frenchman was touching the sleeve of the young elegant Englishman. They did seem quite taken with each other.

'Good evening, Emma.' A small trim man with a small trim moustache took my hand, bowed over it and clicked his heels.

'Kurt! How nice to see you! How did you get in here?' I spoke in German.

'I am the second secretary at the German Embassy with special responsibility for whisky,' the man said with a smile.

I introduced the German diplomat, whose name was Kurt Lohmüller, to Dick. 'Kurt, do you think Cyril Ashcott is a homosexual?' I switched to English for Dick's benefit.

Kurt raised his mobile eyebrows. His face was intensely mobile, unlike his body, which retained a Germanic stiffness. I liked him.

'I have absolutely no idea,' he said.

'Dick here thinks he is.'

Dick blushed rather sweetly, pinkness appearing on his cheeks and reddening his neck. 'I was merely speculating, Emma.'

Kurt looked over the room to where Cyril and the vicomte were deep in conversation. 'I hadn't thought of it, but Dick may be right.'

'It's very clever of him. Mind you, I can spot communists in the same way,' I said. 'Like you, for example, Kurt.'

'I beg your pardon,' said Kurt with mock shock.

'Don't deny it. I've spoken to you enough about politics.' That was indeed the reason Kurt and I were friends. We would seek each other out at the end of diplomatic functions, when we were both a little tipsy and Kurt's diplomatic duties – such as they were – had been discharged. I would explain my ideas about politics, and Kurt would listen with a mixture of amusement at my naivety and interest at what he said were my original opinions.

I liked the attention.

'I can assure you, Mr Loxton, I am not a communist,' Kurt said to Dick. 'I admit Emma and I have discussed Soviet politics at length. Before Paris, I was stationed in Moscow.'

'Bosh,' I said.

'I have no idea what "Bosh" means. I assume something like "Absolutely, Herr Lohmüller"?'

'Double bosh.'

'Unless you mean "Boche" and are accusing me of being German?'

'You know jolly well what I mean.'

'As a matter of fact, Mr Loxton, I am a good National Socialist,' Kurt said.

'More bosh.'

'It's true! I have just joined the party.'

This brought me up short. 'Oh, no. Really?'

'I have to. We diplomats were exempted for a while, but now we all have to become members.'

'But what about your principles, Kurt?'

'My principles are clear. I serve my country. Just like your husband.'

'I say, Emma, isn't that your ma?'

Dick nodded behind me, and I turned.

'Emma, darling! I just bumped into Roland and he told me you were here.'

'And you were invited?'

'I came with Antoine Meyronne.'

He was the new agriculture minister, I remembered, a man whose thick moustache rivalled Clémenceau's. I made sure to memorize all the French ministers as they came and went, which they did with bewildering speed. France had already held two elections that year, and it was only May.

'I had no idea you were coming to Paris.' But I had to admit it wasn't much of a surprise. She almost never warned me of her arrival.

'I have a fitting tomorrow. But perhaps you could join me for luncheon afterwards. At the Ritz?' Then she turned to Dick. 'Aren't you Hugh's friend, Dick? How nice to see you!'

'I am, Lady Chaddington.'

My mother charmed Dick and also Kurt. Dick treated her like his best friend's mother. Kurt showed a different kind of interest.

At forty-five, my mother was still an attractive woman. She wore her hair short and curled; her nose was tiny but pointed and seemed to be constantly sniffing out titbits. She was tall and slim; good clothes looked magnificent on her. Although her milky-white complexion was etched with tiny, barely visible lines, it still seemed fresh.

Frankly, it was hard to tell we were related.

I felt a flash of jealousy at Kurt's interest, and a touch of anger that no one mentioned Hugh's name, after Mama's initial identification of Dick.

I interrupted my mother in mid-sentence as she was discussing a trip to Lake Annecy Kurt was planning to take the following month.

'Did Hugh like whisky, Dick?'

Mama glared at me, whether it was for my rudeness or for the reminder of my brother and her son, I didn't know and didn't care. As Dick answered me, my mother floated off to find her minister.

Chapter 13

'ARE YOU RELATED to the portrait painter?'

Colonel Vivian seemed nonplussed by my question. We were in one of the smallest rooms in the Chancery building. Roland had asked me to meet 'two fellows over from London'. Why, I had no idea.

'Yes, I am,' said Vivian, looking at me suspiciously through his monocle. He wore a toothbrush moustache. I distrusted toothbrush moustaches. He was accompanied by a much younger colleague, Kenneth Heaton-Smith, who was clean-shaven, alert and rather good-looking.

'Comley Vivian?' I persisted. 'I'm not too keen on his portraits, but I once saw a very good painting of a Venetian palazzo by him.'

I realized I had said the wrong thing. I really needed to up my game, especially amongst embassy people, if I was going to avoid embarrassing Roland. I should probably have talked about the weather. 'It's a bit hot today,' I added.

Vivian frowned, and then decided to ignore my babble. 'Thank you for coming to see us, Mrs Meeke,' he said. 'I want to speak to you about a somewhat sensitive issue. When you hear what I have to say, you will understand that you mustn't repeat any of it to anyone.'

'Not even Roland?'

Vivian hesitated. 'Not even your husband. The less discussion there is on this matter within the embassy, the better. Although it was your husband who suggested I speak to you.'

'All right.'

'I've come from London to follow up on indications that sensitive information has been leaked to a foreign power from here in the Paris embassy.'

My mind raced. The foreign power must be Russia! They knew about Hugh. They thought I was a spy.

'I see,' I said, trying and possibly succeeding to keep my tone neutral.

'Naturally we have been interviewing the staff here, but your husband suggested that we speak to you. He said you had particularly strong powers of observation.' Colonel Vivian permitted himself a smile. 'I must say I liked my father's Venetian paintings too.'

'Oh,' I said. It sounded as if I was not to be accused of anything. And neither was Hugh.

'So, have you noticed anything?'

I hesitated. 'It would help if you could tell me to which foreign power you are referring.'

'Oh, yes, of course. Germany.'

'Ah.' My mind darted around the embassy, its diplomatic staff, the other wives, the domestic staff. 'I'm afraid not,' I said. A thought occurred to me. Perhaps I was under suspicion after all. I decided to take the bull by the horns. 'I am rather good friends with one of the diplomats from the German embassy in Paris. Herr Lohmüller. I've always had the impression that he wasn't frightfully keen on the Nazis.'

'Yes, we know that,' said Vivian.

'Is there anything I could say to him?' I asked. 'Obviously nothing directly. But some stratagem?' My brain raced. 'I don't know, perhaps you could plant some false information that only certain people may have seen, and I could check whether Kurt knew it?'

Vivian smiled. 'I like the way you think, Mrs Meeke. But please don't mention any of this to him. For now. But if we do come up with a . . . stratagem, we will bear you in mind. I'm confident we will find the leak. In the meantime, if you do think of something, do let Mr Heaton-Smith or me know. Mr Heaton-Smith will see you out.'

And he did. As we emerged from the old stable block and into the semi-circular courtyard, Heaton-Smith chuckled. 'Nice job, Mrs Meeke. It's rare for people to put Vee-Vee on the back foot like that.'

'Thank you,' I said.

'Here's my card,' he said. 'If you need to get in touch with me back in London. Although I will be based at the embassy here in Paris for the next few days.'

We stopped in the courtyard, and Heaton-Smith looked straight at me. 'You thought the "foreign power" was Russia, didn't you?'

I almost answered 'yes' immediately, but then I hesitated. Was this attractive young man getting me to lower my guard? About Hugh? About my own communist leanings?

At that moment I saw a figure I recognized emerge from the main embassy building.

'Freddie!' I called.

It was indeed Freddie Pelham-Walsh, looking very dapper, his pink silk handkerchief matching his pink silk tie.

'Emma, my dear!' He grinned widely. 'I was rather hoping I might bump into you here.'

I turned to introduce Freddie to Heaton-Smith, but the spy, or counter-spy, or whatever he was, had beaten a retreat back to the Chancery building.

'I had no idea I would bump into you!' I said. 'What are you doing in Paris?'

'Oh, a bit of work, you know. But actually just now I was visiting Lady Clerk. She is an absolute scream. Do you know, she offered to cure my backache? How did she even know I had backache?'

'I think she has faith or something,' I said.

'Her painting is much better than I expected. Some of it I would rate as highly as mediocre.'

'Such a generous critic, Freddie.'

'Always. Mind you, there was one rather lovely nude. I asked her who the model was, but she wouldn't say.'

I could feel my face burning. Suddenly the enormity of my idiocy at allowing myself to be painted naked became very clear to me. Why had I done it? Sometimes I was just very very stupid. As was Lady Clerk.

Freddie grinned. 'Don't worry, my dear. I am quite sure most people won't notice. I have an eye for these things. What are you doing now? Do you have time for a little something?'

So we found a café on the Faubourg, I had a cup of coffee, Freddie took a glass of cognac – even though it was barely eleven o'clock – and he prattled on. I enjoyed listening to him. Partly because I needed a link to Hugh at that moment, partly because he was amusing company.

He was in Paris visiting the offices of an international communist student organization I had vaguely heard of. Some friends in London had recommended he drop in on Lady Clerk, and he was hoping to meet some more fashionable 'indigenous artists', as he called them, while he was in Paris. He asked me whether I knew Gertrude Stein, the American critic, and I admitted I had met her a couple of times, although she probably wouldn't remember who I was. We didn't talk politics, at least not then. I was wary after my conversation with Colonel Vivian. I did tell him that Dick was in Paris, something he didn't know, and gave him Dick's address on the Île Saint-Louis.

But as I walked home over the Pont de la Concorde, I couldn't help thinking about my conversation with Colonel Vivian. Someone had been giving 'sensitive information' to the Germans.

Who?

Chapter 14

June 1979, Paris

Emma and Phil spent the afternoon sightseeing. They started with the Jeu de Paume, a short walk from the British Embassy. It was a couple of years since Phil had visited an art gallery – the National Gallery in Trafalgar Square – and he was amazed by the paintings. He vaguely remembered seeing a couple of impressionist paintings in the National, but he was sixteen at the time, and not that interested.

He must have changed in the last couple of years. Seeing so many fantastic pictures by Renoir, Van Gogh, Monet, Cézanne and all the others overwhelmed him. Emma was amused by his reaction. They spent two and a half hours there. Afterwards, they walked through the gardens of the Tuileries and examined the queue for the Louvre, deciding to leave it for another day. But then Emma took him to an amazing church on a nearby island in the Seine, whose soaring interior was lit up by sunshine streaming through stained-glass windows. Once again, Phil was overwhelmed by the beauty of it.

His parents had traipsed around Wells Cathedral with him the previous summer. Was that as beautiful? Or had he simply not noticed?

Phil felt as if his eyes had been opened, as if for the first time he had been allowed to see all that stuff he had found boring as a child, but as an adult he would appreciate. The idea was exciting. Beyond Paris stretched a whole continent of these pleasures, which had been tantalizingly outlined in the pages of the *Hitch-Hiker's Guide* that he had pored over so thoroughly.

It might have been more fun to be exploring the continent by himself, or with a friend. But Phil didn't want to be ungrateful. It was very generous of Emma to give him this opportunity, when his father would have had him working on a building site or, failing that, filling out a UB40 for the dole like some of his friends were planning to do over the summer.

Emma was tired. They stopped in a café on the way back to the hotel for a light supper of *croque-monsieurs* and salad.

'I'm exhausted,' Emma said. 'I think I'm going to turn in when we get back to the hotel. Read a book in my room. But if you would like to go out and explore Paris, please do. I can give you an advance on your wages.'

So, armed with a hundred francs, Phil set off from the Ritz into the night.

He had consulted the *Hitch-Hiker's Guide*, which had informed him that the neighbourhood to go to meet students was the Place Saint-Michel on the Left Bank.

Armed with a map he had requested from the front desk in successful French, Phil took the Métro and emerged eventually at a junction surrounding an ornate building that turned out to be a fountain. The *place* was indeed filled with people his age.

Actually, they were slightly older than him. They were students; they were already at university. Phil suddenly felt like a schoolboy. The *Guide* had blithely spoken about a great place to meet students, but what exactly was he supposed to do? Walk up to a group of them and say, 'Hi, I'm Phil. What's your name?' Or even worse: *'Bonjour. Je m'appelle Philip. Je suis élève.'* Or something equally dumb.

He needed to buck his ideas up. He decided to find a bar, have a beer and regroup.

He picked a narrow street at random – there were lots of bars. He chose one that was full but not packed, found himself a tiny table, and after considering whether a glass of red wine would be the proper French thing to order, or even a Pernod, settled on a glass of Stella Artois, which most of the men in the bar seemed to be drinking.

Except, wasn't that Belgian? Just like Plastic Bertrand. He grinned. He should have asked Emma for her recommendation.

The bar was full of young people, about half of whom looked French and half of whom were tourists of some kind. Just across from him was a table of three girls, who sounded as if they were Dutch. Quite attractive, especially the small dark-haired one. A little older than him, twenty or twenty-one. If he had been there with a friend he would have given it a go. But how did one school kid chat up three women?

He finished his beer, considered moving to another bar, but decided to stay. He liked the atmosphere of this one, so he ordered another Stella Artois from the waitress.

Through the crowd, he caught a glimpse of a face he recognized – the long-haired guy from the ferry who looked a bit like Frank Stapleton. He realized this was an opportunity to speak to someone. What could be more natural than: 'Hey! Aren't you the guy I saw on the ferry from Plymouth?' If the guy was friendly, and why shouldn't he be, then Phil might become part of the crowd rather than apart from it.

He stood up to try to catch the guy's eye, but he had turned and was pushing his way through the crush to the street. Phil considered following him, but he had a beer on its way.

The waitress weaved her way expertly through the crowd towards him with his beer when a small body barrelled into her, knocking the glass to the floor. It shattered and the noise level in the bar momentarily dropped as the crowd turned to look.

'Scheisse!'

A slight girl with straggly blond hair started to apologize to the waitress in bad French. The waitress was not impressed as she left to get a cloth and a dustpan and brush. The girl turned to Phil and apologized too. When the waitress reappeared the girl helped her clear up.

'Do you want another beer?' she asked Phil in heavily accented French.

'No, that's OK,' Phil replied in German, having identified her expletive.

'You speak German? I owe you another one. I can't believe how stupid I am. You must take it.'

The waitress seemed not only to agree with the German girl about her stupidity, but also to think it was the girl's duty to buy Phil a replacement beer, so he accepted.

The girl sat on the empty stool at Phil's small table. She was holding her own glass of wine. She was really very pretty – small, thin, with bright blue eyes and a pointed chin, strands of hair that was so light it was almost white hanging down against her cheeks. She continued apologizing in German. She seemed to Phil to be agitated, and more than just from spilling his drink.

The waitress returned with another Stella Artois, and Phil raised it to the girl. 'Thank you,' he said.

'Do you mind if I sit here?' the girl said.

'No. Not at all. Aren't you with other people?'

'I was,' said the girl darkly. 'One other person.'

'Oh. My name is Phil, by the way.'

'Heike,' said the girl. But she barely looked at him. She seemed preoccupied.

Phil sipped his beer. The girl, Heike, looked seriously upset and not really in a mood to talk to him. She had taken the chair because it was one of the only spare seats in the bar. Phil thought about giving her her privacy.

But she was very attractive.

'You look like you are having a bad evening,' he said in German.

At first he thought she was going to ignore him. Then she turned to him and smiled. 'You can say that again.'

'What happened?'

'My moron of a boyfriend. Turns out he slept with my best friend from university.'

'He just told you that?'

'He just admitted it. I made him tell me. And then I told him to piss off.'

'Just now?'

'Just now. That's why I barged into that waitress and spilled your beer. I was too upset to watch where I was going.'

91

'I'm sorry,' said Phil. And he meant it. The girl looked seriously unhappy, the corners of her mouth pointed down and she seemed near to tears.

She drained her glass, and looked out at the street. She turned to Phil. 'Do you mind if I stay here a bit? I told my boyfriend to make sure he was out of our hotel room by the time I got back. I need to give him a bit of time.'

'No. Of course not. Can I buy you another drink?'

'I didn't mean that. I'll get it.'

'We'll split it.' Phil somehow got the waitress's attention.

'You're English?' Heike said.

'You can tell?'

'You have the accent. But you speak good German.'

She took out a pack of cigarettes and offered Phil one. He accepted – he barely ever smoked, it seemed ridiculous to him to waste fifty pence on twenty cigarettes, but he grabbed the opportunity to seem that little bit older, that little bit cooler, than he was.

'Are you here alone?' she asked. 'Or have you just dumped your own girlfriend?'

Phil laughed. He was about to claim that he was in his second year at Edinburgh and he was hitch-hiking around Europe by himself, when he thought better of it. She seemed like a nice girl, she'd had a bad evening and she would be a lot easier to talk to if he didn't lie or try to make out he was someone he wasn't. No more cigarettes.

'I'm driving my grandmother around Europe,' he said. 'She's back at the hotel, but she let me out for the evening.'

This went down well. 'Oh, I'd love to drive my *Oma* around. What a great idea! She is this tiny little old lady with the sweetest kitten. She bakes the most delicious cakes for me.'

'That doesn't sound much like mine,' said Phil. 'She's not even really old, and she's a little scary and a little strange.'

'But you like her,' said Heike. 'I can tell.'

'I do like her,' said Phil. He felt a lump in his throat. 'She told me yesterday she is going to die. She has a . . .' He searched for the word and couldn't find it. 'A stone in her brain.'

'*Hirntumor?*' Heike touched his sleeve. 'I am sorry. That puts losing my shithead boyfriend into perspective. I should be happy he's gone. I *am* happy he's gone.' She said the last words defiantly and drank more of her wine. 'This is good stuff,' she said. 'Shall we get a bottle?'

So they bought a bottle. And drank it. Heike was good company. Phil soon admitted that he had just finished school, but that didn't seem to bother her. She came from Braunschweig and was at university studying engineering, but she had read Günter Grass, and was happy to talk to Phil about it. She even laughed at his jokes. Phil found the German coming easily once he warmed up, and with the lubrication of a bit of alcohol.

They bought a second bottle. By this time Heike was becoming quite drunk, and Phil's German was slurring. There must have been a moment when drink-fuelled good humour became sloppy incoherence, but it took a while for Phil to notice it. Eventually, he did, and he suggested that they leave.

'I am seriously drunk,' Heike said deliberately. 'Shitfaced. But at least Jürgen will have cleared out of my hotel room by now. Thank you for entertaining me, Phil.'

'Are you going to be all right getting back to your hotel?'

Heike stood in front of Phil on the street, swaying. 'Maybe not.'

'Here, I'll take you back.'

It was a twenty-minute walk to Heike's one-star hotel; Heike leaned into him the whole way. They found it eventually. Phil considered trying to ask himself in, but decided in a moment of lucidity that one way or other it would screw up what had been a great evening.

'Do you want to meet up again tomorrow night?' he suggested. 'Same place? Eight thirty?'

Heike looked up at him and frowned. Then she smiled. 'OK,' she said, and pushed herself through the hotel entrance.

It took Phil three-quarters of an hour to walk back to the Ritz through the streets of Paris, but he grinned all the way.

Chapter 15

Five and a half hours later, Phil's travelling alarm clock wrested him out of a tumbling sleep. He rolled out of bed, dragged on some clothes and made his way down to breakfast in the Ritz's grand dining room, with its confusing ceiling of blue sky and clouds.

Emma was waiting for him, perusing *The Times* over a pot of tea.

'Philip! You look dreadful.'

'I love you too, Grams. Is there any coffee?'

Emma smiled. 'I take it you enjoyed yourself last night?'

Despite the piston engine in his head, Phil responded with a smile of his own. 'I did.'

'I trust you didn't get yourself into that state alone?'

'No. I, um, I met someone.'

A broad grin from his grandmother. 'I'm very pleased to hear it. What's her name?'

'Heike.'

'German?'

'Yeah. From Brunswick.'

'And did you speak to her in German?'

'I did,' said Phil proudly.

'Good for you.'

Emma refilled her cup of tea, and Phil attacked the chocolate crois-sants. His stomach demanded food urgently.

'Grams, I hope you don't mind. I said I'd meet her again this evening. At half past eight. Is that OK? Do we have anything planned for tonight?'

'We do, as a matter of fact,' said Emma. But then, seeing Phil's disappointment, she continued, 'But we'll get you wherever you are going in time.'

'What are we doing?'

'You'll see.'

After breakfast they retraced Phil's journey of the previous evening, taking the Métro to Saint-Michel. Emma led Phil down towards the river and an old bookshop facing the back of Notre-Dame Cathedral, the words 'Shakespeare and Company' painted on a yellow board above its door.

They entered a warren of little rooms, random steps up and down, musty old sofas, and books, hundreds, maybe thousands of books lining the walls from floor to ceiling. There was a profound smell of dust. The till at the front door was presided over by a middle-aged man with a pointed grey beard reading a novel by Armistead Maupin. Various 'customers', mostly young, lounged about reading the stock. It didn't seem to occur to anyone to actually buy anything.

'Pick something out you'd like,' Emma said. 'I'll get it for you.'

Phil and she split up and wandered around the shelves. Phil was reluctant to buy anything, since he still had over a thousand pages of *War and Peace* to go, but Emma arrived at his elbow clutching *Catch-22* by Joseph Heller.

'I'll get you this,' she said. 'Just in case you get an idea in your head to join the army. Or the air force.'

'I'll join the air force if I want, Grams,' Phil said, partly to wind her up, partly because he didn't like being bossed about even by his grandmother, and partly because although he knew he would never become a jet fighter pilot, just as he knew he would never play centre forward for England, he didn't want to rule the possibility out.

'Of course you will, dear,' said Emma. 'Just read this book first.'

With difficulty, she roused the bloke at the till to take her money for *Catch-22* and a book about linguistics by a man called Noam Chomsky. Or was Noam a woman's name?

They left the shop, with Phil carrying the books.

'I loved Shakespeare and Company when I was here in the thirties,' Emma said. 'But that's not the original shop.'

'It doesn't exactly look new,' Phil said.

'It doesn't, does it? It has its charm, but the original location was on Rue de l'Odéon. I'll show you.'

It was about a fifteen-minute walk. Normally Emma's long legs would have eaten up the distance with no difficulty, but she started veering a little to the right as they walked, and so she threaded her arm through his. A worrying sign of the insidious damage being done to her brain.

The Rue de l'Odéon was a short, straight street that led gently uphill from the busy Boulevard Saint-Germain towards the classical columns of the Odéon theatre. They stopped outside Number 12, a yellow stone house with a small wrought-iron balcony above the front door.

'This used to be Shakespeare and Company. It was run by an American woman named Sylvia Beach. I spent a lot of time here, and also at the French bookshop that used to be right opposite. Sylvia was famous by the time I got to Paris. She had published James Joyce's *Ulysses* in the 1920s, and the likes of Ernest Hemingway used to drop by there. And Gertrude Stein. But by the 1930s the shop was in trouble, and I actually helped bail her out financially. All kinds of writers, French and British as well as American, did readings. I loved it. And I spent *a lot* of money here.'

They walked back down the hill to the roaring traffic of the Boulevard Saint-Germain, and headed towards the tall church of that name.

'The Deux Magots?' Phil said spotting a large café opposite. 'Isn't that where Jean-Paul Sartre used to go?'

'That's right. And the café opposite, where we are going for a cup of coffee now.'

It was the Café de Flore. They took a seat outside on the pavement, watching the cars hurl themselves down the boulevard.

'Back in the thirties, these places were a hotbed of socialism. In those days artists and writers really did wear berets and smoke

Gauloises cigarettes and argue about philosophy or dialectic materialism. It was not exactly forbidden, but it was certainly frowned upon, for diplomats to be seen in places like this, but I used to stop here for a *petit café* after visiting Shakespeare and Co.'

Phil looked around. There were plenty of tourists like him and Emma. There were a few well-dressed, well-heeled Frenchmen and -women. But Phil was pleased to spot an immensely wrinkled old man reading *Libération* with a fag end of ash drooping precariously from his cigarette, a little glass of red wine at his elbow.

'I bet that bloke was here back then,' Phil said.

'Probably.' Emma grinned. 'This is where I met Freddie and Dick.' Her smile disappeared. 'And where I learned something that destroyed my life in Paris.'

Chapter 16

May 1936, Paris

I WAS A little late to the Café de Flore. Dick had telephoned me and suggested that I join him and Freddie there at nine o'clock. I was beginning to appreciate and abide by Parisians' tendency to add a *petit quart d'heure* to any meeting time, and decided to add an extra quarter-hour on top of that to be on the safe side. I had dined alone at home – Roland was on his way back from a day of meetings with ship-owners in Le Havre.

Freddie was already there, as was Dick, but they had somehow inveigled themselves on to a large table of voluble Frenchmen and a couple of Americans, many of whom I recognized from the readings at Shakespeare and Company. As I arrived, Freddie was haranguing a particularly famous and formidable poet in surprisingly good French about the poet's misunderstanding of love. I sat down next to Dick and watched in something approaching fear.

But the poet broke into uproarious laughter, as did his colleagues. They thought the idea of being lectured to by someone whom they assumed was an Englishman on the subject of love a huge joke. An outcome, I realized, Freddie had anticipated.

Freddie saw me and introduced me to his new friends, who expressed varying degrees of enchantment at my presence. There were two women present of about my own age, an American named Frances Piggott whom I had spoken to briefly at the bookshop, and her friend Ellen. I sat next to Dick, and listened to the conversation.

The talk switched to Spain, and the recent elections won outright by the Popular Front coalition, and some discussion and then dismissal of rumours that the army was planning a coup. In France, everyone was sure that a general strike was on its way, of which they all seemed to approve, especially Freddie. It was strange seeing Freddie, so dapper in his well-tailored suit, espousing the cause of the workers with such enthusiasm. The French seemed to like it, and I began to see why Hugh had liked it also.

I was fascinated, although it meant I would be unlikely to get the chance to question Freddie about my brother.

'I'm finding it hard to keep up,' said Dick to me. 'My French isn't quite up to it.'

'It's funny,' I said. 'These are exactly the same topics of conversation the diplomats chat about, but from an entirely different angle.'

'Your friend is quite sure of his opinions,' said Frances, who was sitting on Dick's other side. 'And they are a sight more left-wing than I would expect from an English gentleman.'

Dick smiled. 'They certainly are. But he's Irish. Sort of.'

Dick, Frances and I carried on our own little side conversation in English. I would rather have stayed listening to the others, but I felt sorry for Dick for his lack of French. It turned out Frances was a student at a New England college and was spending a year at the Sorbonne. She seemed nice. I noticed Dick thought so too.

'Oh, I saw your husband today,' Dick said. 'At a restaurant in the Bois de Boulogne. He was—'

'It can't have been him,' I interrupted.

'Oh, it was. I didn't speak to him, but it was definitely him. I don't think they saw me.'

'No. He spent the day in Le Havre.'

'But . . .' Dick hesitated.

I noticed. I wondered.

'Was it him?'

'Um.'

'You said you were sure it was him?'

'Yes. I *thought* it was him.'

'With whom was he lunching?'

'Two men,' Dick said, after a pause. 'Frenchmen, probably.'

The tips of Dick's ears went red. 'The tips of your ears have gone red, Dick,' I said.

'Have they? It must be the wine.'

I fell silent. We listened to the conversation, which had moved on to the German occupation of the Rhineland a couple of months earlier and whether the French government should have kicked up more of a fuss. Except I wasn't listening.

Dick was lying.

Lying about what? About seeing Roland today? No. Why would he lie about that?

If he *had* seen Roland, then Roland's lunch had not been above board. Two possibilities suggested themselves, both of which scared the hell out of me.

'Dick?'

He tried to ignore me.

'Dick!' Louder.

He turned to me reluctantly.

'Was there any chance that the two Frenchmen Roland was having lunch with were, in fact, German?'

'Oh, I don't know,' said Dick. 'Maybe.' He seemed relieved by my question.

He was looking for a lead from me. One of the possibilities, prompted by my conversation with Colonel Vivian, had been that Roland had been lunching with German contacts at an out-of-the-way restaurant to give them secret information from the embassy, and that Dick had realized this and that was what he was lying about for some reason. But his uncertain response, and his relief that I was taking that tack, didn't seem to fit that.

The other possibility seemed more likely.

Should I explore it? Shouldn't I just let it go: pretend Dick had never told me what he had just told me? Dick would go along with that.

That's probably what I should have done. It's what a lot of other married women would have done.

But not me.

'You said Roland was lunching with two other men. Did you really mean that he was lunching with one other woman?'

Dick opened his mouth. Closed it. Kept quiet.

Frances was watching us both. She understood what was going on. She turned away, out of politeness.

I considered forcing Dick to admit it, but he just had.

Roland had lied to me about going to Le Havre. Instead he had gone to a discreet restaurant with another woman, and Dick had seen him.

My husband was having an affair.

I had to get out of there. I pulled myself to my feet, apologized that I was feeling unwell and had to leave, and pushed through the door to the pavement outside. I took a deep breath. My emotions, as yet unidentified, were roiling. Rage. Shame. Embarrassment. Sadness. Despair.

'Emma! Emma, I'm sorry.' It was Dick. He had come out on to the street to follow me. He did indeed look desperately sorry.

'Sorry you lied to me, or sorry you told me the truth?' I said.

'I don't know. That I lied to you. No. Both?'

I touched his arm. 'It's not your fault, Dick. It's Roland's fault.' I took another deep breath. 'Did you know the woman?'

'No.'

'What did she look like?'

'I'm not sure.'

'Oh come on! If you saw Roland clearly, you must have seen her.'

'I didn't, actually. She was facing away from me. She had dark hair and was wearing a cream-coloured dress.' He hesitated. 'That's all I can say.'

'How old was she?'

Dick shrugged. 'I'm so sorry, Emma.'

'Please leave me alone.'

He left me, on the street. Alone.

I walked the mile or so back to our apartment in the Rue de Bourgogne. I walked slowly. It was half past ten. The Paris streetlamps were throwing off their strange purple glow and, in the distance, I could see jags of light flashing from the Eiffel Tower. Roland would probably be home from Le Havre, or the Bois de Boulogne. I didn't want to see him.

So my husband was having an affair. Was it possible? Of course it was. He was in his early thirties, he was good-looking, he was charming. Women found him attractive. And he was in Paris, for God's sake, where everyone was supposed to be having affairs.

And it wasn't as if everyone in England was faithful either, especially in my social set. I didn't exactly have a social set; what I meant was my sister's set, or Roland's. Sarah was constantly telling me about affairs real or imagined amongst her and Tubby's friends. Was Tubby at it too? Was she?

I had trusted Roland. I loved him. I had believed that he loved me. I had believed that he was different from other men.

And what grounds had I for that?

None.

I was a fool. An absolute bloody fool.

The tears came. A couple arm in arm, about ten years older than me, stared at me. I glared at them. They probably weren't even married. Or they were, but to other people.

My pace slowed as I neared my apartment.

What if I was wrong? What if Roland had stayed in Paris, after all? What if he was lunching with another woman for a perfectly legitimate reason?

Maybe. Maybe.

I was clinging to this last desperate hope when I entered the flat. Roland was already in bed, reading.

'How was Le Havre?' I asked. My heart was pounding. Surely he would explain how the trip had been cancelled at the last minute.

'Deadly dull. How was the Café de Flore?'

'Interesting. But I'm terribly tired.'

I got into my pyjamas and slipped into bed. Roland moved towards me.

'Not tonight,' I said.

I closed my eyes tight. You see, not only was Roland hiding something from me. I was hiding something from him.

I was pretty sure that I was pregnant.

Chapter 17

I WAS FORTUNATE that I didn't have to spend much time with
Roland over the next couple of days. His diary was full, which was
par for the course for a diplomat. The following evening he went to
a reception at the Japanese Embassy, and the evening after that he
was dining at the Paris Travellers Club with some British journalists.

Or was he?

I debated grilling Cyril Ashcott to verify Roland's movements,
but decided there was no point. Trying to keep tabs on my husband
for the rest of our married life was not the answer. I had no clue
what was.

The cold light of day didn't bring clarity, just confusion. I
supposed that countless women had found themselves in the situation I was in. But so soon after getting married? It was less than
two years. I wasn't even twenty-two yet.

What would Hugh have said? I had no idea of that either. Before
he had died, I had felt with certainty I would know what Hugh's
opinion on anything was. But after the confusion of his death – his
renunciation of all he believed in, all we believed in, that strange
American woman, Freddie's drunken speculation that Hugh was a
spy – the strength and support he had always given me had dissi-
pated. And then he had died.

Sarah was a better bet. She was a woman of the world, or at
least *this* world of adultery and deceit. I considered telephoning
her in London. Maybe I would. Maybe I should. But I held back.
It was partly a question of pride; I was humiliated, and I didn't
want to share that with my beautiful, successful sister. I knew

Tubby adored her; I knew he wasn't unfaithful, and she would know that too.

The truth was, I didn't know what to think, how to react. I couldn't face talking to Roland about that or anything else, so I didn't. I knew there was a risk that by ignoring him I might alert him to my suspicions, but that might prove in itself a relief. If he gave me a choice, forced me to decide between one path or another, it would be easier to make up my mind. I would avoid him, and hope in time things became clearer.

And then there was the baby, if indeed there was a baby. The thought filled me with an explosive mixture of happiness and dread. I had always wanted a baby. Since he had proposed to me at Boulestin, I had wanted a baby with Roland. But now? Now, I didn't know. I decided to put off going to the doctor for confirmation. I would rather not be certain, at least not yet.

I was fortunate that my mother rang that morning to postpone our promised luncheon for a couple of days, saying she was leaving Paris to see a friend. That nose of hers would have sniffed out trouble.

The second evening, I went out by myself to Shakespeare and Company, and a reading of difficult poetry by an Irish writer in a mixture of English and French. Sylvia, the owner, welcomed me warmly. Not only was I a persistently good customer, but I had joined the whip-round to stave off her bankruptcy the year before. It wasn't just that, or even partly that. Sylvia liked me because I liked books, and I found that comforting. James Joyce was in the audience, dour in his eye patch beneath his glasses; I recalled the poet had been his secretary for many years. Present too were the French writers from the Café de Flore and Frances Piggott, the American student, who took a seat next to me.

'Did you understand that?' she asked at the end of the reading.

'Some of it,' I said. 'Maybe. I still have a lot to learn about poetry.'

'Hmm. Perhaps this guy does too,' said Frances with an irreverent grin.

I decided to sneak out immediately after the reading, but as I was leaving, I heard a voice I recognized from somewhere.

'Miss Brearton?'

I turned. It took me a moment to place the tall woman who was staring at me uncertainly from beneath thick, dark eyebrows.

'Miss Lesser?'

She smiled. 'That's right. I was sitting right behind you, and I was sure I recognized you. Eventually I figured you were Hugh's sister.'

I wanted very much to speak to this woman. Alone. 'I'm just leaving,' I said. 'But I haven't had supper yet. Would you like to dine with me?'

Kay Lesser hesitated. 'Perhaps a drink?'

We found a small café around the corner from the bookshop. We ordered a carafe of red wine.

'What are you doing in Paris?' I asked.

'Learning French. The only reason I went to London was to be near Hugh. After he died I moved here. I've found a job as a photographer's assistant, but it pays next to nothing.' Kay's accent was distinctive; I assumed that Americans had regional accents just like the English, and this was what they sounded like in Chicago. Her face was distinctive also: long, uneven, odd angles of cheek, chin and nose. Intriguing.

'I take it you like Europe then?'

Kay smiled. 'I just love it. And I enjoy learning languages. Like Hugh. And like you, from what Hugh was saying.'

'That's true.' I still liked the fact that Hugh talked about me to his friends, even this one.

'What about you?'

'I married a diplomat. You may have met him at Hugh's funeral. Roland Meeke? Thin moustache?' I almost said 'dark complexion' but something held me back from describing my husband that way. Was it shame at his Indian heritage? I didn't like that idea. 'Dark complexion,' I added.

'There were a hell of a lot of folks at Hugh's funeral,' Kay said. 'I don't recall many of them. But I do remember you.'

'And I you.'

I sipped my wine. There was a question I had been dying to put to her for two years. I put it.

'Miss Lesser. You probably don't remember, but you told me that Hugh asked you to marry him. I asked you your reply, but you never told me.'

The tall American woman leaned back in her chair, studying me. Then her lips twitched into the hint of a smile. An unbending. 'First off, call me Kay.'

'All right,' I said. 'Kay. And I'm Emma. Emma Meeke now.'

'I should never have told you Hugh did that. I haven't told anyone else. I was upset, and I needed to tell someone, to tell his family, to tell *you* that he loved me.'

'So did he ask you to marry him?'

'Oh, yes.'

'And what did you say?'

Kay sighed. 'I said "no".'

I felt an absurd irritation that this woman had rejected my brother, mixed with a slightly less absurd relief that she had.

'Why?'

'See, I'm not sure I believe in marriage. I loved Hugh. But I wasn't sure I loved him in a way that would mean I would never love anyone else. And one day he would have become Lord Chaddington and I would have become Lady Chaddington and that went against everything I believed in. Still believe in.'

'I understand,' I said. 'At least you were honest.'

'I'm always honest,' said Kay. 'That's one of my many failings.'

Strangely, I felt myself beginning to like this woman, even though I couldn't begin to understand her.

'In that case, please tell me: was Hugh spying for the Russians?'

Kay looked away from me, towards the street lights outside the café's windows.

I waited.

She made her decision. She turned back to me.

'Yes.' She nodded. 'Hugh was a spy. But for the Comintern, not the Russians.'

Chapter 18

IT WAS A delightful party in a beautiful house – almost a palace – in the Rue de Grenelle, not far from our apartment: fabulous food, distinguished wine, an accomplished hostess and charming guests. And me.

Roland and I had been invited to a dinner for twelve given by the Comtesse de Villegly. It was part of a diplomat's job to hobnob with the natives, to take the temperature of the host country, and Roland was very good at it. The comtesse had an agenda. Her brother had died in the last war and she wanted to make sure that there wasn't going to be another one. To achieve this she cultivated the British and the Germans in Paris, in an attempt to bring them together. I suspected it went further than that: that the comtesse rather admired the way the Germans had subdued their unruly republic and brought it to order and that she thought France might have something to learn from them.

I had no doubt that Roland was right to engage with the comtesse and her salon, but it occurred to me that he should also have been in the Café de Flore, talking to the French poet and his acolytes. True, it might be difficult for a middling British diplomat to be accepted into that circle. For a moment it occurred to me that I might be the one to do it, and report back.

But I didn't want to report back to Roland on anything.

To my confusion about Roland had been added my confusion about Hugh. The two men whom I trusted most in the world, whom I had relied upon, had turned out to be not at all who I thought they were.

Freddie had been correct after all; my brother had been a spy. An honest-to-goodness spy. A man who passed his country's secrets on to his country's enemies.

A traitor.

It's true that part of me was relieved to learn that Hugh had not renounced his communism after all. I assumed that had been an act for the benefit of the British authorities. I had asked Kay whether that was the case, but she had refused to confirm it, or to say if she knew anything about Hugh's death, or indeed to say anything about him at all. She seemed overwhelmed by the barrage of questions I had flung at her, evading responses to them and quickly excusing herself.

I was grateful she had told me that much.

On the other hand, Hugh was a true communist, but was he a true Englishman? I could understand working towards a communist Britain, but helping a foreign power? I had a vague understanding that technically the Comintern was an inter-national organization but, as far as I knew, it was headquartered in Moscow and funded by the Soviet Union, and the Soviet Union was a possible enemy. That was a step too far, even for me. I was a firm believer that furthering the communist agenda was an act of patriotism – it would lead to a fairer, better Britain. But betraying your country's secrets to a foreign power wasn't.

I had thought that would be a step too far for Hugh too. I wished I had had the chance to talk to him about it. And I felt rejected. If Kay was right, Hugh had still deceived me, this time by including me among the people he had lied to about his changed political ideas. Deceiving my parents was fine, deceiving his new employer, the Conservative MP Sir Patrick Bettinson, was fine, even deceiving Dick was fine. But me? Couldn't he have trusted me?

I looked around the table. There were three Germans there: Kurt Lohmüller, a banker named Schaber, and Otto Abetz, who was a Francophile like Kurt and a young man to watch, according to the comtesse. I was seated between Kurt and the comte, a gentleman who looked to be in his forties, but who acted much older. I liked him. Unlike most of the French aristocrats, who amused themselves with flirting with any Englishwoman they came into contact with, the comte was more interested in animals. Killing animals. A bit like my father, really.

Time to do my job.

'I hadn't realized that there were still wolves in France, Comte?' I said. I had done my research on wild boar, wolves and bears in the American Library that morning. I was hopeless at returning aristocrats' witticisms or simpering at their absurd flattery, but properly prepared I could talk to this man about dangerous animals. I was learning to be a good diplomat's wife.

The comte's eyes lit up, and we chatted happily through the foie gras and the fish course.

As he turned to the woman on his right, Frau Schaber, the German banker's wife, my eyes scanned the table. My husband was charming the comtesse.

She was at least ten years younger than the comte, in other words about Roland's age, and an entirely different kind of person to her husband. She was intelligent, witty and beautifully dressed. I suddenly realized something that had been staring me in the face the whole time I had been in Paris. It wasn't just a case of French aristocrats flirting with Englishwomen. French aristocrats' wives flirted with Englishmen.

I could see it right there. Roland was charmed by the comtesse, and was in turn charming her.

The Comtesse de Villegly's hair was dark. And no doubt she owned a cream dress.

Was this what life was going to be like from now on? Every time my husband charmed a woman, I would look on in a state of uncertain jealousy?

'Are you all right, Emma?'

It was Kurt, speaking to me in French.

111

I was about to assure him I was, when I held myself back. Why not speak the truth?

'No. I'm not.'

Kurt glanced at my husband and the comtesse. 'I see,' he said, his tone studiedly neutral. But at that moment, the neutrality said it all. He did understand my suspicion, but also my uncertainty. He understood my difficulty in speaking about it. And he sympathized.

I smiled at him. For a moment I felt absurdly grateful to him. I felt as though I had a friend.

He smiled back. Then his expression hardened slightly.

With the wine, the volume around the table had risen, and the party had broken into a number of separate animated conversations. 'There is something I need to tell you, Emma,' Kurt said in murmured German. His lips smiled, but his eyes were deadly serious.

'Yes?'

'Before I do so, you must understand it is very important that you don't tell anyone else you heard it directly from me – certainly not your husband. If you do, you may place me at considerable risk.'

'All right,' I said. A few days before I might not have taken his warning seriously. Now I did.

'This is how you will say you heard it. After the meal, I will ensure that I spend a couple of minutes speaking to Herr Abetz alone. I want you to approach us as if you mean to speak to me, but in such a way that you are behind my back and I don't see you. You pause, and pretend to have overheard our conversation. That will be your explanation. Do you understand?'

'Yes, I do,' I said.

'Good. Now smile. Or laugh. Or something. What I am going to tell you is serious, but you shouldn't make it appear as such.'

I understood. 'Kurt, that's ridiculous!' I said, with a look of mock horror.

Kurt smiled. 'Very good. Here goes. It's about your favourite third secretary, Cyril Ashcott.'

Chapter 19

I TELEPHONED HEATON-SMITH at the embassy the following morning, half an hour after Roland had set off for work. He agreed to meet me immediately at a café on the Rue Saint-Dominique near our apartment. Apparently, Colonel Vivian had left Paris for Rome, where someone had pinched the ambassador's wife's necklace, leaving Heaton-Smith in charge in Paris.

I told him that I had overheard Herr Abetz and Herr Lohmüller discussing Cyril, and I had also overheard the word '*Erpressung*', which is German for 'blackmail'. I decided to let the secret-service man join the dots. If Dick could tell that Cyril was a fairy, then Heaton-Smith could too. And Heaton-Smith could work out that it was Cyril who was passing secrets to the Germans. Codebooks, according to Kurt.

Heaton-Smith seemed pleased with my story. 'Thank you, Mrs Meeke. I will certainly follow this up. Have you told your husband?'

'No,' I said.

Heaton-Smith raised his eyebrows.

'Colonel Vivian told me not to.'

'So he did. And he was absolutely right; the fewer people who know, the better, especially within the embassy.'

'I say. If it turns out that Cyril is completely innocent, you will let me know, won't you? It's just that I like him, and I don't want to be suspicious of him with no cause.'

'Yes, I will,' said Heaton-Smith. He smiled, displaying a disconcerting gap between his two front teeth. He shook my hand. 'Your husband was absolutely right to urge us to talk to you. You did well.'

As I walked back to my apartment, I wondered if I had done the right thing. With everything else that had been going on, I hadn't questioned what Kurt had asked me to do, I had just done it. It seemed like the 'right thing'. But what did it say about my loyalty? About whom I trusted?

I liked Cyril, but if he was betraying his country, even his right-wing capitalist country, he should be caught and punished. Maybe not punished if he was a victim of blackmail. But he should be stopped.

He probably would be punished severely. I didn't understand homosexuality, nor did I understand society's reaction to it. Everyone, apart from me, seemed to know when people like Freddie or Cyril were homosexuals, which they all seemed to tolerate or even find amusing, until the poor men were caught by an official, whereupon they somehow deserved severe criminal punishment and social ostracism. It didn't make sense. And more concretely, it meant the likes of Cyril Ashcott could be blackmailed.

My brother had betrayed his country. Would I have sold him out as I had just sold out Cyril?

Then there was the way I had trusted Kurt. Not just that the information about Cyril was correct, but, more importantly, that I should hide from the British authorities that Kurt had given me that information intentionally. Why hadn't I told Heaton-Smith that Kurt was willing to betray his country to the British? It was an opportunity for Heaton-Smith to recruit Kurt as a spy for us.

Because Kurt had asked me not to. Because he had put himself in great danger by telling me what he knew, and he trusted me more than the British secret service to keep his name out of it.

But why was Kurt betraying *his* country?

I knew the answer. Despite his protestations, he, like me, was a communist. It takes one to know one. As a communist, he hated Fascism. He hated Hitler. And he recognized that in me. By exposing Cyril, he and I together were doing a little bit to restrain a loathsome dictator.

I liked that.

Maybe I had done the right thing after all.

When I returned to the flat, the telephone was ringing. I picked it up.

'Emma? It's Dick.'

'Oh, hello, Dick.' I was actually glad to hear his voice. We hadn't spoken since the Café de Flore.

'Look, I'm sorry I mishandled things the other night. Can I take you to the cinema tonight to make amends? Or partial amends?'

Suddenly, that idea seemed very attractive to me. I would like to see Dick, and a film would stop me stewing and help stave off awkward conversation between us.

'That would be lovely. What's on?'

'There's rather a good western that has just got to France. *Blue Steel*. Have you seen it?'

'I don't think I have ever seen a western in my life,' I said, somewhat coolly.

'Well, it's jolly well time that you did,' said Dick. 'The cinema is on the Champs Élysées.' He gave me the address. 'Seven o'clock.'

I hesitated, trying to think what Roland was doing that evening. Then I realized I didn't care.

'I will see you then.'

I was looking forward to the cinema. But I had to deal with luncheon with my mother first.

Mama varied venues for our meals in Paris between Larue's and the Ritz, but I suspected the Ritz was her favourite. She liked the mixture of grandeur and high-society wickedness that the place exuded at that time. I hoped if I could get her chattering I might avoid any searching questions about why I was looking down in the dumps. But if she did ask, what would I say?

Perhaps I would tell her the truth?

If anyone might have good advice on how to deal with this situation, then it would be my mother. She must have oodles of friends in the same boat as me. The thing was, if I was humiliated by the idea of admitting Roland's infidelity to my sister, the idea of telling my mother was mortifying.

And then there was the fact that she was about to become a grandmother. While many mothers would be overjoyed at the news, I knew my mother wouldn't like the idea that she was on the cusp of grannyhood at all. I couldn't tell her, at least not yet.

I decided to walk to the Place Vendôme. As I crossed the Seine, I came up with a stratagem.

My mother seemed in fine fettle, as she ordered a gin and It before lunch. To her surprise, I ordered one too. The Ritz's opulent dining room was full of Paris's beautiful people, some of whom even I recognized: the Italian ambassador lunching with one of the legions of former French cabinet ministers, and a famous French actress toying with a millionaire motor manufacturer.

I had slightly lost touch with my mother's whereabouts, but it turned out she had spent a couple of days in the Loire Valley at the chateau of an old school friend, Googoo. I had heard about Googoo on and off for all of my life, but it sounded a ridiculous name for an adult woman when uttered in the dining room of the Ritz. I think her real name was Gertrude. She was a Scotswoman who had married a French aristocrat.

'Do you think Googoo's husband is faithful to her?' I asked.

'What an extraordinary question!'

I realized that, as usual, I had been a little too direct. Still, my mother should be used to that. 'Is it?'

My mother smiled. She was wearing a new cloche hat, a pale blue dress I also hadn't seen before and her favourite everyday pearls. She had perfected the art of lipstick – her lips traced a perfect bow. She looked the equal of any of the other women in the room, except perhaps the actress, which wasn't bad for an Englishwoman.

'No, I suppose it's not so extraordinary.' She glanced at me, deciding whether to confide. 'I don't think Jean-Pierre has been faithful, no.'

'And how does Googoo take that?'

My mother sighed. 'She puts up with it. It's almost inevitable in this country.'

'Does she speak to you about it?'

'She has done, sometimes. Over the years. Why do you ask?'

I paused while the waiter took our orders.

Time for part two of the stratagem. 'I have a friend at the American Embassy. Her name is Frances. She's married to a diplomat, like me. And she has just learned that he has been unfaithful. She's frightfully upset and I am the only one she has confided in. I don't know what to advise her. Should she confront him? Should she throw him out? Should she leave him? Should she divorce him? Or should she just ignore it and pretend it didn't happen?'

My mother's small nose was twitching. 'Is she sure her husband has been unfaithful?'

'Yes.' I swallowed. Somehow that one question had undermined my confidence, which until that point had been going strong.

'Oh, my poor darling!' My mother reached out for my hand. I gave it to her and she squeezed it. 'My poor, poor darling.'

'It's not me,' I said, fighting to control the tears. 'It's my friend. Frances.'

'Of course it's you, darling. If someone asks for "a friend" it's always them. Don't you even know that?'

The 'even' emphasized my naivety. But I *was* naive. I was only twenty-two for God's sake! I wasn't *supposed* to know about all this stuff.

'Do you know who it is?' she asked.

I gave up any pretence that I was talking about anyone other than myself. My mother's sympathy seemed genuine, and now at least I could get the advice of someone more experienced in life than me.

'I'm not sure. I think it might be Sophie de Villegly. Do you know her?'

'I do slightly. She's very pretty. She *is* his age. And she does have a bit of a reputation.'

I withdrew my hand. This was not what I wanted to hear.

'I'm sorry, darling, but it's much the best if you know whom you are dealing with. How long has it been going on for?'

'I have no idea. I only became suspicious in the last couple of days. But you know how I sometimes miss things. It could have been carrying on for months. Years, maybe.'

For some reason, I hadn't considered this before. Perhaps the affair had started before we were married.

'I thought Roland loved me,' I said, despising the self-pity in my voice.

'He probably does love you,' my mother said. 'I'm sure he's very fond of you; I can see that.'

'Then why does he take a . . .' I searched for the word. 'A mistress?'

'Who knows why men do that? The thrill of the chase? The danger? The excitement? I sometimes wonder whether humans were meant to be monogamous at all.'

'So you think it's possible for Roland to love me and love Sophie de Villegly as well?'

'Having seen this many times, I would say it is perfectly possible. And he may not even love Sophie de Villegly.'

That hadn't occurred to me.

'You said she had a reputation. Does Roland?'

'He did, a bit, before you were married. There were a couple of married women he was rumoured to have seduced. NSIT.'

I remembered that from my deb days. Not Safe In Taxis.

'So what do I do, Mama? Do I divorce him?'

'God no. It will cost heaps of money, there will be a scandal and then you will get married to another man who will just do exactly the same thing.'

'But that's a dreadful idea! It's too horrid.'

'It's the truth. So don't do it.'

'So I don't do anything?'

'I didn't say that. You need to lay down the rules of the game and enforce them. What those rules are is up to you, but I would suggest at a minimum nothing in public. You don't want him to make you look a fool. If possible try and let him know you know without actually telling him. Roland is clever; he'll catch on.'

'So I let him carry on?'

'He will carry on. This way you let him carry on, but on your terms. That's what Googoo does, and it works.'

'For him, you mean.'

'And for her.'

'Does she sleep with other people too?'

My mother didn't answer.

'I don't know,' I said. 'It all seems so sordid. I'm not sure I could ever just "carry on".'

'My poor darling! You are upset and angry, of course you are. Don't do anything rash. Let it settle. And then you will see I am right.'

Our soup came, consommé, and I mulled over what my mother had said as I sipped it. I wasn't sure that I could ever follow her advice. But it was meant well. And I had a horrible feeling that she might be right.

Chapter 20

I FELT DREADFUL when I left the Ritz. I still didn't know what to do. Or, part of me knew what I should do – take the pragmatic option my mother was suggesting – and part of me rejected that. It was tearing me apart.

I resolved to treat myself to some books.

I walked across the river to Shakespeare and Company. The books all around me calmed me down, as did the familiar faces of the browsers. I went to the philosophy section, but that wasn't where the answer to my dilemma lay. Fiction?

Perhaps I needed escape rather than answers.

'Emma?'

I recognized the voice. It was Kay.

'Hello,' I said. We were in an out-of-the-way corner of the book-shop, alone apart from an old lady reading a detective novel by the window.

'I'm glad I bumped into you,' the American said. 'I'm sorry I left when you had so many questions for me last night.'

She was very tall. Her expression was earnest, sympathetic even, as she looked down on me.

'It was rather a bombshell,' I said.

'If you want me to answer your questions now, I can.'

We went to the same café we had visited the night before, and ordered the same carafe of red wine. I didn't usually drink in the middle of the afternoon, but I needed one.

'OK. Shoot,' she said.

'All right.' I scrambled to get my thoughts in order. 'I suppose I was relieved to learn that Hugh was still a communist when he died. But I am surprised that he spied for the Soviet Union against England. He always seemed in favour of international socialism, rather than Stalin's socialism in one country.'

'He liked what he saw in Russia,' said Kay. 'I was with him.'

'That's true. But to betray his own country?'

'I guess he didn't see it that way,' said Kay. 'You're right, he believed in freedom for the workers of the world, and not just Russia. He was also worried about Fascism. Mussolini, the Nazis. The Cagoulards here in France. But most of all he wanted to actually *do* something, rather than just talk about it. Also, he wasn't actually spying for Russia; he was spying for the Comintern.'

'Is there any difference?'

'Hugh thought there was.'

'But isn't the Comintern based in Moscow?'

'Of course it is! Where else could it be based? The Soviet Union is the only communist country in Europe. In the world. But it's a truly international organization. It's devoted to spreading Marxism throughout the entire world. There are delegates from all over Europe and from America and China and India. If there is to be a world revolution, then it has to be nurtured in Russia.'

'I remember Hugh saying that.'

'The whole point about Marxism is that it aims to encourage the workers to rise up everywhere. That's what the Comintern is doing. Class consciousness is something that transcends national borders, just like monopoly capitalism does. The British worker has more in common with his German or French or Russian comrade than he does with an English capitalist. That's what Hugh believed, anyway.'

It was true. That was what Hugh believed.

'So that's why he applied for the Foreign Office?' I asked. 'To be able to spy for the Comintern?'

'Sure. And to get in he had to demonstrate that his communism was no more than a student phase. He had to deny it.'

'I just wish he had told me what he was really up to.'

'He wanted to. He used to speak about you plenty. He said you talked more sense than most of the socialists he knew at Cambridge. But they wouldn't let him.'

'"They"? Who are they?'

'I don't know. The people from the Comintern he was speaking to, I guess.'

Kay was watching me closely under her thick black eyebrows.

'What about you?' I said. '"They" let him speak to you?'

'That's true,' she admitted.

'Why? Are you one of "them"?'

'Not exactly,' said Kay. 'But I did put Hugh in touch with them.'

'*You* did.'

Kay nodded.

Who was this woman? 'How long have you been a communist? I didn't know there are communists in America.'

Kay smiled. 'Oh, there are. Plenty. There are communists all over the world. That's why we need the Comintern to bring us all together. You, me, Hugh, Freddie, Rosa Luxemburg, Maurice Thorez here in France and, yes, Comrade Stalin.'

She hesitated. 'I've been a communist all my life. As has my father. My grandfather emigrated to America from Lithuania in the 1880s. The entire family ended up working in factories in Chicago. I went out to work at the age of twelve.'

'But you escaped?'

'I sure did. My father was self-taught and he taught me.' She smiled. 'A bit like Hugh teaching you. I got myself involved in labour organizations and I ended up in Europe.'

'Is Kay your real name?'

'It is at the moment.'

I had more questions. 'So how did Hugh die? Do you believe it was an accident? Was Freddie right? Did the British secret service kill him?'

'I don't know,' said Kay, for the first time looking troubled herself.

'They may have done. It was very convenient for them, after all. And you said yourself you didn't think Hugh's death was an accident.' She took a deep breath. 'If they did kill him, I cannot forgive them.'

I was reminded that this woman loved my brother too.

'Nor can I,' I said.

We sat in silence for a moment.

Kay spoke. 'You know I said I put Hugh in touch with people?'

'Yes.'

'I could do that for you. You could continue Hugh's work.'

'Don't be ridiculous! Anyway, what possible use would I be?'

'Your husband is doing real well in the diplomatic service. He will go far. I'm sure he trusts you.'

'You want me to betray his trust?' The words were out of my mouth before the irony hit me.

Kay shrugged.

'And betray my country?'

'These are the people who killed your brother.'

'So you say. You don't know that.'

'I believe it's likely.'

Was it? I didn't know. I remembered Dick's assertion that that wasn't the kind of thing that happened in England, and I wanted to believe him, not Kay.

But . . .

'Anyway,' Kay went on. 'You wouldn't be betraying your country. Not really. You would be helping the world's workers. The poor. The people whose lives are being destroyed by the capitalist system every single day. British people, your countrymen. And you would be stopping the Fascists, the Fascists who hate Jews like me and who are just as keen to suppress the working classes but will use even worse methods than the capitalists.'

I didn't say anything. I was listening.

'Hugh did it. I'm just suggesting you should too.'

I took a gulp of my wine and shook my head. 'No. I won't be a traitor. I know you mean well – I know Hugh meant well.' I leaned back in my chair. 'It's rather a lot to take in. Especially with every-thing else that's going on.'

Kay watched me carefully.

'You mean your husband?' she said.

'My husband?' Something close to panic rose in my chest. 'What about my husband?'

'You spoke about betrayal?'

'You know? How do you know?'

Kay shrugged. 'I know. I just wasn't sure you did. But it makes me wonder.'

'Wonder what?'

'Wonder why you would shy away from betraying your husband? After what he did to you, what he's still doing to you.'

I swallowed.

'And who he's doing it with.'

I leapt on that. 'Who with? Do you know who he has been seeing? Is it the Comtesse de Villegly?'

'You don't know?'

I shook my head. It clearly wasn't the comtesse. Suddenly I wasn't sure I wanted Kay to tell me.

But then I knew who it was. Who would be worse than Sophie de Villegly? It was all suddenly so clear.

'It's my mother.' I said the words quietly.

Kay nodded.

'Are you sure?'

Kay nodded again.

It all fitted. Everything fitted. Once you accepted the premise that in the real world anyone could be unfaithful to anyone, then Roland could be unfaithful to me, and Mama could be unfaithful to Papa. Of course there was their age difference, but my mother was unquestionably still a beautiful woman, and Roland liked beautiful women.

My mind raced. My mother had been visiting Paris much more frequently since Roland had been posted here. She was in Paris the day that Dick saw Roland with another woman. Dick had said that that woman had had dark hair, but he must have been lying to protect me. I recalled that when he had first mentioned he had seen my husband in the restaurant he had been about to tell me whom Roland was with when I cut him off. If it had been a woman Dick hadn't known, rather than simply his mother-in-law, Dick would have been more suspicious, and wouldn't have told me about it so blithely.

How long had it been going on? It must have been soon after we were married. Or perhaps before? Since Roland had come to stay with us in Devon the weekend Hugh had died?

Then a darker thought occurred to me. Was the whole thing camouflage? Had their affair already been going on when my mother invited Roland down to Devon? Which meant his wooing of me was just an elaborate cover; by getting Roland respectably married off to me, they were enabling the two of them to see each other whenever they wanted.

I knew the way my mother thought. She would love that. It would be a means of controlling him, and asserting her total superiority over her useless bluestocking daughter. Me.

I pulled some francs out of my purse and put them on the table. 'I'm sorry, Kay. I have to go.'

Chapter 21

June 1979, Paris

'But, Grams, that's terrible!'

'It was.'

'I can't believe he did that to you. And with your mother! Yuk! I'm glad I never met her. Or at least I don't remember meeting her.'

'You didn't. She died when you were two.'

'No wonder no one talks about her. Does Mum know all this?'

'No, she doesn't. We didn't talk about it in the family. My generation are experts at sweeping things under the carpet. I'm sure she realizes something went badly wrong, but she doesn't know what. That's probably why she never told you much about our history. You might understand now why I brought you along instead of her.'

Phil did some quick sums in his head. 'She was the one you were pregnant with?'

Emma nodded.

'Do you want me to keep it from her?'

'When I'm alive, yes. When I'm gone, it's entirely up to you. I didn't want my story to die with me, which is why you are here.'

She pulled some francs out of her purse for the bill. 'Let's go.'

They left the Café de Flore and walked along the busy Boulevard Saint-Germain. Phil was still trying to get to grips with what he had heard.

'But I *liked* Grandpa.'

'I know you did, darling.'

'I can't believe he did that to you. What happened?'

'You'll find out.'

Phil was tempted to insist Emma fast forward to the end of her story, but he knew his grandmother wanted to tell it in her own way, at her own pace. He felt privileged that she trusted him to hear it.

There had been no mention of Lothar yet, the Russian spy whom Swann had mentioned. Nor of any mole.

And there was that revolver in her suitcase. Somehow that was related.

They left the boulevard and walked down increasingly chic streets of yellow stone buildings bearing intricate wrought-iron balconies. Boutiques sold fabric, women's dresses, antique furniture, art, old books and exuberant flower arrangements. This was the Paris of wealth, sophistication and style. Midday was approaching, the streets were hot and, here, mostly empty. Every now and then they passed a woman in sunglasses, a silk scarf around her neck, browsing the shops, her subtle scent following them along the pavement for a few yards.

They turned into a street lined with high walls and imposing buildings, many given over to government business.

'This is the Rue de Grenelle,' said Emma. She stopped outside a wall above which, set back from the road, stood what looked like a mansion. A complicated multicoloured flag hung from a pole pointing out towards the street, the insignia of an oil-rich Middle Eastern nation. 'This was the Comtesse de Villegly's house,' she said. 'Seems it's an embassy now.'

'Wow,' said Phil. 'Very grand.' It was hard to imagine real people living there. But then the Comtesse de Villegly didn't sound like a real person, or not like any person Phil knew.

They walked down towards the river, past an abandoned railway station and then on to the buildings of the National Assembly, guarded by policemen with sunglasses and machine guns, who seemed to be staring at them. Creepy. And not at all like the lone bobby in front of 10 Downing Street.

They turned up a narrow street, the Rue de Bourgogne. This was less swish than the others, the buildings and the shops were less grand: a butcher, a greengrocer, a *tabac*, a hairdresser.

127

They stopped outside a thick wooden door. 'This was our building,' Emma said, looking up at some large windows protected by blue shutters, closed at that moment to keep out the sun. 'We lived on the first floor.'

'Looks nice.'

'It was.'

Phil took a couple of steps back, to let Emma remember.

After a minute or so, she turned to him. 'Are you hungry?'

'Always.'

'Let's go to the Voltigeur. It's just down the road. I used to drop in there for a cup of coffee sometimes.'

The Voltigeur hadn't changed much, according to Emma – a simple cramped café on a corner – although the leather-jacketed guy playing the pinball machine was definitely a 1970s addition. They ordered *croque-monsieurs*, which Phil was becoming partial to, with a beer for Phil and a glass of Evian for Emma.

'What did you do about Roland?' Phil asked.

'It was an agonizing decision,' Emma said. 'And even now, I'm not sure I did the right thing.'

Chapter 22

May 1936, Paris

I BLUNDERED DOWN the street towards the river, and took the steps to the bank. I found a spot free of fishermen, sank down to the ground and sobbed.

I don't know who passed me, who saw me, and what they thought. I didn't care.

Eventually, the sobbing dried up. I looked up at the back end of Notre-Dame cathedral. A tug chugged past, dragging a long barge behind it, a young boy watching me curiously from on top of a pile of what looked like coffins secured to its deck. Dozens of coffins – new, not used, presumably.

I couldn't pretend I hadn't heard what I had just heard. I couldn't follow my mother's advice, however worldly-wise. I had to deal with this my own way.

Directly.

I climbed the steps up to street level and hailed a taxi. It dropped me off outside the Hôtel de Charost. I nodded to the porter and made my way to the Chancery building.

I strode past Muriel, Roland's secretary, and into his office. He was on the telephone. He saw my face and hung up.

'What is it, darling?' His smile was innocent, concerned.

'I know who your mistress is,' I said.

His eyebrows rose. 'What mistress?'

'My mother. Your lover.'

'I beg your pardon? I don't understand what you mean.'

'Yes, you do. You're . . .' I searched for the word I wanted and couldn't find it, so I settled on a poor substitute. 'You're fornicating with my mother. Your mother-in-law. It's disgusting. You disgust me.'

Roland pulled himself to his feet, his face full of concern. For a second I doubted myself, but only for a second.

'I think you must have got the wrong end of the stick, my darling. Why do you think your mother is my mistress? That's absurd.'

'Because you were seen with her when you were supposed to be in Le Havre talking to some shipping tycoon.'

'Oh, that!' Roland smiled reassuringly. 'I can explain that. Let me tell you what happened.'

'No, Roland. I don't want to hear your lies about what happened. I don't want to speak to you ever again. When you get home this evening, I won't be there. Goodbye.'

With that I turned on my heel and left his office. I passed a preoccupied-looking Cyril on the stairs on my way out to the court-yard, but I ignored his half-hearted greeting.

I made my way to Dick's flat an hour before we were supposed to meet at the cinema, lugging my suitcase. I had his address: it turned out he lived at the top of an ancient, unsteady building squeezed into the middle of the Île Saint-Louis. An ancient, unsteady concierge let me in, and pointed up to some stone steps. I climbed them and rapped on a door under the eaves.

'Emma?' he said as he opened it. 'I thought we were meeting at the cinema?'

Then he saw my suitcase, and his expression changed from surprise to concern. 'Come in.'

His flat was really nothing more than a room with a bed, a wash-stand, two armchairs, a gas heater and a hob. And a desk bearing a typewriter with a view over the rooftops to the river and the buildings of the Left Bank beyond. It reeked of pipe tobacco.

It was the classic Parisian artist's garret; evidence of Dick's writings lay all over the desk.

'Sit down, Emma,' he said. 'I take it you've found out?'

I sat down. 'It was my mother,' I said. 'Roland was seeing my mother.' I looked up at him, almost in supplication, praying that he would inform me I was wrong.

But he didn't. I could tell immediately from the expression in his eyes, a mixture of kindness and pain. 'Yes. I saw him with your mother.'

'Then why didn't you tell me?'

'I was going to. In fact, I almost said "I saw your husband and your mother today," but you interrupted me. Then when you said that you thought Roland was in Le Havre, I shut up. It became clear that you thought he had been seeing a woman, a mistress, and I suddenly realized that he *had*, and that that mistress *was* your mother.'

'So why hide that from me?'

'I didn't want to hurt you. I thought admitting he was seeing another woman was bad enough.'

I was determined not to cry again in front of Dick.

'Look, Emma, I can tell you are having a rotten day. Let me give you a glass of wine.'

I nodded. Dick opened a bottle of simple rough red, and poured us both a glass. He sat down opposite me. 'How did you find out?'

I looked at those kindly eyes. Hugh's friend. I wanted him to be *my* friend too. I badly needed a friend.

And so I told him. About meeting Kay at Shakespeare and Company. About how she had claimed that Hugh was a spy for the Russians, or at least the Comintern, and then how Kay had told me not only that Roland was betraying me, but that he was doing it with my own mother.

'Do you believe her?'

131

'I do,' I said. 'As she was telling me, it all slotted into place. In fact, I even suspect that this was their plan right from the beginning. To invite Roland down to Devon to meet me and marry me. I suspect my mother arranged the whole thing.'

'But that's grotesque!' exclaimed Dick.

'It is, isn't it?'

'And what about that bit about your brother being a spy?'

'I think that's true too. Don't you?'

Dick blew out through his cheeks. 'I'm not so sure: I don't think Hugh would do that. Unlike Freddie, I always thought Hugh loved his country. Why did Kay tell you all this?'

'She wants me to be a spy for the Comintern too. Like Hugh.'

'Are you going to?'

'No. Of course not.'

'Are you going to tell the authorities about her? Someone at the embassy? The French police?'

'No. I'm not going to do that either. But I did go and see Roland to say I knew about him and Mama.'

'Was that wise?'

'I don't know. I didn't think I had any choice.'

'Did he deny it?'

'He acted confused. He was convincing. Roland is always convincing.'

'You don't believe him?'

'No,' I said. 'I don't.'

'Look,' said Dick. 'We can't go to the flick now. There's a *traiteur* just around the corner. I'll be back in a moment with some food for supper. Stay here.'

He left me, and ten minutes later returned with some bread, some pâté, some *rillettes*, some *cornichons* and another bottle of red wine.

We ate and we drank and I talked. Dick was kind to me.

Eventually he and I crossed the street to the small hotel opposite. They had a single room. It was cheap and basic and the bed sagged alarmingly, but it would do. Exhausted, my brain fogged with the wine and the emotions of the day, I bade Dick goodnight and fell almost instantly asleep. But then I woke up, just as the bells of Notre-Dame struck midnight, and I lay on my back staring up at the ceiling until morning came.

Chapter 23

I WATCHED AS a thin strip of colour slid beneath the shutters of my room, grey then yellow. A bug scurried across the floor and stopped for a think beside the washstand. It turned out he had friends. I hadn't noticed them the night before.

I slipped out of bed, put on some clothes and emerged into the street. Although the Île was bang in the middle of Paris, it felt more like a medieval village than a city centre. A cockerel tucked away in a courtyard somewhere vigorously reminded me it was dawn. A tortoiseshell cat explored the new day. A mongrel, part-poodle part-sheepdog, eyed the cat suspiciously, before raising its leg on a lamppost. The street smelled of early-morning Paris – the stale garlic from the previous night's cooking lacing the aroma of that morning's bread seeping out of countless ovens throughout the city.

None of the cafés was open yet, but the street cleaner was out with his extra-long-handled broom and his buckets, washing the main road that ran along the middle of the island. A horse and milk cart clopped past, the horse leaving a little something extra on the cobbles for the cleaner to work on. I wandered down a narrow alley and leaned on a wall overlooking the river. Shrouds of mist twisted and turned a couple of feet above the water as it flowed urgently by on its long journey to the English Channel.

Thoughts that had jostled incoherently in my head began to settle. I couldn't live with Roland a moment longer. Nor could I stay with my mother in Chaddington. I could hole up in a hotel for a few days but eventually I would have to go somewhere. England, probably. To stay with my sister Sarah, probably. I was sure she would have me.

But that decision brought questions, questions with no good answers.

And there was the baby. What kind of family was the baby coming into?

The baby would be all right. One way or the other, I'd make sure of that. I smiled. I could use a tiny ally in this complicated, bewildering world.

The baby would be all right.

A few yards down the street the moustachioed proprietor of a café was opening it up, winding down the awning and arranging tables and chairs, all the while favouring a gammy leg – a war wound no doubt. An old woman, her sabots clattering on the cobbles, sauntered by, muttering to herself and ignoring the gruff greeting from the café owner. A boy of about twelve pedalled up with a bicycle cart piled high with the bread I had smelled baking, and made his delivery to the café. I took a table outside, ordered a cup of coffee and some of that fresh bread, and tried to think.

Should I divorce Roland? Should I make our split public? Should I tell Sarah who the other woman was? Should I tell my father?

Should I tell Papa?

He was the person who would be hurt the most if the affair became public. I would cope with the humiliation; it was not as if I had heaps of friends who would gossip about me. I hoped that a scandal might hurt Roland and my mother, but in reality, knowing the circles they moved in, the affair would just add to their illicit glamour.

Sarah would be upset. She was strong; she would cope in the end.

But my father? It would destroy my father.

I loved my father very much, even though we were very different people and barely understood each other. He liked farming – the old way. The old ways were always better. He liked hunting and shooting and drinking late into the night with old friends from Devon, barely speaking. He never read a book. I had the feeling that I had much more in common with his father, my grandfather, the man who had built the library at Chaddington and stocked it so well, the man who had astutely sold a couple of farms on the estate before the war and invested the proceeds in Standard Oil in America, which was where most of the family's income still came from these days. That investment was something that would never have occurred to Papa.

My father never understood me, but he always loved me, and loved me for who I was – a queer bookish girl with few friends. Unlike his wife, he loved me no less than his other two children: his brilliant son and his glittering elder daughter.

A burst of rage burned through the despair and confusion I felt. My mother and my husband had conspired together to ruin my life and quite probably the lives of those others whom I loved. I hated them. I hated them both. It was wrong: wrong, wrong, wrong!

What would Hugh have done?

An idea began to form.

I popped into Shakespeare and Company a few minutes after it opened, putting as bright a face on as I could with Sylvia. I spent twenty minutes browsing the shelves looking for something to entertain myself for the day with. I needed something familiar, comforting. I chose *A Tale of Two Cities* and settled myself in the corner where the woman had been reading the detective novel the day before.

I had just reached page thirty when Kay showed up, as I knew she would. I could tell she was pleased to see me. We repaired to what was becoming our habitual café around the corner. This time, I eschewed the glass of red wine but stuck to a *petit café*.

'Well?' said Kay.

'Tell me what I can do.'

Chapter 24

I MET 'LOTHAR' two days later by the Mare de Saint-James, one of the ponds in the Bois de Boulogne. Kay had given me detailed instructions on how to get there, including where to walk, where to hail a taxi, and where to take the Métro. As far as I could tell, I wasn't followed.

I thought I had spotted Lothar when an elegant man wearing a straw boater and swinging a cane strolled by, all the time looking at me. For a moment I thought he was about to speak to me, but he seemed to think the better of it, and wandered on. Just another French gentleman staring at a young woman, I realized.

'Excuse me?'

I turned to see a tall man with thick blond hair brushed back from a broad forehead. He was wearing a light grey summer suit, and a striped tie.

'Yes?'

'Can you tell me the way to the Porte Dauphine?'

'Certainly, monsieur,' I said. 'It's that way, past the Royal Pavilion.' I then pointed in the wrong direction as instructed.

The man sat next to me and smiled. 'Good morning, Mrs Meeke. My name is Lothar. Kay has told me all about you.'

We spoke French, but Lothar spoke it with a German accent – Austrian possibly – rather than Russian. There were plenty of Russian émigrés in Paris at that time, and I was pretty sure he wasn't one of them. He was friendly, and a very good listener. He examined me with intense eyes of the darkest blue as I spoke. His chin, which jutted outwards, gave his face an aura of quiet strength. He asked me all about myself, about my childhood, my family, and Chaddington. He seemed to know quite a lot about me already – more than Kay could possibly have known or told him.

We had been talking about Sarah and Hugh, and I felt it was time for me to ask a question. 'Did you know my brother?'

Lothar smiled. 'Yes, I knew your brother. And I am very sorry that he died. He was a good man.'

'Did he work for you?'

'Yes, he did. He had only just begun. The intention was that he would join the Foreign Office and work his way up.'

'Did he give you any secrets?"

'He never got the chance. We knew we would have to wait several years before he could provide anything of use. But Hugh was willing to commit to that. He was prepared to devote his life to the cause. I admired him.'

'Do you think he was killed?'

'Murdered, you mean?'

'I suppose I do.'

Lothar paused, considering his words carefully. 'We don't know for sure. But we think so – by the British secret service.'

Could that really be true? Could Hugh have been killed by his own government?

'Do you have any proof of that?' I asked.

'No absolute proof; that's rare in our game. But we have strong indications.'

'What exactly are "strong indications"?'

Lothar shrugged. He wasn't telling. I noticed that he was missing the tip of the little finger of his left hand. In those days there were a lot of Britons, Frenchmen and Germans missing bits and pieces of their body, and Lothar seemed to me to be just about old enough to have served in the war. Presumably for the Austrian army, or perhaps the German.

'What exactly do you want me to do for you?' I asked. 'And who are you? The Comintern? The Russian secret service?'

'Those are fair questions, and I will answer them in time,' Lothar said. 'But first I need to ask you something. Why do you want to work for the cause of international communism?'

'Lots of reasons,' I said. I had expected the question and had thought through my answers. 'My brother taught me that the workers are systematically exploited by the capitalist classes throughout the world and I happen to believe that's both true and deeply wrong. I understand Hugh helped you; perhaps I can too. I have read a lot about communism and socialism and inequality and injustice. I believe in it all, but I am the daughter of a landowner. I don't work, my father doesn't work really, we don't consider ourselves to be particularly rich, but I know we are. I realize I am a hypocrite. Working for international communism would give me a chance finally to *do* something to help the cause. I am pretty sure that must be why Hugh became a spy.'

'I think you are right,' said Lothar. 'Hugh told me he wanted to do something rather than talk about other people doing something. He was very worried about Mussolini and Hitler. I think he liked Russia, but he wasn't spying for Russia against Britain. He was doing his bit to fight Hitler and Mussolini and stand up for the working class, and he thought working with Russia, rather than for Russia, is the best way to do this. And he's right. That's what I'm doing. To answer your earlier question, I work for the Comintern, not the Soviet Union. I'm not Russian.'

'Where are you from?

'Lemberg, as was. It was part of the Austrian Empire; it's now in Poland and it's called Lwów.'

'So you speak Polish?' I suddenly had a strong and rather odd desire to know what language this man spoke.

He smiled. He understood. 'There are a lot of languages spoken in Lemberg. From what Hugh told me about you, you would like the city. I speak Polish and German, and a bit of Ruthenian, but we spoke Yiddish at home.'

'Yiddish? Are you Jewish?' He didn't look it.

'I'm a citizen of the world,' he said. 'As is Kay. As was Hugh. As you are.'

I didn't contradict him; I understood what he meant.

He looked at me closely. 'Is there anything else? Any other reason you want to work with us?'

'Should there be?'

'I don't know,' said Lothar. His dark blue eyes were studying me; I had the feeling they would miss nothing.

I hesitated. 'There is,' I admitted, my voice suddenly wobbling. 'Kay probably told you that my husband has been unfaithful with my mother? Actually, you probably told her.'

'I did know that,' said Lothar.

'Right. Well, I did have some misgivings about betraying my country. But I have no misgivings at all about betraying Roland. He represents all that I hate about the ruling classes; after all, if you are right, it's people just like him who murdered my brother. What I'm doing isn't betrayal – it's vengeance. It will be my pleasure to give his secrets away to those who can make good use of them to help the workers from Britain or France or even Russia – from wherever.'

'You know this means you will have to go back to your husband?' Lothar said. 'You will only be of use to us if you are married to him and living with him.'

'I know. But I am willing to do that. You see . . . if I leave Roland then people will learn everything. There will be a scandal – my sister will find out, as will my father. I don't want to hurt them. But I also don't want to be the poor foolish wife who isn't brave enough to leave. Especially since . . .'

Lothar waited.

'Especially since I think I am expecting a baby.'

Lothar smiled. 'Congratulations,' he said tentatively.

'Thank you.' It struck me how absurd it was that the first person I had told was a complete stranger. Except I couldn't trust anyone closer to me, and for some reason, I did trust him.

'But this way, I stay with Roland, my child has a father *and* I keep my self-respect because I will know that I am helping you and hurting him. Do you understand?'

'I think I do,' said Lothar. 'That's enough for today. Let's meet again next week. In the meantime, work out how you can return to live with your husband.'

'That's going to be difficult.'

'Very difficult. Can you do it?'

I nodded. 'I can do it.'

He made me memorize a complicated procedure for meeting the following week at an address in the Marais, and then we parted.

It was the first of many meetings between us.

I decided to walk all the way back from the Bois to my hotel on the Île Saint-Louis. Walking helped me think, and I had a lot to think about.

I liked Lothar. I trusted him. I liked that Hugh had trusted him.

And I was coming increasingly to believe that the British government had killed Hugh.

Sometimes, when I have a difficult decision to make, I choose a path and then immediately doubt myself. This was not one of those times. In a situation of extreme murkiness, betrayal and distrust, deciding to work for Lothar and the Comintern felt like simply the right thing to do. It was as if I had fallen into a dark river, with weed tangling my legs, and silt stirred up in the water all around me. I had caught a glimpse of the surface and sunlight and kicked upwards. Soon I would be free of the mud and water, break the surface into fresh air and breathe.

There would be consequences. I would have to live with Roland. I would have to speak to my mother as if nothing had happened. I would be giving my country's secrets to a foreign power: despite Lothar's protestations about working for the Comintern, it was safest to assume that everything I gave him would eventually get to the Soviets. I ran the risk of being caught; I wasn't sure, but I believed that traitors faced the death penalty in England. Or I might find myself wrapped around a tree on a country road like my brother.

But it would be a just cause, a cause my brother had believed in, a cause he might even have died for, and I would be proud to follow that cause in his stead. I would be doing it for him and for me, and for all the millions of the poor all over the world, people who were infinitely less fortunate than me, who were being exploited by a capitalist system that was demonstrably broken.

I would be free.

Lothar had asked me how I would get back together with Roland. There was no need to rush that. In fact, too immediate a rapprochement would be suspicious, which was fortunate because right then the very idea of him made my skin crawl. I would hole up in the hotel for a few more nights.

It would be good to see Dick during that time, but I decided not to tell him my decision. In retrospect, I was glad I had rejected the idea of spying for Kay so firmly when Dick had asked me about it.

In my haste to leave the flat the previous afternoon I had forgotten some things: make-up, another pair of shoes, my address book, writing paper. It was early afternoon, so Roland would either be at the office or – and the thought reignited a flare of rage – in a hotel room with my mother. Either way, it should be safe to stop by there for a few minutes to pack another, lighter case.

I climbed the stone stairs to the apartment. When I pulled out my keys I realized that the door was unlocked. I was pre-occupied, and I assumed that Roland had simply forgotten to lock up properly when he had gone to work that morning, so I was shocked to see him sitting in his favourite armchair in the sitting room. He looked dreadful – the skin around his eyes, already dark, was now a purplish shade of black, as if some thug had beaten him up.

He leapt to his feet and took a step towards me.

'Stay away from me!' I told him in something just short of a shout. 'Don't you touch me!'

Roland backed off, raising his hands. 'All right. All right.'

'What are you doing here?' I said. 'Shouldn't you be at the embassy? I only came here now because I thought the flat would be empty.'

'I understand. I told them you were ill and I had to be home to look after you. I hoped you would drop in.'

'Well, that's jolly big of you.'

'No, it's not. I've behaved abominably towards you.'

'You certainly have.'

'And I don't expect you to forgive me.'

'Good.'

'All that I ask is that you listen to me – hear what I have to say for the next couple of minutes. Then I will let you do whatever you want to do.'

'If you are trying to persuade me to stay, it won't work.' As I said this, carried along by my anger, I meant it, but a little voice told me to listen. If I decided to go back to him, I might be able to use whatever he said now as a plausible reason. Though, at that moment, the thought filled me with disgust.

'I saw Lavinia last night,' he said. Lavinia was my mother.

'I don't want to know that.'

'I told her you knew about us. She told me that when you and she lunched you had suspected something, but didn't know it involved her.'

'That's true.'

'I told her we had to finish it. We had an almighty row.'

'Good.'

'Afterwards . . . Afterwards, it was as if a spell had been lifted. I have been under the spell of your mother for three years now.'

'Before I met you, then?'

'Yes.' Roland swallowed. 'Before we met.'

'Just as I thought.' I was speaking in a dull monotone; my fury was numbing me. 'You only married me so you could be with her.'

'Yes,' said my husband. 'It was her idea. I didn't like it, but it was the only way I could keep her. I probably wouldn't have gone through with it, except I actually enjoyed spending time with you. I thought it might be rather fun to be married to you.'

'Oh, because you could make love to my mother at the same time?'

'No, of course not . . .' Roland's voice was raised, but then he paused. When he spoke again, his voice was low, infused with shame. 'Yes. Actually. Yes, I did think that.'

'But that's monstrous. Don't you see that?'

'Yes, I do. The thing is . . .' He looked down at the floor and then up at me. 'The thing is, Emma, I love you.'

'That's absurd! After what you've done to me, how can you possibly love me?'

'I agree it sounds absurd. But last night, the spell was broken. I saw Lavinia and me for who we really are, what we have really done. And you – you are a much better person than she is. I knew that from when I first met you, really. You are kind, generous, highly intelligent. Everyone underestimates you, but I don't. I actually really enjoy being with you.'

'Rot! You expect me to believe any of that?'

Roland looked as if he did really mean it. His eyes were desperate, and held a sincerity I had never seen in them before. But, although I was naive, I wasn't that naive.

'No, no. Of course I don't expect you to believe it. I've been up all night trying to work all this out. I'm sure it's the way I feel and I decided I should tell you in the knowledge that there was no chance you would believe me. At least not now.'

'What can I say?' I said. 'I don't believe you.'

Roland looked away. Clearly some part of him, some poor irrational section of his brain, had hoped for a different response.

'I understand. So tell me what you want me to do. I would like it if you came back to live with me, but I understand there is little chance of that. We can live separately. I can give you a divorce – arrange for me to be caught with some tart.'

'You mean my mother?' I couldn't resist it.

'No, I didn't mean your mother. But if you want it to be your mother, then I can do that too. It's up to you. I won't press you for an answer now – you can go back to wherever you are staying – but let me know when you are ready.'

My mind was in turmoil. Mostly, I was furious that he expected me to believe any of what he was saying after the way he had deceived me over the previous couple of years. Yet I also realized that if I was going to work for Lothar I would have to at least appear to be swayed.

That should come later.

'All I want to do, Roland, is get out of here as soon as I jolly well can.'

Chapter 25

THE ADDRESS LOTHAR had given me was a six-storey block in a narrow street in the Marais, the Jewish neighbourhood of Paris just over the river from my small hotel on the Île Saint-Louis. Although I could have walked there in ten minutes, it actually took me an hour, as I scrupulously followed Lothar's instructions, dawdling on the Pont Marie, taking the Métro pointlessly to the Opéra and then the Place de la République, before walking from the broad Boulevard Beaumarchais into the warren of ancient streets that was the Marais.

This was a very different quarter of Paris from those frequented by Roland and me. The streets were narrower and dirtier, the people poorer, the shops less sophisticated, yet they had a vibrancy that I found exciting. There were craftsmen of every description plying their trade in small workshops-cum-stores: tailors, milliners, glove-makers, furriers, silversmiths, leather-workers, carpenters, pawnbrokers. On the streets, Yiddish mixed with French, and men in long black coats with wide-brimmed hats, full beards and curls dangling from above their ears scurried about their business.

I wondered whether Lemberg was like this.

With one last look over my shoulder, I rang the bell marked '6' as instructed.

'Kay?' I exclaimed as I recognized the woman opening the door. 'I didn't know you lived here?'

'Well, I do,' said Kay. 'It's cheap and it's easy to keep an eye on; we have comrades here. Lothar is upstairs.'

She led me up to a tiny flat at the back of the house one floor beneath the top. Lothar was waiting for me. I was pleased to see him; I was pleased to see her. But after bringing us some coffee, Kay left, saying she would be back in a couple of hours.

'Kay is a cut-out,' explained Lothar. 'She doesn't know my real name; she doesn't know what we talk about or whom I report to. She is the one who rents this flat. If ever she was arrested she wouldn't be able to divulge much of use.'

'She knows who I am,' I said.

'She does,' admitted Lothar. As he sipped his coffee, I noticed his mangled finger. 'The idea is that Kay won't be arrested. But if she is, we will look after you. We look after the people who work for us.'

'Except for Hugh.'

Lothar nodded his acknowledgement. 'That took us by surprise. We have lost very few agents.'

His intense dark blue eyes met mine. 'I don't want to deceive you, Emma. This is a dangerous business, and you should know that from the outset. You've had a few days to think about it. Do you want to work for us?'

'Yes,' I said. 'I do.'

We discussed details for two hours. I found what he told me fascinating – exciting, even. Counter-surveillance techniques, such as waiting for a tram, letting it pass, then jumping on the next one as it was leaving; or stopping to look at a shop window and examine the street behind in the reflection. Emergency contact procedures, places where a coded message could be left, and the codes themselves, which involved six hours being added to any time mentioned and three days subtracted from a date. Phrases to be used at meets with unknown agents, the back-up plans in case a meet was missed, signals that either I or Lothar had been discovered. Lothar gave me a camera and showed me how to use

147

it to photograph documents. We discussed how I would credibly return to Roland.

My first assignment was to photograph papers from Roland's briefcase. I knew Roland often took papers home from the embassy to work on; at this stage I didn't know what they were. Lothar wanted me to photograph whatever was there; in due course he would become more specific about what I should look for. He told me to be very careful: better I arrive empty-handed at our next meeting than not arrive at all because I had been arrested.

I returned to the Rue de Bourgogne the following night after eleven days away. I had filled my days with reading, and had spent a couple of evenings with Dick, on one of which we went to the cinema to watch the western. He seemed to love it; I found it banal. But he was good company. I didn't tell him what I was up to, or even that I was planning to go back to Roland.

I had decided to stay at the hotel on the Île Saint-Louis despite its simplicity, or rather because of its simplicity. I was feeling more and more guilty about my coddled life; if Dick could handle his bugs in his garret, I could handle mine in my hotel. At least they scuttled rather than bit.

One evening, I persuaded Dick to take me with him to a bistro he had discovered in a scruffy street in the Latin Quarter near the Panthéon. It was frequented by the poor workers and the workless, by the hopeful and the hopeless. The proprietor was as wide as she was tall, and wielded a knife-edged tongue. Dick seemed to have made friends with a group of serious drinkers, including a muscular brute who worked in the sewers, a Breton porter at Les Halles, a Polish dishwasher at the Hôtel Meurice, a Russian émigré who claimed he was a former cavalry officer, but who barely had enough to eat, and an Arab navvy who had taken a particular shine to Dick. Dick played the part of a penniless

English writer. With a shock, it occurred to me that he might not, in fact, be playing that part, but might be actually living it.

I had worn my simplest clothes, but they could tell I had money.

Wine was drunk by the litre. The Pole and the Russian shook dice to decide which of them would pay for their drinks. As everyone became drunker, the singing started, led by the sewerman who burst into 'Les Fraises et les Framboises'. The Marseillaise was followed by the Internationale, in which I tentatively joined. Despite his shortcomings in French, Dick had no trouble making himself understood, and he seemed popular.

Dick was there to research his subject, of course. He genuinely wanted to chronicle the daily lives of these people. But although I was for a few moments caught up in the alcohol-fuelled excitement and the bonhomie, most of the time I felt apart from these men, and the women who drifted by the table. I was an onlooker, an observer, a tourist of poverty. A hypocrite.

This was why I had to help Lothar.

Despite the drink and the singing, I couldn't get Roland out of my mind.

I had given careful thought as to how I was going to treat him. I couldn't pretend to love him or even show any affection for him. That might work for a night – or a week at most – but not for the years that would be required if I was to help Lothar. I was wary of trying to come up with a logical, consistent pretext for returning to him. Roland was clever. He would question my motives; I would slip up.

I needed to keep him on the back foot. Inconsistency would be my watchword, illogicality, mystery. I needed to make sure that he didn't understand me. I hated him and I wouldn't pretend otherwise.

I telephoned Muriel, his secretary, asking her which evenings he would be in that week, so I could give him a surprise. I don't know what Muriel suspected – she had heard us arguing and she was no fool – but she told me there was nothing in his diary that evening. I bought some veal chops and celeriac at the market and started cooking.

I heard his key in the door.

'Emma?'

I didn't answer. He came into the kitchen. 'Emma? What are you doing here?'

'I'm cooking you supper.'

'Oh. Thank you. I'm very pleased you're home.'

He moved towards me.

'Don't touch me!' I warned him.

He withdrew and poured himself a pink gin. 'Thank you for coming back.'

I didn't answer, but cooked dinner and took our two plates to the table. Roland poured us both a glass of wine.

'How are you?' he asked.

I didn't answer.

We ate dinner in silence, and then I put my knife and fork together on the plate.

'This is how it's going to be,' I said, remembering the advice from my beloved mother about setting down the rules of whatever game he was playing. 'I am going to live here. I am going to be civil to you but no more. I doubt we will speak to each other much.'

'All right.'

'You are never to touch me. But you are also never to touch my mother either, ever again.'

'I understand.'

'In public I will be polite to you, but you are never to take advantage of that and touch me in front of other people.'

Roland listened, his face pained.

'If you find you have physical needs, I expect you never to take them out on anyone I know. Preferably you should just pay for them.'

'What do you mean?' Roland said.

'I mean go to a brothel. But don't tell me about it. And above all, remember one thing.'

'Yes?'

'I hate you.'

Chapter 26

I MADE MY move two nights later. Roland was in the spare bedroom, and the camera Lothar had given me was in my underwear drawer. I woke in the middle of the night and checked the alarm clock. Five and twenty to three.

I crept out of bed, took out the camera and slunk into the hall, where Roland's briefcase was lying. I took it through to the kitchen, turned on the light and opened the case. There was a 'circulating file' in there. I had seen these before. It was an odd procedure in the Foreign Office where a memorandum would be initiated by a junior third secretary and would meander its way upwards through an office, a series of typed minutes or handwritten comments embellishing it as it passed over each desk, before leaving the embassy by King's Messenger on its journey to a desk in Whitehall, where it would be pummelled and primped in turn. Each contributor up the chain would take the opportunity to show off his erudition, publicly humiliate a subordinate and, occasionally, add a good idea. That was how you ran an empire.

This file concerned the differing views of the three most recent French prime ministers, Flandin, Laval and now Sarraut, on the Italian invasion of Abyssinia. An important, but complicated, topic – in December the revelation of the secret Hoare–Laval pact on how to deal with Mussolini's East African ambitions had brought down the Laval government in France and finished Samuel Hoare's tenure as Foreign Secretary in Britain.

I clicked away with the camera. There were dozens of pages, and although I was accurate, I was slow.

I was carefully replacing the file in Roland's briefcase when I heard the floorboard creak.

Roland.

The camera was on the kitchen counter. I tossed it into a cutlery drawer, grabbed the papers, and shoved them back into Roland's briefcase, which was standing on the tiny kitchen table.

'Emma?'

I looked up at him. He was wearing the green pyjamas I had given him for Christmas. His eyes, red-rimmed, were blinking in their dark sockets. He looked confused.

'Emma? What are you doing?'

What was I doing? Stupidly, I hadn't thought of an excuse in advance. What possible logical reason could there be for me to be rooting through his briefcase in the middle of the night? I couldn't think of one.

I glared at him, playing for time.

'Emma? What are you doing in my briefcase?' His voice was stronger now. He wasn't yet suspicious, but he was very close.

I remembered my strategy. I shouldn't look for a logical explanation; I should look for an illogical one.

'I'm looking for letters,' I said. 'Or notes.'

'From whom?'

'Who do you think?'

'But why would I put notes from Lavinia in my briefcase?'

'Why wouldn't you? If she contacted you at work. I've searched your suits.'

'Have you? Did you find anything?'

'No,' I said, hoping that there wasn't actually anything incriminating in his jackets, because I hadn't in fact searched them. 'That's why I'm looking here.'

'But I told you I don't have anything to do with her any more.'

'You did tell me that, but I don't believe you.'

Roland looked at the briefcase. 'Well, there's nothing there. As you now know.'

I was regaining the initiative. I pushed it further. 'Do you have any letters from her?'

He looked uncomfortable. He was tired and bewildered. He didn't answer.

'Well?' I demanded.

He sighed. 'I have some.'

'Show them to me.'

Roland ran his fingers through his hair. 'I really don't think that's a good idea.'

'Why not?'

'Because they will hurt you.'

'Do you care?'

'Yes. I care now.'

In reality, I had no desire to see the letters at all. But I didn't want to do the reasonable, logical thing. I wanted to keep Roland confused.

I glared at him. 'I want to see them.'

'How about I destroy them? I don't want them. I think it is better for both of us, but especially you, if you don't read them. I will burn them.'

That sounded like a good idea to me. 'I'll think about it,' I said. 'Now I'm going back to bed.'

Roland destroyed the letters. I delivered the film to a *tabac* in the Rue Saint-Dominique the following day. It was barely a ten-minute walk from the flat, but I took half an hour over it, trying out the various counter-surveillance techniques Lothar had suggested. Once I had dropped the film, I took a more direct route back, aware all the time of who was behind me.

So aware, that I forgot to look in front. I was only thirty yards from my building when I noticed a young man waiting outside it, and only twenty yards when I realized it was Kenneth Heaton-Smith. I stopped in my tracks, but before I could turn on my heel and walk back down the street, he had spotted me.

He smiled and waved. I smiled and walked as confidently as I could towards him.

My heart was thudding in my chest. Had the British secret service rumbled me already?

It rather looked as if they had.

Roland must have put two and two together and told Colonel Vivian and Heaton-Smith. Had Heaton-Smith's colleagues tailed me going to the *tabac*? I had done my best to check for followers, but I was an utter novice at this game. I could easily have missed them. In which case they would soon be in possession of the film I had taken the night before.

Oh Lord.

I smiled as brightly as I could manage – too brightly probably. 'Mr Heaton-Smith? Are you still in Paris? I thought you'd left ages ago.'

'I've been in Rome a couple of days, but there were a couple of things I wanted to attend to before I returned to London. May I come in? I rang your bell, but I had just about given up.'

'Of course.' Heaton-Smith followed me up the stairs, and I led him into our flat. 'Can I get you some coffee?'

'I say, you don't have any good old-fashioned English tea, do you?'

'I do, as a matter of fact. I'll just put the kettle on. Have a seat while I make it.'

I tried to compose myself as I made the tea, but it was very difficult. I was trying to come up with a plan. Brazen it out was the best thing. And then don't say anything. It was all looking very rum.

Heaton-Smith wasn't acting as if he was about to arrest me. But he did look concerned.

My hand shook and the saucer rattled as I placed his cup of tea down beside him.

'Are you all right, Mrs Meeke? You look upset.'

So much for brazening it out. My first instinct was to insist that I was perfectly fine. Fortunately, my mind cleared quickly enough to realize that firstly I needed a good explanation for why I was flustered, and secondly that I had a ready-made one.

I forced myself to hesitate. Look down at my own cup. 'Oh, you know,' I said. 'Roland and I have just had the most frightful row. I suppose it happens all the time in marriages, I'm just not used to it myself yet.' I smiled quickly. 'Sorry, I don't know why I'm telling you that. It's just you did ask, and, well, I hoped a walk would clear my head, but it's done just the opposite. I feel worse, really.'

'Oh, I am sorry,' said Heaton-Smith. 'And it's absolutely none of my business. I'll be gone in a tick.' He seemed more embarrassed, in a rather charming way, than suspicious. He was a charming man.

I smiled politely.

'I really came to tell you about Cyril Ashcott.'

'Oh yes?'

Perhaps I wasn't rumbled, after all. But I would keep my wits about me.

'Yes. You asked me to let you know if it turned out he was innocent of giving information to the Germans.'

'And is he?'

Heaton-Smith sighed. 'I'm afraid not. It looks as if you were right – he has been passing secrets to the German Embassy. They were blackmailing him over his involvement with a German boy here in Paris. It's likely the whole thing was a set-up – a "honey-trap" we call it.'

'Oh dear.' I felt a huge wave of relief sweeping over me, one I was desperate to prevent Heaton-Smith noticing. 'I'm sorry to hear that. As I told you, I like Cyril. I'd rather hoped he was innocent. Have you arrested him?'

'No. And we're not going to.'

156

'You are not going to?'

'We are going to turn him.'

'What does that mean?'

'It means we keep him in post and he continues to feed information to the Germans. Most of it will be accurate but unimportant. But just occasionally we will give him something else to slip in, something that will mislead them.'

'So he won't be prosecuted?'

'It doesn't look like it.'

I was very glad to hear that. Especially since it looked like I was not going to be prosecuted either.

Over the coming weeks and months Roland and I settled into a new routine for dealing with each other, the rules of which were set by me. We were polite, sometimes even considerate. We rarely argued, but that was because we rarely spoke. When he was home, I read.

I was less rude to him, partly because I didn't want to scare him away, and partly because I didn't feel the urge. Whenever I remembered what he had done with my mother, I also remembered that I was stealing his secrets. When I thought of Hugh, and his death, I remembered that I was giving away the secrets of those who had killed him.

I went to the doctor, who told me that there was indeed a life wriggling around deep inside me, and that it would emerge into the world that December. I told Roland as perfunctorily as I could; he couldn't hide his pleasure.

I avoided my mother. She stopped coming to Paris. We never wrote to each other, apart from once when I informed her she was to become a grandmother. She never replied. Roland and I briefly visited Chaddington for a day in August on a week's home leave, but she had been detained in London, so we missed her.

I wrote to my father frequently, and he replied. I felt so sorry for him. Not just because of my mother's betrayal of him, but also because it was clear he missed his son terribly. He never stated this directly, but Hugh was mentioned in every letter. He clearly hoped that my child would be a boy.

At that time, my father was fifty-one, but since Hugh's death he had aged ten years. He had become an old man.

In September, Dick went back to England, having written most of his novel. Now all he had to do was find a publisher. I spent some time with him over that summer, and also with Cyril Ashcott, whom I now saw as something of a kindred spirit.

And I saw a lot of Lothar. I provided him with some more documents I had photographed from Roland's briefcase, and also with diplomatic gossip I heard, or overheard, at the various parties I attended. In the past, Roland and I had discussed politics at some length, and I passed on what he had told me then. But an unfortunate consequence of my treatment of Roland was that those conversations ceased. So, as the summer progressed, I began to talk to him again, mostly about his work, under the guise of my unquenchable curiosity.

Relieved, he talked to me. I relayed it all to Lothar.

That summer, General Franco led a military revolt against the republican Spanish government. The countries of Europe had to decide which side to choose in the coming civil war. I was able to give Lothar important details about the thinking of the different factions within the British government and diplomatic service about whether to support Franco or remain neutral. This was a topic of heated debate between the British and French governments. Léon Blum, the new French prime minister, was inclined to support the republicans. Roland was intimately involved in the discussions and knew all the details of what was going on. He was happy to discuss them with me.

I knew who was in the right – the Spanish pro-republican workers – and Russia was supporting them. By ensuring the

Russians knew what the British government was planning, I was supporting them too.

I was doing my bit. It felt good.

And in December, two days after Christmas, Caroline was born.

Chapter 27

June 1979, Paris

They left the Voltigeur and walked back across the river towards the Ritz. Emma said she was getting tired, and she had started to sway a little, so she grabbed Phil's arm. A reminder of that growth in her brain interfering with her balance. Phil left her at the door of the hotel and doubled back to have another look at the impressionist paintings in the Jeu de Paume.

He wanted to see them again. He also wanted to think about what he had just heard.

His grandmother had spied for the Russians. To some extent, he understood why. He understood that her brother had been a communist; he understood why she hated her husband. But the Russians were the bad guys. There was a war on – it might be a cold war, but it was still a war. Marx and Lenin had spoken about international communism taking over the world, and as far as Phil could tell, that was what the Soviet Union was still trying to do. There were tanks massed on the borders of East Germany; there were nuclear missiles pointed at London and Washington.

And it wasn't as if things had been much better in the thirties. Phil had studied Lenin and Stalin in A-level history, he knew about the gulags where hundreds of thousands were locked up and the unnecessary famines where millions died.

Emma had spied for Russia against Britain.

He remembered the conversation with the enigmatic Mr Swann in the Three Castles back home. Phil wondered how much of Emma's activities Mr Swann knew about already. Did he know about her spying? Her treachery.

Probably.

No wonder he didn't want Phil to tell her about their conversation.

Now Lothar had made his appearance in Emma's story. From what Emma had said, it was quite plausible that Lothar had also run an agent in the 1930s who was still undercover – Swann's mole.

Is that what Phil and Emma were doing now? Looking for this Lothar?

But her story wasn't over. Phil should hold his tongue and listen to it until the end, wherever that would take them.

He spent most of the afternoon in the museum, letting the fabulous paintings imprint themselves on his consciousness, lingering in front of each one. Then he headed back to the hotel.

He met Emma in the lobby at a quarter to six. They had a mysterious appointment to keep before Phil returned to the bar at Place Saint-Michel to meet Heike, something he was anticipating with a mixture of nervousness and excitement. Emma looked much fresher than she had at lunchtime, and her eyes were bright.

'Come on, Philip,' she said. 'It's not far.'

She set off at a surprisingly fast pace back towards the Place de la Concorde, and turned into the entrance of a large, grand building of pale yellow stone whose facade was lined with columns. The Hôtel de Crillon.

As they entered the lobby, the crash and roar of petrol engine and metal died behind them. They went through to the bar, where the only sounds were the low murmur of voices, the occasional clink of crystal glass, and a man in a white dinner jacket behind a grand piano softly playing tunes from Simon and Garfunkel. Emma scanned the room and then headed towards a tall man in his sixties, sitting at a low table, reading the *International Herald Tribune*, a pipe and a glass of whisky at his side.

'Dick!' Emma cried as she approached him.

The man stood up and grinned broadly, kissing her on the cheek. She introduced him to Phil. As Phil shook his hand, he could see what Emma had meant when she said his blue eyes, set in a tanned face, were kindly.

Phil liked him immediately.

Dick summoned a waiter and ordered a glass of champagne for Emma and, after a few moments of hesitation as Phil tried to decide what he should be seen to be drinking, a gin and tonic for him.

'Did you fly in this morning?' Emma asked.

'Yes. From Washington. I've got a meeting with a client here. I'm very glad you could coordinate your holiday with my trip.'

'So am I,' said Emma. 'What sort of client?'

'It's a subsidiary of one of the big American multinationals. I'm advising them on reorganizing themselves. They are never happy unless they are reorganizing themselves.'

'I never understood how you got into that line of work,' Emma said.

'You remember I was working for the Ministry of Information during the war? It was stuffed full of poets and novelists, most of them a lot better than me. I ended up writing stuff for some big businesses. Then when the scriptwriting didn't work, I looked up some of my old wartime contacts. And I became a management consultant. I'm surprisingly good at it.'

Phil had vaguely heard of the term 'management consultant', but he had no real idea of what they did. His dad would know.

'Shame I never saw any of your films,' Emma said.

'Probably for the best,' said Dick. 'B-movie westerns. More like C-movie, really. Turned out scriptwriting wasn't really my thing.'

'I've told Philip a little about you, or at least about you in Paris.'

'Grams is feeding me the story bit by bit,' said Phil. 'We've just got to the part where you came to France.'

Dick winced. 'Painful,' he said to Emma.

'Yes,' said Emma. 'But it's good for me to remember. And Philip is my accomplice on this little trip. I was sorry to hear about Frances.'

'It will be two years in September. It doesn't really get any easier, does it?'

Phil assumed Dick was referring to Roland, but Emma didn't answer. He wondered whether that was the same Frances as the American student Emma had mentioned at Shakespeare and Company. That would explain Dick's move to America.

Dick puffed at his pipe.

'That's a familiar smell,' said Emma. 'Your tobacco. It reminds me of the Île Saint-Louis.'

Dick grinned. 'What have you been up to, Emma?'

Emma replied in generalities. Phil got the impression she didn't want to say too much in front of either him or Dick, he didn't know which.

They finished their drinks, and Dick ordered refills.

Emma sipped her champagne and looked coolly at her old friend. 'Tell me about Kurt.'

Kurt? That must be Kurt Lohmüller, the German diplomat.

'I met him in Crete, last year. I went for a week's vacation there last September. We were staying in the same hotel. He recognized me; I suppose I haven't changed that much. I didn't recognize him at all. The moustache has gone, his hair is grey, and he's put on some weight. But he was very friendly. I remember that about him.'

'He was always friendly,' said Emma. 'A natural diplomat.'

'Anyway, we spoke about Paris and Berlin. And you, naturally. A lot about you. I think he rather liked you.'

'I rather liked him,' said Emma. 'In your postcard you mentioned he had seen Kay?'

'Did I?'

'Yes, you did.' Emma was looking at Dick intently.

'Yes, perhaps I did.' Dick glanced at Phil.

'Don't worry,' said Emma. 'You can talk in front of Philip.'

'Kurt said he was still a diplomat, but I wondered if he was a spook. A retired spook.'

'For whom?'

'For West Germany, I assume. I didn't ask. You don't think he could be working for the East Germans, do you?'

'I have no idea,' said Emma. 'It's possible. So how did he see Kay?' She drew a postcard out of her bag: a picture of a ruined tower standing next to an unnaturally blue sea. She flipped it over. 'You say here: *Kurt told me he had seen Kay.*'

163

'Yeah, he did say that. Let me think,' said Dick, drawing his brows together in concentration. 'I asked him something like, "And have you seen Kay?" and he said, "Yes. She's living in East Berlin now." But he didn't say how or when he had seen her. I thought it wasn't surprising she ended up there. Or Moscow.'

'So you don't know whether Kurt spoke to her?'

Dick shook his head. 'No. Sorry.'

'What about Lothar? Did Kurt mention a man called Lothar by any chance?'

'Who is Lothar?' said Dick.

'A friend of Kay's,' said Emma. 'From before the war. You probably didn't know him.'

'Well, no, he didn't mention that name.'

Emma glanced down at the card. 'Have you got Kurt's address?'

Dick shook his head. 'Sorry. But he did tell me where he lives. He's retired from the German government, and lives in France now. In a village overlooking a lake. He says it's beautiful. His wife was with him in Crete. She's French; Martine, I recall her name was.'

'I remember Martine. He didn't say which lake?'

'I'm afraid not. If I had realized you were so keen to see him, I would have asked for his address. Do you have something specific you want to ask him?'

'Yes,' said Emma. 'Yes, I do. There are still one or two loose ends from that time before the war.'

'I see,' said Dick. 'Speaking of which, have you seen anything of Freddie? I saw he resigned as a minister last year. Presumably he's still an MP?'

Phil's ears pricked up. He hadn't realized that Freddie had become that important. But then the name Frederick Pelham-Walsh did sound vaguely familiar.

'Yes, a backbencher.' Emma turned to Phil. 'After the war Freddie became a Labour MP. He was a junior defence minister for a couple of years in Wilson's government but, as Dick said, he resigned. Had second thoughts about nuclear deterrence, apparently.'

'But I thought you said Freddie was a communist?' Phil said.

'We all were, then,' Dick said with a grin. 'Although Freddie was more hard line than most of us. But not as hard line as Denis.'

'Denis Healey?' Phil asked. 'The bloke who was Chancellor of the Exchequer?'

'And a good friend of Freddie's,' said Emma. 'Then and now.'

'So how is Freddie?' Dick asked.

'Fat,' said Emma.

'Married?' Dick asked, with a wry grin.

'No. Unlike Cyril. Do you remember him?'

'Yes, I think I do. That third secretary from the embassy here?'

'Who is now Her Majesty's ambassador to France. With a glamorous ambassadress. We saw him yesterday.'

'You really are revisiting old times.' Dick smiled again. 'I'm glad you included me.'

'And I'm glad you got to Paris to meet me.'

Their eyes met.

Phil thought he should be somewhere else. He checked his watch. It was nearly eight o'clock. 'I'm afraid I have to go,' he said, getting to his feet. 'It was nice to meet you, Mr Loxton.'

'You too.'

'Don't get too drunk tonight, Philip,' said his grandmother. 'You'll be driving tomorrow.'

'Really? Where are we going?'

'I'm not sure. We're going to visit a lake. I haven't worked out which one yet. I'll let you know at breakfast.'

Chapter 28

It was a warm evening, and the Place Saint-Michel was buzzing. Phil found the bar and ordered himself a Stella Artois. Nowhere to sit this time. He was dead on time, but he couldn't see Heike. She was late; he should have expected that.

It had been interesting to meet Dick, a character from Emma's story come to life. It was becoming clear that this trip wasn't just about seeing places from Emma's past. It was about seeing people.

Which was probably why she had the gun in her suitcase.

That thought troubled Phil.

'Hi. You made it.'

Phil turned to see Heike coming towards him. Her blue eyes were shining, and she seemed much happier than the evening before. God, she was attractive. What the hell did she see in him?

He had to put that thought out of his mind. He needed to be self-confident if he was going to impress her.

'Hi,' he said. 'Can I get you a drink?'

She asked for a Southern Comfort and Coke, which he bought her. They found an empty patch of floor.

'Has your boyfriend cleared out?' Phil asked.

'Yes. He was gone when I got back last night. Man, was I drunk.'

'We both were,' said Phil. 'But it was fun.'

'Yeah.' She smiled – simply, not slyly. 'I'm glad I bumped into you. And I'm glad I've got rid of that scumbag.'

'How long had you been together?'

'Not long. Only a couple of months. But shagging my best friend? Unforgivable. On both their parts.'

166

'I'm sorry.'

'Don't be. I'm better off without him. And without her, for that matter. I have a whole life ahead of me to enjoy.' She smiled up at him.

'What are you going to do now?' Phil asked.

'I don't know. Explore Paris. Maybe see a bit more of France by myself. Or I might just go home and try another trip in a few weeks with a friend. Where are you off to next? What does your grandmother have in store for you?'

'I don't know. I'm pretty sure we'll go to Berlin. But we may be going to a lake in France first.'

'Which lake?'

'No idea. She said she'd tell me at breakfast. But I do know we're leaving tomorrow morning.'

'Oh,' she said. Just 'Oh'. But it seemed to Phil to signal disappointment.

'Shall we go somewhere else?' he said. 'It's getting crowded here. My guidebook says that there are clubs around here called *caves*, which are a good place to go. Lively, you know.' The *Hitch-Hiker's Guide* had actually implied they were good places to meet people of the opposite sex, but Phil was planning on bringing his own.

'Yeah, I went to one with Jürgen a couple of nights ago. That's a good idea – let's just make sure it's a different joint.'

So they left the bar, and walked along a narrow street thronged with students. Unlike the previous night, Phil felt part of the crowd, not a schoolboy looking on from the outside.

He started telling Heike all about the *Hitch-Hiker's Guide*. She listened with mild amusement at his enthusiasm. 'Does it say anything about my home town – Braunschweig?'

'I don't know, I'll check. Don't you have a duke there? We call it "Brunswick".'

'I know you do. We were big allies of the British. Soldiers from Braunschweig fought for your Duke of Wellington at Waterloo. Unlike more recent times.'

Phil grinned. 'I'm definitely in favour of more friendly relations.' The moment the words were out of his mouth he worried that they might seem creepy, but Heike seemed not to take offence.

They found a likely place: dark, smoke-filled, with low, arched ceilings. Phil shelled out twenty francs each to get in, and was grateful when Heike shoved a note into his hand to pay for her half. They were near the back and could only just see the tiny stage, on which a black woman with an amazingly sultry voice sang blues in English.

They drank slowly – the drinks were expensive – listened to the music and chatted. Phil found Heike easy to talk to, and soon relaxed. The conversation was in German, but he managed very well, and if he got stuck over a word, Heike patiently guided him to the correct choice. They ordered food: chicken and *pommes frites*, the cheapest thing on the menu.

'Is your grandmother enjoying your trip?' Heike asked.

'I think so,' Phil said. 'It's bringing back memories, not all of them good.'

'What kind of memories?'

'She was a diplomat's wife before the war. And a communist.'

'A communist? She sounds like an interesting lady. Tell me more about her.'

So Phil did. He told Heike about her marriage to Roland and about how Roland had cheated on her with her mother. Heike looked suitably horrified. Then he told her about Kay and how Kay had asked Emma to spy for Russia.

And then he told her that Emma had agreed. Phil didn't think it mattered. It was ancient history, and what difference would it make if a twenty-year-old German student knew about it? It was a great story, it was good to tell it to someone, and Heike was definitely impressed.

'She certainly is an interesting lady,' she said. 'I'd love to meet her.'

'I'm sure she would like to meet you too.' But Phil wasn't exactly sure she would. He had no idea what Emma would think of Heike. He did know that she would be unimpressed that Phil had told her so much. 'Trouble is, we are leaving tomorrow morning.'

'Yes, of course. Do you think where you are going has something to do with the story she has been telling you?'

'I'm sure it has. I wouldn't be surprised if we don't try to find a German diplomat she knew back then. And Kay, the woman who recruited her as a spy. She's in East Berlin, apparently. Which makes some sense, I suppose, for a spy for the Russians.'

'And that's why you think you'll be going to Berlin?'

'Maybe.'

Heike was silent, staring at the stage. She glanced sideways briefly at Phil and then looked straight ahead. A smile crept across her lips.

'What is it?' said Phil.

'Look. This is a long shot, but do you think I could join you and your grandmother? It sounds fun, and I don't have anything else to do. Would she mind?'

Phil's heart leapt. At that moment there was nothing he would like more than to spend the next few days with this girl. But the truth was, his grandmother *would* mind. Emma hadn't chosen Phil to go with her on this, the final trip of her life, so that he could bring a strange German girl with him, however much he fancied her. Although Phil couldn't see any harm in telling Emma's secrets to a stranger, Emma would definitely have a different view.

He searched for arguments he could use to persuade Emma, but he knew the idea wasn't going to fly. Plus there wasn't room in the TR6.

It was still an encouraging sign that Heike wanted to come.

'It's a nice idea,' he said. 'But there isn't room in the car. It's a two-seater.'

Heike nodded. 'Yes, it was a silly idea. I'll just travel around by myself. Maybe go south to Avignon and Arles?'

Phil almost offered to lend her his *Hitch-Hiker's Guide*. But although he fancied her, he didn't fancy her *that* much.

They left the *cave* around midnight. They were standing in shadows on the side of the street just outside the club. Heike rummaged in her bag. She pulled out a biro and an old envelope and tore the envelope in half. She scribbled furiously on one half, and gave it to Phil.

'OK. Here is my home address in Braunschweig, and my address in Bonn next year. Write to me, OK? And maybe we can meet up somewhere in Europe next year? I could show you Braunschweig, although that won't take very long.'

She waited while Phil wrote down his home address in Buckinghamshire – with difficulty because of the darkness.

He handed her the scrap of paper.

She reached up and kissed him on the cheek. 'Bye, Phil.'

'Bye.'

She was about to turn away when she paused. She reached up and kissed him again. On the mouth. Slowly.

'Write,' she said, and she was gone.

Heike took a cab back to her hotel. A tall man with longish dark hair was waiting for her a few metres up the street from the entrance.

She ignored him, went up to her room, and let herself in. Two minutes later, there was a soft knock at the door. She opened it.

'How did it go?' the man asked her in his accented German once he was inside the room. He was supposed to sound like a Yugoslav guest worker, but Heike thought she could detect a Russian tinge to his accent.

'Good. He told me a lot about Emma Meeke. For a moment I thought he would try to bring me with him, but he didn't go for it.'

'Why not?'

'He said there wasn't enough room in the car. What kind of car is it?'

'It's a sports car. British. A TR6.'

'Right. Well, that idea of yours was never going to work then, was it?' Sometimes Heike had her doubts about Marko, even though technically she reported to him. She would much rather be working with a colleague from the Stasi than the KGB, but this was their operation and they had asked for her, or someone like her. She was sure Phil had spotted him in the bar the evening before.

Her comment stung the man. 'Did you fuck him?'

'No, I didn't fuck him,' she said. 'There was no need. He has fallen for

170

me anyway. He's very naive; I wouldn't be surprised if he's a virgin. He seems to think I'm only twenty.'

'You do look young. How old are you?'

'Twenty-six.'

'Well, if you need to fuck him, fuck him.'

Heike really didn't like Marko. She got the impression he would quite like to fuck her. That certainly wasn't happening.

'I'll brief you on everything that Phil told me about his grandmother, and then you can be on your way.'

Chapter 29

Emma was waiting for Phil in the Ritz dining room the next morning, yesterday's copy of *The Times* resting on her Michelin road atlas of Europe.

'Did you have fun last night?'

Phil grinned. 'Yes, I did. And I managed to drink a lot less than the night before, you'll be glad to hear.'

'What's she like, this Heike?'

'She's um . . .' Phil could feel his face getting hot. 'She's really nice. She's a couple of years older than me – she's studying engineering at Bonn. She comes from Brunswick.'

'Oh, I know Brunswick. I visited it before the war. Nice place. I don't know how badly bombed it was.'

'She didn't say. It didn't make it into my *Hitch-Hiker's Guide*. I checked.'

'Philip. One of the things I will hope you will learn travelling with me is that there are places in Europe worth visiting that are not in your guidebook.'

'I don't believe that,' said Phil with a grin. 'But I'm willing to see for myself if Brunswick is one of them.'

'Is she pretty?' Emma asked.

Phil nodded and smiled. 'Yeah. She's very pretty.'

'Well, good for you,' said Emma. 'I'm sorry to tear you away from her.'

Phil shrugged. He was sorry too. There was no point denying it to himself. It seemed such a shame not to see her again after that kiss. He wondered whether he should have asked her if he could go back to her hotel with her. Was that what she wanted him to do?

Probably not. She had walked briskly away from him. If she had wanted him to come too, she would have dawdled. She hadn't really given him a chance.

But what if he had asked her? And what if she had said yes?

The waiter brought some croissants, and Phil helped himself to one.

'Did you have dinner with Dick last night?' he asked.

'Yes. We went to a simple little bistro near the Latin Quarter I remembered from before the war. The one I told you about. It's still there, although it's much cleaner and a lot less rowdy than it used to be.'

'He seems like a nice guy.'

'He is. He always was.'

'I assume the Frances he married is the one he met here at the Café de Flore?'

'That's right. I went to their wedding in Durham – a rush job. There were a lot of those during the war. As he told you, they moved to America afterwards, Hollywood and then Washington. We've exchanged the occasional letter over the years, and we send each other Christmas cards; in his card a couple of years ago he told me Frances had died. But this is the first time I've seen him for nearly forty years.'

It occurred to Phil that Emma was looking much livelier this morning than she had so far on the trip.

'So we both had good evenings last night?'

Emma grinned. 'It sounds like it.'

'Dick's postcard mentioned Kay was living in East Berlin. Is that who we're looking for?'

'It is.'

'Hang on. I didn't realize Kurt knew Kay?'

'Ah. Very perceptive. No, I haven't told you that yet.'

'So we're going to meet Kurt next? To ask about Kay?'

'That's the plan.'

'And why do you want to find Kay?'

'You'll see.'

Phil grinned. 'I can be patient.' He wouldn't be at all surprised if it had something to do with Lothar.

'Good,' said Emma. She touched his hand. 'Thank you, Philip. You are being a good sport about all this.'

'It's fun, Grams. And I'm happy to do this your way.' He nodded to the road atlas. 'Have you figured out where this lake is?'

'I can have a good guess,' said Emma, opening the page at the east of France. 'There aren't actually that many lakes in France, and we're looking for one where someone might retire to.

'There's Lake Geneva. Part of its shore lies in France, so that's a possibility, but I somehow think Kurt would have referred to that by name. I think our best is here.'

She stabbed the map, her finger covering a sliver of blue between mountains. 'Lake Annecy. I remember Kurt went on a cycling holiday there, and he said he loved it. So, that's where we start, and if that doesn't work we may try Lake Geneva, or the Lac du Bourget a bit further to the west, here.'

'OK. Have you planned a route?'

'I have.'

'Then let's go.'

PART THREE

ANNECY

Chapter 30

June 1979, Annecy

It was a long drive from Paris to Annecy, about six hundred kilometres. It took them longer than it might have done because Emma decided to follow the autoroute for only the first part of the journey. The weather had turned cooler – little balls of cloud spurted rain at them before hurrying on – but they managed to keep the top of the TR6 down for most of the trip.

They stopped for a late lunch at a tiny restaurant overlooking a vineyard in Burgundy. Phil ate snails for the first time in his life, and he liked them, or at least he liked the garlic and the butter. He enjoyed the driving, although he was tiring by the end of the day. It was almost dark by the time they arrived at Annecy, the ancient capital of Savoy – as Emma informed him – guarding the foot of the lake of that name. Although she had explored much of France with Roland over the years, this was her first visit.

Emma had asked the Ritz in Paris to book them rooms at a small hotel in the middle of the old town, right on the River Thiou. They dumped their luggage, wandered through the ancient narrow streets lined with timbered houses and covered arcades, and found a bustling restaurant for dinner, overlooking one of the canals that ran through Annecy. It wasn't quite yet the *grandes vacances* in France, but the place was already full of tourists.

It rained overnight, but the weather was crisp and clear the following morning. From their breakfast table they could see the hulking medieval prison with its high stone walls standing on a narrow island in the river, and behind it, above the rooftops, the jagged peak of a mountain.

Phil had had an idea overnight. 'Grams, Brunswick is near the border with East Germany, isn't it?'

'It is,' said Emma, a smile playing on her lips. She had read his thoughts, which wasn't that difficult.

'I assume we're going to Berlin after this?' he said.

'I don't know, but I expect so.'

'Do you think we could stop in Brunswick on our way back? By then Heike may have returned home.'

Emma smiled. 'I can't promise anything because even I don't know exactly where we're going, but if we can, we will.'

'Thanks, Grams,' said Phil. 'I'll send her a postcard today to warn her.'

'Maybe I'll get to meet her?'

'Maybe you will.'

Emma pulled out a small map of Lake Annecy she had taken from the hotel reception that morning, and spread it out on the table.

'How are we going to find this guy?' Phil said. 'There must be tens of thousands of people in Annecy.'

'If you remember, Kurt told Dick he lived somewhere *overlooking* the lake. We needn't worry about Annecy. It's completely flat – you don't look down on the lake from here. You see there are two roads around the lake?'

Phil leaned over the map. 'Yes?'

'The bigger one, on the western side, hugs the shore, as do the villages, which means you don't really look down on the lake from there either. But on the eastern side, the road climbs up into the hills. From these villages you could easily overlook the water.'

She pointed out Veyrier-du-Lac, Menthon-Saint-Bernard and Talloires. 'Talloires is famous – there's an old abbey there. From the map, it looks like most of the village is down by the lake shore, but part of it is higher up.'

'So what do we do? Stand in the village square and shout Kurt's name?'

'We ask around. There can't be that many Germans living in the area, and the locals will probably know who they are.'

Phil bought a postcard, wrote a quick note to Heike and posted it to her home address. It might well turn out that she wasn't back in Brunswick by the time they arrived there on their way from Berlin, but it was worth a shot, and it gave him something to look forward to.

Then they set off along the small road around the eastern side of the lake.

Lake Annecy was indeed beautiful; Phil could see why someone might want to retire there. Clear green-blue water lay between steeply wooded slopes that higher up turned to rock. Down below, the town of Annecy stood at its foot, where the River Thiou rushed down towards the Rhône. In the other direction, the lake wound around a bulbous headland out of sight.

The road climbed swiftly and they were soon in the village of Veyrier-du-Lac. They found a café and a restaurant, Emma asking in each if anyone knew an old German friend of hers named Kurt Lohmüller who lived locally. The proprietor of the café was wilfully unhelpful, and the waiter in the restaurant had no idea. But they had more luck at the pharmacy. The pharmacist said that a German woman popped in regularly to pick up a prescription. Emma suggested that was probably Kurt's wife, and the pharmacist described where the lady's house was.

'But didn't you say Kurt's wife was French?' Phil pointed out.

'Indeed I did. My guess is that one German will know where another one lives.'

Emma was right. The German lady was named Frau Redlich, a comfortable and friendly woman in her fifties, originally from Dortmund, who did indeed know Kurt. Emma described truthfully how she had been a diplomat's wife before the war, and how Kurt and she had been friends in Paris and Berlin.

Kurt and his wife Martine lived in Talloires, a little further along the lake. Frau Redlich gave Emma the address and directions.

The house stood alone on a little road which climbed high above the village. It had been built relatively recently: white stucco walls and a steeply pitched roof with a two-car garage nestling beside it. Phil pulled up behind a large white Mercedes, and Emma rang the doorbell.

The door was opened by a small, rather plump man in his seventies, whose surprised face broke into a broad grin when he saw her.

'Emma! How wonderful to see you!' he said, in French.

Emma smiled and hesitated, but Kurt pulled her to him and they hugged.

'How did you know where I live? What are you doing here?'

'Dick Loxton sent me a postcard from Crete saying he met you there on holiday. He told me you lived by a lake in France, and I tracked you down.'

'You know how I've always loved France. But you didn't even have my address?'

'No. But we had clues.'

Kurt laughed. 'And that's all you needed. Come in, come in. And who is this?'

Emma introduced Phil, and Kurt led them into a large, open-plan living room with a huge picture window looking out over the lake.

'This is gorgeous!' Emma marvelled. And it was. Talloires stood halfway along the lake, at the point where the water squeezed through steep mountainsides at its narrowest point. Opposite Kurt's house, the bulbous hump that they had seen earlier rose out of the water, at the foot of which an absurdly romantic chateau perched on a small island jutting out into the lake.

'We like it. Martine isn't here – she's in Dijon looking after her mother, who is still alive, but only barely. You remember Martine from Berlin?'

'I do,' said Emma.

Kurt bustled about in the kitchen making coffee, talking all the while. Emma suggested they switched to German, and explained that Phil understood both languages.

'Is he going to be a diplomat then?' Kurt asked.

'I certainly hope not,' said Emma.

'I have no idea what I'm going to do,' said Phil. 'I'll just focus on getting through university first.'

As he answered he was startled to see an object drift up in front of his eyes just outside the window. It was a triangle of bright red fabric, under which dangled a man. 'Is that a hang glider?' he asked, using the English word.

'It is indeed. They like it here. Lots of thermals coming off the lake. They jump off a cliff further up the mountain and then just hang about.'

'Wow.'

'You get used to them,' said Kurt. 'After a while they become annoying. They spoil the view.'

Another couple of hang gliders drifted into sight. They performed an elegant dance as they twisted in the unseen thermal, slowly gaining altitude.

'I want to do that,' said Phil.

'You should try it. You should both try it.' Kurt smiled encouragingly at Emma.

'Maybe we should.' She sounded like she meant it; Phil was impressed. She sipped her coffee. 'I'm sorry I haven't been in touch, Kurt. We never quite ended up in the same city. I heard you were posted to Buenos Aires just after Roland and I left?'

'I enjoyed BA. I ended up in Budapest. Ambassador.'

'Roland retired in sixty-seven. He died five years ago.'

'I'm sorry,' said Kurt.

Given what he had just learned about Roland's behaviour to his wife, Phil was looking out for a hint of bitterness on Emma's part. He couldn't detect any.

'Your friend Cyril Ashcott did very well for himself,' Kurt said. 'Sir Cyril now, I believe?'

'And ambassador in Paris.'

'I'm surprised,' said Kurt. 'After getting caught in Paris. When he stayed in place and continued to pass us material, I guessed your people had turned him. But I would have expected them to have dropped him afterwards.'

'There was a move to turf him out of the diplomatic service after the war, but Roland argued in his favour, and won. You are right: some of the information he gave you was false. Including that the D-Day landings were going to take place in Pas-de-Calais and not Normandy, according to Roland. So the Foreign Office kept him on. After which, he had a glittering career, I'm glad to say. Very few people know about his indiscretion, or about his redemption.'

'Good for him.'

Emma smiled. 'Yes. Good for him. What about you? The West German diplomatic service kept you on despite your left leanings?'

'It turned out I wasn't a very good Nazi after all. And they needed some professionals.'

'You were always exceptionally diplomatic.'

Kurt acknowledged the compliment with a nod. 'There was a group of us, young lawyers who really didn't like Hitler or the Nazis. We formed a kind of loose network, in the Foreign Office, and even in the Abwehr, the German secret service. Some of us were lefties, like me, but there were also good Prussians – right-wing law-and-order people who thought that Hitler had gone too far. We teamed up with some officers in the army. A couple of plots were hatched to get rid of Hitler just before the war. They never came to anything; at the last moment the generals lost their bottle. But it was close. You may have heard about them?'

'I did hear rumours,' said Emma. 'But people say it was just German officers and civil servants trying to claim they weren't really Nazis, after all.'

'I know they say that. It's frustrating,' said Kurt. 'And completely wrong. A lot of people risked their lives – lost their lives – to stop him. It all culminated in the bomb planted in Hitler's bunker in East Prussia in 1944. Most of the plotters were rounded up. Some were executed; a few survived the war in prison. Like Fabian von Schlabrendorff – he was a friend of mine. He became a judge in West Germany's constitutional court. And I became an ambassador.'

'Did you end up in jail?'

'No. They missed me, thank God. I was in Paris again at the time, out of the way.'

Kurt and Emma talked about the diplomatic lives they had both led, and Phil did his best to follow. Kurt's face was animated as he spoke, his mouth contorting itself from one expression to another – surprise, mock horror, amusement, serious consideration and laughter.

'Kurt?' Emma said, her voice taking on a serious tone. 'Can I ask you something? It's something Dick mentioned.'

'Fire away.'

'He said you had seen Kay Lesser, and that she now lived in East Berlin.'

'That's right. It was about four years ago, in Hungary. I saw her at a party given by a Hungarian businessman.'

'What was she doing there?'

'I've no idea. We said hello and chatted for a few minutes. It was awkward for me because I worked for the West German diplomatic service.'

'And she worked for the Stasi?'

'I don't know that for sure. But I assume so.'

'Was she still called Kay Lesser?'

'She was still called Kay, or at least she answered to that name. She said she had married a German she met during the war, and lived in East Berlin, her German is very good now. I don't actually know if she is in the Stasi, it's just that given her history it's safest to assume that she is. Or was.'

'Did she say where she lived in East Berlin?'

'No. We only spoke for a few minutes. She hasn't changed much. She's older, of course, her hair is silver – she must have been seventy at the time – but she was still very tall. We had a nice chat; but as I say I didn't want to be seen with her for too long at a diplomatic function.'

'Would you be able to find out the name she goes under now? And her address in East Berlin?'

Kurt looked at her sharply. 'And how would I find out that?'

'Oh, come on, Kurt, you know people who can answer that kind of question.'

Kurt nodded. 'I probably do. But why do you want to know?'

183

'It's personal.'

Kurt raised his eyebrows.

'Do you think I'm working for someone?' Emma asked.

The eyebrows remained raised. 'Are you?'

Emma sighed. 'No, I'm not. I would hardly bring my grandson along if I was spying, would I?'

'I don't know,' said Kurt. He turned to Phil. 'How old are you?'

'Eighteen,' he replied.

'A bit young. But good cover, grandmother and grandson.'

'All right,' said Emma. 'I could be working for MI6. Or the KGB, or the CIA, or even the BND. But I'm not. And neither is Philip. You just have to trust me.'

'Do I?'

'You've trusted me before.'

Kurt gave a short laugh at this. 'Yes, I have trusted you before.' He leaned forward. 'How important is this to you?'

'Very,' said Emma.

'All right. I'll make some calls. Come back tomorrow. I tell you what, why don't you have lunch here? And then maybe you can go hang gliding if the weather holds. I'll watch you.'

'Thank you,' said Emma. 'I knew you wouldn't let me down.'

Kurt grinned. 'You and I never did let each other down, did we?'

Chapter 31

A thick, heavy blanket of cloud lay over the lake as they set off the following morning for lunch at Kurt's house at Talloires. The blanket hung only a couple of hundred feet above the town, and within a few minutes they were in cloud. Phil slowed down and switched on his headlights: visibility was no more than fifty yards.

The weather the previous afternoon had been perfect. Phil and Emma had settled down on the Pâquier, a broad lawn at the foot of the lake. Phil had plunged into the water, which was quite shallow and less chilly than he had expected. Drying off, he opened *War and Peace* and stared out at the crisp blue lake stretching out before him, wooded mountains rising on each side. A swarm of pedaloes pottered about on the water and sailing boats tacked from shore to shore further out. Next to him, Emma read her own book – *Germinal* by Émile Zola In the original French. Or rather reread; she had told Phil that it was one of the books Hugh had studied at Cambridge. She said every time she read it she felt closer to him. That was no doubt why she had given Phil a copy for his eighteenth birthday the year before.

Phil had read it then: very worthy, but a bit on the bleak side, in his opinion. It was the story of a family of French coal miners working seven days a week in an atmosphere of poverty, violence and deep despair.

That morning, confined to the hotel by the weather, they had installed themselves in the small lounge. This time Phil attacked his *Teach Yourself Gaelic,* working through the first two chapters. Emma hadn't said anything, but he could tell she was pleased.

It was a very strange language, but Phil was surprised to find himself intrigued.

'Did you ever actually speak Gaelic?' he said as they slowly made their way up the mountainside through the fog.

'Hardly ever. To myself, which doesn't count. And then two sentences to Hugh. Do you want to try some out on me?'

'*Ciamar a tha thu?*'

'*Tha mi glè mhath. Ciamar a tha thu?*'

'Well, I am very well, too, thank you very much,' Phil said. 'You do remember it! And now you've spoken four sentences.

'Yes, I have.' There was a catch in Emma's throat as she said this.

'I'm sorry, Grams. I didn't mean to upset you.'

'Oh, no. No. Please don't stop. Having you here does bring Hugh back a bit. I hoped it would. As did going back to Chaddington. I don't want you to stop talking about him, Philip, just because it might upset me. Do you understand?'

'Yes,' Phil said. 'I understand.' He searched for a subject. 'Tell me about Hugh's twenty-first birthday. Was that a big deal in those days?'

Emma smiled. 'I wasn't there; it was in term time. But Hugh sent me a letter about it afterwards. It was in the summer term and Hugh punted to Grantchester, with Freddie and Dick and a couple of others.'

She chattered away happily about that day, and another when Hugh had taken her and her mother punting on the river, the summer before, when she was sixteen, and how she wished she could have gone up to the university, but her parents would never let her. There was a warmth in her voice that made Phil want to smile.

They almost missed the turn-off uphill to Kurt's house. Kurt greeted them cordially.

'We would normally eat outside on the terrace,' he said. 'But there is no point – you can barely see as far as the end of the garden.' The table in the dining area of the living room was laid for three. 'But first, can I get you something to drink? I've opened a good bottle of Burgundy.'

Phil and Emma both indicated that that would do very nicely.

'I called the hang-gliding place for you yesterday, but they warned me that they would be socked in today. I'm sorry about that, Philip.'

'It would have been fun,' said Phil. And a little scary, he added silently to himself.

'It would,' said Emma, whose gleaming eyes suggested her enthusiasm the previous day hadn't been a bluff.

'Can I use your toilet?' said Phil.

'By all means,' said Kurt. 'Just to the left of the front door.'

As Phil opened the lavatory door, the bell rang.

He hesitated, then shut himself in.

He heard the sound of Kurt unlatching the door, and then a crash as it banged open, and a shouted order in German.

'Get back! Get back now! Stand over there!'

Phil froze. What the hell was that?

He opened the toilet door carefully and stepped out into the living room.

The next minute passed very slowly.

A man in a black balaclava was pointing a pistol at Kurt and Emma. He stood with his back to Phil, only ten feet or so away from him. Kurt and Emma were both holding glasses of wine: Kurt's face registered shock; Emma was glaring.

The man was dressed in blue jeans and a grey shirt. Phil couldn't see any of his face beneath the balaclava, but he was of no more than medium height, and slim, and there was something in the muscles of his back that suggested toughness. That, and the gun he was holding.

Phil took two steps forward and launched himself at the man, just as the gun went off. In the enclosed space of the house, the noise was deafening. Kurt let out a cry, and Phil and the man crashed on to the floor.

Phil was on top of him, but the man had still kept a grip of his gun. And he was yanking it round to try to point it at Phil. Phil lunged for the gun, and grabbed the man's wrist with his left hand, his right arm pinning the man's body down.

Although Phil had the better angle, the man was strong. Slowly, inch by inch, the gun was moving upwards, the barrel twisting towards Phil's skull. In a couple of seconds, the man would press the trigger and blow Phil's brains out.

187

Phil had no choice. He shifted his weight and his right arm so that he pinned the gun back on to the floor with both of his own hands.

But that gave the man an opportunity. He bucked, twisted, and kicked, pushing Phil off him with his free hand, and scrambled to his feet.

Phil looked up.

The man was pointing his gun right at Phil's face. Phil stared along the barrel directly at the man's hard blue eyes glaring back at him through the slits in the balaclava, focusing on him over the gun sight.

There was another loud crash of a gunshot in an enclosed space.

Phil closed his eyes, his ears ringing.

He didn't feel anything.

He opened them to see the man slumped on the floor a few feet in front of him, blood pouring out of a messy hole in the side of the balaclava, his eyes still staring at Phil. But the light had gone out of them.

Emma was standing next to Kurt's body, her own revolver pointed at the man on the ground, her handbag open on the dining table.

The room smelled of cordite.

'Are you all right, Philip?' Her voice was surprisingly calm.

'Yes,' said Phil, but he was shaking. 'I'm fine.'

'He's definitely dead, isn't he?'

Phil looked again at the bloody mess of the man's head, and at his staring eyes. 'Yes. He's definitely dead.'

Kurt's slumped body emitted a groan.

'But Kurt's still alive!'

He was. Yet only barely, and only for a minute or so.

As Phil and Emma knelt over Kurt and tried to straighten him up and make him more comfortable, he groaned again. 'Who the fuck was that?' he said in German.

'I don't know,' said Emma.

Blood was seeping from Kurt's chest. He tried to say something else, but the words wouldn't come. His breathing was weaker and shallower, but then he seemed to take one last rasping gasp, and he was silent.

Chapter 32

'Jesus Christ!' Phil stared at the carnage. 'He's dead. They're both dead.'

Emma slowly put her gun down on to the dining table.

Phil scrambled to his feet. 'Where's the phone? We need to call the police. What's the number? It's not 999, is it? What's the number in France, Grams?' He was shouting now.

'We're not going to call the police,' said Emma, her voice low.

'For Christ's sake, Grams! What do you mean, we're not going to call the police? They're dead. Look at them!'

'We can't. I can't stay here and talk to the police. It will mess up all my plans, and I don't have much time left.'

'Your plans? Your plans for what?'

'Calm down! I'll tell you.'

'No, I won't calm down!' said Phil. 'Your plans have just involved two people dying. We have to call the police.'

'If that man had escaped, then I'd say fair enough. We'd call the police so they could catch him. But he's dead. There is no murderer to catch. And they'll start asking me questions, questions I can't answer. Much better for us to leave now.'

'Leave now?' said Phil incredulously. 'And go where?'

'Switzerland. Geneva's only fifty kilometres away. With any luck we'll be over the border before the police start looking for us.'

Emma's face was determined. But Phil knew what the right thing to do was.

'No. We call the police.'

He spotted a telephone on a desk in the corner and moved over towards it.

'No, Phil!' Emma raised her gun and pointed it at him.

'Oh, come on, Grams,' said Phil. 'You're not going to shoot me.' He was surprised at his own confidence, but confident he was.

She lowered the gun. 'You're right, Philip. I'm not going to shoot you. But please. Just do as I ask. If we do get stopped at some point, you can say I made you leave without calling the police. I'll back you up.'

Her eyes were pleading. 'You know how important this trip is to me, even if you don't know exactly why yet. If you call the French police, they will stop me. And it's not as if a murderer is going to escape justice.'

Phil stood still and looked down at the two bloody bodies slumped on the floor. This was all spinning out of control very fast. Then he turned to his grandmother. She had brought him along because she trusted him. Now, at the end of her own life, she needed him. He didn't want to let her down, even though he knew he should.

Suddenly, he knew. He was with her. Whatever happened, he was with her.

'All right,' he said. 'What do we do now? Do we just leave them here?'

'Yes,' said Emma. 'Let's quickly wipe down any surfaces we touched today and yesterday. And then let's go.'

'Wait a moment,' said Phil. 'I want to see who this guy is.'

Gingerly, he reached out and gripped the neck of the balaclava. He pulled upwards, trying to ensure that none of the warm blood seeping through it touched his own clothes.

Slowly, a face was revealed.

'Do you recognize him?' said Emma.

Phil nodded. 'He's been following us since England.'

'You can explain in the car,' said Emma. 'Now I want to check if Kurt wrote anything down. Like Kay Lesser's address in Berlin.'

'Be quick.'

Emma searched for five minutes through Kurt's desk, and Phil tentatively checked Kurt's trouser pockets.

Poor man. Phil had only just met him, but he'd liked what he'd seen, and his grandmother was clearly fond of him. And now Kurt was dead, killed by that psycho sprawled on the floor by the door.

190

'Philip. Come here.'

Phil moved over to the desk. A name was written on the back of an envelope, which was lying by Kurt's telephone. *Kay Ortmann.*

'Ortmann must be Kay's married name. Or at least the name she goes under now.'

'Is there an address?'

They looked, carefully, using a biro from the desk and a handkerchief to try to avoid leaving fingerprints on the papers.

Nothing. Or at least nothing obvious.

Emma got two cloths from the kitchen and they began wiping. Fifteen minutes later, Phil and Emma were in the TR6, heading through the fog.

Phil fought to concentrate on the road ahead as the enormity of what he had just experienced crashed around him.

He had just watched someone die.

He had just seen his grandmother blow someone's brains out.

He had risked death by launching himself at a man with a gun.

Nothing in his life up till now had prepared him for this.

But he had to concentrate on the road ahead. On getting out of France safely without the police stopping them. Then he could think properly about what had happened, what was happening.

'For once, I wish I owned a Ford,' said Emma. 'This car is so notice-able.'

'To say nothing of the GB number plates.' Phil was relieved to talk practicalities, to focus his mind on evading the police.

'It's fortunate it's so foggy. It's likely no one saw us at Kurt's house just now.'

'That's true,' said Phil. 'But it's also likely someone noticed the car yesterday.'

'And, once the police start asking questions, Frau Redlich will come forward and tell them we asked her where Kurt lived.'

'That will take them a few hours. Maybe even a day.'

'Poor Kurt,' said Emma with a shudder. 'And poor Martine.'

Phil winced as the image of Kurt slumped next to the dining table, blood pumping out of his chest, flashed before him.

'Who do you think that guy was?' he asked. 'The only reason I noticed him following us was he looks a lot like a famous football player.'

'Why didn't you mention it?'

'I saw him twice: once on the ferry to Brittany, and once in a bar near Place Saint-Michel. I thought he was a student tourist and I assumed it was a coincidence. Do you know who he worked for? He spoke German.'

'No,' said Emma.

Phil didn't believe her.

Emma glanced at her grandson. 'He didn't say much, but from what he did say, I thought he had an accent.'

'What kind of accent?'

'Slavic maybe?'

'You mean Russian?'

'Perhaps. Or Polish. Or Yugoslav. There are lots of Yugoslavs in Germany.'

'Was that the KGB, Grams?' said Phil.

Emma didn't answer.

'We need to get rid of the gun,' said Phil. 'If the police find us with it, they'll eventually be able to tell you shot the man. If we don't have it, even if someone saw us, we can plausibly act as if we didn't see anything. Let them think we left the house before the thug showed up.'

'We should keep it,' said Emma. 'We may need it. It's lucky I brought it with me.'

'I insist, Grams.' He realized his voice was rising. 'I didn't insist that we go to the police, but I do insist we ditch the gun.'

Emma looked across at her grandson. Phil was firm.

'OK,' she said at last. She examined the map. 'Turn right in about a kilometre.'

They were in the village of Veyrier, and Phil took a couple of turnings until he was on a steep track leading up the mountainside through woods. After following a winding road for five minutes or so, they stopped. They were in thick forest, the lake just visible through the trees.

'Wait here,' said Emma. She got out of the car, clutching her handbag in which Phil knew she had stuffed her gun, and climbed up through the undergrowth until she was out of sight.

Five minutes later, she was back.

'Done,' she said. 'No one will ever find that. Now, back to the hotel.'

'The hotel?'

'Yes. It's actually more suspicious if we abandon our luggage there and don't pay the bill. If we collect our luggage, check out and head off for Switzerland, we can just tell anyone who asked that we changed our plans after talking to Kurt.'

Phil pulled up in front of their hotel. In ten minutes they were back in the lobby, packed, and Emma was paying the bill. No sign of any cops. With luck, the alarm hadn't been raised yet.

They loaded the car and headed north to Geneva. They spent the half-hour to the border going over the story they would use if they were stopped. How they were asking Kurt for Kay's address – eventually whoever Kurt had spoken to in the German bureaucracy would mention that. And how when they left Kurt he had been alive and well.

The horror of those seconds in Kurt's house rushed back. The shots. The blood.

Focus.

They reached the border crossing to Switzerland at Saint-Julien-en-Genevois. There were two checkpoints, and a queue: this was one of the most popular entry points between the two countries.

They were stuck behind a Belgian caravan. The French police seemed to be letting through most of the traffic, but they stopped the Belgians to check their documents.

Phil glanced at Emma. His palms, resting on the steering wheel, felt sweaty. He hoped she had their story straight. He hoped *he* had it straight.

He was worried his nerves would give him away. He should relax. He tried to loosen his shoulders, but his hands gripped the wheel more tightly.

Just then, he realized they had made a mistake. Kurt had laid a table for three: he was clearly expecting them to stay for lunch. But they hadn't eaten anything. So why had they left early? It was a question the investigating police might ask them.

As Phil's brain was fumbling for explanations, the Belgian caravan moved on.

He let in the clutch and the TR6 edged forward. The gendarme glanced down at the car and its GB sticker and waved them through.

As did his Swiss counterpart a few yards further on.

They had made it!

PART FOUR

BERLIN

Chapter 33

June 1979, Switzerland

They decided to drive straight through Switzerland, through Geneva and Lausanne, and north to the West German border at Basel. Phil found it extraordinarily difficult to concentrate on the driving. In the streets around Geneva, he wanted to speed up, and on the highway which ran around the north shore of Lake Geneva he had to keep telling himself to slow down. Blood was pumping in his ears, and his hands were gripping the steering wheel in a sweaty death clasp.

Death. He knew the image of Kurt and then the man with the gun crumpling to the ground would never leave him. The sight of the red and grey stuff oozing out of the balaclava and the smell of cordite from the guns mixed with the iron in the freshly shed blood would never leave him. Neither would the man's staring eyes as Phil had lifted his mask.

'Why was that man there, Grams? Was he looking for Kurt? Was he looking for you?'

'I don't know.'

'Will there be more of them in Berlin waiting for us?'

'I don't know.'

'Has this got something to do with why we're in Europe?'

'I don't know.'

'Of course you know! It must have. This isn't some coincidence. These people want to stop you doing whatever it is you're trying to do. It's obvious!'

'I suppose it is.'

Emma's voice was calm, but her face was tense as she stared straight ahead along the road. To their right, Lake Geneva reached into the gloom of the low cloud, its far shore invisible in the murk.

'So what is it we're trying to do? Why are we going to Berlin? To find Kay?'

Emma sighed. 'Yes. To find Kay.'

'And why are we doing that?'

She didn't answer. She just stared straight ahead.

'Are we looking for Lothar?'

Nothing.

After what Swann had told him in the Three Castles, Phil strongly suspected they were.

'Is that why you had that gun? To use on Kay?'

'No, of course not.'

'Then why did you have it?'

'In case we needed it. And it turned out we did need it.'

'So you knew this trip might be dangerous from the beginning?'

'I didn't know it. I thought it might be. I didn't think people would die. I didn't think Kurt would die. You were very brave back there, Philip.'

'What choice did I have?' Phil protested.

'You could have sneaked back into the lavatory.'

'And let him kill Kurt and you?'

'He killed Kurt anyway. And I'm going to die soon in any case.'

'Oh, Grams!' Phil tried to get a grip on his frustration. 'Why are we trying to find Kay? Why can't you just let it all rest?'

But Emma didn't answer. She reached into her handbag, pulled out a packet of cigarettes and lit one. Her hand was shaking so badly it took her several attempts to light it.

Phil's anger and frustration were genuine, but they were tinged with guilt. He should have known when he had seen the revolver in his grandmother's suitcase that whatever reason she had for taking it, she thought there was a chance she might have to use it.

And then there was Swann. Their chat in the pub had added a frisson of excitement to the trip, transforming it from a tame holiday with an older relative into a bit of adventure.

It turned out that that kind of adventure involved bloodshed and death.

Somehow Phil had omitted to ask Swann whether he was likely to watch his grandmother blowing someone's brains out.

To be fair, that wasn't Swann's fault. It was Emma who had got him into this situation; he would be accompanying her now even if he had never met Swann.

They drove through Switzerland in silence. It had started as a silence of anger, but as the TR6 ate up the kilometres, it became a silence of thoughtfulness, each of them trying to make sense of what had just happened and what would happen next.

Phil was unsure what to do. Should he tell Emma about his conversation with the enigmatic Swann? He felt guilty not telling her.

And yet, by her own admission, she had been an ardent communist in the 1930s. She may still be one.

As told by Emma, there had been something heroic about the communism of Hugh and her and Kurt, and the socialism of people like Dick. They were standing up for justice and equality in a world of cruel, broken capitalism.

Yet, now, the communists were the bad guys.

Phil had enjoyed studying history at school, but one of the things he had found hardest to accept was his teacher's precept that good historians didn't see history as the battle of the good guys against the bad guys. You weren't supposed to take sides when you were writing an A-level history essay. Reluctantly, he had grown to understand that the reason why he thought the Protestants were the good guys in the Reformation, and the British the good guys in their empire, was because he was a Protestant Englishman. He was beginning to see that Vietnam, Northern Ireland and Israel were more complicated than they seemed once you dropped the idea that the good guys were the ones who looked most like you.

And yet he wasn't prepared to give up some judgements just because Mrs Hauser, his history teacher, had told him to. The Nazis were the bad guys in the Second World War. The communists, as personified by the Soviet Union and China, were the bad guys now.

Which meant that his grandmother might be one of the bad guys.

Phil didn't like that idea at all.

Swann had said something about how if Emma discovered he had asked Phil to look for Lothar, she might do something she would regret.

At the time, Phil had no clue what that might be. He wasn't sure now, either, but he did see how it might involve the KGB. And, if Swann was correct, it might lead to getting them both killed. He knew Emma had a mind of her own. He knew Emma had been and indeed still might be a Russian spy.

Swann could easily be correct.

He wasn't going to tell her about Swann. At least not yet.

This was all crazy. A week ago, he had been arguing with his father over a minor traffic accident and whether he could join his grandmother on a staid holiday to Europe's capitals. Now it turned out that his grandmother was a Russian agent, that MI6 wanted Phil to spy on her, and that two men had died because of her, right in front of Phil's eyes.

Phil was scared. It was a kind of fear he had never felt before, a fear that there was a realistic chance he and his grandmother might be killed. Soon.

He could easily have lost his life a couple of hours back. It hadn't occurred to him at the time, but maybe he should have crept back into the toilet and left the hit man to kill Kurt and Emma. He didn't want to die, especially for reasons he didn't understand, and that Emma refused to explain to him.

But he was glad he had jumped the man in the balaclava. He was glad Emma was still alive, and he had been responsible for saving her. Deliciously mixed up with the fear was excitement. He had faced danger and he had triumphed.

Emma had tried to tell him that, since she was going to die soon anyway, saving her life was pointless. Phil didn't buy that. He wasn't sure he had completely come to terms with the fact that she was going to die, but if she was, he would make sure it was in bed, not by a KGB bullet.

He would stick with her.

Chapter 34

Emma had other ideas.

They drove into West Germany and turned off the autobahn at a small town on the edge of the Black Forest. The town's only hotel had two free rooms, and they sat in its near-empty restaurant for dinner.

Phil ordered sausages and Emma a trout, together with a bottle of local Riesling.

'We used to drink this stuff by the gallon, in Berlin,' she said. 'Hock, we called it. But it seems to have gone out of fashion now. I don't know why. I think it's rather nice.'

'I like it,' said Phil.

'You'd like anything,' said Emma.

'Grams, I have a sophisticated palate! It might be just a little too modern for you to understand.'

'Oh, Philip, you do talk absolute rot sometimes.'

He did. But it made her smile.

'Philip. I've been thinking. Those were perfectly reasonable questions you were asking me in the car. But I just can't answer them.'

'Can't, or won't?' said Phil.

'Both. I really wanted to bring you with me on this trip. I needed your help, I enjoy your company and I was getting you out of a hole rather neatly. Also, I wanted to tell someone my story before I die, and you seemed the best person to choose.'

She smiled at him. 'And I was right. Mostly. I do like your company. You were useful; I call saving my life pretty damn useful. And you seem genuinely interested in my story.'

'I am.'

'But when we set off, I never really thought either us would be in danger of losing our lives. I expected a hint of excitement perhaps, echoes of a dangerous past, but not men with guns killing people.

'And I thought the story I was telling you was ancient history. I was happy to tell you secrets; I thought in doing that I was keeping the past alive. I didn't want to take those secrets to the grave. But now I think I must. They are too dangerous.'

'Why do you think they're so dangerous?' Phil asked.

'I really don't know,' said Emma. She smiled wryly. 'Of course, the answer must lie in the secrets themselves, and I have just said I am not willing now to divulge those. But I truly don't understand why someone wanted to kill me. Or kill Kurt.'

Phil did. He was pretty sure it must have something to do with Swann's mole. Emma's words implied that she didn't know about the mole. In which case, shouldn't he tell her? For her own safety.

But could he trust her?

Instinctively, he knew that he could trust her not to deceive him in a way that would do him harm. But she had her own agenda, an agenda she wasn't willing to share with him. If he told her about Swann and his desire to find Lothar, he had no idea what her response would be, what she would do. Swann had suggested she would put herself in danger. Phil could believe it.

Very well, she had her agenda and he had his. He was unwilling to betray his country. More than that, if there really was a mole in the heart of the British establishment, and Phil could help reveal his identity, he would do so.

'Philip? You've gone quiet.'

'Yes, I have,' said Phil. 'I was thinking about what you were saying.'

'And?'

'And I understand it, I think. Or as much of it as you're willing to tell me.'

'Good,' said Emma. 'So when we get to Berlin, you should leave me. Take a flight back to England.'

'I can't abandon you, Grams! It's not safe!'

'It isn't safe, Phil. That's the whole point. I can choose to put myself in danger. It doesn't matter much; I haven't long to live anyway.'

'I do wish you'd stop saying that!'

'I do wish you'd let me say it!'

That brought Phil up short. He was beginning to understand his grandmother. She was coming to terms with her death – and her life. His job was to help her do that.

He nodded, lowering his eyes. 'OK. I'm sorry. You can talk about your death as much as you like with me. I get that. You should just understand that I'll be sorry to see you go.' Phil could feel moisture seeping into his right eyelid. He blinked quickly, and was relieved not to feel a tear run down his cheek. Get a grip!

'I know you will, darling,' said Emma with one of her warmest smiles. 'I know you will.' She took a deep breath. 'But there's absolutely no point me telling you all this stuff if you go and get yourself killed right away, is there?'

'No, Grams.'

'Good. That's settled, then.'

But Phil wasn't entirely sure it was settled.

After dinner, going up the stairs to their rooms, Emma stumbled and fell backwards. Phil was right behind her and caught her. Emma glanced at her grandson with gratitude and also a hint of fear, fear of the thing growing within her brain.

No. It wasn't settled.

It was a long drive to West Berlin the following day. They passed within a few kilometres of Braunschweig on the way to the East German border at Helmstedt. Phil wondered whether Heike was back home yet, but he didn't suggest stopping to find out. Maybe on the return journey, if Emma didn't succeed in putting him on a plane back to London.

An autobahn corridor led 170 kilometres from Helmstedt through East Germany to West Berlin. At the border, the West German police and then the East Germans checked all the drivers. The two control points were large complexes, capable of processing the thousands of vehicles that made the trip each day. Phil had made sure the TR6's tank was full of petrol, but that was the least of his worries.

What if the East German authorities realized that Emma had killed one of their agents in Annecy – or if not one of theirs, then an agent of one of their allies? Might they not arrest Emma and him? Why hadn't he thought of this before?

He glanced across at his grandmother's tense face. She had thought of it.

He needed to keep his wits about him in this last day or two he was with her if he wasn't to make a mistake or to fail to catch her making one.

He considered refusing to go ahead. They were several cars back in the queue. She would understand. But she would continue regardless, drive the car herself into whatever trouble was waiting for her.

He took a deep breath. He would stick with her.

The West German police waved them through with a cursory glance at their papers, which showed at least that Interpol wasn't on to them yet. The young East German border guard studied Emma's passport carefully.

'Any guns or ammunition?' he asked Phil in German.

'No,' Phil said, very glad that Emma no longer had that stupid revolver in her bag. The border guard looked as if he was quite capable of taking the car apart. But instead, he asked them to wait, and disappeared through a door, clutching both their passports.

Phil resisted the temptation to exchange glances with Emma. He thought he was doing a better job of looking casual than he had at the crossing into Switzerland, but his heart was pounding.

The young guard returned, handed their passports back to Phil, freshly stamped with transit visas, and told him to drive on.

Phil waited a minute until turning to his grandmother. He meant to chastise her for not anticipating the risk that they would be arrested at the border, but when he caught her eye, they both burst out laughing.

There was no trouble at the checkpoint into West Berlin at the other end of the corridor.

Emma navigated Phil through the suburbs of Berlin with the aid of a map she had brought with her from England, as, unlike Paris, the layout of the city had changed in unpredictable ways since before the war. It had been obliterated by the combined efforts of the RAF and the Red Army. Totally destroyed, and then rebuilt.

He found driving in Berlin much easier than driving in Paris had been. He didn't know whether it was because the drivers were stereotypically more disciplined, or whether he was just getting used to it. Emma guided them to the Kurfürstendamm, the glitzy shopping street in the heart of the western city.

'Let's try here.'

It was the Hotel Bristol, a grand hotel with a modern, curved facade of white stone on the corner of the Kurfürstendamm and Fasanenstrasse, a bright café with a red awning on its first floor facing the main shopping street. Yes, they had rooms for Lady Meeke and her grandson, and the TR6 was once again whisked away by a white-gloved lackey.

'The Bristol used to be on Unter den Linden when I was last here,' Emma said as they waited for the reception clerk to summon a porter. 'Or at least its ancestor was. Unter den Linden is now in East Berlin.'

'I know,' said Phil.

'Your *Hitch-Hiker's Guide* told you?'

'It did,' said Phil proudly.

'Bet it didn't mention the Bristol.'

'No. But there's a good youth hostel in Bayernallee we can try if this doesn't work out. It's expensive though. Fifteen marks a night.'

'That is expensive,' said Emma. 'I think we'll have to slum it here.'

Phil dreaded to think how much his room cost at the Bristol. Probably half his entire holiday budget.

At breakfast the next morning, they discussed plans for the day. Emma wanted to go to the British Airways office to book Phil's flight.

'I tell you what, Grams,' Phil said. 'Before we do that, can you show me around Berlin a bit? Like you did in Paris. And tell me what you can about your time here.'

Emma was about to protest when Phil stopped her. 'I know there are things you can't tell me. But I'd like to hear what you have to say; I want to hear more of the story.'

There may not be another chance for you to tell me, Phil wanted to say, but didn't. Emma heard the thought, though.

'Yes, Philip,' she said. 'I'd like that.'

They picked up a taxi from the hotel and passed along the road that ran beside the Tiergarten, a large wild park in the centre of the city.

'Roland and I had a flat just down there,' said Emma, pointing to a construction site. 'It's all changed now, of course. But it was a good spot. Handy for the park.'

They got out of the taxi and walked into the park, under the scornful marble eye of a gentleman whose narrow beard was slung beneath his thrusting chin, rather like a necklace. He sat high up on a marble plinth, his clothes and a sheaf of marble paper flowing about him.

'Richard Wagner,' said Emma. 'Very popular back before the war.'

'I bet.'

Emma seemed to know her way now, and led Phil along a bewildering network of paths until they arrived at a small garden surrounded by a thick hedge. Roses predominated, but carefully ordered beds of bright flowers, whose names Emma no doubt knew, rivalled them for the attention of the bees, tirelessly toiling at knee height.

'There used to be a giant statue in the middle of this garden,' Emma said. 'An empress in a long dress and a big hat watching over the nannies who used to take their charges here. And me taking your mother, who was nearly two at the time. Otherwise, it hasn't changed much.'

They sat on a bench, letting the sun caress their faces.

'This was where Lothar told me to go for my first meet in Berlin.'

Chapter 35

November 1938, Berlin

ROLAND WAS POSTED to the Berlin embassy in October 1938, as first secretary. The embassy had had a tough time, working flat out in the weeks culminating in the Munich agreement that September, when the British and the French had allowed the Germans to take the German-speaking part of Czechoslovakia in return for a guarantee of peace. Not our finest hour, and something Roland and many of his fellow diplomats were furious about.

But not the ambassador, Nevile Henderson. He wasn't just pro-appeasement, he was pro-German, which was why he had been sent to Berlin in the first place. But right after Munich, he was diagnosed with cancer and sent back to London for treatment. Which was lucky, because Roland couldn't stand the man. Personally, he was fine – charming, considerate, even honest in his own way – but professionally he was a disaster.

My last meeting with Lothar had been in Paris, that September. Lothar had just been recalled to Moscow, and I had learned Roland and I were moving to Berlin. Lothar had hastily come up with a plan for me to establish contact with a new handler in Berlin. I was supposed to turn up at the Rose Garden every Wednesday at 3.30 p.m., and I had the usual idiotic phrases to remember, something about the weather being colder this year than last.

And it was. Colder, I mean. Nobody met me the first two weeks, so Caroline and I had to hang about in the October damp for an hour, waiting. I brought Caroline along as an alibi, on the theory that a young mother looks much less suspicious than a single woman hanging about alone on a miserable October afternoon.

Lots of suspicious things went on in the Tiergarten before the war. In the 1920s and early thirties it was the place for prostitutes and drug dealers to meet their clients and do their business. By the time Roland and I arrived in Berlin that had all stopped, to be replaced by a different kind of furtive behaviour.

Everyone in Berlin assumed that nowhere indoors was safe from prying ears, either electronic or human, so the Tiergarten became the natural place for diplomats to meet. And not just diplomats: German government ministers and soldiers could be seen walking or riding together, deep in mysterious conversation. So why not spies like me?

I persevered. My third attempt was in early November.

I was sitting on a bench, trying to keep Caroline entertained, when I heard a familiar voice.

'Hi there.'

I looked up. 'Kay? Kay! I wasn't expecting you here.'

She grinned. I don't know whether it was my nervousness at meeting the new Lothar, or the general underlying anxiety permeating Berlin at that time, but it felt very good to see a familiar face. I stood up and hugged her. Then I introduced her to Caroline.

'Shouldn't we be discussing last year's weather?' I said.

'Consider it discussed. And thank you for showing up. This must be the fourth week you've been here?'

'Third.'

'Well, I've just moved here from Paris. Arrived last Friday. And I've been promoted! It's now my job to look after you.' I had continued to meet Lothar at Kay's flat in the Marais for the last two years. Sometimes Kay and I would meet briefly there, or at readings at Shakespeare and Company, but it was always Lothar I reported everything to.

'That's marvellous,' I said.

'Sure is. Since I'm American, it's easier for me to operate here than for some of the others. I'm planning on enrolling at the Friedrich Wilhelm University on a language course. And it's Kay Macdonald now.'

'Scottish?'

'Still American. But it sounds a whole lot less Jewish than Lesser. According to my new passport I was born in 1905 in San Francisco and my father was a pastor – also not very Jewish. San Francisco is a fine place to be born in, by the way. All the birth records were destroyed in the 1906 earthquake, so the FBI can't check on me.'

'Well, Miss Macdonald, it's a pleasure to meet you. How's Lothar?'

Kay became more subdued. 'He's back in Moscow. He has been reassigned to a different department.'

'Still in the Comintern?'

'I have no idea. They don't tell me that kind of thing.'

'Kay?' I said. 'Is the Comintern really so separate from the Russian secret service?'

'Sure,' Kay said. 'It's entirely separate. I mean, obviously we are based in Moscow and we get help and funds from the Soviet Union, but we are working for international communism, not just for Russia, I can promise you that.'

I wasn't convinced, but I didn't argue. At that point, Russia was the only communist state in the world, and given the recent spinelessness shown by the British and the French at Munich, the only country that could be relied upon to stand up against the Fascists in Germany, Spain and Italy.

'What kind of stuff do you want from me?' I asked her.

'The same you gave Lothar in Paris,' said Kay. 'Seems it goes down very well with Moscow. Especially the information from your husband. They tell me the low-down you gave Lothar about the Munich negotiations was dynamite.'

I was pleased to hear it. Relations between Roland and me had settled down over the previous couple of years. We never argued; I was unfailingly polite to him. We now shared a bedroom, although we slept in separate beds. The apartment in Berlin only had two bedrooms, and it seemed right that Caroline should have one of her own. But I never let him touch me. Although I smiled, laughed with him even, I knew he could feel my disgust. Yet he seemed to understand it. Respect it.

We did have long conversations, though. Many of them were about politics and the international situation, all good information for Lothar. But, truthfully, I enjoyed those conversations for their own sake; Roland enjoyed them too. I even found myself looking forward to his return to the flat after a day at the embassy.

At that point the Foreign Office was split. On the one hand were those who wanted to take a tougher line on Germany, like Roland but also Vansittart, recently demoted from the post of permanent undersecretary at the Foreign Office, and Ogilvie-Forbes, the new chargé d'affaires in Berlin who was standing in for Nevile Henderson. On the other stood those who believed appeasing Hitler was the only way to preserve peace, like Henderson, and the Prime Minister, Neville Chamberlain, and Roland's bête noire, Horace Wilson, the Prime Minister's right-hand man. The appeasers were gaining the upper hand, but it wasn't always clear-cut. Although the new Foreign Minister, Lord Halifax, had supported the Munich agreement, he had done so reluctantly, and Roland thought he could be persuaded to take a harder line against the Nazis.

Some British diplomats had made their feelings clear in a typically obscure manner. Their dress, which in Paris some had thought quintessentially English but others just ridiculous, comprised black homburg hat, starched white collar, striped sponge-bag trousers and a furled umbrella. After Munich and Chamberlain's famous brandishing of his umbrella in celebration of peace with Hitler, many diplomats no longer carried theirs as a sign of protest. Even when it threatened to rain. Roland was one of these brave souls.

It was all terribly complicated, and Roland enjoyed working it through in his mind with me.

I enjoyed it too, for two reasons.

Firstly, I knew Roland treated my intellect seriously, and he increasingly valued my opinion.

Secondly, I passed it all on to Lothar. I still hated my husband for what he had done to me. Revenge, especially revenge in a good cause, which I believed this was, still tasted sweet. And it made living with him bearable.

I did hate him, didn't I? Sometimes I wondered. Sometimes, when we were at home at the apartment in the Rue de Bourgogne or at our new place in Berlin and he was telling me about some particularly ludicrous episode between the ambassador and his wife, or the Nazi popinjays with whom he now had to deal, I found myself smiling and meaning it. And when he complimented me on my suggestions for how he should deal with the appeasers in the Foreign Office I would occasionally feel a warm glow of pleasure run through me.

No. Of course I hated him. After what he had done to me, how could I not?

'More of that please,' said Kay. 'Also, they've asked for any information you can get on British attempts to undermine Russia – in particular, to support a coup against Stalin.'

'I haven't heard of any,' I said. 'My understanding is that the British government is a lot less suspicious of Russia than they were a few years ago.'

'That's not the way it is. The Munich agreement shows how the British government is willing to ally with the Germans against the Soviet Union.'

'I didn't know that,' I said. 'In fact, I think that's wrong.'

'It's true,' Kay said. 'It's just well hidden. Which is why we would be real happy for you to find evidence of it.'

'All right,' I conceded. 'I'll see what I can unearth. Where do we meet?'

'I've gotten a flat in Kreuzberg. We meet there.' She gave me the address and a date and time the following week. 'By then, I'll figure out fall-back procedures and so on.'

'I've started going to the Staatsbibliothek,' I said. 'It's right next to the university. We can work something out there.'

Kay grinned. 'Trust you to find a library. But it's a good idea. I'll see you next week. And be sure to get your husband to tell you something about the plans to undermine the Soviet Union.'

Chapter 36

I TOOK THE U-Bahn to meet Kay. It was a relief to get underground. Above ground, on the streets, groups of men and some women were gathering. In the distance I could hear shouts. There was trouble in the air.

I had expected to see signs of anti-Semitism when I arrived in Berlin, and I saw plenty of them. Graffiti on Jewish businesses in the shopping streets. Signs of the petty bureaucracy which was designed to entrap Berlin's substantial Jewish population at every turn: the yellow benches for Jews only in the Tiergarten, the special number plates on Jewish-owned cars. It was with some discomfort that I had learned we were renting our flat from a Jewish lawyer who had decamped with his family to Amsterdam. But in the month that I had been in Berlin, I hadn't seen any attacks on Jews directly.

I had a feeling that was about to change.

Two days before, an angry seventeen-year-old German–Jewish student had marched into the German Embassy in Paris and shot the ambassador's private secretary, a young man named vom Rath. I hadn't met him myself, but Roland knew him. I assumed Kurt Lohmüller would have known him well.

Germany was in uproar, goaded by Goebbels' propaganda machine. The newspapers were full of demands that something must be done about the 'Jewish question'. It seemed that the gangs I saw roaming the street near our flat were planning to do just that.

Things were quieter in Kreuzberg, just south of the city centre where Kay lived. It was a neighbourhood full of numerous small shopkeepers who displayed their wares on the pavements: green-grocers, butchers, bakers, coal and potato sellers as well as tailors and cobblers. Bed linen hung out to air from apartment windows higher up. Kay's place was three floors above a printer's shop: in those days most of Berlin's newspapers were located in the area. She welcomed me in. The flat was small and clean, but devoid of any personal touches: no books at all, apart from a large German–English dictionary. A scuffed wireless set stood to attention in the centre of the room.

I was pleased to see her, but also worried about her. Did she look Jewish? It was hard to tell. She didn't conform to the grotesque stereotypes that the Nazi posters proclaimed: the hooked noses, the grasping hands, the greedy leers. But then her hair was dark. Yet so was mine.

I hoped her American accent and passport and her Scottish name would protect her.

We got down to business straight away. I had arranged for the daughter of a French diplomat to look after Caroline three after-noons a week, and I intended to spend most of those at the library, which Kay had now joined. We agreed that if I left two pencils crossed on my desk, that meant I needed to contact her. Similarly, if she left her pencils crossed, she needed to contact me. Three pencils lined up meant that we were blown and shouldn't contact each other.

I liked Kay, but she wasn't the same as Lothar. Lothar had managed to instil in me a feeling of reliability and trust. We would often talk about the subtleties of international politics, or of my relationship with Roland. It had felt like I was working for Lothar personally, that he was the one who decided what was important, and that I was earning his approval when I provided it. I knew that there must be people behind him in Moscow, but somehow they seemed subservient to him, rather than the other way around.

It quickly became very clear that things were different with Kay. Although there was no doubting her sincerity, or her devotion to the cause, she was following instructions, and those instructions were to dig up dirt on British operations against Russia.

The trouble was, there weren't any, or none that Roland knew of, and he knew a lot. I had had two conversations with him about Russia, which had seemed natural enough since he knew of my fondness for the country. He assured me that the British no longer saw the Soviet Union as a threat, and became impatient when I pushed it.

Kay became equally impatient when I told her I needed to be careful about pushing it further. Lothar would have understood immediately. For him, protecting me from suspicion, especially Roland's suspicion, was his top priority. But Kay was insistent. Someone was leaning on her from Moscow.

In the end, I had to agree to question Roland again, a promise I intended to ignore, at least for a while.

It was dark by the time Kay and I finished. We could hear shouts outside.

'Be careful out there,' Kay said. 'How did you get here?'

'U-Bahn.'

'Well, take a taxi back.'

So I did. My taxi driver was a jovial fellow with a fine walrus moustache, and a couple of folds of skin at the back of his neck.

'Are you English? Or American?' he asked when he heard my accent.

'I'm English.'

'And what are you doing in Berlin?'

'My husband works at the British Embassy.'

'Oh, interesting. He must have been very busy recently?'

'I believe they were. But we arrived from Paris just after the agreement was signed.'

'Thank God you British agreed to peace at Munich,' the driver said. I recognized his classic Berlin accent – the 'g's became 'y' sounds. 'For a couple of days there, I thought we were going to be at war.'

'So did I.'

'Well, I am very glad we are not, *gnädige Frau*.' He turned as he was driving and gave me a huge grin, the tips of his moustache pointing upwards. It was quite charming.

'Me too.'

'*Notabene*, no one in Berlin wants to fight the English,' he said. 'We are too similar. All we want is to bring Germans back into the Fatherland. It's good your Herr Chamberlain understands that. Of course, the golden pheasants may feel differently; they want a war.'

'The golden pheasants?'

'The Nazis. The ones who love to dress up and push people around. I was in the last war; I know what it's like, not like these popinjays with their fancy uniforms. Uniforms should be for fighting in, not for preening yourself on the Kurfürstendamm.'

'We don't want to fight you either,' I said, even though I was afraid we might have to.

'The Sudetenland is like if Cornwall was occupied by the French and they were all forced to eat snails and brush their teeth with garlic. That wouldn't be right. Do they really eat snails in Paris?'

'They do. And they like garlic. I'm not sure they brush their teeth with it.'

'Anyway, now we have brought the Rhineland and Austria back into Germany and reunited the Sudetenland, we can live in peace with our neighbours.'

I prayed he was right. It was good to hear that that was what at least one Berliner thought.

The car slowed as a group of young men crossed the road in front of us. The driver raised his hand over the horn and then thought better of it. A moment later we heard the sound of shattering glass.

I peered out of the taxi, and in the light from the streetlamps I saw a man holding a broomstick and thrusting it at the window of a greengrocer. The word *Juden* was scrawled on the wall beside the shop. A group of about a dozen men cheered, and began chanting something I couldn't make out.

'Where are the police?' I asked.

'In their police station playing cards.'

'Won't they stop this?'

'The Jews have it coming to them. You read about how they assassinated that German diplomat?'

'I did.'

'Well, then? It's only going to get worse unless we do something about them.'

'But you can't let people roam the streets and destroy other people's property!'

'Why not? The Jews do it. Of course they are much craftier about it. They take your money without you even noticing. It's the Germans who do all the work, and the Jews who take all the money. It's always been like that.'

I knew it was pointless to get into an argument with a taxi driver, but I couldn't let it pass. I think it was because he had seemed such a genial soul that I wanted him to change his mind. I wanted to believe in the good of the Berliners.

'There are plenty of Aryan businessmen,' I said. 'They are just as wealthy.'

'But they don't go around shooting German diplomats,' said the driver. 'You don't understand. You don't have as many of them in your country as we do. But you should learn from us. Look around you. See what they are doing. Do something about it.'

We both heard the crash of another window shattering.

'Like those guys. They are doing something.'

I'd had enough. 'Stop the car,' I said. 'I'd like to get out.'

'I wouldn't recommend that, madam. It's only another kilometre to your house.'

'I'll walk.'

The driver sighed. 'Suit yourself.'

As I opened the car door he called out to me. *'Gnädige Frau!'* He smiled. 'You don't understand. You'll see, I'm right. We have to do something to stop them.'

I scrambled out of the taxi and slammed the door.

Out on the street, the noise was louder. The shouting, the yelling, the sound of breaking glass. There was even laughter and jeering. And to the west, above the rooftops, an orange glow flickered.

I moved towards it.

I wasn't sure what it was, but I thought there was a synagogue in that direction. I resolved to see for myself.

A couple of years before, there had been incidents where British and American nationals had been arrested, usually for not performing the Nazi salute when troops marched past. This had proved a problem for all concerned, both the Berlin authorities and the foreign consular officials, so a tacit agreement had been reached. The authorities would try not to arrest foreign nationals, and the foreign nationals would try to avoid putting themselves in a situation where they were in public and expected to salute. Diplomats and their families were warned to walk away from Nazi trouble rather than towards it.

But I headed towards that orange glow. The wind was blowing from that direction, and I could smell it. Burning. Burning wood. And something more acrid.

I was walking along a short residential street between two larger thoroughfares. Towards the end of the road, a group of about half a dozen people were crowded on the pavement. I stopped and watched; partly I was nervous about passing them, partly I was curious. A small blond-haired man of about twenty was hammering on the door of an apartment building, a woman of about his own age urging him on. I noticed an arrow painted in red on the pavement pointing to the house, a letter 'J' scrawled above it.

There was no reply. The man hurled himself at the door in an attempt to bust it open, but bounced back into the street and hit the ground with a cry, amidst some laughter. Then one of his mates, a bigger man, pushed past with a crowbar. After a few seconds of tussling with the door, it split with a loud crack, and then swung open. Three of the crowd ran in, and a minute later they emerged with a young woman and an old man, to cheers from those waiting for them on the pavement.

I backed away as they started pushing and shoving the two terrified people. A third, much smaller person ran out yelling 'Mama', but he couldn't get through the crowd.

The old man and the young woman were pushed to the ground. I couldn't see clearly what was happening, but I could see from the way the crowd was stooping and jerking that they were kicking the silent bodies.

The boy stood a couple of yards back from the crowd, unsure whether to run forward to his mother and grandfather, or to run away. He was about five years old, wearing shorts. Under a pool of yellow light from the street lamp, I could see his chubby face stricken with incomprehension, horror and fear, his mouth open, his brows knitted. No one took any notice of him, even when he filled his lungs and wailed.

I should have stepped forward and tried to comfort him. Perhaps I should even have tried to stop them, however fruitless an effort it might have been.

But I didn't do that. I turned and ran all the way home, up the stairs to our flat where Roland was waiting for me home early from work, his face full of concern at where I had been, and I flung myself at him and I held him tight, so tight.

That little boy is with me still.

Chapter 37

June 1979, West Berlin

The offices of the Detektei Pöpel detective agency were above a launderette on a street only a couple of hundred yards from the Wall. Emma and Phil climbed narrow wooden stairs to a cramped cubbyhole, where a young secretary asked them to wait for Herr Pöpel on a sofa only a few feet from her desk.

After ten minutes Herr Pöpel called them into his office. He was a small man, whose face bore the marks of decades of exhaustion. A cigarette drooped from the corner of his mouth, a scrappy moustache sagged on his upper lip, and enormous bags underpinned his small eyes.

He ushered them into an office almost overwhelmed with paper. After instructing Trudi to get them both cups of coffee, and offering them each a cigarette, he sat down.

'How can I help you?' he asked, his Berliner accent so strong Phil struggled to understand his words.

'It's quite simple, really,' Emma said. 'We would like you to find the address of a woman named Kay Ortmann. She lives in East Berlin.'

'And of all the private investigators in Berlin, why pick me?'

Herr Pöpel looked suspicious. Which, Phil supposed, was what you wanted in a private detective.

'You are the second detective we have seen today,' Emma said. 'I offered a fee to the first man to recommend someone who could help us, half up front, and half payable when we had found Kay Ortmann.

221

That way he would only recommend someone who he thought was capable of the task.'

Herr Pöpel's lugubrious face cracked into a laugh. 'I like that. Smart. Well, whoever you spoke to chose well. I make it a bit of a speciality to deal with the *Ossis*. I have contacts there.'

'So you can find Kay?' said Emma. 'I realize Ortmann is a fairly common name, and I don't know her husband's initial.'

'I'm sure I can help you,' said Herr Pöpel. 'Whether I *will* help you is something else. And it depends largely on how you answer the following question. Is there anything I should know about this Kay Ortmann?'

Phil wondered what story Emma would trot out, and was a little surprised when she opted for the truth.

'We suspect she worked for the Stasi. We know her husband did. He may still. She is in her seventies, by the way.'

Pöpel nodded. 'I have heard of Klaus Ortmann. A colonel in the Stasi. Mostly worked overseas. Not a nice man, but by no means the worst. Why do you want to find this woman?'

'I knew her before the war. She's an old friend. I'd like to see her again.'

Pöpel stubbed out his cigarette and lit another one. 'I have my reputation to protect, so I will be discreet. Where I can. But I also need to keep my licence. In cases like this, you should know that if the authorities ask me about your enquiry, I will tell them everything they want to know. Is that all right with you?'

'That's fine,' said Emma.

'Good. Give me any other clues you can, and I should have an answer for you tomorrow morning.'

When they left Herr Pöpel's office it was nearly lunchtime.

'Shall we take a look at the Wall?' Emma suggested.

It wasn't far. They turned a corner and it was right there, a ten-foot-high barrier of white concrete topped with smooth concrete piping. Layers of graffiti had been scrawled on every surface, the words an indistinct jumble.

As they walked parallel to the wall, they passed a row of tacky tourist shops selling Berlin Wall tat, and an observation deck, which was open to the public.

From there they could look over the barrier to a flat strip of tarmac and grass two hundred yards wide, on the far side of which stood another wall. Watchtowers gave the East German border guards a clear sight over the no-man's-land; tall posts planted at regular intervals bore powerful lights to illuminate the ground after dark. Phil shuddered at the thought of desperate East Berliners trying to creep or run between the walls and being gunned down. And all in the middle of one of the largest cities in Europe.

'That death strip used to be the Potsdamer Platz,' said Emma. 'The heart of the city, with shops and restaurants and hotels. The busiest junction in Europe. The first traffic lights in the world were installed here. And now look at it.'

Phil looked. The Nazi Germany on the eve of Kristallnacht that Emma had just described had sounded deeply unsettling, but then so was this.

'There's the Brandenburg Gate,' said Emma, pointing to the north.

The mighty columns of the gate stood alone and proud, penned in on the western side by the outer wall, which flexed outwards into the woods of the Tiergarten at that point. On the eastern side there was nothing.

'The Adlon Hotel, the smartest place in Berlin, was right there,' said Emma, pointing to the emptiness behind the monument. 'And behind that, the British Embassy on Wilhelmstrasse, where many of the government buildings were, including the Reich Chancellery. Now there's nothing except a car park.'

She shook her head. 'It's strange. Paris is almost exactly the same as it was when I lived there. But Berlin? Berlin is totally different.'

They took a taxi back to the Kurfürstendamm and had lunch at the Café Kranzler, which overlooked the Kaiser Wilhelm Memorial Church, or the 'Hollow-Tooth Church' as the locals apparently called it. Like every other building in the city, the church had been badly bombed in the war, but the tower had been left standing, its spire snapped off with a jagged break halfway up. The nave had been replaced by a modern honeycomb block of concrete and glass.

'Café Kranzler used to be on Unter den Linden too,' said Emma as she examined the menu. 'Just down from the Russian Embassy. I used to go there quite often for a cup of tea on my way back from the Staatsbibliothek.'

'Did you stay in Berlin all the way up to the outbreak of war, Grams?'

Emma's dark eyes examined her grandson. He knew she was trying to decide whether to tell him more. Then she smiled.

'Yes, I did. Those last few months were . . . interesting.'

'Tell me.'

Chapter 38

June 1939, Berlin

I HADN'T SEEN Dick for nearly three years, since his stint in Paris writing his novel on the Île Saint-Louis. We met for coffee and cakes at the Café Kranzler, in its old incarnation in Unter den Linden. He hadn't changed over the three years. I suspected I had. Motherhood and the strain of leading a double life had aged me. My waist had thickened slightly, and lines were laying down permanent foundations above my brows and around my mouth. I was still only twenty-four.

We took one of the white tables outside on the pavement, a good spot for watching Berliners going about their business. Comfortable, stout middle-aged men with their facial hair arranged in a multitude of different styles: large moustaches waxed or left to grow thick, pointed beards, and yes, the occasional toothbrush above the upper lip. Stout middle-aged women with bags of shopping, much less stylish than their slimmer Parisian counterparts. And then the younger generation, lean, purposeful, in a hurry. A sausage seller at his brightly coloured cart yelled at all of them, cheerfully indifferent to their indifference. Yellow trams and motor cars thundered past, marshalled by a tall traffic policeman in a blue uniform with white gloves. There were all kinds of uniforms mingling with the pedestrians on Unter den Linden: the brown of the SA, the grey and green of the army, the blue of the Luftwaffe and the sinister black of the SS.

225

'How long have you been in Berlin?' I asked him.

'Just since yesterday afternoon. I'm off to Dresden tomorrow.'

'To interview whom? Your letter was vague.'

Dick grinned. 'I wanted to be careful. I doubt the Nazis would be bothered to read a letter from me to you, but I didn't want to take any chances.'

'Very wise.'

'Have you heard of Dietrich Bonhoeffer?'

'The Confessing Church pastor? Yes, I have. No wonder you were careful. I don't think the Nazis like him very much.'

'They don't. He was chucked out of Berlin last year. He is going around the country setting up seminaries for future pastors. I believe he's in a town near Dresden now. I want to interview him about his new book. For the *New Statesman*.'

The Confessing Church had split away from the official German Evangelical Church, promoting the modern heresy in the Third Reich that the leader of the Church was Jesus not Hitler. The Gestapo didn't like that much; the Confessing Church's day of reckoning would come soon. Like the trades unions, the Communist Party, the homosexuals and now the Jews.

'I'll be curious what he tells you,' I said. 'You're writing magazine articles now? No more novels?'

'I'm afraid not.'

'Thanks for sending me *Capital Palais,* by the way.'

'Did you enjoy it?'

'Not really. You laid on the politics a bit thick, I thought. I felt like I was being lectured to. You use the word "furthermore" much too much, did you know that? And the title is idiotic.'

Dick pursed his lips; too late, I saw that I had hurt him. But then he relaxed, smiling. 'You haven't changed much, have you, Emma?'

'Haven't I?'

'You do say what you think.'

'Oh dear,' I said. 'That was a bit cruel.'

'The cruel thing is you are right.'

'Didn't it sell?'

'No.'

'Oh.' I searched for something good to say. 'I did like the scene in the bistro with the aristocratic young English lady. That wasn't me, was it?'

'Of course not,' Dick said, reddening. 'No resemblance to any person living or dead.'

'Because there seemed to be quite a lot of intimacy between her and Leonard.' Leonard was the young hero of the book.

'Hmm,' said Dick. 'I suppose there was, rather. I tried not to be too explicit.'

'You did,' I said with a wicked grin. 'You left just the right amount to the imagination. I rather liked those bits. Leonard seemed frightfully keen on her.'

'Yes, he was.' Dick cleared his throat. 'Has Roland read it?'

'Not his cup of tea.'

'That's probably for the best.'

A small squad of boys, no more than ten years old, marched past in brown shirts and black shorts, looking as serious and grown-up as they could. I hated the way the state was grabbing the youth of the country and moulding them into little Nazis.

'Do you think they play conkers in Germany?' I said, remembering Hugh at that age.

'I have no idea,' said Dick. 'Why? Do you think that's the SS Conkers Battalion?'

I laughed. 'German conkers are probably bigger and more modern than ours.'

'But not as plucky.' Dick sipped his coffee. 'You are still with Roland, I take it?'

'I am,' I said. 'Are you surprised?'

'I suppose I am. But you have your daughter to think of. He is a frightful cad. You may have forgiven him, but I can't.'

'That's sweet of you,' I said, and I meant it. I was suddenly overwhelmed by an absurd sense of gratitude to Dick. I realized

I needed someone to agree with me about how appalling Roland's behaviour had been; it was even better that Dick had volunteered his opinion without me asking for it.

Roland *was* a frightful cad.

'I don't know whether there is very much stigma to divorce these days,' Dick said. 'If you left him, people would understand.'

'Perhaps. But I've decided to stay.'

I could see Dick wanted to ask me why. And frankly, I wanted to tell him. But I couldn't do that without explaining that I was spying for the Comintern, and that I couldn't do.

Just like Hugh.

Dick had disapproved of the idea that Hugh was a spy.

'Have you joined the party?' I asked.

'The Communist Party?' said Dick, surprised. 'Oh, no. I suppose you could say I'm still a socialist, but I'm nowhere near as left-wing as Freddie.'

'Do you still see him? What's he up to?'

'Occasionally he invites me to some deeply outrageous parties in London. He likes to shock in politics and in other things. How do you find Berlin compared to Paris?'

'Totally different. It's disconcerting living in a police state with uniforms everywhere telling everyone what to do. In France no one seemed to obey anyone; here everyone does.'

I grimaced. 'I was here for Kristallnacht last November. I saw not just windows broken, but Jews badly beaten up, and the state encouraging it. And it just gets worse. In Paris the Cagoulards would start the odd scuffle and sometimes the police would look the other way, but in Berlin it's much nastier.' I shuddered. 'It's terrifying how this can happen in a country that seems on the surface so civilized.

'A friend of ours at the university just lost his job. He's a lecturer in English Literature. He wrote an article about George Bernard Shaw several years ago – I think it was before Hitler had even come to power. A colleague of his sneaked on him: told the Ministry of

Propaganda that it was a socialist tract. So Christoph was out, and he can't get a job anywhere else. He swears the article was nothing about politics at all, just a criticism of *St Joan*. I looked it up in the Staatsbibliothek. It had gone.'

'Presumably it would have been worse if he was Jewish?'

'Much worse.' I sighed. 'I do feel as if I am on the diplomatic front line.'

'And from the diplomatic front line, do you think there will be war?'

'Probably. The British government has more or less decided it's inevitable since the Germans took the rest of Czecho in March. The ambassador here still believes in appeasement; he's desperately trying to find things we can give away to the Germans for more empty promises of peace.'

Nevile Henderson had recovered from his cancer and returned to Berlin as ambassador in February, changing the tone at the embassy and putting Roland in a tricky position. A couple of junior diplomats from the embassy had resigned in protest, but Roland felt his duty was to stay and do what he could to encourage his country to stand up to Germany. And his umbrella remained resolutely in its stand by the front door of our apartment.

'I agree appeasement hasn't worked, but it was worth a try,' Dick said.

'You think so?'

'Anything is worth a try if it's going to stop a war. Now all we can hope for is that we stand firm enough to force Hitler to back down from a war he thinks he can't win.'

'The trouble is, he thinks he *can* win,' I said. 'That's the gossip here. Some of the generals aren't so sure, but Hitler seems pretty determined. Danzig is next. And then Poland.'

'So I'll be wearing a uniform too this time next year,' said Dick.

'I fear you will. Probably by Christmas.'

A stray thought struck me unawares. Hugh would have looked very handsome in uniform.

Chapter 39

ROLAND AND I had been invited to a reception at the American Embassy. It was a beautiful summer's evening, and we decided to walk from our flat along the edge of the Tiergarten: the embassy was in Pariser Platz right next to the Brandenburg Gate. It had been a warm day, but a gentle breeze of the famous *Berliner Luft*, the brisk Berlin air, rustled the trees and cooled the temperature. An unseen multitude of birds in the park discussed the day's events. While the cars still hurtled along the Tiergartenstrasse, the pedestrians seemed less hurried than usual, under the spell of the soothing evening sunshine.

'I saw Dick Loxton today,' I said. I thought it best to be open with Roland; I had secrets I needed to keep from him, but the fewer the better.

'Oh, really? Nice chap. What's he doing in Germany?'

I explained Dick's plan to interview Dietrich Bonhoeffer.

Roland frowned. 'Bonhoeffer is definitely *persona non grata*. He would have been locked up long ago if it wasn't for his Prussian Junker friends. Hitler is still wary of tussling with them. You should tell Loxton to be very careful.'

'Too late,' I said. 'He's off to Dresden tomorrow. But I will see him when he comes back here.'

'I wish him luck,' said Roland. 'I doubt very much Bonhoeffer will tell him anything interesting. He won't want to get arrested himself.'

We walked in silence. Two girls passed us. One of them, a tall woman trailing thick blonde plaits like sledgehammers, flashed her striking blue eyes at Roland, allowing them to linger there before she saw me staring at her.

I glanced at my darkly handsome husband. He was indeed attractive, and as he reached his middle thirties, his attractiveness was, if anything, growing.

And I was impressed with what he was doing in Berlin. He talked a lot about his work with me now. Somehow he managed to tread what seemed an impossible path working for an ambassador hell-bent on grovelling to the Germans, yet still putting forward the revised policy of the British government, which was now to persuade Germany that Britain really, really would stand behind Poland if Germany attacked her, honest.

He was working hard. And his reputation was rising; I knew his colleagues thought a lot of him, as did the diplomats from the other embassies in Berlin. He was going places, my husband, and I would be there to tell the Comintern all about it. At that moment the British were conducting tortuous secret negotiations with Russia to form an alliance against Germany. Being in Berlin, Roland wasn't directly involved, but he was aware of what was going on, and he found in me a receptive audience for his thoughts on the matter.

Kay told me her bosses were very interested in Roland's thoughts, reflecting as they did the position of the British officials with whom the Soviet diplomats were negotiating.

I don't know whether Roland had noticed me noticing the girls noticing him, but he turned to me.

'You know, Emma, you are looking lovely this evening.'

He had that smile. Roland had many smiles, which had varying degrees of superficiality and charm, but this was *my* smile. It was just for me.

'Don't be silly,' I said, blushing. I couldn't help it. This handsome man genuinely found me attractive. He wasn't pretending: he meant it.

'I'm not being silly.' His fingers reached for mine. I clasped them.

I felt good. I felt happy. I almost felt loved.

I wondered whom Roland was having sex with. Not with me. And not, I thought, with anyone I knew. Berlin differed a little from Paris; diplomats here were more likely to have mistresses among the showgirls and hostesses in all those clubs they frequented, rather than wayward aristocratic ladies or their friends' wives.

Who knew? Maybe he even paid for it, as I had told him to.

I let his fingers go.

Sex was too important to Roland for him to ignore.

Yet he was a patient man. I knew that his patience was one of the reasons my relationship with him was tolerable.

Whereas there was none between me and my mother; our split was dramatic. She had seen her granddaughter only twice since Caroline had been born. Between the two of us, we managed to ensure that she was in London whenever Roland and I visited Chaddington.

Over the last couple of years, I had learned the insult in Italian – and Spanish and Portuguese for that matter: *figlio di puttana*. Son of a whore.

Well, I was the daughter of a whore. Why wasn't there a phrase for that?

I was getting better at being a diplomat's wife. Lothar had encouraged me to pass on diplomatic gossip, and to be able to do that I needed to cultivate a group of people willing to gossip with me beyond just Kurt. I had built up a group of confidants in Paris, and I was doing well building up a similar crowd in Berlin.

Most diplomats thought it absurd that a twenty-four-year-old girl could have any views on politics worth listening to, but a minority found my bluntness bracing and my unorthodox ideas intriguing. Foolishly, some of them appeared to believe they could trust me with indiscretions that they would never have shared with a fellow diplomat. They could come from any country and be any age: a fifty-five-year-old first secretary from the Brazilian Embassy was an incorrigible gossip about diplomatic life in Berlin, and was also one of my best sources.

I was speaking to him about the scandalous love life of the daughter of a previous American ambassador when I recognized a familiar face.

'Kurt! How wonderful to see you!'

Kurt clicked his heels and bowed, his familiar smile transforming his stiff demeanour. I introduced him to my Brazilian friend, who did the tactful thing and withdrew to let us talk.

'Are you on home leave?' I asked.

'Oh, no,' said Kurt. 'I was transferred back to the Foreign Ministry here in March. Working for Herr Brickendrop, as you English call him so disrespectfully.'

I smiled, recognizing the nickname of the Foreign Minister, Ribbentrop, who had earned it in London during his stint as German ambassador there.

'I haven't seen you about the place?'

'I'm not in that kind of department,' Kurt said. 'But I wangled an invitation to this evening's reception in the hope that I would bump into you.'

'I'm flattered.'

Kurt bowed. 'It is nice to see you, but I have something rather important to discuss with you.'

'This is where I have to keep smiling and nodding,' I said, smiling and nodding, but intrigued.

'Yes, but not here. Perhaps we could bump into each other in the Tiergarten tomorrow afternoon? Around one o'clock?'

'The Rose Garden?'

'That would be perfect. Until tomorrow.' Kurt bowed, clicked his heels, and withdrew.

It was much nicer hanging around in the Rose Garden with Caroline in June than in November. The giant statue of the Empress

Auguste Viktoria looked over the mothers and the nannies and their charges with the benign attentiveness of a headmistress of a small but strict elementary school. Her husband had arguably started the First World War, and there were certainly echoes in the Third Reich of the militarism of Wilhelmine Germany. But in her long Edwardian dress, she seemed a symbol of a more civilized time.

Out of the corner of my eye I saw Kurt stroll past, enjoying the lunchtime sunshine, puffing on a thin cigar. He noticed me, stopped and raised his hat. 'Mrs Meeke? How nice to see you! May I join you for a couple of minutes before I return to my office?'

'Of course you may, Kurt,' I said, attempting an expression of polite surprise.

He made immediate friends with Caroline.

'Don't you miss Paris, Kurt? I do.'

'Berlin is dreadful. It's very tough on poor Martine.' Martine was Kurt's bubbly French wife. They had been married just over a year.

'We were at a dinner party last week, and the butler refused to serve one of the other guests! Claimed she was Jewish – he had somehow found out her maiden name was Goldstein. Afterwards our hostess said she couldn't sack him because he knew things about her.'

'What sort of things?'

'She didn't say. My guess is she's part-Jewish too.'

'Why do you put up with it, Kurt?'

Kurt shook his head. He reached down and chucked Caroline's chin. 'What choice do I have?'

'Can't you resign?'

'And then what would I do?' He sighed. 'I've always hated things that are unfair, even as a child. Especially as a child – I drove my parents mad. That's why I became a lawyer, to sort out all the unfair stuff. And it's why I became a socialist. Society is unfair. It's not fair that some people are rich and powerful and some people are poor and starving. At university I learned how to phrase all this in terms of jurisprudence and justice, but, basically, it's just not fair. It's wrong.'

'And yet you ended up working for a Nazi government,' I said.

Kurt gave me half a smile. 'There are some little things I can do.'

I understood. 'What do you have to tell me?'

'You remember how you passed on my message about your friend Cyril Ashcott in Paris?'

'I do.'

'I have a similar request. Once again, I would rather you didn't tell your husband if you can. From what I know of your current ambassador, he will want to squash what I have to say. Ideally, you should find a way of getting my message directly to the right people in London.'

'I understand,' I said. I wasn't sure exactly how I was going to do that. It would depend on the nature of the message, but I would find a way.

'This may shock you. It certainly shocked me. It's about a country that I know is close to both our hearts.'

'France?'

'No.' He looked me in the eye. 'Russia.'

Chapter 40

BERNADETTE, THE FRENCH babysitter, was due to look after Caroline that afternoon anyway, so I was able to visit the Stabi, as the Staatsbibliothek was affectionately known by those who toiled in her. I had become interested in the nineteenth-century writer Heinrich von Kleist, who had sought solace from a life plan he had drawn up for himself at the age of twenty-one, but from which he had diverged when he had shot himself and his terminally ill girlfriend at the age of thirty-four. I found him fascinating, and his stories wonderful. I had ordered up a biography and a couple of pieces of literary criticism.

I had difficulty concentrating on the words as I turned the pages, one pencil lying across the other on my desk, waiting for Kay to stroll past and spot the signal. My habitual desk was located in one of the many crannies off the large octagonal central reading room, which, while partially hidden, was easy for Kay to pass naturally.

She didn't come in every day, but she usually visited the library two or three times a week to check on me. Presumably there were other spies she dealt with in Berlin other than just me. I probably had equivalents from other countries – France, maybe, or America.

She strolled past my desk shortly after four. She took a book out from a nearby shelf, and ten minutes later she replaced it. I waited ten minutes and then removed the same book. Inside, I found a scrap of paper with two numbers. I subtracted three from the first number to get that day's date, and added six to the second number to get eight. Eight o'clock at her flat that evening.

Roland and I were due to see *Coriolanus* as the guest of an official in Goebbels' Propaganda Ministry. Shakespeare had always been popular in Germany, and in recent years *Coriolanus* had become the Nazis' favourite play. All those opportunities for Roman salutes.

I telephoned Roland at the Chancery to tell him that I couldn't come because I would be out with a friend from the American Women's Club, and bribed Bernadette to babysit Caroline. Kay had suggested that I join the Women's Club – there were also a small number of British women members – as a cover for making her acquaintance. They gave occasional literary talks, which I found interesting, as well as the odd concert. I left the teas and bridge to others.

Roland wasn't happy about me chucking him and his Nazi friend at such short notice, but I told him that was the kind of diplomatic incident he was qualified to deal with. Inconsistency and unpredictability were still my watchwords in my dealings with him.

At five past seven I set off on my roundabout route to Kreuzberg, as certain as I could be that I wasn't being followed.

'What have you got for me?' asked Kay.

'Russia and Germany are in talks about an alliance.'

'What?' Kay frowned. 'You're kidding me, Emma. The Russians are negotiating with the British and the French, you know that. Comrade Stalin's greatest enemy is Hitler. Who told you this?'

'Kurt Lohmüller. He was a second secretary at the German Embassy in Paris. Now he works for the Foreign Ministry in Berlin. He's reliable. He's also upset. He can't believe that the Soviet Union would ally with Germany.'

'And why does that upset him? Because he's a Nazi?'

'No,' I said. 'I think he's a communist. He's certainly a socialist. That's why we know each other. That's why I trust him.'

'OK,' said Kay. 'I'm sure there's nothing in this, but I'm going to have to report it to Moscow. Give me the details.'

So I told her what Kurt had told me. That Litvinov, Russia's Jewish and profoundly anti-Fascist foreign minister, had been sacked at the beginning of May and replaced by Molotov. That Molotov had severe doubts about an alliance with France and Britain, but seemed to like the idea of cooperation with Germany. That the German government believed that they could persuade the Russians to look the other way when they invaded Poland, in return for the Russians helping themselves to Polish territory and maybe the Baltic States.

'How advanced are these talks?' Kay asked.

'They are just at the initial stages, Kurt says.'

'I can't imagine Hitler doing a deal with Stalin,' said Kay.

'It bothers me more that Stalin would even contemplate doing a deal with Hitler. I mean, Nazi Germany is the enemy! You live here. You see what they do to the Jews. And the communists. They are evil, so much more evil than the capitalist West. The idea that the Soviet Union would overlook Fascist crimes just for a chunk of other countries' territory fills me with disgust. As it does Kurt. That's why he told me. He wants me to tell the British government.'

I remembered Kristallnacht. I remembered that boy watching the crowd of thugs kick his mother and his grandfather on the ground.

It was easy enough to hate Fascism when reading *The Times* in the library at Chaddington. But it was impossible not to loathe Fascism when living in Berlin. It was bad for the British to negotiate with Hitler. For the Russians to do so was to betray the whole point of communism.

'I'll check with Moscow first whether you should,' said Kay. 'If there's nothing in this rumour, they may not want you to confuse the British.'

I had known this would have been Kay's response.

'I think I'll do what Kurt asked.'

'You can't,' said Kay. 'Not without Moscow's permission. It's impossible for you or me to have the big picture. We're individual agents. For world socialism to succeed, there must be discipline. Discipline from people like the both of us.'

'If it's true, if the Soviets *are* doing a deal with the Nazis, then Moscow won't give me permission.'

'Of course it's not true. I strongly advise you do as instructed. Otherwise, Moscow may have to enforce discipline.'

'Are you threatening me?'

Kay had become a good friend over the last seven months. I trusted her. We had been through a lot together: both loving and then losing Hugh, my using her flat as a rendezvous with Lothar in Paris, and now these sessions where I discussed with her what I had heard from Roland and the diplomatic circuit, and where I passed on the occasional film of documents I had photographed for developing. I didn't trust Kay in the same way I had trusted Lothar. It was more that, despite our very different backgrounds, I saw in her a kindred spirit.

'I don't want to threaten you, Emma. But I do need to tell you about consequences. This is just baloney.'

'Is it?'

I looked directly at Kay.

'Is it?' I repeated.

Kay didn't answer. She was thinking. Hard.

'Can you contact Lothar somehow?' I said. 'Ask him what he thinks?'

Kay swallowed. 'Lothar's dead.'

'What?'

Kay got up and went to a cupboard next to her empty bookshelf. She extracted a bottle of vodka, grabbed two glasses, and filled each.

She knocked hers back in one. She winced. 'I learned that in Moscow.'

'At spy school?'

'Spy university.'

'So what about Lothar?' I said, sipping my own vodka and wincing. I was unused to neat spirits.

Kay collapsed into her armchair, holding on to her glass.

'You know he was recalled to Moscow last September?'

'Yes.'

'He wasn't the first. He told me three other NKVD illegals that he knew of had been recalled over the previous year. And they had all been arrested when they returned. Lothar knew one of them had been shot for sure; he suspected they all had.'

'Yet he went anyway?'

Kay sighed and took a gulp of vodka. 'I tried to persuade him not to go. But he said they were his orders. He had always put his own life behind the cause, and he wasn't going to change now. He said he knew that one day he would die for world communism.'

'But that's ridiculous! Why would they execute him anyway?'

'Comrade Stalin is sore. You may have read about the show trials of the last few years? Zinoviev, Kamenev, other Trotskyites, the generals? Well, there was a parallel purge of the NKVD. Those are the people you and I work for – the Comintern is nothing any more. There were a couple of executions in Paris when I was there: Trotsky's son went into a White Russian hospital with appendicitis and never came out, and another guy was found floating in the Seine. Without his head. Stalin is convinced they were all planning to overthrow him, helped by the British. That was why I have been asking you all year for evidence that the British secret service is conspiring against the Politburo. That's all Moscow is interested in these days.'

'But there's nothing there! I keep telling you!'

'And I keep telling them. But they don't believe me. And they don't believe you. Some of them think you are a double agent working for the British.'

'That's insane!'

'It sure is,' said Kay, staring into her glass.

'Will they recall you?' I asked. And execute you too, I could have added.

'They might. I'm hoping that I'm too unimportant for them to notice. But telling them what you've just told me won't help.'

'My source is a good one,' I said.

'Oh, yes. I know that.'

A thought struck me. 'Do you know Kurt?"

Kay hesitated, and then nodded.

'In the same way you know me?'

Kay nodded again. 'You put us on to him. I made contact and Lothar recruited him. Lothar handled him in Paris, and I've taken over handling him here in Berlin.'

I had known that Kurt had communist sympathies, but I hadn't realized they were that strong. As strong as mine.

'And did he tell you about the Soviet–German talks?'

'No,' said Kay. 'No, he didn't. Which poses its own problems.'

'You mean because he told me rather than you?'

'Precisely. It suggests he doesn't trust us any more. Which is hardly surprising if the Soviets really are in secret negotiations with the Nazis.'

'I trusted you,' I said. But there was regret in my voice. Perhaps I had made a mistake. Had I got Kurt into trouble with the Russians?

But Kay smiled. 'You did. And I trust you. We both trusted Lothar. But Moscow? I'm not so sure.'

She looked up at me. 'I had heard about these talks from another source. Not Kurt. I've already told Moscow and they denied it. They suggested my other source was a double agent spreading disinformation.'

I considered this. 'If you tell them that Kurt warned me of these talks, they are not going to be happy, are they? With any of us?'

'No,' said Kay. 'I was thinking that. They will say that you are lying. They'll say that Kurt has turned to the British by talking to you. And they might decide that I'm working for the British, just because that's the way they think. And then they will recall me to Moscow and it will all be over.'

She exhaled. 'I need another drink. Want one?'

She topped up our glasses. My head was beginning to feel woozy – from the vodka, and from what Kay was telling me.

'You know,' she said. 'I'm beginning to believe it might be best not to tell Moscow any of this. What do you think?'

'I think that sounds about right,' I said carefully.

We were silent. I was trying to make sense of what I had just heard. Lothar's recall to Moscow to be executed. Kurt working for the Russians just like me. The mistrust that the people in charge in Moscow felt towards all of us: me, Lothar, Kay, Kurt. That made me angry. We were all putting our lives on the line for the cause of the international proletariat, and this was how they thanked us. With distrust. With death.

'It might be true, mightn't it?' I said, quietly.

'That the Soviets are speaking to the Nazis? Who knows?' She sighed. 'Yes, it might be true.'

'At least Hugh didn't see any of this.'

Kay winced. An unexpected tear leaked from her left eye. I was surprised; Kay didn't seem the weeping type. I reached over and squeezed her hand. 'You miss him, don't you?'

Kay put her hand to her mouth. 'It's not that. I do, but it's not that.'

'What is it?'

'Hugh knew.'

'Knew what?'

'Knew that the Russians were not to be trusted.'

'Then why did he decide to spy for them?'

'He didn't.'

'What do you mean?'

'I haven't been straight with you, Emma,' Kay said. 'Hugh didn't work for us.'

She blinked.

'He wasn't a Russian spy.'

Chapter 41

I STARED AT her blankly. That didn't make any sense. The whole point was that Hugh *was* a Russian spy. That he had agreed to work for Lothar. That that was why he had denied his communism to me and his friends.

That was why he had been killed.

That was why I had agreed to spy for the Comintern for the last three years.

'I don't understand,' I said.

'I recruited Hugh. I told you that, right?'

'Yes.'

'It wasn't easy, but I persuaded him. I had gotten to know him on that Moscow trip, and he was very taken with the Soviet Union. But he had second thoughts: I think Dick had gotten to him. Dick had a professor at Oxford who was from the Ukraine and told him baloney about famines and the Russians locking up counter-revolutionaries. At least, I thought it was baloney then. But Hugh believed him. And he was reluctant to betray his country.'

I listened. It was possible.

'So he told me and Lothar he wanted out. He tried to persuade me to stop working for Lothar too, but I refused. I was angry with him; we were both angry with each other. Hugh had just asked me to marry him, like I told you, but after he decided to back out, it was over between us. The irony is, a few days later the British killed him anyway.'

She winced. 'I wish we had had a chance to make up before he died. Although I'm not sure we ever would have.'

'Why didn't you tell me this?' I demanded. 'I would never have started working for you if you had told me.'

'I know,' Kay said. 'That was exactly why I didn't tell you. I'm a spy. I lie. I lie all the time.' She looked at me with regret.

I felt an intense surge of fury rise up in my chest. Fury that I had been led to believe a lie about my brother. Fury that when I thought I was walking in his footsteps, he had actually turned around and faced the other way. Fury that Kay hadn't told me any of this, had manipulated me shamelessly. And Hugh, probably. No doubt she had been sent on that Intourist trip to Moscow to entrap promising young Englishmen, and Hugh had been her victim.

Kay opened up her hands and shrugged. 'You know why I lied to you. What's stranger is that I'm telling you the truth now.'

The anger evaporated, or rather it retired, waiting for a new target. Yes, I had been misled. But so had Kay. Both of us had been misused, drawn to betray our countries on the basis of false promises. As had Lothar. Who was now dead.

Hugh had seen sense, right at the end.

I had a thought. 'Was it the Russians who killed Hugh? When they realized he wasn't going to spy for them?'

'No,' said Kay. 'It was the British. Lothar told me.'

'And you trust him?'

'Yes, I trust him. He and I were very close.'

I understood. Oddly, my first response was a flash of jealousy: Lothar was an attractive man, and he had earned my trust. Then suspicion: had she been Lothar's lover and Hugh's at the same time?

Kay read my expression. 'It was in Paris. Just for a few months and just before he was recalled. I barely knew Lothar when Hugh and I were together.'

Everything was falling apart. Everything.

'So what do we do now?' I said.

Kay picked up the bottle of vodka. 'We deal with it the Russian way. We get plastered.'

I didn't get home till after midnight.

Roland had waited up for me, and he was furious. 'Where the hell have you been?'

'I told you,' I said, kicking off my shoes. 'I've been to see an American friend.'

'Oh yes? And what was her name?'

I had no idea what her name was. I tried to scramble my brain into some kind of order. Nothing.

'Frances,' I said.

Roland frowned. 'Wasn't Frances the name of your American friend in Paris?'

Oops. I nodded wisely. 'Yes. So's this one. It turns out heaps of American women are called Frances.'

'Are you tight?'

I nodded again. 'Me and . . . Frances had a little drink. To celebrate.'

'Celebrate what?'

Roland's tone was sharp. He was rarely angry with me; that wasn't the way we behaved to each other.

I didn't know what we had been celebrating, and I couldn't be bothered to make something up.

'Don't be so bloody, Roland!'

He opened his mouth to say something, and thought better of it, turning away from me. I stumbled off to our bedroom and wriggled sloppily out of my clothes. There was a knock at the door.

'Yes?'

Roland's anger was gone, replaced with what looked like fear.

'Emma?'

I tried to focus on him, but the room was spinning. He was spinning.

'Yes?'

'I thought they'd got you. I thought the Gestapo had got you.'

Chapter 42

June 1979, West Berlin

'So Hugh never spied for the Russians after all?' Phil stared at his grandmother wide-eyed over their empty lunch plates. The café was bustling.

'No. He didn't.'

'I'm sort of glad to hear that.'

'You might be now. I was furious. I had lived three years of my life on the understanding that my brother had worked for the Comintern. I had become a traitor to my country because I thought he had been. And he hadn't.' Emma shook her head. 'It was all a lie.'

Phil winced. 'Yes, I can see that must have been a bit upsetting.'

'More than a bit, Philip.'

Phil drained his beer, thinking through what he had just heard.

'So, who did kill Hugh?'

Emma took a deep breath. 'I don't know. But I mean to find out.'

After lunch, Emma suggested they take a swift look at the Hollow-Tooth Church just up the street, before going to the British Airways office. It was a unique site, encapsulating the drama of West Berlin over the previous ninety years. The tower itself exuded the late-nineteenth-century assertiveness of the Wilhelmine Empire, ostentatious brickwork on the outside, dramatic murals decorated with gold leaf on the inside. Yet its tower was broken, snapped in two by the war, and the brickwork was blackened by fire. And next to it was the modern, geometric hall, a concrete skeleton with small glass scales.

'What do you think, Philip?' asked Emma.

'I'm not sure,' said Phil. 'It's ugly, but there's something striking about it.'

They entered the hall. Phil corrected himself. 'No. It's beautiful.'

Inside, the brutal concrete has been transformed into a delicate blue net of stained glass, illuminating the vast, simple interior, all focused on a dramatic golden figure of Christ on the cross suspended above the altar.

They sat down. Phil studied the glass around him, noticing the little patches of red, green and yellow glass dotted amongst the blue. He said a quick, silent prayer along the lines of: 'Please God, get me out of this alive.' His grandmother, he knew, was an atheist. Was she a communist still? After what she had just told him, he wasn't sure.

He took advantage of the peace to try to process what he had just heard, to see if it made sense of what had happened in Annecy. Emma had been betrayed: not just by Roland, but also by Kay and Lothar and the Russian communists. So had her brother Hugh, probably. In turn, Emma had betrayed her country and her husband. It was clear she had unfinished business from that time. It was also clear that was why she and Phil were in West Berlin. Now it seemed that Lothar was dead, it was not clear what that unfinished business was.

It wasn't unfinished business just for Emma. There was also the mole that Swann was trying to track down. And it was no doubt the unfinished business that the KGB or the Stasi were trying to finish to their own satisfaction.

Finding the mole was going to be a lot harder now they knew Lothar was no longer alive. But at least now Phil would be able to tell Swann where Lothar was. Six feet under the ground somewhere in Moscow.

A small blonde girl walked down the aisle and sat in a chair near the front of the hall. It looked just like Heike. It *was* Heike.

Phil's heart beat fast.

'Grams? Will you excuse me a sec?'

Phil walked as coolly and casually as he could down the aisle. 'Heike?'

She turned and then smiled her brilliant smile, her blue eyes sparkling. 'Phil! I'm so pleased to see you.'

'May I join you?'

'Of course.' She shuffled along to the next chair to make room for him.

'What are you doing in Berlin?'

'I was going to travel south from Paris to Avignon. But then I decided to see a bit of my own country. I came to Berlin with my parents as a kid, but I decided to take another look. So here I am. What have you been up to? Did you get to that lake?'

'We did.'

'How was it?'

Phil desperately wanted to tell Heike all about it, but he was aware of his grandmother a few rows behind, no doubt watching them closely.

'It was disappointing,' he said.

'Sorry to hear that. What do you think of Berlin?'

'Fascinating. We saw the Wall this morning. It's seriously weird.'

'I know. It's even weirder if you're German. Knowing that the people on the other side of it are just like you, but are only there because of an accident of geography. And of history, I suppose. Whether they were liberated by the Russians, or the British and Americans.'

Phil thought the use of the word 'liberated' was interesting. The Germans had lost the war: weren't they 'occupied'?

'Let me introduce you to my grandmother. Just don't tell her I said *anything* to you about her or why we're here.'

'Have you figured out why you're here?'

Phil shook his head. 'Not really. I'm getting a few more clues, but it's still a mystery.'

He led Heike back and introduced her to Emma. Fortunately, his grandmother didn't act weird, but gave Heike one of her charming smiles.

'What a coincidence!' she said.

'Yes, it is,' said Heike. 'Extraordinary.'

Emma raised her eyebrows.

Heike noticed, and blushed. She glanced at Phil. 'OK. I admit it. I was rather hoping I would bump into your grandson.'

'Is that why you came to Berlin?' Phil blurted, astonished.

Heike looked sheepish. 'I enjoyed your company. After that arsehole of a boyfriend. Oh! Pardon my language, Frau . . . I'm sorry, I don't know your name.'

Emma grinned. 'It's Meeke. But please call me Emma. I think your interest in my grandson shows extreme good taste.'

Heike smiled with shame and relief. 'Yes. Well. I'm really embarrassed, now. My plan was to play it cool.'

Emma laughed. 'I too tend to embarrass easily. Embarrass other people, that is. It's one of my sins, don't you agree, Philip?'

'I do agree.'

'We're just on our way to the travel agent to get Philip his flight back to London. Would you join us for a cup of coffee?'

'I'd love to,' said Heike.

They dropped into a café on Tauentzienstrasse, one of the streets leading from the Hollow-Tooth Church. Heike did an excellent job of charming Emma, and put up with Emma's interrogation of her about Brunswick and her engineering course at Bonn University. Phil was not at all surprised by how much Emma knew about civil engineering, but it delighted Heike.

Phil arranged to meet Heike at seven that evening, in front of the Hollow-Tooth church.

'What a charming girl,' said Emma as they parted from Heike. 'And she's very pretty.'

'I know,' said Phil, grinning with pleasure. 'I can't understand what she sees in me.'

'No,' said Emma, frowning.

Jesus! thought Phil. Sometimes his grandmother could be so blunt. But he could handle it. He was just looking forward to seeing Heike that evening.

'You haven't told Heike anything about why we are here, have you, Philip?'

'Oh, no, Grams. Certainly not.'

Phil felt slightly guilty as he said this. He was no doubt misleading his grandmother, but compared to the wholesale deceit she was describing to him, it was nothing.

And besides, what threat could a twenty-year-old engineering student pose?

Chapter 43

They bought Phil's one-way British Airways ticket back to London and returned to the Bristol. Emma had a word with the concierge about finding a way to get the TR6 back to England, now Phil wouldn't be around to drive it. The concierge seemed undaunted by the task, and promised to work on it.

There was a message in reception that someone was waiting for them in the bar.

Phil was almost expecting to see Dick, but the man who climbed to his feet when he saw Emma entering the room was much larger. His thinning grey hair was brushed back above a fleshy face and impressive jowls. A three-piece suit fitted snugly over a large stomach, a gold watch chain adorning the waistcoat and a patterned pink silk handkerchief brightening up the jacket. Two pink spots flashed on the man's cheeks as he grinned.

'Emma!'

'Well, Freddie. What a surprise!'

'A nice one, I trust?'

'Oh, a very nice one. This is my grandson, Philip.'

The large man ordered gin and tonics for Phil and himself. Emma stuck to sparkling water.

'Since I found myself in Berlin, I thought I'd drop in on you.'

'Found yourself?' said Emma. 'You don't expect me to believe this is a coincidence?'

Freddie laughed. He had a deep, fruity voice, with just a hint of Irish about it.

'I would travel the length and breadth of Europe for you, Emma.'

'I'm flattered. How are you finding the opposition benches? What is it, a month now?'

'I can't stand that bloody woman,' muttered Freddie. 'I do hope you didn't vote for her.'

'Of course not. But I fear Philip did.'

Freddie looked at Phil. 'I can't understand the young people of today. What happened to the hippies and free love? What was wrong with that? Sounded fun to me. Now look at you – short hair and thin ties, and you all vote for Margaret Thatcher.'

Phil quite enjoyed being teased by an MP. 'Someone's got to drag our country out of the mess it's in. I'm comfortable to stand by my vote.'

'Leave my grandson alone,' said Emma. 'If he wants to vote like a moron, I'll fight to the death for his right to do it.'

'I'll drink to that,' said Freddie, raising his glass. He examined Phil. 'I say. He does look rather a lot like Hugh, doesn't he? A good-looking lad too.'

'Yes, he does,' said Emma, with a small smile of affection. 'I'm glad you see it as well.'

'I never knew Hugh existed, that I had a great-uncle at all,' said Phil, ignoring the attached compliment. 'Grams has been telling me about him; I think I would have liked him. You were friends at school?'

'Yes. We were rebels together. School was quite barbaric in those days. Beating and buggery. We tried to inject a bit of civilization. It's all changed now, thank God. Where did you go?'

'The local grammar school,' said Phil.

This seemed to temporarily nonplus Freddie. 'Ah. Jolly good too. Anyway, Hugh and I published a little magazine. Complaining about the patriotic teaching of history, compulsory Officer Training Corps, precocious criticism of modern poetry and art. It was banned eventually, much to our joy. Then we both went up to Cambridge together: he went to King's, I went to Trinity.'

'And you both became communists?'

Freddie glanced at Emma.

'It was a long time ago,' she said. 'He needed to know. I needed to tell him.'

Freddie hesitated, but decided to answer Phil's question. 'Yes, we did. There was a lot of it about then. And it made some sense. Capitalism had failed the working classes. As far as I am concerned, it still has. I joined the party, and Hugh chose not to. As a matter of fact, it looked as if he was drifting away from communism altogether just before he died.'

It was interesting to Phil to see how Freddie was corroborating Emma's story.

'It's always a tragedy when a young person dies,' Freddie went on. 'But it was a damn shame about Hugh. He was a brilliant man. He could have been a great leader of something. Business, maybe, or even politics. He was applying for the Foreign Office, but he was always a man of independent thought, not someone else's mouthpiece like a diplomat has to be.'

He caught Emma's eye. 'Here's to Hugh.'

'To Hugh,' she said, sipping her water, and Phil raised his glass.

'We saw Dick in Paris,' said Emma. 'I hadn't seen him for years.'

'I bump into him occasionally,' said Freddie. 'Or I did when I was a minister in the MOD. Dick docs a lot of work for defence contractors all around the world. He's well thought of; he's rather good at the management consultancy, which surprises me a little. He was always a clever chap, but I thought writing was more his thing.'

Emma winced. 'Did you ever read his novel?'

'Yes,' said Freddie with a grin. 'Enough said.' He sipped his gin. 'And you saw Cyril?'

'Yes. I wanted to show Philip the embassy. You *have* been checking up on me.' Emma hesitated. 'Did you know Cyril? Back then?'

'Oh, you mean because he and I are confirmed bachelors? Or he was then.'

'Yes. I rather thought you all knew each other.'

'We did bump into each other once or twice,' Freddie admitted. 'Cyril was a good-looking young man. Always elegant.'

'Did you hear about his indiscretions in Paris?'

'Darling, we all have indiscretions in Paris. That's what Paris is for. Berlin too, in the good old days before the Nazis.'

'These were spectacularly indiscreet indiscretions.'

'Blackmail?'

'I'm afraid so.'

'The Russians?'

'The Germans.'

Freddie winced. 'I'm surprised Cyril recovered from that.'

'I believe he redeemed himself during the war,' said Emma.

'Good for him,' said Freddie. 'We all do our best to redeem ourselves. I know I have.' He looked at Emma closely. 'Is that what you are trying to do now? Redeem yourself?'

'How do you mean?' asked Emma.

Freddie didn't answer the question. 'I heard about Kurt Lohmüller,' he said.

'Kurt?' Emma was watchful.

'He died,' said Freddie. 'In Annecy. After you came to see me in London to talk about old times before the war. And after you set off to Europe with young Philip here.'

'Have you been sent here to ask me about him?'

'I have.'

'By whom? MI6? C?'

Freddie grimaced, glancing at Phil. Emma was clearly talking secret stuff Phil wasn't supposed to be hearing. Freddie decided to ignore her question.

'The French police don't know about you. Yet.'

'Will they find out?'

'That depends. Lohmüller was found shot. With a KGB agent, also killed. Were you there? An Englishwoman and a young Englishman were seen the day before, asking about him.'

'We did go and see him. We asked him where we could find Kay Lesser in East Berlin.'

'Did he tell you?'

'He was going to. But he never got the chance.'

'Because he was shot?'

Emma didn't answer.

'Did you see him the day he was killed? You know he was killed?'

'I can't talk about it.'

'Why not?' said Freddie.

'Because it's not wise.'

'What about you?' Freddie asked Phil.

'Same here,' said Phil.

'I see.' Freddie sipped his drink. 'You realize you may have to tell me? Or someone from MI6? Or the French police?'

'No,' said Emma. 'We don't. We won't.'

Freddie raised his eyebrows at Phil.

'And neither will I,' he said, surprised at his own conviction.

Freddie considered this information, but decided not to push them further. 'Next stop East Berlin to look for Kay Lesser?'

'For me,' said Emma. 'Philip is flying back tomorrow.'

'Is East Berlin safe?'

'Probably not. That's why Philip is leaving me.'

'You are a brave woman,' said Freddie. 'You always were.'

Emma went up to her room to rest. Phil opened *War and Peace* in his own bedroom, but he found it impossible to concentrate on the doings of Pierre, Prince Andrei and Natasha.

He had questions for his grandmother.

He gave her an hour and then walked down the hotel corridor to Emma's room, and knocked. She let him in.

Phil sat in one of two armchairs in the room; Emma took the other. Outside, traffic on the Kurfürstendamm rumbled.

'Thank you for backing me up with Freddie,' she said. 'It was good of you not to tell him what you know.'

Phil smiled. 'If you can be stubborn, I can be stubborn too.'

'You are my grandson.' There was a note of pride in Emma's voice, which Phil rather liked.

'Was Freddie a spy for the Russians like you?' he asked. 'And how come he is an MP?'

'I don't think he ever was a spy,' said Emma. 'Although I can't be certain. The NKVD made sure that their spies didn't know of each other's existence. We never met each other, at least not knowingly. Kay broke all the rules when she told me about Kurt.'

'So he could have been a spy?'

'I do know Freddie was a friend of Guy Burgess. And he knew Kim Philby a bit too, at Cambridge; they were both Apostles as well. When Burgess and Maclean fled to Russia, Freddie helped MI5. I think he helped them with Philby. Redeemed himself, as he put it.'

'I get confused,' Phil said. 'What's the difference between MI5 and MI6?'

'MI6 is abroad – they do the spying. MI5 is domestic – they find enemies' spies.'

'And when the enemy's spies turn out to be your spies?'

'Turf war,' said Emma. 'It was because I knew that Freddie was so well plugged into the intelligence services that I spoke to him earlier this year.'

'About Lothar?'

'About my time in Paris and Berlin. He wasn't particularly helpful.'

'Who's "C"?' Phil asked. 'The head of MI6? Or MI5?' It sounded rather like a cross between Ian Fleming's 'M' and John le Carré's 'Control'.

'MI6. I got the definite impression that Freddie had been talking to C. Which surprises me, a little.'

'Why?'

'I don't understand why MI6 would care so much what I was up to.'

So it was Freddie who had tipped off Swann! That was why Swann had approached Phil. Freddie had known what Emma was up to all along.

Phil knew why MI6 cared.

'You're definitely going to East Berlin tomorrow, Grams?'

'Yes. I just got a message from Herr Pöpel; Kay Ortmann lives in Prenzlauer Berg. I've got her address.'

'And you're sure I can't come with you? I'm worried about you.'

'Quite sure, Philip.'

Phil took a deep breath. No point in arguing.

'There's a chance I might not see you again, Grams. After tomorrow. What with one thing and another.' Like you either might die of a brain tumour or the KGB might blow your brains out.

Emma reached out for his hand. 'Yes, I know, darling. It's been wonderful travelling with you this last week. I don't know how I can thank you. Actually, I did have a little idea. I've written a letter to my lawyer telling him that I want you to have the TR6 when I'm gone.'

Phil grinned. The thought made him sad, but happy at the same time. He wanted Emma to see his happiness.

'Dad won't like that,' he said.

Emma laughed. 'I know.'

'Grams. I know you want to be careful about what you tell me, and I understand why. But you *have* to finish your story. There's so much I don't know, stuff that someone needs to know once you're gone. Like did you continue spying for the Russians? What happened between you and Grandpa?' And why we are looking for Kay, he wanted to add, but didn't. He understood now she wasn't going to tell him that.

And besides. He had a little plan.

Emma studied her grandson for a moment. 'All right,' she said. 'I'll finish the story. But promise me you won't tell anyone else about it. And certainly not your friend Heike.'

'I promise,' said Phil.

Chapter 44

June 1939, Berlin

I GOT TO the restaurant first. It was the Taverne, a perpetually crowded Italian restaurant in Kurfürstenstrasse, near the Memorial Church. Ostensibly Italian, but actually it was run by a large German man and his small Belgian wife. It was late, nearly ten o'clock, and I recognized a couple of the American journalists who used to gather there after they had filed their copy to gossip. Gossip in which I had occasionally joined.

I had told Roland where I was going, and whom I was meeting. But I hadn't told my husband what I was going to say.

'I'm sorry I'm late,' said Dick. 'My train just got in half an hour ago. They are not always as punctual as they claim, these Germans, are they?'

'The economy is at full war production, and troops are shuttling around everywhere,' I said. 'Even the famous Deutsche Reichsbahn is stretched.'

We ordered veal, and a bottle of Italian wine.

'How was your pastor?' I asked.

'Wary about any direct questions to do with present-day Germany. But fascinating about his book: *The Cost of Discipleship*. You should read it. I only just caught him – turns out he is on his way to America next week.'

Dick talked animatedly about Dietrich Bonhoeffer and the article he was going to write about him.

'I didn't get a chance to tell you, because you had already left,' I said. 'Roland warned me you should be careful. Bonhoeffer is on the Gestapo's naughty list.'

'I didn't see any signs of trouble,' said Dick. 'As I say, he was very circumspect. Looks like I made it out safely. My train to the Hook of Holland is tomorrow morning.'

I sipped my red wine. It was good. The journalists' *Stammtisch* was filling up, and the noise levels were rising. I recognized Sigrid Schulz from the *Chicago Tribune*, Bill Shirer from CBS and Selkirk Panton from the *Daily Express*, as well as one of the editors of a German newspaper. Sigrid caught my eye and gave me a quick smile. I liked her; ordinarily I would have introduced Dick to the journalists, people were always coming and going at their table eager to share gossip, but I wanted him to myself that evening.

I glanced over my shoulder, the classic *deutsche Blick*, checking for others overhearing us. The tables were crammed close together, but the noise level was high. I knew the Gestapo employed lip-readers, presumably even lip-readers who spoke English, but I doubted they would be bothered to go to that effort for Dick and me. There was something I had to tell him.

'You know Kay told me Hugh was a Russian spy?'

'In Paris? I remember. I found it hard to believe,' Dick said.

'It turns out you were right. Or half right.'

'What do you mean?' Dick leaned forward, interested. I paused for the waiter to serve us our veal.

'Hugh did agree to spy for the Russians, just like Kay said. Or the Comintern. That was why he applied for the Foreign Office. And that was why he told everyone he had changed his mind about communism. He didn't want to arouse suspicions.'

'Right.'

'But the thing is, Hugh really did change his mind. Just before he died. And Kay thinks you and your Ukrainian tutor persuaded him.'

'Really?'

'Kay and Hugh had a big fight about it. Hugh wanted to stop working for the Comintern, and he wanted her to give up as well.'

'But she wouldn't?'

'No.'

'And then Hugh died?'

'Yes.'

Dick's food lay untouched in front of him. He attacked it as he considered what I had been saying. He looked irritated. 'I *told* you I never thought he could be a Russian spy.'

'And I thought he was,' I said. *And became one myself,* I wanted to add, but didn't. 'It's awful. I thought I knew Hugh so well, but even now I'm struggling to discover who he really was. Especially around the time he died.'

'I know what you mean,' said Dick. 'It's very frustrating. If what you say is true, we were both wrong. The poor chap must have been so confused. I wish he had confided in me. Or you.'

'He confided in Kay,' I said.

'How do you know all this?'

'I saw Kay recently. She's moved to Berlin.'

'I say,' Dick said. 'You never took her up on her offer, did you?'

'To work for the Russians? Oh no, of course not. Although I did consider it back in Paris when I was so angry.' I had no intention of telling Dick the truth: that I was working for the Russians and had been for three years. He didn't need to know that; no one did.

And I didn't want to lose him as a friend. If he hadn't approved of Hugh becoming a spy, he certainly wouldn't approve of me doing so too.

'But you still see her?'

'I like her,' I said. 'I was unsure of her at first, as you may remember. But in some ways she is a bit like me. And we both loved Hugh.'

'Does she still think Hugh was killed by the British secret service?'

'She does.'

'Couldn't it have been the Russians? I mean, if he changed his mind about spying for them . . .'

'I know. I asked about that. But she insisted they didn't.'

'And you believe her?'

'I think so. She was very frank with me about everything else. I think she would have told me.'

The alternative was too horrible to contemplate. Not only that both Kay and Lothar had lied to me. Not only that I had spent three years spying for Russia on the assumption that my brother had too.

But that I had spied for the man who had killed him.

A man who was now dead. Shot by the people *he* worked for.

I *wanted* to believe Kay. But how could I be certain she was telling me the truth this time?

'Do you think it was just an accident after all?' Dick said.

'Maybe it was. I suppose I'll never know for sure.'

Dick shook his head. 'This is all very messy. Poor Hugh.'

'It is. I wish he were here so we could talk to him about it.'

Dick nodded. 'So do I.'

'Where are you staying?' I asked after Dick had paid the bill.

'A little hotel in Augsburger Strasse. I think it's quite close.'

'It is,' I said. 'Walking distance. I could walk with you. I've got a favour to ask.'

'Certainly.'

Dick had come to the Taverne straight from the station, so he retrieved his small suitcase from the cloakroom and we headed out into the night. It was spitting lightly, but the cool air felt good after the crowded restaurant.

He lit his pipe. 'What's your favour?'

'I have a message I would like you to deliver. To a man named Heaton-Smith. This is his number.'

I reeled off the Sloane telephone number Heaton-Smith had given me in Paris, which I still remembered three years on.

'Can you memorize that?' I said. 'Don't write it down.'

He repeated it a couple of times. In those days phone numbers were just the exchange plus four digits.

'Make sure you speak to him face to face,' I said.

'And what do I tell him?'

'Give him this.' I handed Dick a sealed envelope.

Dick looked at it. It was unaddressed.

'Are you sure this is a good idea? I mean, I might be searched.'

'When?'

'At the Dutch border. They didn't search me coming into the country, but you never know. They may well know I spoke to Dietrich Bonhoeffer. Perhaps you should just tell me what's in it, and I can tell this Heaton-Smith?'

I felt such an idiot. It was basic tradecraft. Three years of meeting with Lothar and now Kay should have made me more careful.

'Of course. You're right. Give me that back.' Dick handed the envelope back to me and I stuffed it in my handbag.

We were on a side street not far from Augsburger Strasse. 'Slow down,' I said. 'And I'll tell you. It's about Russia. And Germany.'

I repeated what Kurt had told me. I didn't give Dick Kurt's name, but I did tell him to let Heaton-Smith know my information came from the same source as Paris. Heaton-Smith would realize that meant Kurt.

Dick listened closely, taking it all in. At the end, I asked him to repeat the telephone number, which he did correctly.

'Why don't you tell your husband?' he asked. 'Surely this is something he would be very interested in.'

'Because he would have to tell the ambassador,' I replied. 'And Henderson will want to either suppress the information or pooh-pooh it, and Roland will have to follow his ambassador's instructions. Whereas Heaton-Smith will know who will actually do something. He has proved himself before.'

We arrived at Dick's hotel.

I didn't want to let him go. I was leading a ridiculous life with a husband whom I didn't love and who had betrayed me horribly. I was betraying my own country for a group of people whom I had trusted and shouldn't have.

I still didn't know what had happened to Hugh and why.

There was no one I could trust. Kay perhaps, but who was to say that Kay wasn't lying to me now?

Just the tall man with the kind blue eyes standing in front of me now.

I threw myself into his arms. He pulled me close and squeezed. It was immensely comforting.

I looked up into his face, which was full of concern for me.

I wanted to kiss him. But what if he rejected me? I couldn't bear that. My life was too complicated as it was.

So I pushed myself away from him, turned and walked rapidly up the street.

It had felt so good, those few seconds when I had been enveloped in his arms. It was years since anyone had held me like that, and that had been Roland.

I shuddered.

Why should I let my marriage to Roland stop me from having the comfort I craved? Even the love I craved?

Dick might reject me. But I would take the risk. I had to take the risk.

I took several deep breaths and turned back towards the hotel.

Three men in raincoats were walking purposefully into the building. I had been in Berlin long enough to know who they were.

Gestapo.

I stepped away from the yellow glow of the lamppost into the shadow of a doorway, and watched.

A couple of minutes later, the three men appeared. One was carrying a suitcase, the other two leading someone between them. I couldn't see clearly, but I could tell from his height and build and the shape of his hat who the man they were escorting was.

Dick.

Chapter 45

I WAVED DOWN a passing taxi and went straight home. Roland had gone to bed, but I woke him.

'Emma! What's the matter?'

'It's Dick. He's been arrested.'

'By the Gestapo?'

'Looked like it. Men in raincoats.'

'Did he see Bonhoeffer?'

'Yes, he did.'

Roland swung his legs out of bed and quickly flung on some clothes. 'Don't worry,' he said. 'I'll sort it out.'

'Where are you going?'

'Prinz-Albrecht-Strasse. Gestapo headquarters.'

I changed into my pyjamas, but I couldn't go to sleep. Usually it was the consul's job to spring errant Englishmen from jail, not the first secretary's, but I knew Roland was formidable with bureaucrats, even Nazi ones.

But why had Dick been arrested? Presumably it had been because of his interview with the clergyman. Was there any way that the Gestapo could have suspected what I had told him about Kurt and the German talks with Russia? Were they on to Kurt too?

If they had somehow got wind of that, then they would beat it out of Dick, or at least try to. I was confident Dick would keep quiet, at least for a while. Although the Gestapo's interrogation methods were notorious in Germany, Dick was a British citizen, and Roland would be there to protect him.

I was so glad that Dick had refused to accept the envelope I had thrust in his hands. Whatever reason the Gestapo had for arresting him, they would have been sure to read any correspondence on his person and to have been very interested in the contents. Not only that, but it would also have immediately condemned Dick as a spy. And me, for that matter.

It had been about midnight when I returned home and woke Roland. It was four fifteen when the telephone rang.

'It's me,' said Roland. He sounded exhausted.

'How is he?' I asked.

'He's all right. They haven't touched him. I think they just wanted to put the wind up him for meeting Bonhoeffer. To discourage other English journalists from coming here and trying similar tricks. They didn't expect anyone from the embassy to turn up so quickly.'

'Have they released him?'

'They will. I'm waiting for him now. Don't worry – I won't leave here without him. I've negotiated that we go straight to Zoo Station from here. I'll put him on the train to the Hook of Holland.'

'Thank God for that.'

Three days later, I received a telegram from Dick from London: *FLOWERS DELIVERED SAFELY. PLS THK ROLAND. DICK.*

I thanked Roland.

Two months after that, on 23 August, the Molotov–Ribbentrop Pact was signed. Initially it seemed that the pact simply pledged that the Soviet Union and Germany would not attack each other. On 1 September, Germany invaded Poland. On 3 September, Britain and France declared war on Germany. On 4 September, Roland, Caroline, I and the rest of the embassy staff left Berlin by train to the Hague, and from there we were packed on to a boat to Gravesend and another train to Victoria.

On 17 September, as anticipated in a secret protocol of the pact, the Soviet Union invaded eastern Poland and grabbed a large chunk of their territory. On 30 November Russia attacked Finland, and in June 1940 she invaded Latvia, Estonia and Lithuania.

As Kurt had warned me, the Soviet Union had teamed up with the Nazis to carve up north-eastern Europe, and everything I had done for them over the last three years was betrayed.

Chapter 46

September 1939, London

ROLAND, CAROLINE AND I took up residence in my family's town house in Mayfair; Mama had scarpered to Devon. A heady mixture of fear, panic and excitement overcame London. The population was diligent in taping up windows, digging up parks, carrying around gas masks and preparing for the hail of bombs that never came. Children were carried off to the countryside and soldiers were transported in aimless circles around the country. Newspapers were read from cover to cover and every story was discussed at breakfast tables, St James's clubs and pubs. The blackout was imposed and London's first casualties of the war were sustained: cars pranged into lampposts and pedestrians flattened.

Kay had given me instructions to meet a new handler in London involving park benches in Regent's Park, but I had no intention of following them, and Kay knew it. She said that the London branch of the Comintern was a shambles since all its controllers had been recalled to Moscow to be liquidated. I had continued to give Kay snippets of embassy gossip in Berlin, mostly relating to Britain's pointless negotiations with Russia. We agreed it was best for the long-term health of both of us if Moscow continued to see me providing Kay with information, and Kay passing it on.

Kay was in real danger of being recalled to Moscow and suffering Lothar's fate. Since meeting Lothar in the Bois de Boulogne, I had been very aware of the danger to myself from the

British secret service and even the French and German authorities. To them was now added the Comintern, or rather the NKVD, the very people for whom I was doing all this.

After what I had learned about Hugh and Lothar, and following the signature of the Molotov–Ribbentrop pact, I was finished with spying for Russia. I knew it and Kay knew it, but neither of us said anything about it. War was coming, and with it, my time in Berlin would come to a natural end. What Kay would do, I didn't know and we didn't discuss.

I was looking forward to returning to England for many reasons. It was only when I arrived in London that I realized which was the most pressing. To see Dick again.

We had corresponded after his return, but only a few times, and our letters were friendly but more restrained than I would have liked. Dick had attempted to join the RAF but failed, due to some minor problem with his eyes. His next stop was the army, but he had received a summons from the new Ministry of Information, where a clique of his friends was gathering. He wrote to me that he was in two minds about accepting it. On the one hand, he wanted to fight for his country against the Nazis. On the other, he thought of himself as a pacifist who believed war was wrong. Fighting with words was a compromise. I could tell he wasn't really happy about it, though.

I read and reread his letters to me in Berlin, until I knew every word by heart. They were full of friendship and affection.

By now I knew I wanted more.

The day after we arrived at the house in Hill Street, I sent him a note asking him to telephone me. This he did. We arranged to have dinner the following week at Simpson's in Piccadilly.

I didn't tell Roland.

Dick seemed pleased to see me, and in good spirits all around. He described how he had passed my message on to the mysterious Mr Heaton-Smith at a pub in Pimlico. Heaton-Smith had been duly grateful, but we agreed it didn't seem to have made a blind bit of difference to Britain's diplomacy. It probably hadn't been believed. After subtle probing on my part, Roland had revealed that the Foreign Office hadn't received any warning as early as the end of June when Dick had met the MI6 officer. I wondered whether I should have told Roland myself; perhaps he could have found a way around the ambassador after all. But then Kurt had made me promise I wouldn't, and, strangely, I trusted that German diplomat more than the British.

Dick and I agreed that the Soviet Union had proved herself utterly untrustworthy.

Dick regaled me with stories of the hapless Ministry of Information, which was based at the University of London in Bloomsbury. He mentioned a number of names I had heard of, writers whose books I had read or whom I had seen reviewed. But I could tell there was something wrong.

'You would like to be fighting, wouldn't you?'

'I don't know,' said Dick. 'Maybe. I am jealous of all those other fellows who are putting on uniforms and square bashing. Oh, I know war isn't glorious. But this time, we are truly fighting against evil. Or they are. I'm coming up with slogans about potatoes.'

'Can you leave?'

'Not right away. I'll give it a couple of months and see.'

Simpson's was crowded, and the menu was still pretty good. We had both ordered partridge: it was shooting season in the fields and copses of the country's estates, estates like Chaddington, even if it wasn't in France. Yet.

'It's good to see you,' Dick said.

The time had come to say what I was going to say. I assumed lots of women, married women perhaps especially, would know exactly how to proposition a young man. I was sure that my mother, for example, was an expert at it. But if there were such things as 'feminine wiles', I didn't have any.

'Dick?' I said.

'Yes?'

'Do you think we could find a hotel after dinner?'

I had expected one of two reactions. A smile of happiness, perhaps a complicit good-humoured laugh, and then an equally good-humoured discussion of the practicalities. That's what I had hoped for, and what over the previous week I had persuaded myself I was most likely to receive. But I also knew there was a chance of a kind, gentle but firm rejection. If that happened, I would accept it, and Dick and I would remain good friends.

What I got was something quite different. A look combining shock and surprise. Dick's mouth opened, and then he closed it again.

I felt instantly humiliated. What had I been thinking? I had assumed that Dick would be a man of the world like all the other men of the world I knew, or at least like Roland.

But Dick *wasn't* a man of the world.

'But I thought . . .' he stammered. 'I thought you had decided to stay with Roland. That's what you told me in Berlin.'

'Yes, I know. And I have. But . . . It seemed . . . Everyone else . . .' I was floundering badly.

'Oh, Emma. I'm sorry. I'm so sorry.'

'No, it's I who should be sorry.'

'Emma, I'm engaged.'

'Engaged? To be married? To whom?' This was an eventuality that hadn't occurred to me.

'To Frances.'

'Frances? American Frances? The one I introduced you to in Paris?'

'That's right. We've been writing to each other. She came over here for the summer to stay with an aunt.'

'But why didn't you tell me?'

'I'm telling you now.'

'But why not before?'

'We only got engaged last week. It was either that or she was going to have to go back to Philadelphia.'

271

'But . . . Oh! I've made such a chump of myself!'

'No, you haven't. I'm sorry if I have led you on.'

'Oh, Dick! You have been a perfect gentleman – always. It's me making an idiot of myself. I always make an idiot of myself.'

'Here. Don't worry about it. Have some more wine.'

He reached for the bottle. But the humiliation was boiling up inside me. I couldn't stop it. I couldn't bottle it up. I couldn't take back what I had said.

'I'm sorry, Dick. I have to leave.'

To my surprise, Roland was home when I got back. I had expected him to be at the Travellers.

'You're early,' he said.

I ignored him and rushed up to my room. It was *my* bedroom, the one I had used as a child whenever the family decamped to Hill Street. Roland was in my parents' bedroom, alone.

I slammed the door, threw myself on to my bed and wept.

How could I have been so stupid! To throw myself at Dick like that. To give all those secrets to a foreign country, betraying my own. For someone who considered herself to be reasonably intelligent, I was a chump. A perfect chump.

There was a knock on the bedroom door.

I ignored it.

Another knock.

'Go away, Roland!'

The door opened.

'I said go away!'

But he sat on the bed next to me. My face was buried in my pillow, but I could feel his weight.

'Were you seeing a man?' Roland said.

I had simply told him I was having dinner with a friend. I hadn't specified the sex. For the first time, it occurred to me that part of me had wanted to make Roland jealous. What was the point of that? Idiot!

I nodded, my head moving up and down deep in the pillow.

'And it didn't go well?'

I nodded again.

'Move over,' he said, tapping my knees.

I bunched them up, and he shifted to the end of my bed.

I sat up. It was ridiculous. Me sitting at one end of my childhood bed, crying, and my husband at the other. My husband whom I hated.

'I love you,' he said.

'What's that supposed to mean?'

'I love you.'

'Don't be ridiculous!'

But I looked up at him. Those deep, dark brown eyes were gazing at me with something that looked to me a lot like love.

'I don't believe you.'

'Well, it's true. And it's a problem.'

'Oh. Because I don't love you,' I said sarcastically.

'Don't you?'

'Of course not.'

Roland gazed at me steadily. 'I think you do.'

'You're mad.'

'I didn't realize it at the time, but I think I loved you from the moment I saw you. Or pretty soon afterwards.'

'You definitely are mad.' But I was watching him closely, my chin on my raised knees.

'Over the last five years, I have got to know you really well, and the more I see of you, and the more I know you, the more I love you.'

Why is he doing this? I thought. Why is he going all out with his seduction technique? But I listened.

'I love your enthusiasm for life, I love your intelligence, I love the way you think, I love your sense of humour, I love your kindness. And I love your eyes. Your smile. Your body.'

'Don't you say this to all your women?'

'No, Emma. No, I don't. Because I didn't love any of them. Extraordinary as it may seem, you are the only woman I have ever loved. Sometimes I think you are the only woman I ever can love. Which, as I say, is a bit of a problem.'

'I'll say,' I said. But then the obvious question flashed in my mind. 'Even . . .?'

Roland nodded. 'Even her. Oh, I was infatuated with her. At the time I thought I loved her, but I didn't really. I know that now. Because of you.'

Golly, Roland was good at this stuff. I could feel myself slipping. I shored up my defences. 'What about the other women?'

'There haven't been any other women.'

I stayed silent.

Roland looked away. Then he looked straight at me. 'Not for two years. And not *her*. Not since you found out about us. Not her.'

'And the other women? More than two years ago. Who were they?'

'I paid for them. Like you suggested.'

'And then you stopped?'

'I stopped. I was ashamed. All those affairs with married women I had in my twenties. I don't know what I was doing, what I was looking for. But I do know what I am looking for now. I wanted to win you back. And I knew it would take some time. But the time is now.'

'You want me to take you back? But don't we live together anyway? Isn't that good enough?'

'Not as man and wife. Yes, at first I wanted you to take me back. But now I realize what I want is for you to answer that question.'

'What question?'

'Do you love me?'

I had forbidden myself from asking myself that question ever since Kay had told me that Roland was having an affair with my mother. But over the years I had grown used to Roland. He had been considerate. He had been respectful. He had been under-standing. He had even been affectionate in as open a way as I would let him, which was not very open. He was reliable. I trusted him. Grudgingly, I admired him. He was always there. Despite myself, I loved our conversations.

I remembered the flash of jealousy I had felt when that blonde German girl had stared at him.

He *was* very good-looking.

I remembered how he had sent my heart into palpitations when I had first met him. I remembered the ride up to Dartmoor, the way he had treated me so seriously. Later, I had assumed that was all for show. But I knew some of it, at least, was real.

Now I was no longer spying for the Russians, there was no reason to remain with Roland. I could walk out and leave him tomorrow.

Or I could stay.

'Don't ask me to forgive you,' I said.

'I'm not asking you to forgive me. I hope you will one day, but I'm not asking you.'

'Because I can never forgive you.'

Roland swallowed. 'I understand,' he said. 'But do you love me?'

The dam was cracked. The dam of my justified suspicion and mistrust, which I had shored up over the last three years, broke.

'Yes, Roland.' I smiled. 'Yes. I love you.'

I said it not because he had sweet-talked me into saying it, but because I knew it was true, and I couldn't hide it from myself any more, and I didn't want to hide it from him.

He leaned over and kissed me – gently at first.

Then I grabbed him, and he was mine and I was his.

Chapter 47

June 1979, West Berlin

'So, you and Grandpa got back together?'

'Yes, we did,' said Emma with a smile. 'You were right. It's important I told you about that. I know you liked him.'

'I did. I was very fond of him.'

'So was I,' said Emma. 'Oh, I don't want to say it was all plain sailing, especially at first. I found it very hard to trust him; I had second thoughts a couple of weeks later and we parted for a bit before I had third thoughts and we got back together. I always found it hard to forgive him what he did with my mother. But I did love him.' She smiled. 'And he loved me. I know he did.'

'But no more children?'

'No. At first I didn't want any more. It took me a while to believe that Roland would always be around. And then . . . Then it just didn't happen.'

'I'm sorry.'

'We had Caroline. The rest you know. Roland became a successful career diplomat and I was a dutiful diplomat's wife. Roland was knighted; we retired to Cornwall; you and Mel came on the scene.' She paused. 'Roland died. And now I'm going to die.'

Phil resisted the urge to contradict his grandmother. She *was* going to die. Soon.

'One last thing you need to know about Roland,' Emma said with a wicked smile. 'The sex was good. Very good.'

'Grams! Did I really need to know that?' Phil protested.

276

'Someone did. And like it or not, that someone is you. Now be off with you! But don't tell Heike any of this – you promise?'

'I promise.'

Phil knew, as soon as they sat down in the Turkish restaurant in Kreuzberg, that Heike wanted to sleep with him.

It was the way she talked, the way her eyes flashed, the way she touched his hand unnecessarily. There was an enthusiasm about her, a determination, that she hadn't displayed before.

It made Phil nervous. Nervous that he would screw it up and put her off. Nervous that he wouldn't put her off, and then screw it up.

It also made him excited.

She talked a lot, very fast, and Phil struggled to keep up with her German, but she was patient when he admitted defeat, repeating things slowly for his benefit. She was funny; *he* was funny, or at least she seemed to think so. They drank a bottle of Turkish red wine and then ordered another. The food was delicious – skewers of lamb on a stick, known as a *kebap*. Phil had never been to a Turkish restaurant before. Apparently there were loads of Turkish guest workers in West Berlin, and Kreuzberg was where many of them lived.

'My grandmother was telling me about coming here before the war,' Phil said. 'She had a friend who lived around here somewhere. Above a printer's shop.'

'I'd have thought this would have been a bit scruffy for diplomats, even then,' said Heike.

'Oh, her friend wasn't a diplomat.'

'What was she?'

Phil didn't want to sound evasive, although remembering his promise to his grandmother, he didn't want to say too much. 'She was American. A student, I think. Not much money, at any rate. Grams had known her in Paris.'

'Oh. Was that the woman you mentioned before? The one who asked your *Oma* to spy for the Russians?'

277

Phil hesitated before answering. 'It may be,' he said, with an attempt at indifference. He had forgotten how much he had told Heike in Paris.

'Your grandfather was a diplomat in the British Embassy here?'

'Yes. Just for a year. Until war broke out.'

'It must have been wild then. All those Nazis.' Heike shuddered. 'Not our greatest moment.'

'No.' But Phil didn't want to refight the war with Heike. 'West Germany seems to me to have done an excellent job of becoming a democracy.'

'I suppose we have,' said Heike. 'But I sometimes wish we had chosen a more socialist path. You said your grandmother actually spied for the Russians?'

Phil remembered he had said that. He couldn't deny it now, no matter what he had promised Emma.

'That's what she told me.'

'She can't have been happy living here with the Nazis?'

'No. I don't think many British people were then. Apart from the ambassador at the time. He liked them, apparently.'

'You know, my grandfather was killed by the Nazis? In Dachau in 1938.'

'I didn't realize you were Jewish?' Phil said.

'It wasn't only the Jews who died in the concentration camps,' said Heike. 'My grandfather was a member of the KPD, the German Communist Party. The Nazis locked him up. He was only forty when he died. They said he fell over and hit his head, but of course nobody believes that.'

'I'm sorry.'

'He was a very brave man; I would have liked to have met him.' Heike sighed. 'I wonder if I had been alive then whether I would have looked to the Soviet Union for support against Hitler. Like your grand-mother did. I like to think I would. I can't believe I wouldn't have seen through him.'

Phil was severely tempted to tell Heike all about Emma's flirtation with communism, and he couldn't for the life of him see what harm it would do. But he had promised.

'I think she thought Russia was just as bad,' he said. 'She saw through Stalin.' Eventually.

'I liked her,' Heike said. 'She is really smart, isn't she? You can almost see her brain fizzing.'

'I know.' Phil laughed. 'She certainly keeps me on my toes.'

'Are you going to East Berlin?'

'She is. I'm going home tomorrow.'

'That's a shame.' Heike's eyes betrayed disappointment. But also something else.

Desire.

'Yes,' said Phil. 'That is a shame.'

Heike was staying in a friend's squat close by. Apparently Kreuzberg was full of squats. Phil had never seen a squat before, and yes, he would like to see Heike's friend's place.

It was the ground floor of what had once been a workshop of some kind, perhaps even a print shop. The walls were covered in graffiti, the windows draped with makeshift curtains of blankets and even newspaper.

The interior design was open-plan: sleeping bags on the floor. After briefly introducing Phil to a couple of long-haired guys sharing a joint, Heike took him through to a small room at the back of the space in which lay two mattresses. On one of them, a pretty dark-haired girl was reading a book by the light of an Anglepoise lamp resting on the floor.

'Hi,' she said, giving Phil a friendly smile, and without another word, she gathered up her book and left them.

'That was nice of her,' said Phil.

'She's a nice girl,' said Heike.

Then she reached up and kissed him.

Two hours later, Heike flicked the edge of the blanket that acted as a curtain and watched the English boy's silhouette as it disappeared down the pavement. She couldn't help smiling to herself when she saw him take a little skip.

Naked, she lit a cigarette and sat on the mattress.

She never liked doing this kind of stuff. In many ways this had been so much better than the last time she had slept with an Englishman – a forty-five-year-old married RAF officer who turned out to have a well-suppressed fetish for blonde German women, the SS and whips. That had been deeply unpleasant.

Yet in some ways this had been harder. In her job, it was better not to become emotionally involved. That had been dead easy with the RAF officer. But it was difficult to seduce someone like Phil without opening up something of yourself, without becoming emotionally involved. She had known it would be his first time, and it was. He was overenthusiastic, but he had a certain natural talent. Heike grinned to herself.

He hadn't told her very much, at least not at first. Nothing about Annecy at all. It wasn't even clear whether Phil and his grandmother had come across the dead bodies of Marko and Kurt Lohmüller. The KGB didn't know what had happened. They assumed that there had been some kind of shootout between Lohmüller and Marko, although how Marko had managed to get himself into that situation with a target in his seventies was beyond Heike. That guy really had been incompetent.

His replacement as Heike's boss, Rozhkov, was older and tougher. Heike was happier with that; she knew where she was with men like him. She knew she shouldn't care, but she hoped that Phil wouldn't end up dead like Marko. She had no doubt that Rozhkov would order his killing if necessary; she just hoped it wouldn't be necessary.

And she liked the sound of Phil's grandmother. A woman who had understood that, with capitalism broken and Fascism on the rampage in Europe, communism was the only way to go. Heike had been telling the truth about her grandfather dying in Dachau; she had hoped to tempt Phil into opening up about his grandmother. It had nearly worked, she was sure.

Her grandfather was really why she was doing all this, lying on her back for the cause. Her father had clung to his own father's beliefs during the war, and afterwards, in the Russian sector of Berlin. Her mother was convinced that the West had rejected solidarity with the poor and the working classes, and that that would eventually destroy them. Heike was seeing a lot more of the West than her parents had ever done, and although she found some of the wealth and the good things seductive, she knew those were only available for the rich. She was glad she lived on the right side of the Wall: the side where the people took priority over the rich and powerful.

It was her cause, her family's cause, her country's cause, and she would continue to do what was necessary for it.

She had a report to make, and it couldn't wait. She made a quick phone call: unlike a real squat, this building still had a phone line. She pulled on some clothes and let herself out into the dark street, searching for a passing cab to take her to Rozhkov's apartment.

She had something to report. Finally, she had broken down Phil's defences. After the sex, she had playfully talked about Phil's grandmother spying again, and whether she was going to East Berlin to meet an agent, but Phil had steadfastly refused to rise to the bait. He had explained that he had promised Emma that he wouldn't repeat any of what she had told him about her time as a spy to Heike. He was feeling bad about what he had already said.

Heike had withdrawn, offended, muttering something about how ridiculous that was. Phil had touched her thigh, but she had stiffened and he had removed his hand.

Then she had made her breakthrough.

'Of course, she didn't say anything about not telling you things she knows nothing about,' he had said.

Heike turned to face him. 'Like what?'

'Like a strange man in a pub back in England asking me to look out for a mole.'

'What's a mole?' Phil had used the German word, *Maulwurf.*

'It's spy slang for an agent who burrows into an enemy country's intelligence agency or government. Kim Philby was a famous one, but there were others in Britain. I don't know about West Germany.'

'That's exciting!' said Heike, touching him. 'Have you found this mole?'

'No. I was told not to ask Grams directly. I hoped that it would become clear through her stories.'

'And has it?'

'Not really. Maybe Grams will find something out tomorrow, in East Berlin.'

'But you won't be there.'

Phil hadn't answered her. Just before he had walked off into the night, she had asked him if there was any way he could stay in Berlin instead of flying back to London. She wanted to see him again.

He had smiled. 'Maybe. Do you have a phone here?'

She had given him the number, resolving to ensure someone stayed at the squat for the next couple of days to be there to take a message if he called.

'I might call you tomorrow,' he said. 'I have a little idea.'

Chapter 48

Phil struggled to wake up the following morning. Emma was quiet at breakfast in the Hotel Bristol. She asked cursorily whether he had had a good time last night. She was thoughtful; she seemed anxious, scared even. And well she should.

Her fear made Phil feel happier with the decision he had taken on his way back to the Bristol the night before, although that decision made it more difficult to say goodbye. He went upstairs to his room to pack; he stuffed the clothes he had originally brought with him into his rucksack and rolled the new clothes they had bought together in Paris into a couple of laundry bags for Emma to add to her luggage. Her plan was that he should check out and take a taxi for the airport, and then she would set out for a day trip to East Berlin to meet Kay, returning to the Hotel Bristol that evening.

Phil had a different plan.

They stood together in the lobby, Emma having paid Phil's room bill.

'Thank you so much for coming with me, Philip,' she said, her face stern, her tone matter-of-fact, despite her words. 'I don't know what I would have done without you.' She hesitated. 'You saved my life. I shall miss you.'

'I shall miss you too, Grams,' Phil repeated, somewhat lamely.

Then her reserve crumbled, and she threw herself at him, burying her head in his chest. He put his arms around her.

After a little while she stepped back. 'All right. Have a good trip back. And give my love to your mother and your sister. Oh, and your father.' This with a smile.

'Bye, Grams.'

Phil turned and left the hotel. Emma had got the doorman to procure a taxi, and it was waiting for him.

'Tegel?' asked the driver.

'No, I don't think so,' said Phil. 'I've changed my mind. Where is a good place I can store this rucksack for the day?'

'Zoo Station has left luggage.'

Zoo Station was only a couple of minutes away. The taxi driver waited while Phil dumped his rucksack, and then took him eastwards to Friedrichstrasse and the Wall.

The Wall actually ran west to east at this point, Friedrichstrasse bisecting it south to north. Checkpoint Charlie was the crossing place for foreigners entering East Berlin; it was situated between the American sector and the southern edge of Mitte, the former city centre around Unter den Linden, which was now in the Russian sector. On the Allied side, the checkpoint comprised a hut, some sandbags and two signs: one declaring 'Allied Checkpoint' and another announcing 'You are leaving the American sector' in English and then repeated in Russian, French and German. An American military policeman waved Phil through.

He walked past a red-and-white-striped barrier and over the narrow strip of no-man's-land to the more extensive obstacles on the other side. Watchtowers overlooked a large shed where the border formalities took much longer. An East German border guard in a forbidding grey-green uniform took Phil's passport. The guard checked him for guns, ammunition and printed papers; the *Hitch-Hiker's Guide* had warned him of this, and so Phil had reluctantly left the book with his rucksack at the station, having memorized all it had to say about East Berlin. He was required to change six Deutschmarks fifty for a similar number of flimsier East German marks. The five-mark note he received bore a picture of some sixteenth-century preacher in a floppy hat: not very communist, although on the back a combine harvester did its stuff for agrarian productivity. Tourists were supposed to spend all their currency during the day – it could not be exchanged on return to the West.

Phil then spent forty minutes hanging around the northern, East German section of Friedrichstrasse, waiting for Emma and avoiding the occasional suspicious glance from the border guards. If someone was watching him more discreetly, he couldn't tell.

Eventually he saw her tall figure marching along the street towards him. She hailed a taxi, and Phil moved quickly. The taxi was tiny, with no rear doors, so as Emma climbed in over the passenger seat, Phil bundled in after her.

'Philip!' she said.

'That's me,' said Phil, grinning.

'What on earth are you doing here?' she demanded.

'I couldn't let you do this by yourself,' Phil said.

'But I expressly forbade you from coming with me. It's not safe, Philip!'

'I know. That's why I'm here, Grams. I can help. You know I can help.'

'But I don't want you to!' said Emma, genuinely angry now. 'I insist you get out of this taxi.'

'No,' said Phil. 'I'm with you on this, Grams. Wherever it takes you.' He smiled. 'You'd have done the same when you were my age. You can't deny it.'

'Excuse me, comrades,' said the driver in German. 'Where do you want to go?'

'One moment,' said Emma. She looked at Phil. 'Oh, all right,' she said. She smiled back at him, reluctantly at first, but then resorted to a full beam of relief. 'Prenzlauer Berg,' she said to the driver. 'And take us along Unter den Linden.'

The taxi was tiny, with an engine that sounded like a lawnmower. The driver was large and spoke with the by-now recognizable Berliner accent.

'Is this car made of plastic?' Phil said, tapping the roof. It was very different from the Mercedes in which he had arrived at Checkpoint Charlie. The little vehicle was, however, identical to almost every other car on the road.

In a couple of minutes they turned right on to a grand, broad street of old imperial buildings interspersed with more modern structures.

And a dual line of small trees running down its centre – lindens, no doubt. Above and a little to the left rose a tall needle with a large ball two-thirds of the way up. A TV tower, Phil remembered from the *Hitch-Hiker's Guide*.

'That's the Stabi,' Emma said, pointing to an imposing grey stone facade, through whose arches Phil could just see a courtyard with a fountain.

Phil looked around eagerly. He had never been in a communist country before. Some things were different: the modern, dreary blocks, the tiny cars, the TV tower watching over everything as if monitoring the movements of the East Berliners below. But the people appeared pretty much the same, although very few wore jeans. And, frankly, a lot of the modern architecture in West Berlin was pretty dire too.

'It's not *that* different to West Berlin,' Phil said.

'It's very different from Berlin in 1939, believe me,' said Emma. 'Then there were giant red swastika flags hanging from the buildings, and men in uniform marching everywhere. And no trees.'

'No trees?'

'Hitler tore them down to build the S-Bahn.'

That explained why the new lindens were so small.

They passed through a large square, Alexanderplatz, which had become the centre of East Berlin. A group of workers in hard hats beamed down on them with unbridled joy from a massive poster. The address Emma had given the driver turned out to be a five-storey block of flats, built since the war, opposite a row of older tenement buildings that had survived the bombing and the Red Army.

A column of buzzers guarded the door to the building.

Emma hesitated. 'I don't want you to listen to this.'

'Too late,' Phil said.

'I will have to talk about things I have kept from you up till now. Things which will be dangerous for you to know.' Emma paused, relief at his presence mixing with worry for her grandson. 'She might not even let us in.'

'Then we'll think of another way to talk to her.'

'All right.' Emma pressed the buzzer.

'*Hallo?*'

'Oh, hello, Kay,' Emma replied in English. 'It's Emma. Can I come in?'

'Emma Meeke?'

'Yes.'

There was silence, or rather a hum of static. It seemed to go on forever, but Emma waited. Whether to let these strangers from the West in was a difficult decision for a former agent of the Stasi.

Phil checked the short street for watchers; it seemed to him to be empty now their taxi had driven off. You could still see the tall needle of the TV tower from Prenzlauer Berg. There was a distinct smell of cabbage in the air.

He realized that he would have no chance of spotting professional surveillance in a strange city.

'I've come a long way,' Emma said.

'UK,' said the voice. 'Come on up. Fourth floor. Apartment twenty-seven.'

Chapter 49

Kay's apartment turned out to be the third floor, but then Kay was American, Phil remembered.

Number 27 was opened by a tall, striking woman with silver hair cut short above her ears. She was wearing a necklace of heavy green stones and large hooped earrings. She didn't look happy to see Emma.

'Hello, Kay,' Emma said. 'Can I come in?'

Kay hesitated, and then let them into the small apartment, which had a dreary view over the tenements opposite. The bookshelves were groaning with titles, mostly in German. A large black-and-white framed photograph of skyscrapers dominated one wall. Chicago, presumably. But that was the only hint that one of the occupants was American, not East German.

'You are lucky that my husband isn't here,' she said. 'He's just left for lunch with some of his old colleagues from the Stasi.'

'I assume he's retired?' Emma said, as if discussing a bank manager.

'Oh, yes. But you know what they say? Once a secret policeman, always a secret policeman.' Her accent was American, but with a certain clipped Germanic tinge.

It seemed to Phil that Kay wasn't exactly being friendly. He remembered what Herr Pöpel had said about the reputation of her husband: *Not a nice man, but by no means the worst.* And Emma was trusting his wife?

'And you?' said Emma, taking a seat on a brown sofa. 'Have you retired?'

Kay permitted herself a wry smile. 'Oh, yes.'

'But you were still working when we met in Brussels in 1965?'

Phil tried not to show surprise; he hadn't realized Emma had met Kay since the war. One of those pieces of information Emma had omitted to tell him that were now coming out. He anticipated more.

'Only a little. Helping my husband, who was a commercial attaché at the East German Embassy. I was a diplomatic wife then. A bit like you.'

'I heard you were also stationed in Budapest? Kurt Lohmüller told me he met you there a few years ago.'

'Yes, he did,' said Kay. 'How is Kurt?'

It seemed to Phil that Kay's ignorance of Kurt's fate was genuine, but then presumably Kay was an experienced and skilful liar.

As was his grandmother, it turned out. 'He's quite frail at the moment,' she said. 'I'm not sure he has long to live.'

'That's a shame. I liked him,' said Kay in her first sign of unbending.

'It's good to see you, Kay,' said Emma.

Kay gave a quick smile but didn't repeat the sentiment.

'Why are you here?' she said. 'You know I will have to report your visit? I doubt it will reflect well on me.'

'Oh, yes. I am sorry, Kay. I'm here to talk to you about Lothar. Do you know where he is?'

'Lothar? But he's dead.'

That's what Phil thought too.

Emma frowned. 'But you told me in Brussels that you had seen him. On an operation in Geneva a few years before. Must have been the early sixties. You said he was an art dealer operating under an assumed name.'

'Ah, yes, I did, didn't I? But I was mistaken.'

'How could you be mistaken about that?'

'Easily. This man looked a lot like Lothar, or what you might expect Lothar to look like in his sixties. We learned later it wasn't him. It was just an Austrian art dealer.'

'I don't believe you, Kay.'

Kay shrugged. It was a shrug that said: I don't care what you believe. I may be lying to you, but so what?

'I've been thinking a lot about Lothar recently,' said Emma. 'And about Hugh.'

Kay listened.

'It makes no sense at all that the British government would have killed Hugh, even if they suspected him of being a spy. That's just not the way they behave. They might have arrested him, or they might have tried to turn him, or they might simply have watched him, but they wouldn't have executed him.'

'How can you know?' Kay asked.

'I was a senior diplomat's wife. Over the years I have met people I can ask. I asked them, not specifying Hugh of course. And they all said the same thing. The British didn't kill spies on their own territory. They didn't kill Hugh.'

Kay didn't reply.

'Which means Lothar did,' said Emma. 'Or if not Lothar, then someone working for him. You know that, don't you?'

'Lothar didn't kill Hugh,' Kay said. 'I am one hundred per cent certain.'

'How can you be so sure?'

'Like you, I have had contact with people in Lothar's line of business over the years. And they have confirmed that Lothar didn't kill Hugh.'

Phil could see Emma trying to contain her frustration.

'You and I were good friends, Kay,' Emma said. 'Back in 1939. You were my one reliable ally when everyone else was letting me down. I know you were as upset as I was about the Russians' pact with the Nazis. I know how fond you were of Hugh. What happened back then was wrong.'

Kay listened impassively.

'I don't have long to live,' Emma said.

'I guess none of us do,' said Kay.

'No, I mean I have very little time to live.' Emma tapped her forehead. 'There's something growing in here, and it's going to kill me. But before it does, I want to see Lothar. Confront him with what he did to Hugh. I need to do this before I die.'

So that was what all this was about, thought Phil. But as a plan it did rather rely on Lothar still being alive, and as far as he could tell, that wasn't the case.

Kay and Emma stared at each other. They both had equally intense brown eyes. Something was passing between them, Phil thought. Not just memories of fleeting meetings in pre-war Europe, but their lives since. What had been important to them then. What was important to them now.

Then Kay raised her index finger slowly. She moved it in front of her lips in a shush signal.

'I'm sorry to hear that, Emma. But I really can't help you. Lothar is dead.'

Emma kept quiet.

'But it is good to see you. Let's have some coffee, and you can tell me what *you* have been up to. Philip, can you help me?'

Phil followed Kay through to the kitchen, where she prepared a metal pot of coffee and stuck it on the stove. 'Can you get the cups, please, Philip?' she said, pointing to a cupboard.

Then she picked up a notepad on the kitchen counter, and a pen. Holding a finger to her lips, she began scribbling as they waited for the coffee to brew, its gentle gurgling hiding the scratch of pen on paper. Phil read over her shoulder as she scrawled left-handed, with spiky, backward sloping letters.

This apartment is almost certainly bugged.

Lothar is alive. He didn't go back to Moscow in 1938. He escaped to Switzerland. The KGB found him in the 1960s under the name Werner Strobl. I was sent to Geneva to track him down. I think the KGB intended to kill him. I met him. He got scared and disappeared again before the KGB could get to him.

For a long time I never believed he killed Hugh, or rather I believed his denial. But you must be right. Hugh was a threat. He knew who Lothar was and also some of the other people the KGB had recruited, probably including Philby and Maclean. Lothar didn't want Hugh to tell MI5 this. There is no other explanation. It's obvious. I just refused to believe it.

Lothar killed Hugh.

Chapter 50

The coffee pot emitted a triumphant final gurgle, and Kay poured out three cups, asking Phil to take them through to the living room. She handed the notepad with her scribblings to Emma.

As Emma read, Kay spoke.

'I apologize for the lousy quality of the coffee. It's never been very good here, but it's gotten a lot worse in the last year or two. They call this Kaffee-Mix. I dread to think what it's mixed with; it's only fifty per cent genuine. Think of it as an experience.'

Phil sipped the brown liquid: unpleasant, with a strong taste of chicory. He was watching Emma for her reaction to Kay's note. Her eyebrows rose as she read. She glanced quickly at Kay and then Phil, her face setting in determination.

She began scribbling a response. Phil could read the words from where he was sitting.

I thought so! Do you know where Lothar is now? And what is his current identity?

'So, Philip,' Kay said, reading the note. 'Tell me about yourself. Are you at university?'

'I'm going to Edinburgh in September,' Phil said.

Kay made a circling motion with her hand, urging him to continue talking as she wrote. Which Phil did, with Emma making occasional proud grandmotherly interjections to keep him going.

I don't know his current ID.

Kay hesitated. Emma mouthed the word 'Please.' Kay took a breath and began to write as Phil gave a blow-by-blow account of his A-level papers.

Three years ago, the Stasi sent me to look for him again. And I found him. I found where he lived. I visited him. The Stasi and the KGB don't know. He persuaded me not to tell them. So I decided to tell the Stasi I had checked and he wasn't there.

Emma wrote:

Where?

Kay scribbled:

Spain.

Phil started talking about hockey.

Where in Spain?

Kay hesitated.

A town called Jávea. I forget the precise address. His house was at the end of a road, on top of some cliffs overlooking a cove. I think the road is called Calle Cabo Negro. Small place, but there is a large stone lion outside the gate.

Kay quickly asked Phil whether he had been to West Germany before, and how he liked it. She began writing again:

It's really important the Stasi don't discover I found him. They know I went to Jávea to look for him and believed me when I said he had moved. So make sure they don't follow you there.

Emma glanced at her sharply.

Do you think the Stasi are watching us now?

Kay wrote:

Probably. A man came here yesterday to say you might be visiting, so I expect they will be watching this apartment now, and they will listen to the surveillance tapes. If you go to Spain, you must lose them. They <u>must not realize</u> I told you where Lothar is. Of course, he might have moved since I saw him.

Emma nodded. Kay glared at Phil, who nodded also.
Then Kay wrote two more words:

Good luck!

Emma put down her cup, which was still almost full of the dark brown liquid. 'Thank you for the coffee. As you say, an experience.'

'I'm sorry I couldn't help you with Lothar,' Kay said. 'He's dead, Emma. You just have to accept that.'

'I find that difficult,' said Emma stiffly.

As they moved to the door, Kay grabbed Emma and pulled her into an embrace. They stayed like that for several seconds.

'So Lothar's still alive,' Phil said as they emerged from the building entrance out into the street.

'And he killed Hugh. I knew it! I spent three years of my life spying for the filthy murderer!' Emma glared at her grandson, her eyes alight with fury. 'I tell you, Philip, it makes me so angry I could . . .'

'You could what, Grams?'

Emma shook her head. 'Nothing. Let's find a bus back to Friedrichstrasse.'

But Phil couldn't help thinking once again of the gun in Emma's suitcase, the gun that was now safely out of reach in the woods above Lake Annecy.

Chapter 51

Back at the Bristol, Phil followed Emma to her room while the hotel was getting a new one ready for him. She sank into an armchair and closed her eyes. She looked exhausted.

'Do you think they were following us?' Phil asked. 'The Stasi?'

Emma sighed. 'Probably. I expect they were on the lookout for us when we crossed at Checkpoint Charlie.'

'And was Kay's flat really bugged?'

Emma opened her eyes, suddenly alert. 'I doubt it.'

'But . . .' Phil was stopped in his tracks by Emma raising a finger to her mouth in exactly the same way Kay had. Phil realized what she meant, and let his gaze wander around the room, examining the telephone, the nightstand, the ceiling.

He nodded to show he understood.

'I fancy a cup of coffee in the bar,' he said. 'Do you want to join me?'

'I'm tired,' said Emma.

'Please, Grams. I have some questions I need to ask you. We could discuss them here?' He looked around the room meaningfully.

'Oh, all right. Let's go downstairs.'

It was early afternoon, and the bar was emptying of those having coffee after lunch. They found a quiet corner, and spoke in tones barely above a whisper.

'So you think your room might be bugged?'

'It might,' said Emma. 'I suspect bugging a West Berlin hotel is easy for the East Berlin secret police. Best to assume it is.'

Once they had crossed back into the West, Phil had believed they were safe. Wrong.

'Kay said they warned her we might visit, didn't she?' Phil said. 'They could have arrested us on the other side, or worse, if they wanted to.'

'Yes.'

'I wonder why they didn't?'

'I don't know,' said Emma.

'Now we know Lothar is alive, we are looking for him, right?'

'Right.' Emma examined her grandson. 'Are you coming with me to Spain?'

'I am,' said Phil. 'Even if you don't want me to.'

Emma closed her eyes. Phil wasn't sure whether she was thinking or resting. She smiled, and then opened them. 'Thank you. I shouldn't let you do it, but I am grateful. I need your help.'

'That's OK,' said Phil. 'But I really would like to know what's going on.'

Emma nodded. 'I owe you an explanation.'

She took a deep breath and paused for the waiter to serve them their coffee. 'During the war and afterwards I came to believe that Lothar must have had Hugh killed, or done it himself. But I also believed that Lothar had been executed by Stalin in 1938. So when I met Kay in Brussels fifteen years ago, and she told me she thought Lothar was still alive, it brought everything back.

'Of course, there was nothing I could do about it, so I just tried to forget it. Roland retired, we moved to Cornwall, Roland died. And then I got this diagnosis. I am going to die. I asked myself, what do I want to do before I go?

'My thoughts kept on coming back to Hugh, and what had happened to him. I didn't want to die and him to be erased from history. I wanted to revisit the places I had lived just before the war, when I was trying to make sense of his death, and do something about it. And then Dick sent me that postcard from Crete.'

Emma sipped her coffee. 'I realized I might have a chance of finding Lothar – if I could find Kurt and Kurt knew where Kay was. I hoped Kay would confirm what I suspected: that Lothar had killed Hugh.

'Once I'd had that thought, it wouldn't go away. I knew Dick was coming to Paris on business, and I thought I could perhaps meet him there. I wasn't confident of finding Kay by myself, especially with the tumour, but I also wasn't sure I could ask Dick to help me. I was dithering about what to do.

'Then, at Sunday lunch at your house, you mentioned you had had to cancel your hitch-hiking holiday in Europe, and I realized I could go after all if you went with me. I liked the idea of passing on what had happened to Hugh and to me to the next generation. That is to you. So I asked you to join me.'

'To help you find Lothar?'

'To find Lothar.'

'Why didn't you tell me all this?'

'I intended to tell you most of it. Bit by bit as we travelled around Europe. But then when Kurt was killed so horribly . . . well, I realized it was a lot more dangerous than I had thought, and I should keep you out of it.'

'What do you think the KGB have to do with this?'

'I'm not sure,' said Emma. 'Presumably Lothar has managed to evade them for decades, and they still want to find him.'

'Why?'

'He still has secrets. He may have been the one who recruited Burgess, or Philby, or any of the other Englishmen who spied for the Russians. Or if he didn't recruit them directly, he might know about them.'

Like Swann's mole, Phil thought. It seemed unfair that Emma didn't have the knowledge that there was still another mole burrowing underneath the British establishment and that MI6 thought Lothar knew his identity. Phil considered telling her right then. But he wasn't sure, yet. Swann had been adamant that he shouldn't.

He would wait and see.

'What are you planning to do if we find Lothar?' Phil asked.

'Look him in the eye and ask him whether he killed my brother.' There was iron in Emma's voice.

'And when he denies it? He'll deny it.'

'I'll know,' said Emma.

She sounded certain. But . . .

'Is that why you brought that gun with you, Grams?'

'What do you mean?'

'To shoot Lothar.'

Emma was about to deny it but then decided not to.

'I don't have the gun any more,' she said. 'You made me throw it away.'

Thank God for that, Phil thought. 'So. Spain next?'

'Tomorrow morning.'

'Do you think they'll follow us? The Stasi or the KGB or whoever they are?'

'Let's hope they don't know what Kay told us. In which case they might not. But, yes, I think they probably will try to follow us. And we will try to lose them. We have a whole continent to do it in.'

'As long as they don't decide to stop messing about and just kill us.'

Emma frowned. 'I know. You can still back out, Philip. In some ways, I wish you would.'

She lifted her eyes to Phil, her expression a mixture of fear, hope and pleading.

Phil grinned as reassuringly as he could. 'No, Grams. I'm coming too.'

Emma gave a small smile of relief. 'Philip?'

'Yes?'

'Promise me you won't be in touch with Heike before we go?'

'Why not?'

'I'm sorry to say this, but I fear she might be working for the East Germans. For the Stasi.'

'But she's only twenty!'

'She's older than that, Philip. She's twenty-five at least.'

'No she's not.'

'And it was quite a coincidence she found you at the Hollow-Tooth Church yesterday.'

'She said she was looking for me,' Phil said. 'She likes me.'

Emma raised her eyebrows. 'I wonder why a gorgeous twenty-five-year-old German woman would travel across Europe to meet an eighteen-year-old schoolboy.'

That hurt. That hurt a lot. It was true that Heike was way out of Phil's league, but he felt that he and she had had a real connection. She understood him. And she wasn't twenty-five, she was twenty. And why did his grandmother have to be so bloody offensive, when Phil had done so much for her?

'You just don't understand, Grams,' Phil muttered, getting to his feet. 'I'll see you at dinner.'

Chapter 52

Phil was fuming as he went down to reception to get the key to his new room. He knew he had only met Heike a couple of times, but he really really liked her. They understood each other. Sure, she was a couple of years older than him, but she *got* him. It was nice to talk to a girl like that. And there was the sex. He wanted more of that. He just did.

There was a message waiting for him in an envelope. He opened it as soon as he got up to his room. Inside, there was a note, handwritten on the headed paper of another Berlin hotel, the Hotel Zoo.

Dear Philip,

I hope your trip to East Berlin was interesting. If you have something to report to Mr Swann, I would be happy to pass it on to him. Can you get away to meet me this evening? I am staying at the Hotel Zoo, address above. It's very close. Please telephone the hotel number to let me know when you can come. It's important.

And don't let your grandmother know you are meeting me. I apologize for the necessity for secrecy, but I am sure you understand.

Yours sincerely,

Freddie Pelham-Walsh

So Freddie was in cahoots with Swann after all. No surprise there.

It did surprise him that Freddie knew he had joined Emma in the east. It turned out the Stasi were not the only people watching them.

But what to tell Freddie? Phil did have something to report, that Lothar was alive and living in a town in Spain. But to do that would be to betray his grandmother. Yet wasn't he betraying his grandmother already by omitting to tell her about Swann's interest in her?

Could he trust Freddie? Sure, Freddie had been a government minister, but he had also been a communist. As had Emma, for that matter.

Shouldn't he, in fact, be telling Emma about Swann?

The truth was, Phil didn't know whom he could trust.

He decided to see Freddie and play it by ear. If Freddie could convince him that he really did know Swann and would pass on Phil's message to him, then Phil would tell him about Lothar. It would be useful to have British intelligence on their side in the next couple of days. But if Phil's doubts remained, he would keep quiet for now.

So he rang the number of the Hotel Zoo, which he had noticed stood a little further up the Kurfürstendamm, and asked to be put through to Freddie. There was no reply from Freddie's room, so Phil left a message that he would meet Freddie in the hotel bar at 6.30 p.m. He didn't leave his own name.

He was sitting on his bed, staring at the phone, still wrestling with the problem of what to say, when it rang.

He picked it up. 'Hello?'

'Phil! You're still here!'

Phil couldn't help smiling at the sound of Heike's voice.

'I am.'

'You hinted you might not be going back to London after all, so I thought I would call you at your hotel on the off-chance. What happened?'

'I decided to stay.'

'And did you go to the east?'

'I did. I actually surprised my grandmother in a taxi on the other side.'

'How did she take that?'

'She was a bit pissed off, but then she seemed happy.'

'Great. Look, can we meet up this evening?'

'I'd like to.' Once again, Phil wasn't sure what to do. He had promised to see Emma for dinner and it would be hard to ditch that, especially if he said he was meeting Heike. He could sneak out of the hotel afterwards. Or he could see Heike for a quick drink before he met Freddie.

'Tell you what, I have to see someone at the Hotel Zoo at six thirty. Can you meet me before then?'

'I can do that,' said Heike. 'How about that café in Tauentzienstrasse where your grandmother took us before? Half past five?'

'That's good. See you then.'

Chapter 53

Phil had time to pick up his rucksack from the left luggage office at Zoo Station before he met Heike, all the time stewing over what his grandmother had said about her.

Heike was waiting for him at the café, wearing a yellow *Atomkraft? Nein Danke* T-shirt and tight black jeans. She looked gorgeous. Images of her naked in the dim light of the squat the previous night slid their way to the forefront of Phil's brain.

She didn't look anything like the men in hats and raincoats of the classic spy film, or even the pneumatic women with enormous breasts and tight-fitting dresses of the Bond films.

But she didn't look twenty. Phil's friend Mike's older sister Rachel was twenty-one, and Heike looked older than her.

They kissed each other hesitantly, a quick brush on the lips. Phil ordered a beer, and Heike a glass of wine. She did seem pleased to see him.

She asked all about his trip to East Berlin, and he admitted he had seen Kay, the woman he had told her about in Paris and Berlin before the war. He told Heike Emma had asked Kay about the man who had 'handled' her on behalf of the Russians, but Kay had insisted the man was dead.

Naturally enough, Heike was fascinated. It was a fascinating story.

'So are you staying in Berlin?'

'No. We're off tomorrow.'

'Where?'

'Grams discovered from someone else where this guy is. And we're going to see him tomorrow. It's going to be a very long drive.'

'Really? Where are you going?'

Phil strolled past the Hollow-Tooth Church down the Kurfürstendamm to the Hotel Zoo, which was a flashy hotel only half a block from the Bristol. He was five minutes late, but Freddie was not in the bar.

Phil sat down, somewhat uncomfortably. He felt what he was, a scruffy boy in a hotel for international jet-setters. After he had twice turned down a disapproving waiter trying to offer him drinks, he left the bar and headed for the front desk in the hotel lobby. Something was up: a ripple of suppressed anxiety surrounded the half-dozen men and women conferring behind the desk.

Phil stood politely next to the desk while they ignored him. Finally, a woman came over and smiled stiffly.

'I'm waiting for a guest in your hotel. Herr Pelham-Walsh,' Phil stated in German. 'Can I telephone his room, please?'

The smile disappeared. 'One moment.' She turned to the group of staff. 'Herr Klauber? This gentleman is supposed to be meeting Herr Pelham-Walsh.'

An immaculate man of about fifty, with perfectly groomed hair and a neatly trimmed moustache, instantly detached himself from the group and introduced himself as the manager.

He led Phil through to the recesses of an office behind the desk and bade Phil sit down.

'I am sorry to say that Herr Pelham-Walsh was killed this afternoon in a road accident,' the man said in English. 'Just a couple of blocks from here. It was a hit-and-run.'

'Oh my God!'

'Is he a relative of yours?'

'No. No.'

'A friend perhaps?'

Phil's brain fizzed. He wasn't going to waste time speculating whether Freddie had been killed by accident; the MP had been run down deliberately, probably by the Stasi or the KGB. Possibly to stop Phil talking to him right now. Phil couldn't think through all the implications of this immediately, but his instinct was that it would be better if the West German authorities didn't know who he really was.

'Godfather.'

'And you were supposed to meet him?'

'Yes. He contacted me to say he was staying in Berlin for a couple of days and he knew I was here, and could I meet him this evening? So I said yes I would.'

'I'm very sorry, sir.'

Phil realized he should be looking sad. He also realized he was probably looking as stunned as he felt, which would do fine.

'We understand that Mr Pelham-Walsh was an important man in Britain? A member of parliament?'

'Not just that. A government minister. Or he used to be.'

The hotel manager absorbed the information, no doubt ratcheting up the problem a notch.

'We have been in touch with the British Embassy. Do you have his wife's contact details, perhaps? Or his home phone number?'

'Freddie wasn't married,' Phil said, with some degree of confidence. 'And my address book is back at my hotel.'

'I see. I am sure the police or someone from the embassy will be here shortly. Would you mind waiting until they arrive?'

'Not at all,' said Phil.

'Thank you, sir.' The manager got to his feet. 'Oh, forgive me, sir. What is your name?'

'Oh. Um. Eustace. Eustace Parsons.'

Eustace? His French teacher Eustace? Get a grip, Phil told himself. But the truth was his brain was tumbling. First Kurt, and now Freddie.

Who next?

Phil had an uncomfortable feeling it might be him. Or Emma. Or both of them.

Fear was seeping into his brain, seizing it up, preventing rational thought.

Get a grip.

'Thank you.' The manager scribbled the name down on a piece of paper. 'And where are you staying?'

'The youth hostel in Bayernallee.' Better.

The manager's nose remained unwrinkled as he wrote this down. 'And your home address?'

Phil spelled out a random address in Marlow, the closest town to Wittingcombe.

The manager floated off, and Phil hung around in the lobby, doing his best to overcome his agitation.

He did mind waiting for the police or a man from the embassy, actually. Once he got himself ensnared with the authorities, it would be impossible for him and Emma to get away to Spain.

So, while the bodies behind the reception desk were conferring, he slipped unnoticed out of the front entrance and hurried down the street towards his own hotel.

Heike was strolling along Tauentzienstrasse when a battered green BMW pulled up beside her. She jumped in. Rozhkov was in the driver's seat.

'What happened to the other car?' she asked. Rozhkov had been driving an equally battered grey Mercedes.

'I had to get rid of it.'

'Pelham-Walsh?'

'Yes. I got him on a side street. Only possible witness was a young woman with two children, and I'm sure she was looking at them, not me.'

'Dead?'

'Dead.'

Traffic accidents were better than more blatant liquidations, especially for high-profile targets like Pelham-Walsh. A shooting would have stirred up a hornets' nest. The problem was, hit-and-runs weren't always reliable; at least this one had been successful.

'How did it go with young Phil?' Rozhkov asked.

'Well. He confirmed he and Emma saw Kay Ortmann yesterday.'

'We know that. But the surveillance tapes show she didn't tell them anything.'

'That's true. But Phil said Emma knows where Lothar is.'

'Did he say how she knows?'

'No. But he did tell me where. They are planning to track Lothar down tomorrow.'

Heike was glad Phil had spilled the beans about Lothar's where-abouts. After the debacle in Annecy, the plan had changed, at Rozhkov's suggestion. The idea now was to let Phil and Emma lead them to Lothar, and then kill him. And them. And the agent buried deep within the British establishment for the last forty years would remain safely buried, as would the couple of others still in place that he had recruited in turn.

She really must do a better job of dealing with Phil. He was going to die – she knew it, and she should be able to handle it if she was to be the professional agent she aspired to be. She had done a lot for her country; there was a lot more she could do.

She was glad she hadn't had to sleep with him again that night. Phil had declined her suggestion, saying he had a long drive the following day.

As, therefore, did she and Rozhkov.

'Well done,' said Rozhkov. 'So where are they leading us tomorrow?'

Heike told him.

Chapter 54

Phil's tiny travelling alarm clock went off at 4 a.m. He was in a deep sleep, and it took all his willpower to drag himself out of bed and stand under a shower for five minutes. He was supposed to be meeting Emma in the hotel lobby at 4.30 a.m.

As soon as he had returned to the Bristol the evening before he had knocked on Emma's door and forced her out and down to the bar for a drink. He was more inclined than ever to believe that her room was bugged. She had seen from his face that something important was up, and under the murmur of the cocktail-hour crowd, Phil had explained that Freddie had summoned him to his hotel, and that he was now dead, run over on a side street.

A succession of emotions swept across Emma's face: shock, sadness, fear and then resolution.

'It was the KGB, wasn't it?' Phil said.

'Must have been. Do you know why Freddie wanted to talk to you?'

'No idea,' Phil lied.

'We need to leave this city,' Emma said.

Phil heartily agreed. Freddie's death had badly shaken him; he didn't want to spend a moment longer than he had to in Berlin. 'Shall we go right now?'

'Yes.' Then Emma hesitated. 'Maybe not right now. We're both tired and we have a very long journey ahead of us.' That's when she came up with the plan of getting up at four in the morning.

Emma was waiting for him in the lobby, looking as resolute as ever. She had summoned the TR6 to the hotel entrance. It was already light outside, but the Kurfürstendamm was quiet. Out on the street the sun was rising behind the broken spire of the church, painting stripes of rose and gold along the upper floors of the buildings along the street.

The roads were empty. But as they approached the western suburb of Zehlendorf, and the checkpoint from West Berlin back on to the autobahn corridor through East Germany, a number of lorries began to accumulate.

It was here that they were most likely to be stopped, either by the West German authorities if they had realized Phil knew something about Freddie's death, or by the East German border guards. Phil and Emma had discussed this, and decided that if the East Germans had been happy to follow them to visit Kay without arresting them, they would be likely to allow them out of Berlin.

The reasoning sounded plausible. But it could be wrong. The only way they would know was when they were safely driving along the corridor itself.

Both sets of border guards let them through, the East German taking longer than his western counterpart, but that in itself wasn't suspicious. And then they were off on the autobahn, heading to Helmstedt, Braunschweig and Hanover.

Emma and Phil were wrapped up in their own thoughts. It was too early to talk. On the open road, with no speed limit, Phil put his foot down, nudging the speedometer past a ton.

He checked his grandmother, who caught his eye and grinned. The sun hung low behind them, urging them on.

It appeared that giving a false name to the manager at the Hotel Zoo had worked, at least for a little bit. Swann would hear of Freddie's death soon enough. The British Embassy had already been told, and presumably the news would spread around Whitehall to reach him. Phil had considered trying to telephone him, reverse charges, the night before, and telling him that Lothar was in Spain.

But Phil was cautious. The safest choice seemed to be to keep as low a profile as they could until they actually found Lothar. Then he would telephone Swann.

Who was this damn mole anyway? Of course, it could easily be someone Emma had never met, someone who hadn't been part of her story yet – someone like Denis Healey – or more likely someone of whom Phil hadn't even heard. In which case there was no point in Phil trying to speculate.

But if it was someone Emma knew from the 1930s, then that would explain Swann's insistence Phil keep their conversation from her.

If the mole was a friend of Emma's.

Or if Emma had recruited the mole herself.

That would mean Emma had not been completely open in the stories she had told Phil; she had held things back.

It was possible. In fact, she had always admitted she was holding information back, information that it would be dangerous for Phil to know.

So if Emma knew the mole, who might it be?

Kurt would have been a good guess. He had risen in the ranks of the West German Foreign Ministry. But he was dead; almost certainly killed by the KGB.

What about Roland? Had Emma recruited Roland at some point, maybe after their reconciliation?

But Roland, too, was dead. It sounded as if Swann was looking for a mole that was still burrowing.

There was another obvious possibility.

'Grams?

'Yes.'

'You know you said Freddie spied for the Russians before the war?'

'Yes, darling.'

'Do you think he might still have been working for them?'

Even as he was driving, Phil could feel Emma's sharp brown eyes studying him closely.

'Why do you ask?'

'I was trying to figure out why he was killed.'

'You mean, you think it might have been the British? Because he was a Russian spy?'

'I don't know, Grams,' Phil said. 'I'm just trying to make sense of this.'

'I suppose he might have been working for the KGB. But I think it unlikely. He did help MI5 track down Burgess and Maclean, and I think Philby.' She sighed. 'That's the problem with this spying business. You never really know. Even when it's your own brother.'

A tear crept down her cheek. 'Freddie was exasperating, but I liked him.'

'I'm sorry, Grams,' said Phil.

But his mind continued to roam. 'What about Cyril?'

'Cyril?'

'Do you think he has anything to do with Kurt's death?' Phil asked. 'Kurt did know Cyril was a spy, after all.'

'I don't think so,' said Emma hesitantly. But it was clear the idea hadn't occurred to her.

Emma was thinking too.

'If you're looking for a spy, I don't think you need look much further than Heike.'

Phil glanced at Emma and swallowed. 'I saw her last night, Grams.'

'You what?'

'I slipped out to see her for a drink. Just before I went to meet Freddie at the Hotel Zoo.'

'But I told you to stay clear of her!'

'I know you did. But I thought you were wrong; I was sure you were wrong.'

'You fool, Philip!'

'Until I was with her. Then I realized you were right. She's not twenty. And if she's not twenty, she probably isn't a student at the University of Bonn. And much as it pains me to admit it, she probably doesn't fancy me. And when she quickly turned the conversation to where we were going today, I knew for sure why she was interested in me.'

'You didn't tell her?'

'I did tell her.'

'Phil!'

'I told her Lothar was on a Greek island. Skiathos. It was the destination we planned to head for when we were hitching across Europe. The *Hitch-Hiker's Guide* is very complimentary about it.'

Emma grinned. 'Did she believe you?'

'I think so.'

'Maybe you're not such a fool after all.'

Phil smiled. 'Maybe I'm not.'

Emma touched his arm. 'I'm sorry. I know you liked her. It must be awful to know you were being deceived all along.'

There was something in her touch, in the tone of her voice, that made Phil realize this sixty-four-year-old woman did understand. And then he realized that at about his age she too had slept with someone who was deceiving her.

'All right,' said Emma. 'We need a plan.'

'Don't we have a plan? We're driving to Spain.'

'The KGB will be watching us. Following us. They will be expecting us to head towards Greece. Which we will do. Until we lose them.'

'How are we going to do that?'

'I'll think of something.' Emma pulled out her road atlas and studied it closely.

They had no problem at the border and stopped for breakfast at a service station on the other side. They sped past Braunschweig, both of them ignoring the signs, and then turned south on an autobahn heading to Munich and Austria, and ultimately Yugoslavia and Greece.

Half an hour south of Nuremberg, in Bavaria, Emma announced it was time for lunch. They pulled off the autobahn and stopped at a garage with a little shop which sold sandwiches and local maps. They bought both.

Phil had been looking out for cars following him, but couldn't spot any. More accurately, there were dozens of cars following them on the long journey, and there was no way of telling if any of them contained KGB agents.

Much easier on a straight stretch of country road. Which, by examining her newly purchased map closely, Emma found.

They pulled over on the verge of a straight on a back road a couple of kilometres west of the garage. A blue van, a silver Opel, and a green BMW with a single male driver passed them and disappeared around a corner a kilometre away. They munched their sandwiches, checking each passing vehicle carefully. On one side cows grazed a low hill; on the other, tidy Bavarian farmland stretched into the distance.

'Ready?' Emma asked, once they had finished their sandwiches.

'Ready.'

'Let's go.'

Phil drove as fast as he could along the country roads, Emma giving him a bewildering series of directions. He called out the type and colour of any vehicle that appeared in his rear-view mirror; Emma suggested this as an aide to spot a particular car reappearing. None did. They spent a frustrating two minutes trapped behind a slow-moving tractor before Phil accelerated past it on a blind corner. In ten minutes they were back at the entrance to the autobahn, which headed south to Munich.

'That way,' said Emma, pointing to a sign.

North.

Chapter 55

Heike and Rozhkov stood beside their BMW on the low hill overlooking the distinctive green British sports car, Rozhkov training his powerful binoculars down on them.

'They know they're being followed,' he said in his Slavic-accented German.

'They can't have spotted us,' said Heike.

Rozhkov had planted a radio tracker in the TR6 in the hotel's garage, and Heike had followed Phil and his grandmother on a heavy portable display plugged into the BMW's cigarette lighter. Rozhkov had kept at least a couple of kilometres behind the British sports car the whole way. The only time they had got close was when they had driven past the stationary TR6 on the lane down there, and Heike had slipped down low in the passenger seat out of sight.

'It's all very well stopping for a picnic somewhere,' Rozhkov said. 'But they have just pulled over on to a verge. It's not a natural stopping place. They want to lose us.'

'They are not doing a bad job of it,' said Heike. 'But they don't know we know they are heading to Greece.'

'Phil knows,' Rozhkov said.

'Phil knows I know,' Heike said. 'He doesn't know you do. He doesn't suspect me, I'm sure of it.'

'Perhaps you're right,' Rozhkov said. 'In which case they will be on the autobahn heading south in half an hour or so.'

Rozhkov stiffened. 'They're off. And they're not going back the way they came. That means they *are* trying to lose us.'

Rozhkov and Heike jumped in the car. Heike put the bulky display on her lap and tried to read it. The display showed bearing and approximate range, which was fine on a straight autobahn, but was very difficult on winding country roads, especially without a detailed map.

They spent a frustrating fifteen minutes doing their best to keep up, Rozhkov letting his impatience show. Heike had had no training on the system. She suggested that they switch and she drive, but Rozhkov wasn't having any of that. He was the man, so he had to drive.

Turned out Rozhkov was just as much a jerk as the hapless Marko, just in his own special way.

It was with relief that they crested a low hill and saw both the autobahn, and a green sports car moving towards it.

'That's them!' Heike said, and put the display to one side.

A 'well done' would have been appreciated.

Rozhkov drove steadily to the junction and joined the highway heading south.

'OK. How far ahead of us are they? I want to get the separation right.'

This was easier. Heike checked the display. It didn't make sense. The dot was at the bottom of the concentric circles.

'Hold on. They're behind us!'

'They can't be.'

'Look.'

Rozhkov leaned over and looked.

'Damn it!' he said. 'They're heading north! We'll have to double back at the next junction.'

He glared at Heike and muttered something in Russian.

Russian was compulsory in East German schools and Heike had been good at it.

He had just called her a stupid female dog.

At the next junction, they veered off the autobahn and rejoined it heading north. After a frantic twenty minutes of seriously fast driving, a blip appeared on Heike's screen, this time where it should be. At the top. Ahead of them.

They followed it on what was to be a long journey north, and then west, and then south through France.

To Spain.

PART FIVE

SPAIN

Chapter 56

July 1979, Jávea, Spain

Lothar's house stood at the end of a road which wound up a hillside of rock and surprisingly green forest. The blue of the Mediterranean flashed between the trees as they drove.

Emma studied the local map they had bought in the old coastal town of Jávea, a few kilometres to the north. After their picnic manoeuvre in Bavaria, they had driven for the rest of the day and holed up in a hotel near Lyon in France. The following night, they had stayed in Valencia, so that they could meet Lothar at a reasonable hour in the morning.

They drove past the villa slowly. It was a single-storey building with a red-tiled roof behind a low white wall rimmed with purple flowers. There was indeed a stone lion grinning at them by the iron gate on the short driveway leading down to a garage.

'Turn around and park a bit further down the hill,' said Emma. 'We don't want to make the same mistake we did in Talloires – leaving the car outside the house.'

They had passed a few other houses on the road, and a number of building sites. It was a beautiful spot; something the local developers were clearly taking advantage of. Phil turned around at the end of the road, drove down the hill past the villa and parked in a lay-by next to a footpath leading down to the sea.

They walked back up the road. It was scarcely ten o'clock but the July sun was already beating down hard from a blue sky. Phil wore shorts and a T-shirt, and the sweat was beginning to form. Emma looked fresh in a yellow sundress and seemed to be taking the climb in her stride, clutching her handbag. The tumour was leaving her alone, at least for now.

Several hundred feet beneath them, they glimpsed a cove surrounded by lush green vegetation, a rocky headland rearing up on the far side. This was all much greener than the rest of Spain through which they had driven. It wasn't the sun, sand and beach umbrellas Phil had been expecting; Emma's road atlas had shown Benidorm not far to the south.

Phil was wondering how he could persuade Lothar to divulge any clues about who Swann's mole might be. He had thought of trying to recruit Emma to help him, but that would involve admitting he had been keeping his conversation with Swann from her the whole time. She wouldn't like that.

The key thing Swann had wanted to know was where Lothar lived. Phil would at least tell him that, and then MI6 could take it from there.

They reached the house and opened a small iron gate through which a stone path led down to the front door. With a nervous glance at Phil, Emma pressed the bell.

They waited a full minute before the door was opened by a tall, stooped man with a stick. He looked at Emma and Phil with intense dark blue eyes over half-rimmed spectacles tied to a cord around his neck. His hair was thick and white, his face strong, but crumbled around the edges by age.

'Lothar,' Emma said, simply.

'Emma? Emma Meeke?'

'That's me,' Emma said in German.

For a moment a cloud of surprise passed over the old man's face, followed by a grin. He opened his arms, his stick clasped in his left hand.

Emma hesitated and then stepped forward. He embraced her with his arms and with his charm, which was almost palpable.

'I should say this was a surprise, but that would be understating it. This is a shock. A good shock. Come in, come in.'

He led them through to a sitting room, whose windows looked down through trees to the sea and the cove. The walls were covered in brightly painted pictures – modern art from the early part of the century, Phil thought. Some looked like Matisses. Maybe they were Matisses; Phil remembered Kay had said Lothar had become an art dealer.

Lothar lowered himself into what was clearly his favourite armchair, an ashtray and a novel in Spanish by Gabriel García Márquez on a side table within easy reach.

Phil perched on a sofa opposite, and Emma on a wing chair.

'You found me. How on earth did you find me? Let me guess. Kay?'

'That's right. We just saw her in East Berlin. She said she had tracked you down here a few years ago. She also said she hadn't told her former employers where you are.'

'I'm very glad to hear that. I thought I could trust her. I am surprised she told you, but then you and she always had some kind of connection, however unlikely that may seem.'

'You mean Hugh?' said Emma.

'Hugh. And a belief that the world could be a better place.'

Phil could see how Emma had trusted this man so completely. Even in his eighties, for that was how old he must be, he oozed reliability and strength. His steady voice, his steady dark blue eyes, his sense of calm purpose.

'This must be your son. He looks a lot like Hugh.'

'Grandson,' said Emma. 'And he does, doesn't he? I brought him with me on a little trip around Europe to revisit old times. He has been most helpful.'

'I'm glad to hear that,' said Lothar with a smile at Phil. 'I do hope he's the only person you brought with you.'

'We weren't followed, if that's what you mean. I believe the KGB are interested in our movements, but Philip cleverly led them astray. They think you live in Greece.'

'So they are still looking for me,' said Lothar, frowning now.

'I believe so,' said Emma. 'What have you been up to? I thought you had been shot in Moscow, until I met Kay about fifteen years ago; she said you were still alive. And when we saw her last week, she said you were living here, but she didn't have a chance to say much more. She was being careful.'

'Good,' said Lothar. 'I almost did return to Moscow back in 1938. It was actually Kay who persuaded me not to go, but I didn't want to endanger her by letting her know I had listened to her. It was safer for her if she believed I had gone.

'I took on a new identity and disappeared to Switzerland, to Zurich. You probably never knew this, but I was for a time a cobbler, a forger of identity documents. I was pretty good at it. There was work in Zurich for people like me during the war. And after the war, I discovered that there was a lot of wayward art floating around Central Europe, prised loose from museums and castles. Some of it was real, some of it was forged, a lot of it had been stolen. It turned out I had the necessary skills to untangle all that, and I set up a business in Geneva dealing in art. Quite a successful business.

'That was where Kay first found me, sometime in the sixties, and I had to retire in a hurry. Franco's Spain was a good place in those days for people like me to disappear to. Still is, really.'

He nodded thoughtfully to himself. 'Then Kay found me a few years ago. I persuaded her to tell her bosses I had left, and she assured me she would. I trusted her.' He grinned. 'I found trusting Kay usually worked. I should probably have reinvented myself yet again and disappeared somewhere. But I was too old at that stage. If they find me, they find me. I'm surprised they still care.'

'They must think you still know things,' said Emma. 'Things that Russia's enemies would find useful.'

Phil's pulse quickened. Was there a way he could prod the conversation towards moles?

Somehow, God knows how, Lothar noticed Phil's interest, even though Phil could have sworn he hadn't moved.

His steady blue eyes latched on Phil's. 'Was it wise to bring your grandson along with you, Emma? There's a risk he might hear things that are not good for him.'

324

'You're right,' said Emma. 'A few days ago, I realized that this little trip was significantly more dangerous than I had expected. So I tried to send Philip back to England.' She glanced at her grandson. 'I failed. He's a stubborn boy. Besides, I want him to know what I did. What we did. Before I die.'

Lothar snorted. 'But you are still young. What are you, sixty?'

'Sixty-four. I have a brain tumour. I am going to die. Soon.'

'I'm sorry to hear it.' The old man meant it; his commiseration seemed genuine and heartfelt, but also, curiously, encouraging.

He pulled out a packet of cigarettes from the yellow cardigan he was wearing, and after offering them to Phil and Emma, who refused, lit up. Phil noticed that he was indeed missing half of his little finger.

'So that's why you have come to find me. Because you are dying.'

Emma nodded. 'I want to ask you about Hugh.'

'Hugh.' Lothar sighed. 'He would have made a wonderful spy. I'm sure he would have got to the top of the diplomatic service. Ambassador to Russia one day. That would have been useful. Or he could have moved across to MI6.'

'It must have been disappointing for you that he changed his mind, then,' said Emma, calmly.

Lothar paused. 'Kay told you that, I suppose.'

Emma didn't answer. 'When he told you he wouldn't spy for Russia any more, it wasn't just a lost opportunity, was it?'

'What do you mean?'

'He was going to talk to the British secret service.'

Lothar remained silent. He waited.

'And if he had talked, he would have told them about you. And about the fellow Cambridge students you had recruited.'

No answer.

'So you had him killed.' It was a statement, not a question.

The words hung heavy in the room.

'A few years ago, I would have denied it,' said Lothar. 'But now? We are both old. You have a right to know. For what it's worth, I am sorry. He was a good man. At the time I believed that helping the cause was everything. Actually, I still do believe that. The Soviets let down the cause of international communism as much as Hugh was planning to.

'I'm sorry, Emma,' he repeated.

'Who did kill him?' Emma asked.

'A policeman. One of your bobbies. We had quite a few agents in the Metropolitan Police in those days, did you know that? Recruited them in the nineteen twenties after the police strike. This man used to do the occasional difficult job for me.'

'What was his name?'

'Does it matter? He's long dead.'

'In that case, maybe it doesn't matter.'

Emma thought for a moment, and then reached down for the handbag by her feet and placed it on her lap. She opened it.

And pulled out a gun.

A gun Phil recognized: the revolver that he thought she had slung into the woods above Lake Annecy.

She got to her feet, cocking it and pointing it at Lothar.

'What is this?' said Lothar. 'Revenge?'

'Justice,' said Emma. 'For Hugh. Before I die. I'm sorry you have to see this, Philip.'

So was Phil. Then it occurred to him that if Lothar died, so would the identity of Swann's mole.

'Lothar,' he said.

Lothar switched his glance to Phil. As did Emma.

'One of the agents you recruited is still working, isn't he? Deep in the heart of the British secret service. That's why the Russians are after you. Who is he?'

'Philip!' Emma was clearly unhappy with Phil's interruption.

'I won't tell you anything about anyone I recruited,' said Lothar.

'Where did you get that idea from, Philip?' demanded Emma. 'Who has been talking to you?'

Phil ignored her. He needed Lothar's answer. 'If you don't tell us, Lothar, Emma will shoot you.'

'Emma is going to shoot me anyway, Philip. Aren't you, Emma?'

Emma nodded.

Lothar took a deep drag of his cigarette. 'It was always going to happen some time. I have cheated death for forty years. I'm an old man now. And I am glad it's you and not some KGB hit man in the middle of the night.' He raised his hand. 'But before you do it, let me repeat. Your brother was a good man. I am sorry he is dead.'

Emma stared. There wasn't hatred in her expression, or even anger. But there was determination.

And Phil knew his grandmother well enough to know that when she was determined to do something, she did it.

She pulled the trigger. And then she pulled it again, and again.

Chapter 57

Heike heard the three shots, as did the startled pigeons perching in the trees on the hillside, who took to the air in a flurry of beating wings and rustling branches.

She and Rozhkov had stationed themselves a few metres above the road, looking down on the villa. They had hidden the BMW behind the wall of an empty construction site between the TR6 and the villa, having managed to keep tabs on Emma's car all the way from Bavaria, maintaining at least two kilometres' distance. They hadn't had much sleep on the way; they had had to spell each other keeping watch over the hotels in France and Valencia where their targets had spent the night, in case they decided on another departure in the early hours.

'Who shot who?' said Rozhkov.

'Maybe she's killed Lothar,' said Heike. 'Sounded like three shots from the same gun.'

'Or maybe he shot the two of them.'

'Has anyone heard it?' The nearest neighbouring house was fifty metres down the hill, but that looked shut tight as a drum. The gunshots had been fired within the building, which had muffled them somewhat.

'We have to assume someone will call the police,' said Rozhkov. 'Let's get down there. If they come out of the front door, shoot them.'

Heike followed the KGB agent down to the road, her gun hanging by her side, so it couldn't be seen from anyone at a distance.

Still no sound of an alarm being raised, or sign of a curious neighbour. But all it needed was for one person to pick up the phone and call the police.

They opened the gate, and crouched behind a bush, waiting for someone to emerge. From there they couldn't see clearly into the villa through the windows, although Heike thought she spotted something move inside.

'Did you see that?' she whispered.

Rozhkov nodded. 'All right. We're going in. Shoot to kill. Let's make it fast.'

'Jesus!' said Phil, his ears ringing from the gunshots in a confined space as he watched the blood pour from Lothar's chest.

His grandmother had just shot someone. Again. That's not what grannies were supposed to do.

And with Lothar had gone all hope of finding Swann's mole.

Emma slumped back into the armchair, still holding the gun.

'What now?' said Phil, leaping to his feet.

'Leave me here,' said Emma. 'I've done what I came to do. I'll explain that you had nothing to do with it.'

'No,' said Phil. 'No. We're going to get out of this like we did in Talloires. Get up, Grams!'

She didn't move.

'Up!' He hauled her to her feet.

Phil scanned the room. 'I think we've barely touched anything since we've been here.' Lothar had opened the front door for them, and the living-room door had been open. He hadn't given them anything to drink. All they would have touched was the fabric of the sofa and the chair Emma was sitting in. Phil wasn't sure, but he thought fingerprints needed hard surfaces to come out clearly.

'Someone might have reported the shots. We need to get going before the police come.'

'Don't worry about it, Philip,' said Emma.

Phil ignored her and moved through to the hallway, where there was a window looking up to the road. He saw two figures, a man and a woman, running across the road, guns hanging down by their sides.

He recognized the woman.

Heike.

He dashed back into the living room. 'KGB!' he said. 'Come on, Grams! They've got guns. You might be happy to die, but I'm not.'

He knew that would snap her out of it.

'There may be a way out of the back garden,' she said. She moved over to a window. 'Yes – there's a gate.'

'Let's go!'

They found the back door and hurried through it, across the garden and out of the gate at the back. They scrambled down the path into the woods.

Rozhkov went first, flinging the front door open and storming into the villa, Heike following, her gun raised. Adrenaline was pumping in her system. There were armed foreign agents in there; if one of them turned out to be Phil, she would shoot him, if Rozhkov didn't shoot him first. Their orders were clear. Phil, Emma and Lothar all had to die. The KGB's agent in Britain had to be protected at all costs.

The body of an old man was slumped in an armchair, blood oozing from his chest through the torn fabric of his shirt and cardigan. The lenses of a pair of glasses hanging from his neck were spattered with blood.

That must be Lothar.

His eyelids flickered open.

'Where have they gone?' Rozhkov shouted at him in German.

The man managed to shake his head.

Rozhkov shot him between the eyes.

More noise.

'Check the bedrooms!' Rozhkov ordered.

Heike moved through the villa, her weapon raised.

She kicked open first one door – a guest bedroom – and then another. Lothar's bedroom. Heike scanned the room for possible hiding places. Behind the bed and a wardrobe. She checked. Nothing there.

She glanced out of the bedroom window. The view was spectacular. A steep wooded slope dropped down to a quiet cove of blue and green.

There was a small garden behind the villa. It was enclosed by a high white wall, to which all manner of shrubs and vines clung. A small black gate stood in one corner.

Open.

She could just make out a footpath winding among the trees, heading down to the cove.

'Rozhkov!' she shouted. 'They went out the back!'

She joined Rozhkov as he found a back door from the kitchen out into the garden and followed him through the gate.

The path was steep, but they took it as quickly as they could. Phil might be difficult to catch, but they should be faster than Emma. She noticed Rozhkov limping a little as if he had twisted an ankle, and so she squeezed past him.

A hundred metres or so below them, the trees briefly opened up, revealing the path. She kept her eyes on the spot and, sure enough, she saw a flash of yellow as first Emma and then Phil ran along it. Emma was moving fast for a grandmother, certainly as fast as the limping Rozhkov.

Phil stopped and glanced upwards. For a second, he stared right at her; then he was gone into the trees.

She rushed on.

She was pretty sure she was catching them up. They were getting close to the foot of the hill and the cove, which was rimmed with a narrow pebbly beach.

She emerged from the trees at a spot about twenty metres above the shore. Emma was running headlong through the pebbles. There was no sign of Phil.

Emma slipped and fell.

Heike stopped, and raised her gun, fighting to control her breath. The range was only about fifty metres, but that was difficult with a handgun, especially if you were panting as heavily as she was.

She could hear Rozhkov behind her.

'Shoot her,' he commanded.

Despite her age, Emma was moving fast. But probably not as fast as the two KGB agents.

They came to an opening in the trees and Phil looked back. He saw one of the agents staring at him.

Heike.

They needed a plan. Phil had one.

He caught up with Emma.

'Give me your gun, Grams!'

'Why?' she called back.

'Just give it to me.'

She paused and handed Phil her gun. In a rushed couple of sentences, he explained his plan.

He could hear them behind him. He was searching for the perfect spot. They didn't have much time – the beach was nearing. Once out on the beach, they would be sitting ducks. Emma would be a sitting duck.

He found his spot and pushed himself into a bush.

Twenty seconds later, Heike appeared in front of him, breathing heavily. She paused and looked out over the beach, where Emma was running.

Phil could hear the sound of her colleague scrambling down the path a few yards above him.

He raised the revolver, cocked it as quietly as he could, and pointed it at Heike's back.

Just for an instant, an image of Heike's lively smile, of those glittering blue eyes, leapt to the front of his mind. But only for an instant. Heike was about to shoot his grandmother. And she would shoot him too, if she got the chance.

He had to time this right. He had to take out Heike's KGB colleague as well.

Two seconds later, the man arrived next to Heike, limping.

The man spotted Emma on the beach. 'Shoot her,' he commanded in German.

Phil squeezed the trigger.

The bullet hit Heike between her narrow shoulders from ten yards. The recoil surprised Phil.

He steadied himself and moved the barrel of the pistol towards the other guy, who was turning towards him and raising his own gun.

Phil shot him in the head.

And then he shot Heike again, just as Emma had done, to make sure she was dead.

And then he was out of bullets.

EPILOGUE

Chapter 58

July 1979, Buckinghamshire

Phil sipped his pint of Brakspear with pleasure. It was good to be back in a proper English pub, especially if it was the Three Castles.

He had arrived a few minutes early for his meeting with Mr Swann. He wanted to have time alone with a pint to try to process what had happened over the last couple of weeks.

It would take much longer than ten minutes to process; it would take a lifetime. He was still buzzing from the adrenaline of it all. He had avoided death not once, but twice. He had saved his grandmother's life. He had plunged into the world of spies and spying.

He was also grateful for getting to know Emma better. Not only his grandmother as she was now, but also as she had been forty years ago, as a young diplomat's wife.

He had left England a schoolboy, less than three weeks before. He didn't feel like a schoolboy now.

He had slept with a woman for the first time in his life.

And then he had shot her.

He had had no choice about Heike and her colleague; it was self-defence, and defence of his grandmother. But he had had his first bad dream the night before. He knew it would be the first of many; perhaps a lifetime's worth.

Emma had killed someone in cold blood. Murdered him. Sure, she had a reason to kill him – to avenge her brother's death – but revenge wasn't a justification for murder. This woman, whom he had grown to love over the last couple of weeks, was a murderer. What was he going to do about that?

Nothing. Until the tumour got her. Then he would think about it.

They had left the two bodies where they had fallen and hurried back up the path, which forked left to where they had parked the car. They heard the sound of a police siren as they were driving down the hill, and just managed to pull off into a driveway before a small Guardia Civil police car sped up the road towards Lothar's villa. They didn't pass any other police cars as they headed out of Jávea, pausing to dump the gun in a rubbish bin off a side road. There were plenty of GB registered cars on the Spanish roads in July, so they felt less conspicuous than they had elsewhere.

As soon as they had reached Dover, Phil rang the number Swann had given him. He was put right through. He told Swann that Lothar was dead and that he didn't have the name of the mole, and he agreed to meet him the following lunchtime at the Three Castles.

He had come clean about Swann to Emma; after all that had happened, she didn't seem to hold it against him.

After much thought, she had asked Phil about Mr Swann's teeth.

The return home the evening before had been difficult. On the one hand, it was wonderful to be once again surrounded by the security and minor irritations of his family. On the other, he and Emma had told lie after lie to his parents, with his sister Mel looking on sceptically. She knew something was up.

'Phil!'

Phil recognized Mr Swann immediately, still wearing a suit, still with tufts of hair sticking out above his ears. Phil wondered whether he looked the same to Swann as he had the last time they had met. Or whether killing someone changed you on the outside as well as the inside.

'Can I get you a drink?' Phil asked politely. He was flush with cash; Emma had paid him the three hundred she had promised for accompanying her. He had earned it.

'That's all right. I'll get it,' said Swann.

He was back with his own pint within a couple of minutes.

'You have been in the wars, haven't you?'

'You've heard?'

'One KGB agent killed in Annecy, another and a Stasi agent killed near Valencia, plus a former West German diplomat in France. And, of course, a retired NKVD agent from before the war. Are there any I've missed?'

'I don't think so. We didn't kill Kurt,' Phil said. 'And I'm sure you heard that Freddie Pelham-Walsh was run over in Berlin. That wasn't us either, but I'm pretty certain it wasn't an accident.'

'So am I. So, Lothar is dead, and he took the name of the mole with him?'

'That's right,' said Phil.

'Tell me what happened.'

'Why don't you ask my grandmother?'

Phil looked up behind Swann, who turned to see Emma coming towards him.

'Hello, Kenneth,' she said.

Swann scrambled to his feet. 'Emma? I wasn't expecting to see you.'

'I thought it unfair to leave Philip to explain everything. And I suspected it would be you.'

'How?' said Swann.

Emma touched her front teeth. After much thought, she had asked Phil whether his Mr Swann had a gap between his front teeth. Phil had confirmed he had.

Just like Kenneth Heaton-Smith.

'Well, you are easily recognizable after all these years,' said Swann, as Phil still thought of him.

'Are you still working for MI6?' Emma asked.

'That's not the sort of question I can answer.'

'Don't be coy, Kenneth.'

Swann nodded. 'They drag me out of retirement every now and then.'

'"They" being C?'

Swann nodded again. 'After you spoke to Freddie a few months ago, Freddie came to C. C drafted me in because I had a good relationship with you going back a long time. It was good, wasn't it?'

'I suppose it was,' said Emma. 'At least I helped you.'

'And your country. For which I am very grateful.'

'But why did you approach Philip and not me? And why did you ask him to keep quiet about it?'

'We suspected that you were sympathetic to the Russian point of view before the war,' Swann said carefully. 'Rightly or wrongly, we were concerned that you still might be.'

'Wrongly,' said Emma.

'I can vouch for that,' said Phil. 'As can those bodies of Russian agents we left about the place.'

He was surprised to hear himself talking so casually about the people he and Emma had killed, but he meant to defend her from the British secret service as much as the Russian one. He was committed now.

'So you think there is another mole? Beyond Anthony Blunt.'

Swann winced at the mention of the name. Phil had never heard it before.

'Anthony is Surveyor of the Queen's Pictures,' Emma explained to Phil. 'And for many years it's been widely known that he was a spy for the Russians.'

That didn't sound like a particularly sensitive job to Phil. Did this Blunt bloke keep the Kremlin up to date with the pictures hanging in the royal toilet? He was coming to realize that the British establishment was a very curious beast.

'It's not widely known,' said Swann. 'That, young man, is still a secret. But yes, Emma, C has a suspicion that there is yet another spy hiding somewhere. He thinks he was recruited by Lothar before the war.'

'I see,' said Emma.

'But Lothar didn't tell you who?'

'No,' said Emma. 'Phil did ask him. Phil is a loyal citizen; he seems to do what you tell him. But Lothar refused to say who it was.'

'What happened next?'

'I shot him,' said Emma. 'Lothar killed my brother Hugh before the war. I needed to put that right.'

'Meanwhile, we lost any chance we had to find the spy.' Swann's tone was calm and matter-of-fact, belying the frustration he must have been feeling.

'Sorry,' said Emma, not sounding in the least bit sorry.

'Do you have any idea who it might be, from back then? Anyone you knew whom you think Lothar might have recruited?'

Phil had been asking himself the same question. He was anxious to hear Emma's answer.

Emma seemed to take the question seriously. 'The only person I can think of is Freddie,' she said. 'But I am sure that has occurred to you.'

'It has. We think Freddie dabbled for the Russians for a couple of years before the war, but the Nazi–Soviet Pact in 1939 put him off. He helped us extensively after the war. That's not the man we are looking for.'

'Then sorry. Nothing.'

Swann turned to Phil. 'Do you have any clues? Any suspicions from what you have heard?'

'Just Freddie,' said Phil.

But then someone else popped into his mind.

'Phil?' Swann had noticed.

'No. I was racking my brains, but no.'

'All right,' said Swann. 'Let's order some lunch.' He passed the simple pub menu card to Emma.

'You two have left quite a mess behind you,' he said as she read it. 'Interpol has been in touch about a young man who said his name was Eustace Parsons, who was enquiring after Freddie in Berlin and claimed to be his godson. Fortunately, the real Eustace found the local police's questions amusing, once I had assured him that you were safe. He denies being eighteen years old, or being in Berlin a couple of weeks ago.'

Phil winced. Not his brightest moment.

Swann continued. 'The French police have questions about a green British sports car seen at the house where Kurt Lohmüller was killed.

Nothing from Spain as yet, but we must be prepared. Don't worry; we will protect you both. But I do need to know exactly what happened.'

'All right,' said Emma. 'But before we go into all that, will there be any retribution, do you think?'

'From the French and German police?'

'No. From the KGB. I'm more worried about Philip than myself.'

Swann smiled. 'No. The KGB will not want to carry out a vendetta against an old lady and a schoolboy. It's an embarrassment. They will want to forget all about it. The relevant officers will be blamed and disciplined, and it will all be swept under the carpet, I am quite sure of that. There's a lot of stuff under that carpet, believe me, but there is always room for more.'

Chapter 59

July 1979, Cornwall

It was raining the whole way from Reading to St Austell, which gave Phil a chance to polish off *War and Peace*, the last section of which seemed to be an extended essay on Napoleonic warfare and the theory of history. Which Phil found fascinating.

The rain cleared as the train entered Cornwall, and Phil put down his book. Emma had rung earlier in the week, angling for him to visit her, while at the same time giving no hint to her daughter that there was anything wrong with her. He had got back his labouring job on a building site starting the following Monday, so Phil had decided to visit his grandmother for a few days before then.

He was looking forward to seeing her. He also wanted to talk to her about the idea that had lodged itself in his brain in the Three Castles.

He thought he knew who the mole was.

He didn't have much evidence, he certainly didn't have proof, but it fitted. And he needed to talk to his grandmother about it.

She wasn't waiting for him at the station.

Dick was.

He grinned and waved when he saw Phil, grabbed Phil's rucksack and slung it into the back of the TR6.

'I didn't know you were staying with Grams?' Phil said.

'She is so secretive, your grandmother,' said Dick. 'Yes, I rearranged things. I'm planning to stay with her until . . .'

'Until?'

'Until.'

That shut Phil up for a bit. 'Is it close, do you think?'

'She had a brain scan when she came back. The tumour has grown. Her balance is really bad now, and often she can't grip things or do up buttons. She gets headaches, especially early in the morning, but nothing too persistent. Yet.'

'Do they say how long?'

'No. They don't know. It could be any time. Or it could be weeks.'

'Oh.'

'Still. She is in very good spirits. And she's so pleased about you coming.' Dick grinned. 'I do like this car, by the way. It must have been fun driving it around Europe.'

Fun? Could you call fleeing halfway across the continent from homicidal KGB agents fun? And yet.

'Yes,' said Phil. 'It was fun.'

'We've been talking a lot,' said Dick. 'About her life. About her brother – my time at school with him, university. About you even. She's been enjoying it. And so have I.'

They drove through the narrow streets of Mevagissey and then high up the hill overlooking the fishing harbour to his grandmother's familiar house. He found her in the conservatory, which overlooked the garden and the white houses of the village down below. She looked pale and exhausted, but her eyes lit up when she saw Phil.

'*Ciamar a tha thu?*' she said in Gaelic.

Phil screwed up his face in concentration. '*Tha mi glè mhath.*'

She smiled. She was sitting in a wicker chair, a copy of *The Black Prince* by Iris Murdoch next to her.

'Would you like some lime cordial?'

Rose's lime cordial with ice was the drink she used to fix for Phil and Mel when they came to stay in the summer as children.

'That would be lovely, Grams.'

She struggled to get to her feet.

'I'll get it,' Phil said.

'Don't worry, I will,' said Dick.

He returned with a glass a minute later, and then left them alone, explaining that he was going to walk out to the cliffs.

'I'm so pleased you came,' said Emma.

'Dick said there might not be long to go,' said Phil. He had learned over the last month not to beat about the bush with his grandmother.

'I know. That's why I wanted to see you.'

'You really must tell Mum,' said Phil. 'Or let me do it.' His mother still had no idea that her own mother was terminally ill.

'No,' said Emma. 'Please no. You know, I'm really enjoying these last few days. With Dick. And you. I don't want Caroline bustling about here bossing me around.'

Phil felt sorry for his mother. He knew she would want to know, and would be furious with Phil for not telling her. But he supposed it was Emma's right to decide whom she told.

'All right, Grams. If you insist.'

She smiled her thanks. She insisted.

Phil realized that with Dick gone for his walk, he had an opportunity that might not reappear.

'About Dick.'

Emma gazed into Phil's eyes, searching, finding, affirming.

'You think so too?' said Phil.

'That he's Kenneth's mole?' said Emma. 'Yes.'

'I can't be sure,' said Phil. 'He's the only one you knew back then who isn't accounted for. We know it's not Freddie, we know it's not Kurt. Dick's a management consultant working with international defence companies, plus he worked for some dodgy ministry during the war, so he would be well placed to spy for the Russians.

'There is a chance that the mole is someone you've never met, but that doesn't quite make sense. Swann must suspect that the mole is someone you knew, which is why he told me and not you about him; he was afraid you might warn whoever it is. You and Swann trusted each other. Why else wouldn't he have spoken to you directly?'

Emma nodded.

'I know it's not exactly proof,' Phil went on. 'But it's a good guess.'

'I always wondered why Kurt's warning about the Molotov–Ribbentrop Pact never got through to the Foreign Office,' Emma said. 'There is only really one explanation. It was never delivered. Dick never delivered it.'

'Because the Russians told him not to?'

Emma nodded.

'We could just ask Swann,' said Phil.

'We could. But I'd rather we didn't.'

Phil had been afraid of this. 'How long have you known?'

'I don't actually *know.*'

'All right, how long have you suspected?'

'Since Spain.'

'Wait a moment,' said Phil. 'Did you shoot Lothar so that he couldn't tell me about the mole?'

Emma nodded. 'Sorry, Philip. You took me quite by surprise when you brought that up. I thought Lothar would refuse to tell you, but I couldn't take the risk. I was always going to shoot him; that just made me pull the trigger sooner.'

'But Dick's here! He's here with you now!'

'I know. And it's wonderful.' She reached out to take Phil's hand. 'I know I have asked a lot of you, Philip. But I have just one more favour. Keep this to yourself. For me. Just so I can enjoy my last few days.'

'But he's a spy, Grams! Don't you care? He's spying for the Russians and they're our enemies.'

'I don't care, Phil. I was a spy, once, remember? Dick is a good man. He is doing what he is doing because he believes in it. Because he believes that capitalism ruins the lives of the masses. Because he loves his fellow human beings. I admire that.'

'Oh, Jesus,' said Phil. 'Does he know you know?'

'No,' said Emma. 'And I strongly suggest that you don't let on that you know either. It might not be good for you.'

Because the bastard might kill me, thought Phil. He was angry with his grandmother. Angry that after all this she would put him in such an awkward situation. Again.

'Promise me, Philip. Promise me you won't tell Kenneth about Dick? Even after I'm gone.'

Why shouldn't he? Why the bloody hell shouldn't he?

He glared at his grandmother. She held his eyes, pleading, trusting.

Emma, Freddie, Dick, Kurt, Kay: they had all betrayed their countries at various times, all from a genuine belief that what they were doing was right for humanity. Phil disagreed with them. History had proved that they were wrong; the Soviet Union *was* evil.

He might be only eighteen, but he loved his country, as so many eighteen-year-olds had done before him.

But he also loved his grandmother.

'OK, Grams,' he said. 'I won't tell anyone. I promise.'

Chapter 60

July 1979, Buckinghamshire

The phone call Phil had been expecting came the Friday after he got back from Cornwall. He returned home from his first week on the building site filthy and exhausted. His mother was waiting for him in the hallway, her eyes red.

'Grams is dead, Phil.'

'Oh.' Phil had anticipated this news, but it still stunned him.

'A man called Dick Loxton has just rung. Who is he? He says he's been staying with her.'

'Yes,' said Phil. 'We met him in Paris. He knew her before the war.'

'And he's staying with her now?'

'Yes. I saw him last week.'

'And you didn't tell me?'

Phil didn't answer.

'He says she had a brain tumour and that she knew about it. Did she tell you?'

'Not at first,' said Phil. 'But eventually. When we were driving through France.'

'And you didn't tell me that, either?'

'She made me promise not to.' He looked at his mother, whose face was crumpling in front of him. He felt guilty and he felt angry. Guilty that he had kept his promise to his grandmother, and angry that she had made him do it. 'Sorry, Mum.'

'Phil!' The tears were streaming down his mother's face now. 'Phil, she was *my* mother. I had a right to know. I should be down there looking after her, not this dick.' She spat out the last word in all its penile ambiguity.

Phil's father emerged from the sitting room; he must have come home early from work. He put his arms around his wife and glared at his son.

Phil stumped upstairs, and sat on his bed in his jeans, filthy with dust from the building site. His eyes roamed around his room and settled on his copy of the *Hitch-Hiker's Guide* lying on the floor.

He thought of his grandmother beside her brother's grave at Chaddington; sitting beside him in the TR6 lecturing him on Plastic Bertrand; showing him that church with the amazing windows in Paris; crammed in the back of the tiny taxi travelling through East Berlin. He imagined her as a young diplomat's wife confounding all who met her, diplomats and spymasters, throughout Europe.

He smiled. And then a blackness seeped inside him, spreading from somewhere in his chest throughout his whole body, filling every empty cranny with a darker emptiness.

He blinked and felt a hot trail wriggle down his cheek.

There was a knock at his bedroom door.

He didn't answer.

The door opened. His mum appeared, hesitated, and then walked into the room and sat down next to him on the bed. Slowly, she put her arm around his shoulders, and he leaned into her as she hugged him tight.

He felt her lips in his hair.

Phil had had enough of keeping promises to his grandmother.

While his parents were sipping gin and tonics before supper in the sitting room, he made a murmured phone call to a London number, reversing the charges. It took a while for him to be put through to Mr Swann, or Mr Heaton-Smith, or whatever his name was.

'My grandmother just died,' he said.

349

'I'm sorry,' said Swann. 'I know you expected it, but it must be a blow.'

'I have some things I need to tell you. I know who the mole is.'

'Who is it?'

'I need to tell you face to face.' Phil and Emma's proof wasn't cast iron; he wanted to have a proper chance to explain it to Swann.

'All right. I'm abroad at the moment. But I can see you at one o'clock, Sunday. Same place.'

Phil heard a car pull up in the little driveway outside their house. It was Saturday afternoon, and his parents were at the garden centre. Mel was in her room practising her guitar, and he was learning Gaelic vocabulary.

He found it strangely calming. It both distracted him from his grandmother's death and reminded him of her at the same time.

He looked out of his bedroom window to see the familiar shape of the TR6, top down. And Dick at the wheel.

Christ!

Dick rang the doorbell.

Play it cool, Phil thought. Not too cool, though. It would be natural for him to seem upset, agitated even.

'Hello, Dick,' he said as he opened the door, opting for a downbeat tone.

'Hello.' Dick flashed one of those kind smiles that had so captivated Emma. 'I'm so sorry, Philip. I know how fond you were of her. And she was of you.'

'Thanks,' said Phil. 'What are you doing here?'

'I came to deliver the car,' Dick said. 'Emma was very keen you should have it. And you and I need to have a little chat.'

Uh-oh. 'Come in,' said Phil.

'Look, it's a lovely afternoon. Why don't we take her out for a spin?'

Phil couldn't think of an answer why not. 'OK,' he said. 'One moment. I just need to tell my sister where I'm going.'

'I'll wait in the car.'

Phil ran up to Mel's room.

'Who's that?' said Mel, looking up from her guitar.

'It's Dick, Grams's friend. He's taking me out for a drive.'

'Have fun.'

'Mel. I'm dead serious about this. Listen closely.' Phil looked around her room, grabbed a biro and ripped off a sheet from a pad of paper on her desk. He scribbled down a number.

'If I'm not back in an hour, ring this number and ask for Mr Swann. Tell him Dick Loxton took me for a drive and I haven't come back yet. Dick Loxton. Have you got that?'

'Are you serious?' His sister's expression was somewhere between bemused and scornful.

'Dead serious,' said Phil.

'I knew something was up,' she said. 'Now you've got me scared.'

'I am scared,' said Phil. 'Bye, Mel.' And he bent down and kissed her quickly on the cheek.

'Wow,' she said. He never kissed her on the cheek. 'Bye, Phil.'

He left the house to find Dick waiting for him in the passenger seat.

'Where are we going?' Phil asked.

'Is there anywhere we can go for a decent walk around here? There must be, the countryside is beautiful.'

'I know somewhere,' said Phil, and drove off towards one of those small valleys that cut into the Chiltern Hills.

Dick was talking about Emma's last few days, something about how she had been comfortable until the very end when she had complained of a severe headache and then lost consciousness.

Phil was listening with half an ear.

Dick was going to kill him. Take him to some remote spot and kill him.

Phil had no idea how. He probably had a gun.

Phil needed a plan.

The walk was Phil's best hope. Dick was an inch or two taller than Phil, and quite a bit heavier. Phil wasn't sure he could overpower him, especially if Dick had a gun.

But he could outrun him.

So the plan was, wait till they were close to some woods, but don't wait too long.

And then make a run for it, into the trees.

They were driving along a quiet road and parked in a layby near a footpath, which led up through a field to a wood.

They got out of the car.

'Emma said you and she had had a conversation when you came down last week,' Dick said. 'About me.'

'We did,' said Phil, avoiding Dick's gaze.

'She said you had both decided that I was some kind of spy.'

They had crossed a stile and were climbing a low hill beside a hedge, watched by a clutch of bullocks. Behind them, a tiny village dozed in the Buckinghamshire sunshine. The field was exposed to the view of anyone looking out of the windows of their cottage. Not a great place to shoot someone undetected. Dick would have to wait for his chance.

Phil stopped. 'I promised her not to tell anyone, and I haven't.'

Dick grinned. 'I'm sure you haven't. You are the epitome of a loyal grandson.'

'You can trust me not to tell them now,' Phil said. And at that moment he was willing to stick by that promise if Dick could think of a way of enforcing it without killing him.

He was scared, but he was doing his best not to show it.

Dick laughed. 'Don't worry, Philip,' he said. 'I'm not a "mole" as she says you call it. It's not me.'

'Oh, good,' said Phil, happy to be seen to be persuaded.

'Seriously, Philip. It's not me. She and I discussed it a couple of days ago. I convinced her it wasn't me.'

'Good,' said Phil.

Dick frowned. 'You don't believe me, do you? She said I should find you as soon as she died. She also said you would be difficult to convince.'

'No, no, you've convinced me,' said Phil. Unconvincingly.

'Being Emma, she told me how to convince you.'

'Did she?' said Phil. That did sound like Grams. 'I'm listening.' But he was still standing motionless in the open field. At some point he would run.

'Emma says that what convinced her was that the Foreign Office never received her warning about the Russian talks with the Germans in the summer of 1939.'

'That's right.'

'She says that the only possible reason they didn't is that I didn't pass on the message.'

'That's also right,' said Phil.

'It's not quite right,' said Dick.

'What do you mean?'

'I mean there is another possibility. That I did pass on the intelligence, but that the person I told it to kept it to himself.'

'Heaton-Smith?'

Dick nodded. Phil thought about it. It did make sense.

'So you still maintain that you gave the information to Heaton-Smith?'

'I do,' said Dick. 'I remember it well. We were in a pub in Pimlico. It's the one and only time I met him. He had a gap in his front teeth.'

Phil thought about it. Maybe.

Dick was thinking too. 'Why would I have sent a postcard to Emma telling her about Kurt and Kay if I was trying to stop her finding Lothar? Eh?'

'I don't know,' said Phil. 'Why would Heaton-Smith want me to tell him where Lothar was?'

'Emma had an answer for that.'

'Which was?'

'He had been put up to it by C and Freddie Pelham-Walsh – C is the head of MI6.'

'I know.'

'The three of them decided to involve you, and so Heaton-Smith had to. But by recruiting you himself, and keeping Emma out of it, he could follow how her investigation was going. If she found Lothar, and you told Heaton-Smith where he was, he could make sure that the KGB got to him before MI6.'

'But why mention the mole at all? Surely, the less I knew about moles, the less chance that I might find one.'

'Either C or Freddie insisted on it. The important thing from the mysterious Mr Swann's point of view was that Emma didn't find out what you and he were up to.'

Phil thought it all through. 'OK. Heaton-Smith may be the mole, I get that. Or it might be you. How do I know which?'

Dick smiled. 'According to Emma, you have the answer to that.'

Chapter 61

July 1979, Three Castles, Buckinghamshire

This time, Phil was ten minutes late as he walked into the Three Castles. Swann was waiting for him, at the same table where they had met before, between the jukebox and the dartboard.

Phil bought himself a pint and joined him.

'Hello, Phil,' said Swann, smiling. 'Thanks for getting in touch with me.'

Phil smiled, shook Swann's hand, and sat down. He came straight to the point.

'The man you are looking for is Dick Loxton,' he said.

'Loxton, eh?' said Swann.

'Do you know him?' Phil asked.

'We met once, during the war.'

'Oh, was that at a pub in Pimlico? My grandmother told me about that. He had a message for you about the talks between the Germans and the Russians. Was that right?'

'He did have some information for me,' Swann said, carefully. 'From your grandmother.'

'Did the British government take any notice of it?'

'No,' said Swann. 'They didn't believe it. Even though we were nearly at war, there were still some appeasers left in the Foreign Office.' He lit a cigarette. 'So tell me, Philip. How do you know that Loxton is our man?'

Phil launched into a detailed exposition of his earlier suspicions. Swann listened carefully. After a couple of minutes, they were interrupted.

'Hello, Kenneth.'

Two men were standing behind Swann. One, a sixty-year-old civil servant with a suit and tie, fleshy square face and bulging, hard eyes, was doing the talking.

'Do you mind if we join you?'

'Of course not. I was just debriefing Phil here.'

'We heard.'

Swann didn't move. Slowly he drew on his cigarette, not moving his eyes from the civil servant.

'Are you wearing a wire, Phil?' Swann asked eventually.

'He is,' said the civil servant.

'Uncomfortable, aren't they?' Swann said to Phil. 'Just wait till you take it off. The tape they use rips off all your chest hair.'

'You were talking about Dick Loxton,' the civil servant said.

'We were.'

'And how he met you in a pub in Pimlico in 1939 and passed on information about the Molotov–Ribbentrop Pact.'

'That's right.'

'Information that you didn't pass on to anyone in London.'

'Oh, I can assure you I did,' said Swann. Phil had to hand it to him; he was keeping his cool. But he had just confirmed that Dick had indeed followed Emma's instructions back in 1939. Dick wasn't the mole, and it looked very likely Kenneth Heaton-Smith was.

'We've checked the old files,' said the civil servant. 'There is no record of you mentioning your conversation with Mr Loxton to anyone.'

'It will be in the files somewhere,' said Swann. 'Just a question of looking in the right places.'

The civil servant scanned the bar, which was becoming crowded. 'We really need to discuss this further, Kenneth, but this isn't a good place to do it. Why don't you come with me and Roger?'

Phil, and Swann, glanced up at Roger, who was in his late thirties, broad-shouldered and very fit-looking. Phil wouldn't want to have an argument with Roger. And neither did Mr Swann.

'All right,' he said. 'Goodbye, Phil.' And they were gone.

*

Ten minutes later, his wire expertly and painfully removed in an electrician's van in the pub car park where the civil servant and his entourage had been listening to it earlier, Phil returned to the pub. Dick was waiting for him with two pints lined up on the bar.

'Turns out you're not a Russian spy, after all,' said Phil, accepting his gratefully.

'That's good to know,' said Dick.

'Was that bloke "C"?'

'Couldn't possibly comment,' said Dick. He raised his glass. 'To Emma.' He paused. 'And Hugh.'

'To Grams,' said Phil. 'And her brother.' He took a sip.

Nothing tasted better to him at that moment than a good English pint in a good English pub on a summer afternoon.

ACKNOWLEDGEMENTS

I should like to thank Hugh Chawner for his help with Spain, Geoff Skingsley for his help with France and Colin West for his help with the Gaelic.

Thanks are also due to my agent, Oli Munson, to Susannah Hamilton, my editor, and to Richenda Todd and Liz Hatherell for their copy-editing and proof-reading. And to my wife Barbara for accompanying me on the arduous research trips required to write this book.

A Message from Michael Ridpath

Get a FREE 60-page story

I hope you enjoyed reading this book as much as I enjoyed writing it. Thank you for buying it.

To write a book is to communicate directly with the person who reads it. I like to build as direct a relationship as I can with my readers and so I send occasional newsletters with information about my books and any special offers.

If you sign up to my mailing list I will send you a free ebook of a 60 page story set in North East Iceland featuring my Icelandic detective, Magnus, called *The Polar Bear Killing*:

> *A starving polar bear swims ashore in a remote Icelandic village and is shot by the local policeman. Two days later, the policeman is found dead on a hill above the village. A polar bear justice novella with an Icelandic twist.*

To sign up to the mailing list and get your free ebook of *The Polar Bear Killing*, please visit my website www.michaelridpath.com, where you will also find information about my other books.